Pledged To A Highlander

By

Donna Fletcher

Donna Fletcher

No part of this publication may be used or reproduced in any manner whatsoever, including but not limited to being stored in a retrieval system or transmitted in any form or by any means, electronic, mechanical, photocopying, recording or otherwise without permission of the author.

This is a book of fiction. Names, characters, places, and incidents are either the product of the author's imagination or are used fictitiously, and any resemblance to actual persons, living or dead, business establishments, events or locales is entirely coincidental.

Pledged To A Highlander

All rights reserved.

Copyright June 2020 by Donna Fletcher

Cover art
Kim Killion Group

Visit Donna's Web site
www.donnafletcher.com
http://www.facebook.com/donna.fletcher.author

Chapter One

Scotland, The Highlands, 12th century

Her skin felt like the softest velvet and was as smooth as the finest silk. He couldn't stop touching her. He wanted to caress and kiss every inch of her lovely naked body. She belonged to him and only him and that was the only thought that consumed him when he slid inside her and took what belonged to him.

Her virginity.

She was his and his alone, no other had the right. He had waited. They had waited for this moment and he relished it. Her sheath was snug, though it opened for him, welcoming him, accepting him, hugging him as he slipped deeper and deeper inside her.

"I love you, Royden—always."

He cherished those words, held on to them, let them seep deep inside him as his manhood felt the tight barrier that blocked him—her maidenhead.

She was his to claim, always had been, and once he broke the barrier she'd be his always. They would be forever joined as one. Even when separated, they'd still remain connected through this special moment when they sealed their vows.

He looked into her eyes and fell more deeply in love if that was possible, her beautiful smile lighting his heart as she whispered, "Come to me. I'm yours."

Royden woke with a start, jolting up in bed angry to wake from the dream he'd had often in the past five years. Five long years of thinking, dreaming, fighting to get home to Oria, the woman he'd loved since he'd been young and who had loved him—*always*.

He didn't know if she had survived the attack on their wedding day that had torn not only them apart but his whole family, his whole clan. The last time he had seen her, she was helping women and children into the safety of the keep. Her fate was unknown to him and he ached to know what had happened to her. He had no idea if his da had died or survived. He and his brother, Arran, had spent about a year together before they'd been separated. He had no knowledge of what happened to him. And there was his sister, Raven, a handful of a lass. If anyone could survive, she could and he hoped she had since he had learned that she'd never been found.

From the moment he'd been captured, he and Arran had talked of escaping and returning home, finding their family and seeking revenge on whoever was responsible for the devastation to their clan. They'd been taken to the most barren part of Scotland where few men braved to go, the land desolate and unforgiving. At times they'd been transported on ships to fight on foreign soil, though they were always returned home to Scotland. They weren't given a chance once dumped in a battle. It was fight or die.

He ran his right hand through his dark hair that barely touched his shoulders. He swung his legs off the edge of the rumpled bed and grabbed the black leather cuff off the low chest next to the bed. He slipped it on the stub of where his left hand should have been and used his teeth to help tighten the leather strips that kept it securely in place. It had taken time for him to get used to having only one hand and it hadn't been easy. The day of the attack had been seared into his memory. How could he forget it? It was meant to be his wedding day.

He stood and reached for his shirt. He had grown thicker with muscle over the last few years, his chest and arms heavy with it and his legs as well. Muscle wasn't the only thing he had gained. He'd also gained scars, some small ones and others large, from all the battles he'd been in. None, though, were as deep as the scar on his heart. It tormented him that he had failed not only to protect Oria, but to wed her, make her his wife, seal their union. That chance had passed him by and was no more.

Not that he didn't dream or hope that by some miracle Oria had survived and when he was finally able to return home, she'd be there waiting for him.

He turned at the rustle of blankets and shook his head at the woman sleeping in his bed. He hated that after a while he couldn't deny himself the pleasures of a willing woman. He had a need, especially after battle, and women were supplied to the men in abundance. He seldom paired with the same woman. There were no feelings when he coupled just a need that had to be satisfied. Still, his need troubled him and when he saw that some women had more need than he had known, he wondered, with him gone, what Oria might have done to assuage her need. Not that he would blame her. If anyone was to blame, it was he himself.

It was a deep source of anger and guilt, failing to keep her from harm, that he harbored. One that would not leave him soon, if ever.

He added a few logs to the fire pit in the middle of the hut after he finished dressing and without a word to the woman he had been so intimate with last night, whose name he did not know, he left.

Royden bundled his wool cloak around him, the pre-dawn day cold. While spring had arrived, it was still cold this high in the Highlands. His breath came out in large puffs and his stump ached as was its way when too cold. He walked through the village, if it could be called that, the area comprised of several huts, a few storage sheds, and a longhouse.

The amount of warriors that occupied the area had thinned of late and there was talk the few who remained were to be dispersed to other groups. He and Arran's plans to attempt to escape had quickly been brought to an end when all the captives were told the rules.

Attempt to escape and one of your clansmen will suffer for it, attempt again and your clansmen will die, succeed at escaping and you will be hunted down and you and a family member will die. It wasn't until one brave captive attempted an escape that he and Arran knew escape wasn't a viable option. The man was found and returned and all watched as he'd been forced to pick who in his clan that had been taken captive with him would be punished. The man chosen was left chained outside for two days and nights in the cold without food, given only a hot brew. He survived, though barely.

The captives had been given an offer of freedom. They would join the band of mercenaries and fight, earning their freedom, but that would take years. Or they could remain with the group and share in its wealth. Sometimes if one was lucky, a captive was released without explanation, though that was a seldom occurrence.

That's when Royden had begun to discover the power and influence of the person who had forged a band of unwanted warriors into highly-skilled mercenaries for hire.

He entered the longhouse to find Platt there. He didn't like the man. He had been the one who led the attack on Royden's clan, leaving several of his clansmen dead or wounded. He had discovered that Platt owed some kind of allegiance to the overall leader of the mercenaries and followed his command without question.

"I will miss our morning talks," Platt said with a snarling grin.

Royden sat on the bench opposite Platt at one of the many tables, not because he wanted to, but because it was closest to the fire pit. He didn't acknowledge his humor, he and Platt having shared no morning talks only silence when they had eaten.

Unless he was going home, what did it matter where he was sent? Still, he asked, "Where am I to be sent this time?"

Platt retained his smile. "Aren't you going to miss me?"

"You're not going with me?" Royden asked, actually enjoying the small bit of good news.

Platt laughed, a seldom heard sound from him. "You really want to take me home with you?"

Royden wasn't sure he'd heard him correctly or if he misunderstood. He eyed Platt skeptically, but said nothing.

"He has no use for you anymore. You are free to return home," Platt said and raised his tankard, toasting Royden's good fortune.

Royden was still skeptical, Platt not always truthful, and he also wondered if he was possibly dreaming and yet to wake.

"Can't spare you a horse, but I can see you have food for a while, since it will take you a good month or more to reach home." Platt shook his head at Royden's skeptical glare. "It's the truth and I'm glad to be rid of you."

"My brother, Arran?"

"I don't know about him, but with you being set free I don't see why he wouldn't be as well, but then again, he could be dead for all I know."

"That's an outright lie," Royden challenged. "You know more than you ever say."

"The reason I've survived all this time. I keep my mouth shut."

Royden stood. He didn't care if his belly was growling. If he was free, he wanted to leave now. He wanted to get home.

"I'll get that food and leave now," Royden said and went to turn.

"Royden."

He stopped.

"A price was paid for your release. A steep one that few, if any, would pay. You'll need to remember that one day."

Royden turned and walked away. Never had Platt offered any information. Why did he do so now? He didn't bother to ask who it was who had bought his freedom. Platt wouldn't tell him. He'd probably get satisfaction out of not telling him. He wondered, though, who had paid a steep price for his release, what that price was, and why had it been paid?

***

Royden stood looking at the MacKinnon keep. He had approached it from the woods, not sure what he'd find. Once he had caught sight of it, he had to get closer, had to finally get home. The stone keep stood tall and proud and didn't appear as neglected as he feared it might. Although he didn't know what he'd find inside. For now, it didn't matter. He was home. After five long, terrible years he was home.

He turned and looked over the village and the sight disturbed him. The cottages were in disrepair and he saw no one tending to chores or lingering about. He didn't even hear the bark of a dog.

"Few have remained, but the few who have will be happy to see you. Happy to have a chieftain once again."

Royden turned to see Bethany standing just outside the open doors of the keep.

"You stayed," he said pleased to see a familiar face, family of sorts.

"Someone had to be here if your sister returned," she said.

Tears glistened in her eyes that had aged since Royden had last seen her. Her hair had turned completely gray and she appeared thinner, a slight stoop to her shoulders, but the broad smile she wore let him know how happy she was to see him.

"My da, Bethany?" he asked, though feared her response.

"I never saw what became of him."

"Has Raven returned?" Royden asked anxiously, hoping for good news while trying to accept the inevitable—his da was dead.

Bethany shook her head. "No, she hasn't been here and I've heard nothing about her."

"The warriors who remained here probably frightened her away," Royden surmised or more hoped, giving credence that his sister had survived.

"The warriors left about a month ago and have not returned. They were not the same warriors who first remained here. Warriors have come and gone over the years. They all did little while here. Then *he* came one day." Bethany shuddered. "A beast of a man. A metal helmet concealed his face and I was glad of it. Something told me if I looked upon him I'd wither and die. His own warriors—the ones who arrived with him and there were many—kept their distance except for one man. He was called Trevor and he did the beast's bidding." She shuddered again, her whole body quaking.

"Why was he here?"

Bethany shook her head. "I don't know for certain. I did hear some say that he was close to getting what he wanted. Whatever that might be."

Royden wondered himself and intended to find out. "The warriors won't be coming back. I'm free and I'm home to stay."

Bethany's shoulders sagged as if a heavy weight had been lifted off them. "Those who have remained here have struggled to keep the clan together until one of you returned.

No one ever doubted that one of you would come home and return strength and pride to the clan."

"It will be done. The Clan MacKinnon will rise again," he said and with what he had learned while captive, he'd make his clan close to invincible. "I never got to thank you for what you did that day of the attack, Bethany. It took courage to step forward and lie to protect Raven, and I am forever grateful that you did. I am also grateful that you remained here and did what you could to keep the Clan MacKinnon together."

"The clan is my family and I would do anything to protect Raven," Bethany admitted tearfully. "And I'd do anything to find her and help bring her home."

"You have my word. I will find Raven and bring her home," Royden said, intent on keeping the promise he had made those many years ago.

"Will Arran return home soon?" Bethany asked.

"I believe he will," Royden said, sounding and feeling hopeful now that he was home. He'd never forget what his brother had done for him when he'd lost his hand. He owed Arran much and he prayed he'd see him soon. Otherwise he'd... "I'll go find Arran if necessary."

"As he would you," Bethany acknowledged. "Much work is needed here, the fields need to be made ready for summer planting and the cottages repaired along with the storehouses which need stocking. I don't know if there is enough left of the clan to see it done."

"I'll see it done." Royden didn't know how, but he'd let nothing stop him from restoring his clan's power and wealth and providing a thriving home for them all.

"You should be aware that one of the warriors who was here for some time chose to stay," Bethany said. "He fell in love with Emily, Old George's granddaughter, and they wed."

"Emily is so young," Royden said, thinking she was near the same age as his sister.

"Not anymore. She's close to ten and nine years now," Bethany reminded. "And past the age most lassies wed."

Now that he was home, the years he'd been away seemed like only yesterday. But they weren't and nothing was the same. His sister wasn't a young lass on the verge of womanhood. She was grown and had been of marriage age for a few years now. Had she found a man of her choosing and wed?

"Penn seems nice enough and he's good to Emily and she's madly in love with him." Bethany sighed and shook her head again. "I can't help but wonder and worry that Penn was ordered to stay here."

"And keep this leader of his informed," Royden said the obvious.

"It's a thought I can't shake, but look at me going on like this when you're probably hungry and could do with a washing."

"You're right about both," Royden said. "Once that's done, I'll walk through the village and talk with everyone so they know I'm home."

He gave one last look over the quiet village and spotted a lone rider not far off.

"That would be Lady Learmonth. Once a week she visits here to tend the ailing and give what comfort she can to those in need," Bethany said.

"The old chieftain wed? And when did Learmonth have a title bestowed on him?" Royden asked.

"Aye, he has a wife and not long after the attack a title. You nee—"

"Get food and drink ready for our guest. I have much to ask Lady Learmonth," Royden said and turned away from Bethany, failing to see the worry in her eyes and the hesitancy in her steps as she did as she was told.

The rider came to a stop not far from him and before he could offer her assistance, she dismounted on her own and with graceful skill. Her hood concealed a good portion of her face as she approached him.

The woman stopped suddenly, hesitant to approach him, and he couldn't blame her.

He was far from presentable, his garments soiled from his arduous journey and worn from the years and elements. He also needed a good soaking to wash away not only the grime and odor, but who he had become these past five years. A man who had lost all sense of who he had once been. A man he'd become far too familiar with over time. A man who killed far too easily and a man who had laid with women he cared nothing about. A man who had lost all honor.

He reached back to his past, recalling manners he hadn't needed in years. "Please forgive my unpresentable state, Lady Learmonth. I have only returned home after a long journey and I am not as presentable as I should be."

When she failed to respond, he wondered if she was too offended by his appearance to even speak to him. Or was it the shock in seeing that he had lost a hand that kept her silent? Or hadn't he sounded sincere enough? He had had no call to be mannerly while captive and it felt foreign for him to do so now.

Annoyed she refused to speak to him, he held his temper that was rising and tried to engage her again. "You have been most kind to my clan in my absence."

Still she gave no response and she didn't even move. She appeared frozen in place. What did she think he was going to do, attack her? Had his appearance changed that much? Did he look that menacing?

He couldn't keep his temper from erupting. "Since you find the sight of me to reprehensible to speak with me, then get on your horse and go. And don't bother to return." He turned to walk away, anger burning in the pit of his stomach.

"Royden?" the whispery voice asked.

He turned with a scowl at the questionable mention of his name. "Aye, it is me and who is it I know that takes such offense to my appearance?"

The woman raised her hands and lifted her hood, revealing her face.

"Oria." He nearly roared her name, at least in his head, since it came out more gently, and the fire in his gut burned like the fires of hell when he realized that the woman he loved was wed to another man.

Chapter Two

Oria was having difficulty finding her voice. She couldn't believe the man who she loved was finally standing there in front of her. She had prayed every day for his safe return and now that he had finally returned, she found herself speechless. Her instinct was to simply throw herself at him, feel his arms wrap around her once again, hug him tight, and never let him go, but she quelled the urge when he took a step back away from her.

She looked at him then, truly looked at him, and saw a much different man than the one she had loved since as long as she could remember. He appeared far taller and larger than she had remembered him, not that he had grown in height, though he had in width, thick, solid muscle straining at his garments. He also held himself more erect than she recalled, his chest taut, his chin a slight lift to it as if daring anyone to come near him. There were small telltale signs of scars here and there on his chin and neck and one on his brow that had long healed.

They reminded her of her own scar and she was glad her hood hid the hideous scar that ran along her jaw on the right side of her face. They both had been left scarred and not only with visible ones.

"You've wed," Royden said, voicing the only thought that filled his mind.

Betrayal, that's what she heard in his remark and in a way, she couldn't blame him. It was how she had felt when she exchanged vows with Burnell—that she had betrayed Royden.

Raindrops suddenly began to fall and Royden stretched his arm out toward the keep doors. "Come inside."

Oria couldn't hide her surprise at seeing that he had lost his left hand. She had to fight back the tears and the pain to her heart hurt for what he must have gone through, the suffering and having to learn to live with only one hand. She wished she could have been there for him—to help him and to love him.

Royden had grown accustomed to no longer having his left hand, not that it didn't anger him at times, but others sometimes looked with shock upon his covered stump just as Oria did now.

"No need to look with repulsion at my stump, it will never touch you," he said. "Now get inside out of the rain."

There was anger not only in his voice but in the pinched lines around his dark eyes, lines that hadn't been there the last time she had seen him. How could he think that she was disgusted by his suffering? Didn't he realize that she never stopped loving him? Her thoughts churned as badly as her stomach as she lifted the hem of her cloak to hurry up the keep's stairs and inside to the Great Hall.

Royden had learned to contain his anger since it had done little good to unleash it while held captive, though relief had come through battle. He had fought every battle as if fighting the foe who had destroyed his life, his family, his clan. Battle after battle had been like revenge after revenge, though it never lasted long, which was why after a while he had looked forward to the next battle.

Now, however, not only seeing how the woman he loved looked at him with disgust but also seeing that the Great Hall, the place where his family had gathered for meals, for celebrations, the place where he would have wed Oria resembled a battlefield after a battle. Tables and benches lay scattered and broken, while a few were piled on top of each other, and only one table and two benches sat in front of the large, cold fireplace piled with ashes. Tapestries that had once graced the walls were gone and the only light provided in the room was from the two narrow windows and a lone candle on top of the one trestle table.

Bethany entered the room balancing a pitcher and a large wooden bowl in her arms.

Oria was quick to help her set both on the lone table.

"Some of the warriors that stayed here helped, the last lot not so much. They took more than they got," Bethany explained. "Penn has been good about providing meat for the village since the last group of warriors left and the women fish the stream. We've kept up with the kitchen garden. Penn has started work on the fields and the few men left here have begun to help him." Bethany nodded to Oria. "Lady Learmonth kindly supplied us with ale and wine after the last troop took their leave."

Royden clenched his one hand. He wanted to strike out at someone, preferably the person responsible for destroying everything he held dear, everyone he loved. In time, he would have his revenge and he would enjoy making those suffer who had made so many suffer.

"Thank you, Bethany. We'll talk more later," Royden said.

Bethany bobbed her head and with a smile to Oria, she left the room.

"Sit," he said, though he was aware it sounded more an order.

Oria had no choice but to lower her hood so she made sure to sit where her scar wouldn't be visible to him.

Royden filled the two tankards before Oria could. He didn't want her serving him, taking pity on him because he had only one hand.

Oria cupped the tankard in both hands, hoping to stop them from trembling.

Royden downed his tankard of ale and filled it again, remaining silent a moment afterwards. "Thank you for helping my clan."

She didn't know how to respond to that. Did he forget the Clan MacKinnon was to be her clan too? How could he think she would forsake a clan that was like a family to her?

"I would never desert the Clan MacKinnon," Oria said.

"Yet, you wed another," Royden snapped, knowing he had no right to accuse her when she probably had had no choice, but he couldn't stop himself. "Did you even protest the marriage?"

The day she wed Burnell was burned in her memory. She could never forget it. "I had little choice. I did what I was ordered to do."

"Something we all did," Royden said, his anger far from subsiding, though it wasn't directed at her. He was angry at himself for failing to protect her, keep her safe, keep her from being forced to wed another. It was all his fault.

"Royden," she said softly and ached to reach out and touch him, feel his familiar strength and the comfort it always brought her, and offer him comfort.

"Do you know what happened to my sister?" he asked, his tone brusque.

It hurt more than she ever thought possible that he dismissed what had been between them, appearing not even willing to discuss it, as if it was over and done or would never be again. It was like losing him all over again.

Because of a promise she had made, she did something she'd never thought she'd do. She lied to him. "No, I know nothing about Raven."

"She couldn't have just disappeared," he said, shaking his head. "What about my da? Did you hear anything about him? And your da, Oria, how is he?"

Oria's heart went out to him. At least she knew what went on here in the years that had passed. Royden knew nothing of what happened to his family, the people he loved, his clan, his home. He would learn all that had happened, though not all at once. The only thing she could do for him at the moment was give him hope.

"Raven's tenacious nature no doubt got her through this ordeal. I'm sure she'll return home one day. As for your da," —she paused, not comfortable with having to lie to him again— "I heard he was wounded badly and managed to make it into the woods. There's no word after that."

"Five years and not one sign of him leaves little hope that he survived," Royden said.

She heard his ache, his sorrow, and felt it as well, and she wished she could tell him all of it, but she had given her word and for a good reason.

"And your da?" he asked.

"He survived the battle, but not what followed. He died three years ago." She couldn't stop the tears that welled in her eyes, though she managed to keep all but one tear from falling.

Royden wanted to leap across the table and take her in his arms and not only hug all the sorrow and hurt out of her, but he selfishly wanted to feel what he once had with her. That feeling of comfort, warmth, love. Good, God, he ached for her love. Unfortunately, he no longer deserved it. No more was he an honorable man, since an honorable man wouldn't be thinking how he wanted nothing more than to scoop Oria up in his arms, rush her to his bedchamber, strip her naked and do what he should have done five years ago, make love to the woman he loved—a married woman.

He offered the appropriate response. "I'm so sorry, Oria. Your father was a good man."

"He was," Oria said and wiped the single tear off her cheek with her finger.

Royden dropped his one hand beneath the table, not wanting her to see him clench it in anger. He hated to see her hurt and to know he hadn't been there to help her through her da's passing. She had faced it alone and that tore at his heart.

"What became of your land?" he asked, hungry to learn all he could about what had happened in his absence. He hoped it would help him discover who was responsible for it all.

"That's the odd part," she said. "A group of warriors remain there and sees to providing for the clan. My da wasn't replaced as chieftain and when he died no chieftain was appointed. The keep sits empty, though it is maintained, as if it waits for someone."

"That is odd," Royden agreed. "Why were you forced to wed Lord Learmonth and not one of the warriors left at your keep?"

This was not the reunion with Royden she had imagined, endless questions and what seemed like accusations. What had he expected after five years? Neither of them were who they once were. How then was it that she loved him even more today than she did those many years ago?

Bethany entered the room with a man following behind her and Oria couldn't be more pleased, since another lie would have slipped from her lips.

"Pardon, Chieftain Royden, but Penn wanted to speak with you right away," Bethany said.

Chieftain Royden.

Bethany bestowing the title of Chieftain on him made him realize the loss of his father and he felt a stab to his gut, though he didn't let his sorrow and anger show.

Penn stepped around Bethany and Royden ran his eyes over him, taking in all of him. He was a head shorter than Royden, his long hair light, not a usual color for a Scotsman, and his body solid though lean. He stood erect, his shoulders back, a stance of confidence, something Royden had learned while captive. He wore a plaid with a pale yellow shirt beneath and the only weapon he could detect was the hilt of a dagger sticking out of the top of one boot.

"I'm Penn, sir, and I wanted you to know that I chose to remain here of my own accord and I will work to prove my worth and my loyalty."

"Were you taken prisoner and forced to fight?" Royden asked.

Penn shook his head. "No, I joined the mercenaries, hoping to eventually find a place to settle, to call home. I found that here with Emily. I love her and will do whatever is necessary to remain with her."

"Who is the leader of these mercenaries?" Royden asked.

Penn shrugged. "I don't know. His identity is known only by a chosen few."

"So you were part of a group of mercenaries who pillage men's lands, take what isn't yours, and you expect me to accept you into my clan?" Royden asked, glaring at the young warrior.

"I have scrounged for my existence since I've been eight years and knew hunger long before then. I had little choice but to take what the mercenaries offered me, food and shelter, and in an odd way, family. I wasn't proud to pillage, but I also wasn't too proud to survive the best I could. I will do whatever you ask of me to prove my worth to you. I only ask that you give me a chance."

Royden looked to Bethany. "What say you?"

"He was a help while the last lot of warriors were here and much more help after they left. I think he should be given a chance. Besides, Emily is round with his child and she needs her husband."

Royden turned a deeper glare on Penn. "I make no decision yet. You'll go and take stock of what repairs are needed to the village, the storage sheds, and what is needed to be done in the planting fields. You'll report back to me by nightfall."

"I can tell you now," Penn said with a lift of his chin.

"I have no time for you now. I will summon you when I'm ready," Royden ordered.

"Aye, sir," Penn said and followed Bethany out of the Great Hall.

"Do you know anything about Penn?" Royden asked Oria once the young warrior was gone from the room.

Oria was reminded of old times when Royden would sometimes ask her opinion and it was like spying the Royden she had once known.

"Only what I have seen on my visits here. He keeps the village fed, makes what repairs he can on his own since it has taken time for the clan to trust him. And he treats Emily well. You can see how much they love each other when they are together. Love shines in their eyes and in their smiles."

Like ours did once, Royden couldn't help but think.

"I should go see to the few people who are in need of tending," Oria said, it growing more painful to sit there and talk with him as if they were nothing more than acquaintances.

"A few more questions and you can be on your way," Royden said, not that he wanted to let her go, but what choice did he have?

She nodded, though she would have preferred to run from the room, her heart was breaking so badly.

"Do you know Chieftain Galvin of the Clan Macara, his son Bayne or daughter Purity's fate?" he asked.

"Chieftain Galvin survived. Bayne died in the battle." She paused a moment before letting a partial lie slip from her lips. "Purity hasn't been found."

"And the Macara land? Does Galvin still retain it?" Royden asked.

"Aye, he does. Since Purity was never able to be found and forced to wed, Chieftain Galvin's land remained with him. He's encouraged some of your clan members to come join his clan."

"He what?" Royden snapped. "Did any go?"

"Instead of offering help, he preyed on their fears, saying none of the MacKinnon men would return," Oria said, recalling the day she had heard him make such a claim and letting him know what she thought about it. "None believed him and no matter what he said, no one would leave here."

Royden felt ready to kill Galvin Macara. He had searched for answers to the attack that day five years ago. How had the troop of warriors been able to surprise them? Why hadn't their sentinels alerted them? Had they waited for that specific day, his and Oria's wedding day, when so many chieftains would be present to purposely attack? And had Galvin, sending a missive to Chieftain Burnell of the Clan Learmonth, been in any way the catalyst that had started the chain of events?

"Chieftain Thurbane. How has he faired?" Royden asked. These men's lands bordered his land and he needed to know for the safety of his clan. He would take no chances. Not ever again.

"Thurbane does well. The man, Fergus, his daughter Alynn was forced to wed, treats her well. They have two children, a son almost five years and a daughter three years," Oria said, thinking how she and Royden probably would have had two bairns by now if fate hadn't been so unkind.

Royden had the same thought and all that he had lost came rushing back to him like a blow to the face. He wanted to roar out his fury, thrash someone or something, he needed a battle, but there were no more battles and while he was glad for it, he also feared the repercussion of not having an outlet for his anger.

"I should go," she stood quickly so he couldn't stop her and turned with the same haste.

Royden got so fast to his feet that the bench he sat on tumbled over. His face was a mask of pure rage and anger and his tongue so sharp that his words pierced like the point of a blade. "Who did that to you?"

Oria had moved so quickly she had forgotten about the scar along her jaw. Royden had seen it, though it wasn't disgust she saw in his eyes when looking upon it. It was that feral look he'd get when angry, though much worse than she had ever seen it before. It was as if he was more animal than human and it frightened her.

Royden vaulted over the table, landing beside her. He took hold of her chin, turning her head so he could get a better look at the scar that ran along her right jawline, puckering in a couple of places.

"Who did this?" he repeated more demandingly.

Oria reached up and placed her hand on his to ease his hand off her chin, but his grip was firm and she couldn't budge it.

Royden could let go of her, but the gentle touch of her cool hand shot a myriad of feelings through him that brought back a rush of memories reminding him of the deep binding love they had had for each other, and he didn't want to let go of that. He didn't want to let go of her.

"Don't make me ask you again," he warned when she failed to respond a second time.

Never would she think to fear Royden. Feeling safe and comfortable with him was part of what she loved about him. Now, however, a spark of fear ignited within her.

"A man named Firth. I fought him when he tried to pull me away from the keep. I bit him hard on the arm and for that I got this scar," Oria said, touching the scar. "I continued to fight when two other men tried to throw me in a cart. Firth had enough of me and threw a punch to my face I couldn't avoid and knocked me out. I woke in a cart, my hands tied, and my wound still bleeding."

Anger raged like molten fire in him. Somehow he'd find Firth and the man would beg to die by the time he got done with him. He let Oria know what he intended. "I'm going to kill him."

Firth was a ruthless man and she didn't want Royden anywhere near him. "He's long gone."

"I'll find him."

Oria wrapped her hand around his wrist and gave it a squeeze. "Please, Royden, there's been enough hurt and loss."

He lifted his left arm, ready to caress her face as he had once done so often and stopped, realizing he had no hand. He released her chin and stepped back away from her.

Oria took the distance he had put between them as a rejection. He didn't want her anymore, didn't love her anymore. If he had stabbed her in the chest it would have been less painful.

"Go. Return home to your husband," Royden ordered, needing her gone.

Oria raised her hood, covering her scar, and hurried out of the keep.

He warned himself not to follow her, not watch her leave, not lose her again. He lost the battle and hurried out of the keep. She was already riding away. She wanted to be rid of him and he couldn't blame her. He'd come home a far different man. A man she didn't know. A man she didn't love.

"You and Oria have been through a lot. It takes time to heal," Bethany said, having come up behind him.

"She has a husband to help her heal," Royden said, unable to keep the anger out of his voice.

"She didn't tell you?"

Royden swerved around to glare at Bethany. "Tell me what?"

"Oria is a widow."

Chapter Three

Royden looked over the fields with Penn. He had accomplished much in the three days since he'd been home, but had failed to come to any rationale solution about Oria. If she still loved him she would have told him right away that she was free to wed again, but she hadn't. Though, he hadn't been as kind as he should have been, but he had thought her a married woman. What did that matter? He should have at least let her know he never stopped loving her. He had told himself over and over that was the first thing he'd do when he returned home. He'd let Oria know he never, not for one day, one moment stopped loving her.

"We need more men to get these fields fully prepared for summer planting of the oats and barley," Penn said, looking out over the unfinished fields. "You also can use some extra hands with getting the keep in shape, not to mention all the repairs to the village."

"We have who we have. We'll have to make do," Royden said, annoyed that he'd lost so many of his clansmen to the mercenaries.

"I can get extra hands. I know Chieftain Fergus of the Clan MacDonnegal and many of the warriors who chose to stay and make a home with the clan. They would help if I asked."

Royden turned a murderous glare on Penn. "You want me to beg for help from those responsible for the destruction of my home, my clan?"

"It's not begging and those men are not your enemy now, they're your neighbors. They aren't even the warriors who attacked here. If you're not comfortable asking

Chieftain Fergus, then Lady Learmonth would surely lend her clansmen to help us."

That infuriated him even more. Even the thought of asking Oria for help struck a blow to his pride. But he had discovered that pride didn't always serve one well.

"Chieftain Fergus has wanted to meet you since your return home. Why not meet with him and judge for yourself," Penn suggested.

Royden folded his arms across his broad chest. "Tell me, is this what your leader had in mind? Infiltrate the area with his men and eventually take over without having to lift a weapon?"

"I don't know what he had in mind. I do know, though, that he was only interested in claiming this particular area. We were to attack no other clans but the ones designated."

"What specific clans?" Royden asked, eager for another piece to the puzzle.

"Clan Learmonth, Clan MacDonnegal, Clan MacGlennen, Clan Macara, and Clan MacKinnon."

All the clans he mentioned bordered one or more of the others somewhere along their borders. Clan Learmonth was the oldest of the clans and had owned much of the land before battles but disputes changed that.

"You claimed to know nothing yet you tell me this now. Is there more information you'll tell me as time goes on?" Royden asked. Penn seemed like a decent enough man, but it would take time, if ever, that he would trust him.

"I do my best to prove my loyalty," Penn said.

"But who are you truly loyal to?" Royden asked, having wondered that since meeting him.

"Men approach," Penn said, pointing in the distance.

Royden followed where Penn pointed, though kept in mind that he never responded to his question. Had it been convenient or on purpose?

There were three men. As they got closer, it was obvious from their slow gait and soiled garments they had been traveling on foot for a good distance. When they drew even closer, Royden recognized them as members of the clan.

He greeted them with strong hugs and he understood the tears that welled in their eyes. He had felt it himself when he had seen the keep and had seen a familiar face. He knew then he was finally home just as these men did now.

"We were told you were home when we were released," John said.

Short and barrel-chested, John was thicker in the arms and legs than when Royden last saw him, which had been about three years ago when his clansmen had been separated from him.

"And we heard more men are being released," Angus chimed in, hurrying his hand over his eyes before tears could fall. "Some from the Clan Macara and from the Clan MacDonnegal."

Angus had been thick in the middle from all the sweets he'd sweet-talked out of Bethany. No more. He had slimmed down, though his long, dark hair was heavily sprinkled with gray.

"Did anyone tell you the reason you were being let go?" Royden asked.

Stuart, a tall man with bright red hair, said, "I didn't care for the why. I just wanted to get home to my Sara. She was heavy with child when I was taken away. Please tell me she and my bairn are here and safe."

Royden was relieved he could give the man good news. "Aye, Sara is well as is your son, named for you. And the little lad's a hard worker too, helping wherever he can.

Stuart didn't try to stop the tears. "A son. I have a son."

The men slapped him on the back, congratulating him.

"I'm dying for some of Bethany's sweets. I sure did miss them," Angus said.

"He missed Bethany as well, but the stubborn fool won't admit it," Stuart said, and the men laughed when Angus's cheeks blossomed red and he mumbled as he walked off toward the village.

The men followed him and Royden was glad to see the smiles on their faces and hear their laughter. Smiles and laughter were needed here again, though neither would come easily after all they had suffered.

Clansmen hurried to greet the returning men with tears and hugs.

"God be praised, you're home!" Sara cried out when she spotted her husband.

Stuart had her in his arms in no time and the two wept like children. Little Stuart stood nearby staring at them when Big Stuart suddenly scooped him up and announced, "I'm your da, lad."

The little lad looked to his mum, and she nodded. "Aye, he's your da."

The lad threw his arms around his da's neck and hugged him, and Stuart shed more tears.

The bell tolled surprising, frightening, and alerting everyone that warriors approached.

Royden swore quietly, not wanting to show his alarm. There weren't enough men to protect the village and the ones skilled enough to were too exhausted to battle. Somehow he had to grow the clan or it would be far too susceptible if attacked.

"Royden," Angus called out, and Royden's hand shot up and caught the hilt of the sword Angus threw his way.

It had taken time to learn that feat, but he had forced himself to do so and it had been a wise decision, one that had helped during battle. He heard the rush of whispers around him. He'd known, without a word being spoken, that many wondered about his abilities and skills having only one hand. In time, they would see he was a far better warrior than he had once been.

Royden was proud that even though exhausted from a long journey the men drew their swords and gathered behind him, ready to fight. The women even reached for weapons along with a couple of older men whose frailty would never sustain a fight. Still, though, they drew swords.

To Royden's relief, a good-sized man led only six warriors toward the village. They were not under attack and seeing who approached all lowered their weapons, but kept them in hand.

"That's Chieftain Fergus," Penn said, standing next to Royden, sword in hand.

"You invited him without my permission," Royden accused.

Penn shook his head. "No, I would never do such a thing. Fergus comes of his own accord."

Royden waited, his sword remaining firm in his hand, and watched the small troop approach. Fergus sat erect on his horse, his posture one of pride, strength, and confidence, which often signaled a skilled warrior. He looked to be of average height and though he wore a dark, wool cloak draped over his broad shoulders, it was easy to see he was of solid girth. His long hair was a golden red and braids hung on either side. His features were plain, nothing that would turn a woman's head. The warriors that followed behind him sat with the same degree of strength and purpose, though one caught Royden's eye.

A cleric.

What was a cleric doing with this troop?

Fergus stopped the troop a short distance from Royden. He dismounted and approached with a forceful stride.

"I don't wish to intrude, but I've wanted to meet with you and welcome you home," Fergus said, extending his hand.

Royden didn't offer his hand.

Fergus dropped his hand, his face pinched with annoyance. "Thurbane sends his regards. He would have come with me but he hasn't felt well lately."

"Or you didn't want him here," Royden said.

Fergus blew out a hefty breath. "I know this can't be easy for you, but I'm here to stay. We can either be friends or enemies, the choice is yours."

"The choice is mine?" Royden laughed. "When did you give Thurbane a choice or his daughter Alynn? Your leader stole from all the surrounding clans, so don't tell me the choice is mine that we are to be friends or foe. You are my enemy until proven otherwise."

"Then let me prove otherwise," Fergus said. "It looks like you could use some help around here. Let me send some men to help you with your fields and make repairs to your village as the weather allows."

Royden wanted nothing more than to refuse his offer, but with so few men to see to all that needed to be done, it would be foolish of him to refuse Fergus. He needed to make sure sufficient food was made ready for the winter months, the storage sheds stocked, and their shelters sound. He'd never be able to do it all with the amount of men he had. Like it or not, he needed the help.

"Let me prove I am more friend than foe," Fergus said and extended his hand again.

"Prove yourself a friend, only then will I extend my hand to you," Royden said.

Fergus shook his head as he dropped his hand once again. "You're a hard-headed one."

"Cautious is more like it," Royden said.

"The day is young and my men are ready to help. Put them to work while we talk," Fergus offered.

Penn spoke up. "The fields desperately need to be finished in time for planting."

Royden didn't like that Penn let Fergus know the clan was desperate for anything, but the ground needed to be made ready for summer planting or the oats and barley they depended on to feed the clan wouldn't be plentiful.

Fergus turned a grin on Royden. "My men can see to that while we talk and drink."

It was an opportunity to possibly learn more about the mysterious leader. One he couldn't turn down. But first he would have a few words with Angus and John.

"Keep watch over the lot of them, Penn as well," Royden ordered. "I'll see that ale and food are sent to you."

Both men nodded and, though tired, did their duty without complaint.

Royden had had one of the damaged trestle tables from the Great Hall brought outside and placed under the large oak tree. One of the four corners had broken off and a section of the top had a split running down a piece of the wood. It might not serve well in the Great Hall, but it would do outside. Two damaged benches sat on either side and Royden took the side where he could watch over the village. Fergus was stuck with his back to the village or anyone who approached.

As soon as they sat a servant lass placed a pitcher of ale and two tankards on the table, then left only to return moments later with a bowl of salted meat.

Fergus ran the back of his hand over his mouth after downing a whole tankard of ale. "Nectar of the gods." He refilled his tankard and drank half of it. "I have no fight with you, Royden."

"Then tell me who I do have a fight with."

"It's over and done. Let it be," Fergus advised.

"I lost far too much to let it go, including five years of my life," Royden said with a bitterness he didn't try to hide.

"And it took me ten to find a life," Fergus argued.

"You mean rob another of his land."

"And who did Thurbane rob it from?" Fergus spat back. "The strong and the ones willing to fight, to survive, Royden. You fought and survived. You're back home now. Build a clan no one can destroy and friendships that will help you defend it. That's my plan."

Royden glanced toward the village. "I already had that."

"Did you?"

Royden was about to ask him what he meant when he spotted Oria walking toward the keep, Angus holding the reins of her horse as he walked beside her.

"Over here, Angus," Royden called out and he and Oria turned toward him, though Oria alone approached, Angus walked off leaving the horse to nibble at a patch of grass.

"It's wonderful to see that some of the men have returned home," Oria said with a genuine smile.

He'd forgotten how beautiful she was when she smiled. He thought he had seared the memory of that smile in his mind, but seeing it now, he hadn't truly remembered the beauty of it or the joy it had always brought him. And he hadn't felt that sense of joy in five years.

Royden stood and Fergus did the same.

"It is good to see you once again, Lady Learmonth," Fergus said.

"And you as well, Fergus," Oria said.

That she retained her smile while greeting Fergus proved that she truly was pleased to see the man and had Royden asking, "You greet this man as a friend?"

"Lady Oria is a good friend to my wife and to me as well. She helped in the birth of our bairns and Alynn was there for her when Burnell died six months ago, God rest his soul," Fergus said.

Royden's eye went to Oria at that news to see what she would do and her remark annoyed him.

"Burnell was a good man and a good husband."

"And it's another good husband you'll have soon," Fergus said. "The King himself has seen to it."

Royden felt as if a sword had been thrust through his heart. While he thought himself unworthy of her, there was still a spark of hope that in time they could recover what had been lost to them, whether he wanted to admit it or not. Now there was no more time. She'd been given to another once again.

"I will not be forced to marry again," Oria said with an annoyance of someone who was tired of repeating herself.

A slight smile poked at the corners of Royden's mouth at the way her soft green eyes deepened in color when they flared with anger.

"You don't have a choice. Learmonth's land and title pass to his relative," Fergus said. "And you won't retain your title, but I never thought the title meant anything to you anyway."

"It doesn't, and how can I be homeless when my da's keep sits empty?" she asked.

"Your family's land is no longer yours. It belongs to another now," Fergus said. "It's done, the documents signed. You're as good as wed. All that's left are the vows and, of course, the consummation to seal it all."

The idea of Oria lying with yet another man infuriated Royden and he didn't give thought. The words shot out of his mouth with force. "I'll wed Oria."

"You need not sacrifice for me, Royden," she said with a prideful tilt of her chin.

How could she think it was a sacrifice for him to wed her? It didn't matter whether she wanted to or not, he would wed her.

I failed you once. I won't fail you again.

Those words rang in his head but didn't fall from his lips. Instead, he demanded, "You will wed me."

"I've been ordered—"

"I don't care who ordered it," Royden spat, stopping Oria from arguing with him. He'd have his way. To hell with the power hungry fiend. He looked to Fergus. "You brought a cleric with you. Wed us now and be done with it."

"No doubt the orders came from the King. He would just annul the marriage," Oria argued, worried what the King would do to Royden for interfering in his plans.

Fergus burst out laughing and Royden and Oria stared at him in disbelief.

"You claim Oria is a friend, yet you find it humorous that she is being forced to wed once again?" Royden asked anger marking his every word.

"Aye, I do—since it's *you* she's being forced to wed." Fergus laughed even louder.

Chapter Four

"Is this a game you play, Fergus?" Royden demanded, the news having shocked him. Or was it that he was relieved that he and Oria would finally be husband and wife as it had been planned? But it wasn't by choice. Would she marry him otherwise?

"Not at all. I have the document to prove it, the royal seal affixed. While I don't think either of you will object, since you were to wed at one time, I must tell you that it is a condition of your release. You must wed Oria or you will be returned to the mercenaries."

Oria rushed to say, "I'll wed Royden."

Did Oria sacrifice to save him? This wasn't the way they were to wed, forced to save either of themselves. If they loved each other, what did it matter? That was the question that gnawed at him. Much had changed in five years. He certainly had and Oria had had a husband, a good husband from what she had said. How would marriage be for both of them now?

"Good, then we'll get it done," Fergus said.

A thought occurred to Royden. "I was told someone made a deep sacrifice for my release. If that is so, why then would the King interfere?"

"I don't know. I'm not privy to how your release came about. I follow the orders sent to me," Fergus said.

"By the King or the one who commands you?" Royden demanded his temper flaring.

"I won't stand here and argue with you about it. It's your choice. Wed Oria or return to the mercenaries," Fergus said with a touch of anger.

It wasn't lost on Royden that Fergus didn't protest that someone commanded him. There was more to what was going on with his release than he was being told. Had the leader of the mercenaries struck a bargain with the King, but if that was so there was no reason for anyone to sacrifice for his release. None of it made sense and that made him want to find out what was truly going on.

"Wed us now. I will not see Royden taken from his home again," Oria commanded with such strength and determination that both men's brows shot up.

"I don't need you to defend me," Royden snapped out of sheer pride that she would be saving him.

"Since you've gotten so stubborn and prideful, then wed me so I won't be homeless," she said.

That rankled him even more since she sacrificed her own pride for him. "Are you begging me to wed you?"

"Aye, if that is what it will take for you not to be foolhardy," she said, her tongue as curt as his.

"I should—"

"Refuse me and leave me homeless?" she challenged, her green eyes blazing brightly.

Royden didn't hide his anger and he spoke to her as he never thought he would. "Your tongue has grown sharp over the years, woman."

"No, my tongue has grown wiser over the years. It's a shame yours hasn't."

Fergus wisely moved out of the way of the two, stepping to the side and glad he was that he did, since Royden vaulted over the table with the agility and strength of a seasoned warrior. A surprising feat for a man with one hand.

Royden went to stand directly in front of Oria. "You've changed and not for the better."

"And what of you, Royden. Who is it that I marry, since you certainly aren't the kind and loving man I once knew and loved?"

He leaned down, his nose almost touching hers. "You're about to find out." He turned away from her. "Fetch the cleric, Fergus, and let's get this done."

Oria went and sat on the bench at the table, fearful her trembling legs wouldn't hold her up much longer. She kept her head up and her shoulders erect, letting no one see the worry that had taken hold of her. Never had she imagined she'd be forced to wed Royden. Force would never be necessary, not to wed the man she loved. But was he still that man? Did she truly know who she wed?

She took light breaths to calm her turmoil. This was what she had wanted for as long as she could remember—to be Royden's wife. The circumstances were not as she had imagined them to be, but her love for him hadn't changed even if he had. But would her love be enough? Or would she find herself wed to a stranger?

She felt a hand on her shoulder and looked up to see Bethany.

"I am happy for you both. You and Royden were always meant for each other. All will be good now," Bethany said with a joyous smile.

Oria wished she had the woman's confidence. However, as she stood at the cleric's approach, her legs—weak from trembling—reminded otherwise.

It was a quick ceremony. Fergus and Bethany were the only witnesses to it. Royden signed the document Fergus presented to him, and it was done.

She and Royden were husband and wife. She should have been happy but she felt more relieved than anything. Royden was safe and she wasn't homeless. Not thoughts a new bride would expect to have on her wedding day.

"Fergus and I have things to discuss, and there are things I must see to. We'll talk later," Royden said, dismissing her and turned to walk away with Fergus.

"Since the day has you occupied, I'll ride to Learmonth and see to gathering my possessions and return before nightfall," Oria said.

Royden swerved around to face her. "You will not go anywhere. I'll send someone to see to it. You will remain here."

"I prefer to see to it myself and let those at Learmonth know I won't be returning," Oria said, annoyed that he dictated to her.

She had been blessed with the gift of freedom from Burnell. He never dictated to her or made demands of her. In a way, he had spoiled her giving her such freedom and she hadn't realized it until this moment.

"Whether you prefer it or not, I forbid it," Royden ordered sharply and once again dismissed her by turning away.

"You forbid me to go?" she asked, his dictate stirring her anger.

"Aye, *forbid*," he reiterated with emphasis, annoyed she questioned him in front of Fergus.

"Come, my lady, I will fix you a nice brew," Bethany said.

"Oria no longer bears the title," Royden reminded with annoyance. "She's simply mistress now." He turned to Fergus. "Come, there are things to discuss."

Oria hurried after him and once outside she saw him stop and speak to a lad of about ten years and the lad ran toward her horse while her husband and Fergus continued on.

"Come, Mistress Oria, a chill fills the air. Come in and sit by the fire and enjoy a hot brew," Bethany encouraged, having followed her outside.

"Not right now, Bethany." Without a glance toward the woman, Oria hurried toward the lad who was about to take the reins of her horse. "Leave her be, lad," she ordered.

"Chieftain Royden ordered me to tend the horse," the lad said.

Oria took the reins from him. "I will let the chieftain know I chose to do the task myself. Go and see if Bethany has a treat for you." She looked to Bethany. "He needs a treat."

Bethany nodded with a smile and waved the lad to her, though her eyes sent a warning to Oria that she ignored.

Without an ounce of doubt to her actions, Oria mounted her horse and took off, and she didn't take her time going through the village. She set a fast pace and flew right past her husband.

Royden and Fergus stumbled out of her way, almost tumbling to the ground.

Fergus laughed. "You're going to have your hands full with that one."

Royden looked around for a horse.

"Take mine," Fergus offered, pointing to a chestnut colored stallion.

Royden didn't hesitate. He threw himself up on the horse and took off.

Penn approached Fergus and they both watched him.

"He handles himself far better than I expected for a one-handed man," Fergus said.

"He's no fool. He already suspects I am here to provide information to the leader of the mercenaries," Penn said.

"You like your new home, Penn?" Fergus asked.

"I do. And I love my wife and look forward to our bairn being born," Penn admitted.

"Then do what you're told so you don't lose what you love just as I am doing," Fergus said.

***

Royden couldn't believe Oria had disobeyed him. She'd always been compliant, never arguing with him, always thoughtful and agreeable. Where had that woman gone? And how had she learned to ride with such skill and confidence—and speed?

He raced to catch up with her, glad Fergus's horse had speed of his own. They were racing across an open meadow and the land spread out beyond offered slight hills that wouldn't slow her down much. If he didn't reach her before then, he doubted he would be able to catch her.

He crouched over the horse and picked up speed. It wasn't easy to pluck someone off a racing horse or jump onto one from another racing horse, and at one time, he didn't have the skill or the confidence to attempt either feat. But the time came when he had had no choice, necessity had dictated it and anger had driven him. If he hadn't taken a chance, Arran would have died. After that time, he didn't fear attempting either feat again and again and again, until he was skilled enough to do so with confidence rather than fear.

Anger drove him once again. He had forbid Oria to leave and she had defied him. She would learn that was something he wouldn't tolerate.

He caught up with her and it took only a few moments to adjust to her pace and another moment to determine timing and then—he threw himself off his horse to land directly behind his wife. His left arm hooked her around the waist to yank her snugly against him while his right hand took hold of the reins and brought the horse under his control. He worked the reins to slow the mare's pace. Fergus's horse slowed on his own accord to a trot before circling back to join him.

Oria struggled against him to no avail. She didn't recall him being that strong or his muscles that taut. His muscles seemed as hard as the metal anvil the smithies pounded their hammers against. She shivered, realizing it was impossible and useless to defend herself against him.

She was glad when he brought the horse to a halt, though not when he dismounted and hooking her waist once again, he swung her off after his feet had barely touched the ground. She stumbled against him, hitting his hard chest before his hand took tight hold of her arm and shook her.

"Where are your senses, woman?" he berated.

"You have no right to dictate to me," she accused, her chest heaving from her heavy breaths.

"That right became mine when we exchanged vows," he reminded. "You will obey my word. I'll have it no other way."

"Then you'll be disappointed."

His anger had him wanting to thrash her into submission, but he had never raised a hand to her and he never would. Only cowards hit women and he was far from a coward.

He yanked Oria against him and dropped his head so their noses almost touched. "Listen well, woman, you will heed my word."

Oria pressed her nose against his. "Or what?"

Something happened at that moment. She didn't know how, what, or why and she didn't care. She only knew that by some small shred of hope or some miracle she spied the man she loved in Royden and it was like the shattered pieces of her heart began to piece together.

"Royden," she whispered and pressed her lips to his.

Her kiss was like a shock to his soul, it slammed through him battering anything that stood in its way until it hit him deep. He couldn't resist if he wanted to and he didn't want to. He had dreamt endlessly of her lips and how they would feel again and they didn't disappoint.

Her lips were gentle, curious, and aching for more as she urged his lips to respond. If he did, he feared he wouldn't stop, wouldn't let her go. He warned himself to be careful, take it slow, but the unquenched ache he had had for her all those years rose up and took control.

His hand went to the back of her neck, his fingers digging up through her hair to grip the back of her head as his lips took control of hers.

Never had Royden kissed her with such possessiveness. Never had she known such a kiss possible. His lips held such strength and his tongue such purpose as it delved into her mouth and while forceful, by no means did he force her. She responded with equal enthusiasm. Her passion ignited so rapidly that it sent darts of pleasure poking at the most intimate of places. It caught her so unaware it robbed her of her breath and he must have realized it, since to her great disappointment, his lips left hers. She was relieved—her moan—evidence of it when he nibbled along her bottom lip, plump with passion and down along her neck, nipping at her tender flesh with his teeth and lips and sending gooseflesh prickling her skin.

Good Lord, she had missed this man.

His lips returned to hers, his kiss bruising, demanding as if he couldn't get enough, but then either could she. It was as though they tried to make up for the wasted years that had separated them.

Her body ached for him as it had done when he was gone. She had had the memories but they had been torture, recalling his kiss, his touch, and she had berated herself for not having made love with him, for having waited for a wedding night that never came.

His hand left the back of her head and to her surprise he grabbed her hand and reached down with it to slip under his plaid and lay against his hard manhood. He kept his hand over hers, not letting her move it. His shaft swelled against her palm—already so thick she wondered how it could grow any bigger—and seemed to pulse with a life of its own. It was velvet soft and she instinctively squeezed it, and Royden groaned.

He dropped his head back for a mere second, then placed his brow against hers. "I want to throw you to the ground and jam myself deep inside you over and over and over until you overflow with my seed."

She was surprised again that his words thrilled her and at the heavy wetness she felt between her legs. She was as eager to feel him inside her as he was to be there.

He shoved her away from him and took several steps back. "I'm not the mannerly man you once knew and loved. If anything, I'm more a savage. I've killed, beaten, looted, and stuck my shaft into more women than I can recall. Until I can control my savage instincts, you are to stay away from me. Now get on your horse."

Oria took a step toward him.

"Get on your horse!" he shouted at her.

She did as he ordered, the threat in his tone warning against disobeying him, and he got on his horse.

Royden brought his horse near to hers. "Do not challenge me, disobey me, tempt me. Do I make myself clear?"

She nodded.

"We return home."

"Please, let me go to Learmonth and gather my things. I don't have much. It won't take long. Also, a few of your clansmen came to stay at Learmonth and when they learned you returned they asked to go home. I could bring them with me when I return. Please, Royden, I need this." She hated to sound like she begged, but she needed time away from him—if only for a few hours—to try to make sense of it all.

He stared at her, the taste of her still on his lips and his shaft still swollen from the touch of her hand. He didn't want her to go. He wanted her with him—a dangerous thought.

"Go, but don't be long," he said.

Fearful she would fall into a heap of tears, she hurried to say, "Thank you."

"Don't thank me. I do what is necessary, otherwise you would be down on the ground your legs spread wide for me. Remember that when you think to tempt the savage in me."

He rode off and she hurried in the opposite direction, not seeing him stop and look back at her, not knowing how much he hurt.

Chapter Five

Oria stretched herself awake. It had been two days since she wed Royden and he had done everything he could to avoid her. She'd been placed in the chieftain's bedchamber, but Royden hadn't joined her there. He had continued to sleep in his bedchamber, the one she would have shared with him when they first were to wed. She worried that their marriage wasn't truly sealed without consummating it, which meant it could be dissolved far too easily. She didn't want that, but how she would solve the problem, she didn't know.

She had thought endlessly about the incident between them the other day. That he thought himself a savage disturbed her. She didn't believe Royden could ever be a savage. He had been made to do things to survive just as she had been, though he had suffered far worse than she had. That time, however, was over. They could build a good life together. The only thing she could think to do to make that possible was to get to know the man Royden had become and show him that she loved him just as much as the man he had been.

She bounced out of bed eager to start the day, to move forward with the plan to get to know her husband. The first step was not letting him avoid her.

At least, she was happy here amongst people familiar to her, people who cared for her. Burnell's clan had been overrun with warriors unfamiliar to all and they had made little friends with the clansmen. She had never felt at home at Learmonth and it was good to finally feel at home once again.

She hurried into a pale yellow shift and slipped a dark green tunic over it. She pulled on her boots, planning on tracking down her husband who'd been spending a good portion of his day outside, if weather permitted. Otherwise, he cloistered himself in the solar. She gathered her honey-blonde hair up on the top of her head with a couple of bone combs, though couldn't keep several strands from falling free. At least it would be out of her way. She used the water in the bucket Bethany had brought to her to scrub her face fresh, leaving her cheeks glowing. She smiled at the dried mint in the small bowl near the bucket, recalling how Raven had told her about Bethany teaching her how to keep her breath fresh with it. Oria was grateful Bethany had extended her the same courtesy.

She hurried down to the Great Hall, hoping to catch Royden before he left the keep for the day, but she was too late.

"He left some time ago," Bethany said when she saw the disappointment on Oria's face.

Several of the trestle tables and benches had been repaired and arranged in the Great Hall. The room was far different than Oria had remembered it. It felt so cold and empty without the beautiful tapestries hanging on the walls and the long table, with beautiful linens draped over it, that once sat on the dais along with several throne-like chairs. It hurt to see how badly the lovely room had been gutted.

"Sit and I'll bring you food and drink," Bethany said.

Oria shook her head. "I'm not hungry."

"At least take a cloak, mistress, there's a brisk chill in the air today," Bethany called out.

Oria gabbed one of the many wool cloaks hanging on the pegs by the door and swung it over her shoulders to tie at her neck. She was glad that she did. A chill did fill the air and gray clouds dotted the sky. It was one of those unpredictable weather days in the Highlands but then weather was always unpredictable here.

She walked toward the village, smiling at the sound of chatter, laughter, children playing, and work being done. Life was finally returning to the Clan MacKinnon and she was grateful to be part of it.

Before she went to find her husband, she made a stop at Emily's cottage. The young woman had been accompanying her when she had regularly visited here and tended those in need. Oria smiled when she caught sight of Emily stepping out of her cottage, a basket in hand.

Emily saw her at the same time and waved.

Oria wondered how she got around, she had grown so large with child, though it might have been her petite size that made her protruding stomach appear so huge. Her bright red curls bounced out from around her head even though she had tried to contain them with combs, and a spattering of freckles across her nose and cheeks actually added to her lovely features.

"Feeling well this morning?" Oria asked when she reached Emily.

Emily's hand went to rub her rounded stomach. "Well enough, though I'll be pleased when he's born. He so active I barely sleep."

"Two months is it?"

Emily nodded and laughed. "Not soon enough. I can't tell you how pleased I am, as well as everyone else here, that you are the new mistress of Clan MacKinnon. It's what should have been and glad we are that it's finally done." She patted her stomach again. "And soon you'll be carrying the heir to the Clan MacKinnon."

How that could be when her husband didn't touch her, barely acknowledged her, she didn't know. Though, she'd let no one know that.

"Does someone need tending?" Oria asked, pointing to the basket and wanting to avoid any more talk of future bairns.

Emily drew back the cloth covering the top of the basket. "Bread for Mildred, her hands have been more painful than usual and some for Calla. She can use all the food she can get with five lads and a husband to feed. Though, all are confident with Royden's return home that food will once again be plentiful."

After walking with Emily to Mildred's cottage and speaking briefly with the old woman, Oria continued on through the village. There was so much that needed Royden's attention, she now wondered if he truly had avoided her or he was simply too busy to pay her heed.

She got her answer when shortly afterward, she spotted Royden talking with Penn and sent him a wave along with a smile. He acknowledged neither. He turned and walked away, Penn following after him.

She thought to go after him, but what good would it do confronting him in front of others? What was between them was private and she intended to keep it that way.

Feeling a bit removed from things, her routine having been completely changed, she decided to take herself into the woods. She had shared lovely moments with Raven and Purity in the woods. Their friendship with Purity had barely time to form before the attack, yet it had been as if the three of them had been longtime friends. The memory of their friendship had sustained her through difficult times. The three of them shared a special connection, one not only forged out of necessity, but love as well. It was a connection no one could break and the last five years had proven that.

She entered the woods and made her way to the spot she and Raven and Purity had once gathered. It was a spot they had bonded and became friends in a brief but significant time. She thought to go deeper into the woods, but decided it presently wasn't a wise choice.

A glance up had her smiling. The trees were thick with sprouting buds. Soon they would all blossom, creating a canopy overhead and an oasis of privacy. Here is where she would miss her friends the most and also where the memories of that horrid day would too often set in.

She lowered herself to the ground and try as she might not to shed tears, she couldn't help it. That day five years ago had torn family and friends apart, destroyed lives, and altered futures. She would never forget it and she would never stop shedding tears when the memories rose up to torment her.

***

Royden had purposely ignored his wife. Every time he saw her, she looked more beautiful than the time before. And every time he saw her, his loins would stir with such an ache that he had to distance himself for fear of doing something foolish.

He wanted his wife with a fierce hunger. A hunger he had never known before. Even the hunger he had had for her five years ago when they were to wed was nothing to the hunger he had for her now. Perhaps it was because he was now far too familiar with the pleasure of coupling. And he wondered—more ached—to see if he would find the deep satisfaction he was looking for with Oria that he had never achieved with another woman. Whatever it was, he didn't know how long he could fight it.

When he had seen her smile, had seen the way her soft blonde hair had fallen haphazardly around her neck and face, his first thought had been to free her hair of the combs and run his fingers through her silky waves, inhale the fresh scent of her, and taste the minty flavor that forever lingered on her lips.

She was his wife and he had a duty to consummate his marriage. And it troubled him that he delayed it, since she could be taken from him far too easily if he didn't seal their vows. But how did he touch his wife, leave his mark on her, when he had done such horrible things?

"We extended the field as you ordered," Penn said, pulling Royden out of his reverie. "And, the good Lord willing, we'll have a bountiful crop of oats and barely this year."

Clearing his head with a slight shake, Royden responded, "That is good to hear."

"Stuart finished the repairs to his roof's cottage faster than I've ever seen done. He claims it's because he doesn't want the roof leaking on his bare arse while he pokes his wife." Penn laughed. "He's helping repair the other roofs now."

Royden didn't want to hear about bare arses and poking wives since he wasn't poking his wife, but he listened and offered a comment. "Anything that gets the repairs done. Besides, Stuart's been away from his wife far too long."

And I've been away from Oria far too long and I shouldn't waste any time in making love to her. Far too much time has already been lost.

"Have you sent the hunters out?" Royden asked, needing to get away from thoughts of husbands poking wives.

"I did and some have already returned. Today's kill will be spread among the villagers." Penn cleared his throat. "Many have been wondering when the Great Hall will be available for meals once again as it once was in your da's time."

"Soon," Royden said, though wasn't truly certain. More tables needed repairs and the stone walls were so bare without the tapestries. He could only do so much, though it was important the clan had a place to freely congregate and feel like family once again. Perhaps that was why he delayed seeing to the Great Hall. Something was missing... his family. Oria was his family now, but he wouldn't rest until Arran and his sister, Raven, were home, and he found out his da's fate.

"Chieftain," Angus called out.

Royden turned, still not comfortable with the respectful title. It belonged to his da and every time he heard it, his heart broke a bit more at losing the man who had taught him much about being a man.

"What is it, Angus?" Royden asked.

"With all that has gone on, I'm more cautious, wearier than I once was, so seeing Mistress Oria enter the woods alone, by the oak tree, I thought it best you be informed."

Royden's brow rose sharply. "I appreciate your keen eye, Angus."

"A keen eye is needed," Angus said and looked to Penn before he walked away.

"Will I ever be accepted here into the clan?" Penn asked.

"That's up to you," Royden said and walked away as well, his strides strong and fast as he headed to the woods.

He heard Oria's sobs when only a few paces into the woods and it tore at his heart. He hurried forward and spotted her seated on the ground, her face buried in her hands as she wept. He didn't hesitate to go to her.

He bent down in front of her and with his arm around her waist and his other arm slipping beneath her legs, he scooped her up against him.

She gasped but only a moment. Seeing she was in his arms, she laid her head on his shoulder and let her tears fall.

Royden sat on the ground, placing her on his lap, cradling her close and wishing he could take her pain away.

He was at a loss as to why she cried. Was it for the years they had lost? For their forced marriage? Did she believe it was a mistake to wed him?

As much as he didn't want to talk, didn't want to spend time with her for fear of losing control, he had little choice if he wanted to know what caused her grief. For now, though, he let her weep, let her shed whatever pained her.

Oria cuddled against his warmth, his strength, his love. She could tell herself it was what she wanted to believe, that he still loved her, but she knew for certain. He had held her, cradled her, comforted her that way before and he had done so because he loved her just as he did now. There was no way Oria would believe that Royden had ever stopped loving her.

Her sobs subsided, mostly because his strong arms offered the comfort and love she needed. And she remained there contented, never wanting him to let her go—not ever again.

"Tell me why you cry?" Royden asked, needing to know for his own sanity as her sobs eased.

"Memories," she managed to say. "They sneak up on one and stab at the heart."

He knew all too well what she meant. "Far too often."

She nodded against his shoulder.

"Tell me what hurts you?" he encouraged, wanting to know, wanting to ease her pain.

"How do I choose? There are so many," she confessed.

"And there are no rhyme or reason to them."

"Aye, you're right. They come and stab at you at will and no matter how hard you fight, you can't chase them away. They leave when they choose to leave and not before."

Her words could have been his words. She described perfectly what it was like for the memories to intrude at will and remain until ready to take their leave. All the mental fighting in the world didn't help. The memories did as they pleased and hurt with endless vigor.

She looked up at him. "It is good to be in the comfort of your arms once again. I have missed them around me."

Her soft green eyes had turned bright from crying and her cheeks were damp from her tears, and her lips were far too close and far too tempting, and his resolve far too weak.

Oria watched the dilemma play out in his dark eyes, felt it as he tightened his hold on her, and how he struggled to keep control and instinct had her lifting her face just enough so her lips were closer to his as she whispered, "I have missed you so much."

A whiff of mint tickled at his nose and God help him, that was enough—he couldn't resist. It wasn't a demanding kiss he settled on her lips but a light brush of his lips he whispered across hers, taunting and teasing them, torturing them both with delayed but delightful pleasure.

She mewed softly when he nibbled at her lower lip, then brushed his lips across it and felt her shiver. He placed a soft kiss on her lips, keeping it tender, then ran the tip of his tongue along the slight opening between her lips. That was it. Her mouth dropped open inviting him in and he entered with a flourish.

Oria's hand went up around his neck to grip it tight, to hold him captive so that he couldn't change his mind, couldn't break the kiss. His lips grew demanding and she responded with a demand of her own. There was a hunger between them that had gone unsatisfied far too long. And she wondered if their quench would ever be satisfied. For now, however, she would take this moment with him—this kiss—and linger in it.

And she did. She didn't remember him ever kissing her like this, a blend of tenderness and hunger, one feeding the other. It stirred her senses and when his hand moved to her backside to adjust it to nest on his bulging manhood, a tingle settled with a vengeance between her legs. She wiggled her bottom until she fit perfectly against him.

Royden's lips left hers, a moaning growl erupting low in his chest and he turned his head away. He had to stop this or he'd have her on her back and be inside her in no time.

"Don't stop," Oria begged, seeing his hesitation.

He didn't know where the words came from and he regretted them as soon as they left his mouth. "Is it a good poke you need since you've been without a husband these past six months?"

His words cut deep and she scrambled out of his arms and to her feet, her anger surging.

Royden barely got to his feet when he felt her hand slam against his cheek.

"Don't ever speak so rudely to me again. Burnell was a good man."

Royden grabbed her arm, near her shoulder, so tight, that she winced. "Raise your hand to me again and you'll be sorry."

Oria didn't care that he looked ready to kill, she retaliated, "Speak to me the way you did again and you'll be sorry." She went to yank her arm away and couldn't budge it.

"You see and feel my strength, woman. Do not anger me." He shoved her away from him and ordered, "Get back to the keep now."

Oria thought to defy him, her anger raging but she held her tongue and rushed past him, stopping and turning for a moment. "Burnell did something you didn't do. He kept me safe." She turned and ran, tears rushing to her eyes.

Royden felt her words like a punch to his gut that almost took him to the ground. She was right. He hadn't kept her safe when he had promised her he would. He couldn't blame her for feeling that way when he felt that way himself and had for the past five years. What he couldn't understand was how Burnell, a seven ten and five years old man could keep her safe when he hadn't been able to.

Chapter Six

"She's barely eaten in three days and has barely spoken to anyone," Bethany said, wringing her hands with worry.

Royden rubbed his chin, having grown concerned about his wife himself. He'd seen her only once in the last three days and she hadn't even looked his way. Their last encounter had taken a toll on them both. He had berated himself endlessly for having said what he did to her. He'd been wrong, so wrong, especially at such a vulnerable moment. He felt like an arse, but the words were out and he couldn't take them back.

It couldn't go on like this. They were husband and wife and nothing was going to change that, and he didn't want it to. They had to find a way to get along. But would the pain of the past allow them to do that?

"Where is she now?" Royden asked, rising out of the chair in his solar and going to stand by the hearth, a fire blazing in it to chase away the chill of the damp day.

"In her room, the heavy rain keeps everyone inside today," Bethany said. "Her breakfast has gone untouched and she didn't eat supper last night."

"Send her to me," Royden ordered and saw that Bethany hesitated.

"You object to my order?" he asked.

Bethany sighed. "I will do as you say, but first I have something to say."

Royden nodded permission for her to continue.

"You have both been hurt, but have survived. Don't let that hurt defeat you. Your love for each other is stronger than that."

"Is it?" Royden asked as if he truly needed an answer.

"Maybe that's something you both need to find out before you destroy a love that hasn't been given a chance," Bethany said and turned to leave.

"Bethany," he said and she turned. "Tell my wife if she doesn't come here to me in the solar, then I will come to her bedchamber."

Bethany nodded and left the room with a slight shake of her head.

Oria might defy his summons, but threatening to come to her bedchamber—a place he doubted he was welcome—would have her thinking twice.

After several minutes passed, Royden thought she did intend to defy him, but then a soft rap sounded at the door.

"Enter, Oria," he called out.

Oria entered, Bethany lingering in the background.

"Bethany, bring some food," Royden ordered.

"Aye, sir," Bethany said, a quick smile surfacing before she hurried off.

"Sit," he said, pointing to a chair near the fire and waited until she sat before he took a seat in a chair not far from hers.

Two days of not seeing her and he was surprised by the shadows under her eyes. She looked as if she hadn't slept or she hadn't slept well. Her soft green eyes weren't as vibrant as they usually were, but her soft blonde hair was beautiful the way it fell in waves over her shoulders and on her chest. He'd forgotten how much he loved when she let her hair fall free.

"I owe you an apology," Oria said.

Royden hadn't expected that from her and if anyone owed an apology, he did—for everything. She spoke before he could stop her.

"I let my anger get the better of me and said something that was purposely meant to hurt you but was not the truth.

You kept me as safe as you could that day. You fought bravely protecting not only me but the whole clan. I was proud of you then and I still am. And I am proud to be your wife. I hope you can forgive me."

He was stunned by her apology, though more stunned that she was proud of him and proud to be his wife. "It is me who owes you the apology. It is unforgiveable what I said to you. I can blame it on my own anger, but I'm not even sure from where that anger came."

"It hasn't been an easy reunion," she said before he could say any more. "We both have changed."

But what of their love. Had it changed as well, he wondered.

A knock at the door had Bethany entering with a platter of meat, cheese, and bread. She placed it on the chest beside Oria and went to the table and filled two tankards with wine, handing one to Royden and the other to Oria, then she left without a word.

"Tell me about Burnell and your marriage. I'd like to know," Royden said and handed a piece of cheese to his wife. She was in need of food and he intended to see she got it.

Oria took it, though made no effort to eat it. She held it in her hand and she seemed to drift away in thought for a moment.

He didn't think she noticed that she sighed heavily before speaking.

"Burnell treated me well. He was tender and mannerly and soft-spoken. He never lost his temper or raised a hand to me." She ran her fingers over the scar along her jaw. "Burnell had Letha, Clan Learmonth's healer, tend my wound. She did the best she could." Her hand hastily fell away from her face as if she wanted no more memories of that time. "Burnell gave me something I thought I had but until I got it, I never realized I didn't have it in the first place."

"What is that?" he asked, thinking he had always given her what she asked of him.

"Freedom," she said softly and with a smile of a cherished gift she had appreciated. "I could come and go as I pleased."

"That could be dangerous," Royden said, the thought of her going off completely on her own a frightening one.

She swallowed the bite of cheese she had taken and sipped a bit of wine before responding. "I found it exhilarating, not having to seek permission for almost everything I did."

The thought of her going off on her own as she had done when she had gone into the woods would not work with him. He would worry endlessly not knowing where she was, what danger she may be in.

"I will not have my wife going off as she pleases," he said and could hear the command in his voice. It was a necessity for a time and though now not always needed, it was a habit not easy to break.

"I'm not your wife—yet," Oria said.

Her tongue had never been quick or defiant with him. That had changed. She was right. She wasn't truly considered his wife until their marriage was consummated.

"It's not a tender, mannerly husband who will be in your bed this time," Royden warned. "Are you prepared for that?"

There was a time that 'aye' would have spilled from her lips without hesitation. But that would have been to a man she had known well and loved with all her heart. That man was gone replaced by a man she no longer knew, though she still loved even though he was now a stranger to her. She had sought seclusion these last three days, the incident in the woods forcing her to think on all that had happened since his return. He was a man filled with anger and also blame. And she couldn't help but think that he blamed her for marrying Burnell. Much needed to be settled between them, only then would their marriage—their future—have a chance at succeeding.

"Your hesitation answers for you," Royden said with annoyance.

"Let me explain."

"What is there to explain? You either welcome me in your bed or you don't," he snapped.

"I suppose it is that simple," she said with a sadness that tugged at her heart.

"Then I'll have an answer," Royden demanded.

This time Oria didn't hesitate, even though it hurt her to say, "I'm not ready to welcome you to my bed yet."

Royden lashed out in anger, raising his arm that had no hand. "Can't stand the thought of a stump caressing your naked flesh?"

If only he could feel the tingle of excitement and anticipation that raced through her at the thought of his touch, whether it was his hand or his stump, it didn't matter. She'd never stopped aching for his touch. Or dreaming. Good Lord, the dreams of him touching her had driven her mad with desire.

"I have no aversion to your stump, Royden," she said softly.

She spoke as she once did, with a gentleness that also reminded him of her honesty. Was it possible? Was the loss of his hand not repugnant to her?

"How did you lose your hand?" she asked.

Neither knew what had happened to the other, what things had forged new strengths and what things had depleted them, and what had changed them, during the five years that had separated them. Oria wanted to know, but she also knew how difficult it would be to share those things.

"You weren't here to see it?" Royden asked to confirm that she hadn't, hence her question. If that was so, he was relieved. It hadn't been a sight for her to have seen.

"No," she said, shaking her head.

He hesitated. There was no need for her to know.

"Please, Royden, I want to know

He relented. "It was at the end of the battle the day of the attack. I could tell we were losing, but I couldn't surrender, either could Arran." He didn't say how he had hoped, prayed, begged God to see that she had somehow managed to escape. He had feared for her outcome more than he had for himself. "It happened so quickly. I heard Arran warn with a yell and I struck down the warrior I was fighting. My arm instinctively went up to protect me from whoever rushed up behind me. His sword came down and my hand was gone. Arran and I both sent our swords through the warrior and that's how the battle ended. If it hadn't been for Bethany searing the wound when she did and Arran's help, I would have died."

A cold dread ran over Oria at the horrible image his words had painted and the suffering he must have endured. The thought of how close he came to death frightened her senseless. It had been a terror she had lived with until word had reached her and she had discovered that Royden was still alive. A joyous and sad day. She'd been filled with joy for him, but saddened beyond belief that they weren't together.

"I don't need your pity," Royden said, seeing it in her eyes.

"You mistake pity for sorrow."

"I don't need that either," he said, snappishly. "Life goes on no matter what."

"It certainly does, but there is time to grieve."

He huffed and stood, going to refill his wine from the jug on the table. "What good does it do to grieve? It won't change anything. The only thing that matters is to fight and conquer,"

He hadn't thought that way before and his words gave her a glimpse of what life must have been like for him the past five years. He had lived an endless battle to survive, and her heart broke for him.

He returned to his chair, taking a gulp of wine before he spoke. "We're wed and nothing is going to change that, since I won't see you—"

"Homeless," she finished, though wished for a different response.

He shook his head. "Taken and given to another."

Her heart plummeted. For a brief moment, she thought he was about to say taken from him. She wanted to hear that from him. Hear that he never wanted to let her go. Hear that he still loved her or loved her more than ever before.

"You need to eat," he said, pointing to the platter of food. "Bethany is worried about you."

What about him? Was he worried at all about her? She certainly was worried about him.

She picked up a piece of cheese.

"There's much to be done around here. I could use all the help I can get," he said, wanting to keep her from isolating herself in her bedchamber.

"What do you want me to do?" she asked with little enthusiasm.

That she seemed not the least bit interested sparked his anger and he spoke harshly. "Stop feeling sorry for yourself and see to your duties."

She almost let her tongue loose on him, but stopped. She hadn't seen to the duties expected of a wife. How could she when she didn't even feel like a wife? That was no excuse though. She had given herself time to consider everything or had it been grief that had kept her tucked away? Had she needed to grieve for what had truly been lost to her and Royden before she could begin again? She didn't know. She only knew she had to go on living just as she had done when she had lost him on their wedding day.

"I will see to my duties," she said.

He wondered just how well she would when her response lacked emotion. She had once been so eager to be his wife and take over the duties of the keep. But that had all changed. There was no going back, no wishing, no dreaming that things would again be the way they once were. They would never be the same again.

Oria dropped the piece of cheese on the platter not having taken another bite.

"You need to eat," Royden said as if it was an order.

"I'm not hungry,"

"That doesn't matter. You eat to keep up your strength whether you want to or not. You never know where your next meal may come from," he warned.

His remark gave her another view into his time spent away.

She had to ask, "Did you know hunger, Royden?"

"The past is the past, Oria, let it stay there," Royden said. "Now eat."

Oria didn't wish to argue. She took the piece of cheese she had returned to the platter and nibbled on it.

"How long did the mercenaries remain on Burnell's land?" Royden asked, needing to turn the conversation away from them.

"A few remained while a majority of them left after a year. They just packed up and one day were gone." Oria said and shook her head. "It was so strange, though Burnell didn't seem surprised."

"You think he knew they had plans to leave?"

"Many thought him feeble, but I believe he had his wits about him and he knew more than he said."

"Do you know what relative inherited his land?" Royden asked.

"I had no idea he even had a relative. I thought he was the last of his line."

"Too bad you didn't give him a son. At least then you could have remained there."

"I didn't want to remain there. It was never truly my home. I wanted to go home to my clan after Burnell died, but I was forbidden to return there. I was told the King had given it to someone else. All I had known—my family—it was all gone."

"You have me now," Royden said as if it made all the difference.

"And I am grateful," Oria said more than he knew. "Were you ever able to find out who was responsible for all that happened here?"

"No, but I have thoughts," he said.

"Tell me," she urged, "for I have given it much thought myself."

"The leader of the mercenaries seems to be a powerful man, but to attack this area and particular clans had to relate to something—revenge perhaps."

"And he had to have knowledge of this area and the clans," Oria added.

"Or he had to have had help," Royden said.

"A thought I didn't want to consider, but made sense," Oria said, munching on a piece of meat.

Royden was glad she was eating and glad they had found a shared interest to discuss. It also told him that she hadn't accepted her fate as easily as he had thought she had. She had been questioning what had happened just as he had.

"I don't like to think that one of the clans had betrayed the others. But how this was carried out without little trouble tells me otherwise."

Oria looked over to the flames in the hearth.

"What is it, Oria?" Royden asked after a few moments of silence.

"Did you ever wonder if whoever attacked here that day knew in advance that most of the chieftains and lords would be attending our wedding?"

"Are you suggesting our wedding was used as a trap?" he asked, never having considered it.

"Don't you think it too convenient that so many heads of clans were here that day?"

"All but two," Royden said. "Chieftain Thurbane of the Clan MacDonnegal and—"

"My now deceased husband, Lord Learmonth."

They both grew silent at the implications at what that could mean.

"Lord Learmonth sent his apologies for not being able to attend when invited. He explained he was not feeling well," Royden said. "I need to find out why and who destroyed my family and the other clans around us."

"I've felt the same. This wasn't a random attack or unwise decision on someone's part. This took planning and a large contingent of warriors. Warriors who fought for what they could gain, not out of duty," Oria said.

He could see the eagerness in her green eyes for answers, her thirst to solve this as desperate as his own. This had left scars on them both and to heal, they had to solve this puzzle and they had to see that the person responsible paid for it.

"You should come see Learmonth for yourself. Burnell's relative isn't expected there for a month or more," she suggested. "It might do well for you to also visit Chieftain Thurbane and get to know Fergus better."

"I don't trust him or Penn. They fought willingly for the leader of the mercenaries. Their allegiance was to him and I believe it still is. I don't believe this mysterious leader is finished here. He's planted his men wisely and when the time comes there is no telling what they will do."

"I must admit, I thought the same myself, but isn't it better you keep your foe close, know what goes on with them and let them know only what you wish them to know about your plans?"

She had a point and a good one since it was what he had done with Platt. He disliked the man greatly, but he had made sure to keep a good eye on him and engage with him now and again.

"We'll go to Learmonth when this weather dries out," Royden ordered.

"And we'll plan a visit to the MacDonnegal clan. I'll visit with Alynn while you talk with Fergus and Thurbane."

"I need to visit with Galvin as well."

"He's turned bitter, Royden," Oria said.

"Haven't we all. He lost his son and he doesn't know what happened to his daughter, Purity. What's left for his clan if anything happens to him? There is no one to carry on his name. He'll be lost, no one ever knowing he existed. It's not a legacy a man wishes to leave."

Their eyes met and held, each realizing the implications of his remark.

"I will have the Clan MacKinnon name carried on," he said.

He was letting her know that there would come a time he would seek her bed.

"I will let you know when you are welcome in my bed," Oria said.

Royden leaned forward in his chair. "You have a duty as my wife and we don't need a bed to see the deed done." His hand was quick to go up when she went to respond. "Tread wisely, wife, and remember a savage lives within me."

Fear prickled her skin. How would she ever find the strength to tame the savage?

Chapter Seven

Oria waited on the top of the keep steps for her husband. It had taken three days between the weather and things that needed immediate attention before Royden was free to ride to Learmonth with her. They had engaged sparingly in conversation since they had spoken in the solar. She had kept busy, seeing to her duties. She had men busy repairing the table and chairs that had sat on the dais. Repairs were also being made to the trestle tables and benches so once again the room would be filled with talk and laughter. And she was seeing what linens were available to once again have the MacKinnon family table well dressed.

The sun was full in the sky though who knew how long that would last and with a chill in the air, she made certain to wear her wool cloak. She scanned the distance for any sign of her husband. She was eager for this time àlone with him. She couldn't learn more about his time away if they kept their distance. Besides, after their talk in the solar, she realized how much she had missed talking with him.

One thing she had learned about her husband was that he didn't allow having only one hand stop him from doing anything. He lifted, carried, managed to do what men with two hands did. He had learned well to compensate for his lost hand, not an easy task.

"Ready?"

Oria jumped startled that her husband was behind her.

His hand shot out to grab her arm. "Be careful, you're too close to the stairs. You don't want to take a tumble."

She stared at him, for a moment, he sounded so much like the old Royden. The man who she never doubted, not for a minute, loved her with all his heart. And she ached for that man's arms around her again.

Her attention turned to the sound of horses and was a bit surprised to see Angus, John, and Stuart approach. She was disappointed. She had hoped to be alone with her husband, giving them time to talk in private.

She looked from the men to her husband. "I've traveled alone back and forth between Learmonth and here many times without incident."

"Burnell may have allowed you that, I don't," he said and, with his hand firmly at her arm, guided her down the stairs to the horses.

Oria had cherished the freedom Burnell had given her and Royden's remark let her know how different it would be now that she was wed to him. He annoyed her even more when he kept hold of her and wouldn't let her mount her mare on her own. His hand and his arm were at her waist before she could stop him and he swung her up onto her horse. She had always thought him a strong man, but there was a strength to him now that was much different than before.

When they were clear of the village, Royden nodded to the three men and they spread out, though kept a perimeter around her and Royden. A hasty pace was set and no words were exchanged between them as they rode.

When Oria spied the Learmonth keep in the distance, she and her mare did what they usually did, they raced toward home, leaving her husband in her wake. She loved the sensation of flying across the land, the chilled air stinging her cheeks, turning them red, and her hair blowing wildly around her head. It was exhilarating, though the feeling had been quick to die off once she arrived at the keep, her home that had never been a home to her. The ride—at least for a short time—had allowed her to feel completely free.

Oria slowed as she approached the village and her husband drew up beside her and stopped, bringing her to a halt.

"I've warned you about taking flight like that," he ordered harshly.

"It was something I always did when approaching home, a habit of sorts," she explained.

"It's not your home anymore," he said, his tongue remaining harsh.

"It was a harmless habit."

"That you need no more," Royden snapped.

Not used to a commanding husband, she said, "Your tongue need not be so sharp with me."

"And you need to know your place."

"And where would that be?"

"Wherever I command it to be," he warned and his deep scowl threatened.

Oria drew back as if avoiding a hand to her face, not that he had raised his hand. She shook her head. "What has suddenly put you in such an ugly mood?"

"YOU!" he said and rode off.

She shook her head again. She had hoped for a far better day than this was proving to be and followed after Royden.

Oria took note of the way John, Angus, and Stuart spread out through the small village once they entered it. It came to her then that they were here to find out whatever they could. They would talk and share an ale or two or more and learn things. It had been wise of Royden to bring them.

Royden paid little heed to the village. He climbed the hill to the keep. It wasn't a steep hill, but one could feel the pull in one's legs when walking up it. He remembered visiting here with his da. Once up the hill, one could see a distance in all directions. From the narrow windows high up in the keep, the view was endless. There was no way anyone could approach this place without being seen.

"Burnell had to have seen the mercenaries approach. He would have had enough time to send for help." He turned to Oria. "You must have realized that after a while."

She walked to stand beside him, not an ache in her legs, having grown accustomed to the climb. "I did and I asked him about it. He told me he'd been expecting friends and with only a small group approaching, he thought it them. Once distracted by the strangers that arrived, others followed behind them."

"Did you believe him?"

"I wasn't sure. I asked myself if it was a lie, why would he lie? I didn't like the answer. It meant Burnell was expecting the mercenaries."

"He hired them," Royden said with an anger he found hard to contain.

"I don't believe so. The warriors never harmed him, but they didn't pay him much heed either."

"And if he had been the one paying them, then they would have treated him much differently," Royden said, his conclusion leaving him frustrated.

"That was my thought, so I couldn't be sure of anything. Except that Burnell and Thurbane were the only clan chieftains who didn't attend our wedding. That thought refused to leave me."

Royden turned and looked down on the village. "The village has prospered."

"It has," Oria agreed. "It wasn't looted like the other keeps, and warriors made repairs while here and kept the storage sheds full of food and the fields tilled and planted."

"It's been kept in fine shape, perhaps it was the bargain Burnell struck with the leader of the mercenaries for use of his land."

Oria didn't like to think that she had been married to a man who had betrayed the other clans, but Burnell had escaped the turmoil and suffering the others had gone through.

Royden followed Oria into the keep. The fireplace, small for a Great Hall, was sufficient for the size. There was barely room for two tables and the dais held a table fit for only two people. It was clean and a pleasant scent filled the air.

Oria turned and smiled at the old woman, standing not much over five feet, her gray hair braided neatly, who entered the room, and she went over to her. "I'm not *my lady* anymore, Detta. I have come to make certain I have collected everything of mine before the new Lord Learmonth arrives." She turned and looked to her husband. "This is my husband now, Chieftain Royden of the Clan MacKinnon."

"Sir," Detta said with a bob of her head. "Can I get you anything."

"Your hospitality is appreciated but we won't be long," Royden said.

"If there is anything I can do, please let me know," Detta said and bobbed her head again.

"I'll come find you before we leave," Oria said and the old woman left the room.

The stairs were narrow and with the width of Royden's shoulders he had to turn on an angle to climb them to the second floor. Burnell would have had no problem climbing these since he'd been tall and slim.

They made their way to the second floor and entered the master bedchamber. It wasn't large, a bed and a chest or two and a small table with a chair tucked neatly beneath it. The small fireplace heated the room as sufficiently as the one in the Great Hall for its size.

"I don't think there's anything here that would tell us much, but since Burnell didn't have a solar, his bedchamber would be the closest thing to one," Oria said and went to the chair at the table scooping up something draped over the chair. "My shawl. I had forgotten I left it here."

Royden turned away, the shawl a reminder that she had shared this room with Burnell. He tried to avoid looking at the bed, but his eyes seemed to have a will of their own. The blankets were neatly folded back, the pillows plumped, and he tried not to think of Oria sleeping there in Burnell's arms night after night. Unfortunately, his mind thought differently and he couldn't get the image of Burnell driving his manhood into her again and again and again. Though how a man his age and of frail health was capable of it puzzled him. Another thought invaded his mind that flared his anger. Had Burnell made Oria ride him?

Royden wanted to punch something or someone. He held onto his temper, barely, and ordered. "Let's go."

Oria gave one last look around the room and offered a silent prayer. *Rest in Peace, Burnell.*

Royden followed her out the door and when she went up the stairs instead of down, he asked, "Where do you go?"

"My bedchamber," she said and continued up the stairs.

A sense of relief stabbed at his gut that she hadn't slept every night in Burnell's bed. He followed her into her room, bending his head the doorway too low for him, and stopped just inside. It was so small there was no place for him to go. There was barely room for the narrow bed. A chair sat beside the bed and the fireplace wasn't big enough to hold any sizeable log which meant the fire had to constantly be replenished. And the tapestry that covered the lone, narrow window did little good from stopping the cold from getting in. How many cold, winter nights had the fire gone out while she slept, leaving her to wake icy and shivering? She had not had it easy living here and that got him wondering what else she had endured during his absence.

"It's small but it was sufficient for me," she said, knowing what he was thinking just by the questionable look in his dark eyes. "When it got too cold I stayed in the Great Hall for the night."

The image of her cuddled by the fire by herself tore at his heart.

"Why not seek the warmth of your husband's bed?" he asked, not that he wanted to think of her doing so but at least she'd have been kept warm.

"Burnell often didn't feel well and I didn't want to disturb him," she said and lifted the chair.

"What are you doing?" Royden asked and took the chair from her.

"Place it by the window. I want to show you something," she said.

When he saw that she intended to climb up on it, her head just reaching the bottom of the window, he coiled his arm around her waist and lifted her to stand on the chair.

"Look," she said, pushing the tapestry aside.

The bottom of the window reached his chin so he was able to easily see out it. He was amazed at the distance one could see, since no woods blocked the landscape.

"I woke one night, shivering, and was going to add logs to the fire but first hurried to see if it was snowing. Depending on which way the wind blows, the snow sometimes fell past the tapestry into my room. Instead of heating a room I wouldn't be able to stay in, I looked out the window to determine if I should seek the warmth of the Great Hall. A light snow was falling, but it was what I saw in the distance that turned me cold. A troop—a large troop—approached the keep, torches flickering and bouncing as they drew closer. At first I thought it might be an attack, but I realized they rode at a tempered pace, not at all in a hurry."

"Tell me you remained safe in your room," he said, worried for her safety even though the incident was in the past.

Her hand went to her scar. "I wasn't about to leave myself vulnerable. I was already dressed, it being far too cold to sleep in only my nightdress, but I waited since it would take time for the group to reach the keep. When I thought the time right, I took careful and silent steps down the stairs only to find that a warrior was stationed at the bottom. I kept myself hidden and tried to listen to see what I could hear, but there was too much talk to distinguish any particular voice."

While he wished she hadn't taken such a dangerous chance, and relieved she hadn't been harmed, he was glad that she had. It had provided more information, more pieces to the puzzle.

"So Burnell met with this troop secretly," Royden said.

"That was the strange part," she said and held out her hand for Royden to help her off the chair. Instead he slipped his arm around her waist once more and lifted her off the chair. A ripple of pleasure trickled through her and she was reminded again how much she missed his touch. "I stopped at Burnell's room thinking if he had yet to join the group I could find out who it was that arrived so mysteriously in the night. I found him sound asleep in bed and the next morning there was no sign that the group had ever been here."

"That is strange," he agreed. "Could Burnell have simply supplied the mercenaries a central gathering place to operate from in return for leaving him unscathed? Or had he surrendered to them to begin with since his clan had little chance against them? Whatever the reason, we now know that Learmonth most probably was the place it all began."

Their return ride home was far different and far more pleasurable than the ride there. This time she and Royden talked.

"Did Burnell ever speak with you about any worry for the future of the Clan Learmonth once he was gone?" Royden asked, his eyes on his wife while also paying heed to everything around him. It was a skill he had learned quickly, surprise attacks all too common while with the mercenaries.

"One night when the howling wind seemed to penetrate the stone walls, he mentioned to me that even if this keep fell, the Clan Learmonth would never fall. That a Learmonth had been on this land long before a keep had ever been built and a Learmonth would remain here forever."

"It seems that he didn't worry if you didn't bear him an heir, so he had to have known there was someone who would lead the clan and carry on the name."

"It is an old name here in these parts," Oria said. "I remember my da talking about how his da was in a battle that ended with Learmonth land being divided among other clans."

"I would think that that might have something to do with this, but it was a good many years ago, and lands are lost and gained, through marriage and battles. It's just the way of things. Why now at such an advanced age would he decide to seek revenge? It would seem more likely that he was trying to protect what he had by bargaining with the mercenaries and keeping his small clan safe."

"That would mean that Burnell was nothing more than a minor piece to this puzzle," Oria said.

"I wouldn't say minor, more significant since his land provided a place to build up troops and launch their attacks. What puzzles me is why the attacks stopped after the Clan MacKinnon was attacked and nothing more happened for five years. Our area may be remote but news does travel. Why didn't the King do anything? Surely he heard what happened. Yet nothing was done."

Oria offered a sensible reason. "Raven and Purity couldn't be found and forced to wed, leaving Purity's da safe and your land unable to be rightfully claimed."

"Unless the King stepped in and he didn't. Why? And it still puzzles me why Burnell wed you when you could have been wed to another and your land and clan secured." Royden turned wide eyes on her when a thought struck him. "Burnell wasn't meant to wed you, was he?"

"I gave my word to my da and Burnell I would never tell anyone," she said.

"You once trusted me, Oria, trust me now when I say I will never reveal what you tell me to anyone. Besides, your da and Burnell are gone, does it really matter any longer."

"My word is my word, Royden. I dishonor myself if I betray my word."

"I don't think your da would mind you telling me."

Oria recalled her da's words as he lay dying. *Royden needs to know.* Had he meant that she should tell him if she ever got to see him again?

She followed her instincts. "I was taken home after the attack. Burnell was there with his healer and a cleric. My da told me I was to wed Burnell. It made no sense to me and I was in too much pain to object. I wed Burnell without question. Much later I discovered that my da and Burnell had made a pact that if you were killed in an attack or taken captive that Burnell would wed me to keep me from having to wed a stranger and my da from losing his land."

Her da had taken no chances. He had made arrangements for Oria's safety in case something happened to the man she was supposed to wed. Royden had never given thought to such a possibility. He had believed he'd be able to keep Oria safe when he should have considered what might happen to her if he'd been unable to. Royden was glad her da had been wiser than him.

Clouds followed them home and Royden went off to see that much needed work was getting done before the rain started once again.

She watched him stride off. She had enjoyed their time together, talking, trying to make sense of what happened, trying to piece the puzzle together. It reminded her of old times with him, not that it was exactly the same, but there had been something familiar they had shared, and to her that was a start. She had realized by his stance and the troubled look in his dark eyes that he hadn't liked being in Burnell's bedchamber. His eyes had taken on an angry glare when he looked upon the bed and she hadn't had to guess what he'd been thinking.

Oria turned and climbed the keep steps. She had thought to tell him, but how did a married woman admit she had remained a virgin?

Chapter Eight

Royden couldn't sleep. His wife constantly haunted his thoughts. Their return ride from Learmonth had given him a glimpse into the past at a time he cherished, a time when their love was strong enough to conquer anything. That time, that love had been what kept him going when things had gotten unbearable. Oria had been his strength, his reason to survive, and return home. So why, now that he was here, Oria his wife, did he find things so different?

He threw the blanket off and swung his legs off the bed, sitting on the edge, his hand and stump pressed into the mattress on either side of him. He shook his head when he looked at the stump. Sometimes, crazy as it was, he thought he still felt he had his hand.

He stood and wrapped his plaid around himself, a simple task that had taken time to learn once he'd been healed enough. He didn't bother slipping on the leather cuff that covered his stump, no one would be about the keep this late. He rarely slept a full night. His thoughts either leaving him too restless to sleep or nightmares plagued and woke him abruptly. Either way, a good, sound sleep had long eluded him and he had learned to adapt.

He ran his fingers through his hair, letting it fall as it may, then slipped on his boots. He'd go to his solar—*his solar*—was it truly his now? Was his da dead? Would he ever find out what happened to him? And what of Arran? Would he make it home? And what of Raven? He shook his head, his family constantly on his mind.

One thing at a time, he silently warned himself.

Quick steps had him down the stairs in no time and he was about to hurry through the Great Hall to his solar when he spotted her and stopped. He stared for a moment since at first glance he thought her lifeless propped against a section of the stone hearth, the fire's light bathing her lovely face in a soft glow. Then he recalled Oria telling him that she would sometimes go to the hearth in the Great Hall to sleep when at Learmonth, it having been too cold in her small bedchamber. But her bedchamber here wasn't cold, so what had brought her to sleep by the hearth?

Leaving her to remain there wasn't even a thought. He went and crouched down in front of her. He would have wondered how she could sleep like that, sitting up, braced against stone, but he had been forced to sleep in ways and places he never thought possible. They both had learned to cope with what fate had dealt them.

One thing that hadn't changed was her beauty. She would always be the most beautiful woman in the world to him. Even the scar couldn't detract from her lovely features.

Stop staring and take her to bed.

His thoughts jolted him inwardly. *Put her to bed, not take her to bed*, he silently warned himself. He wasn't ready for that yet, or so he told himself, and she had told him he wasn't welcome there—*yet*.

He reached out to wake her with a gentle touch, but pulled his hand back. Not a good idea. Instead, he spoke her name softly, "Oria."

"Royden," she said in a raspy whisper before her eyes spread open wide. Seeing him there so close, she threw herself at him, her arms going around his neck.

His arm snagged her waist as he held himself steady so they wouldn't tumble. She clung tightly to him as if she'd feared letting go and there was something different about the way she felt in his arms. She melted into them, against him, as she had once done. He reacted instinctively, pressing his cheek to hers, keeping her firm against him, never wanting to let her go.

Then something happened. She tensed and eased herself away from him and he had to fight hard to let her go. Her eyes held a look of surprise and he wondered what had happened.

She spoke as if she needed an explanation herself. "A recurring dream, I thought I was at Learmonth and you came for me. I forgot I was here."

So she had dreamt of him as he had of her and she had hoped that he would return to her. But what had she expected him to do when she'd been wed to another?

He let that question go unspoken and instead asked, "What are you doing down here? You have a warm bedchamber."

"I couldn't sleep. And you?"

"I couldn't sleep either," he said and moved to sit beside her against the stone hearth.

A sadness gripped her chest. She had loved the man beside her for as long as she could remember. That hadn't changed one bit. Why then did they act like strangers?

She got the courage to ask, "Did you think of me through the years?"

"I never stopped. You were on my mind endlessly," he admitted.

She asked without thinking or hesitation, "Do you still love me?"

He turned his head to look at her when what he really wanted to do was to take her in his arms and kiss her senseless. "I never stopped loving you, Oria. I never will."

"Then why this struggle between us?" she asked, joyful that he still loved her and yet worried of what stopped them from loving once again.

"I told you. I'm not the same man I once was," he said.

"What does that matter?"

"That man you loved since you were young is gone. A different man has returned to you."

Oria looked him up and down. "He looks the same to me, though a bit larger."

"If only that was all," he said. "You can't tell me you don't see a change in me."

"You're temperamental where you weren't before."

He grunted, his way of agreeing but not wanting to admit it.

"You dictate, though thinking on it that isn't new."

He sat forward and glared at her. "I never commanded you."

She patted his thigh. "You did, but I never realized it since you were always cordial about it. It took being wed to Burnell for me to see it. Now, however, you dictate like a demanding chieftain."

"What else did you learn being married to Burnell?" he asked, trying to keep the demand out of his tone.

"That friendship worked best when there was no love between a husband and wife." She poked him in the arm. "And what did you learn that turned you into a grumpy old man?"

"I'm not old," he argued.

She laughed softly. "So you admit to being grumpy."

"I suppose I can be at times," he admitted with reluctance.

She rested her hand on his arm. "That's one thing I have always loved about you—your truthfulness. And I'm glad to see that hasn't changed."

"So much else has," he said, not looking at her and trying to ignore how good her hand felt simply resting on his arm. Something he had once taken for granted far too much.

"You're being too harsh on yourself, Royden."

"No, I've done things I should have never done."

"You did them to survive. We all did what was necessary to survive," she said.

"And in doing so we altered our lives forever."

"Then we start anew," she said tired of this distance between them.

"And what if you don't like the new me?"

"Then I'll have to learn to live with and love a grumpy old man," she said with a laugh.

"That shouldn't be difficult for you to do since you already had an old man for a husband," he said as if challenging her.

She laughed again. "All the better. I have the experience to deal with you."

He leaned his face down close to hers. "You have no idea who you're dealing with."

She moved her face closer to his. "But I do. You're the man who stole my heart all those years ago and no matter what—I'm not taking it back."

"I'm not a nice man anymore," he warned.

"You always had a wild side. You merely kept it tamed." She gasped when she suddenly found herself in his lap and his arm around her.

"You can't tame what's inside me," he warned.

She rested her hand to his cheek. "No, I can't. Only you can do that."

His hand gripped the back of her neck and he delivered a crushing kiss to her lips.

He stole her breath and when he stopped she could barely breathe.

"Whether I'm welcomed or not, I've gotten used to taking what I want."

"Do you want me, Royden?" she asked her insides stirring madly.

"Aye, wife, I want you. I've always wanted you, and I'll take you when I'm ready. And it won't be an old man you'll feel inside you." He moved her off his lap, leaving her to sit on the floor as he got up and walked away.

"Royden," she called out.

He didn't turn, he kept his back to her.

"I wouldn't know how an old man feels inside me. Burnell never consummated our vows. I'm still a virgin."

Shock froze not only his limbs but his words as well and when he finally turned to face her—she was gone.

"Good, you're awake."

Royden turned to see Angus standing just inside the Great Hall door.

"Someone has word on Arran," Angus said.

Royden hurried to follow Angus, but first chance he got, he was going to find his wife and... damn, he wasn't sure what he was going to do.

***

"Don't get close to him," Angus said as they approached a figure, draped in the dark brown robe of a monk, standing at the bottom of the keep stairs. "He's a leper."

Royden stopped several steps away from the monk. He was hunched over from his illness or the sheer burden of it. The hood of his robe was drawn down over his face as far as it would go and he wore gloves. Royden preferred looking a man in the eye when he met him. Truth and lies could be seen there. This time, however, he didn't mind since there was no telling the extent of damage the illness had caused to his face.

"You have word of my brother, Arran?" he asked and the monk nodded, keeping his head bent.

His voice was raspy, painfully so. "I met your brother on the road. It was late and cold. He and some other men had a fire and food and I took a chance to beg some food from them. Your brother defended me when the others went to chase me off. He even had them build a fire for me a distance away so I could stay warm for the night. When the men slept, he came to me and asked for a favor. I had mentioned I'd been headed this way. He asked me to stop here and tell you that he had one thing that needed his attention, then he'd be home. A month or more in his estimation. He also told me you would spare me some food."

"How do I know the message is from him?" Royden asked.

"He thought you would ask that and he told me to tell you that what needed his attention pertained to the promise that you, your da, and he made five years ago."

Raven.

It had to be. Arran must have gotten some information on her. At least he knew his brother was free of the mercenaries, though he wondered what men were with him. They could be men from their clan since from what the leper had said, Arran seemed in charge.

"I'll see that you get a full sack of food and you will leave at first light," Royden ordered.

"Please, I beg of you, let me stay just inside the woods for at least a day or two. I kept a fast pace to get here and slept little. I need rest before I can continue."

He did sound exhausted and Royden couldn't imagine how unbearable his life must be. "Two days no more and I'll see more food is given to you before you leave."

"Bless you, my son, bless you," the monk said, bobbing his head slowly.

Royden turned to Angus. "Get him some bread, meat and ale, and take him into the woods to where the tangled tree sits. He's to stay there. Warn the others he's there." Angus went to turn away, but Royden caught his arm and spoke in a whisper. "How did he come to find you?"

Angus kept his voice low as well. "I couldn't sleep and stepped outside. He stepped out of the shadows, scared the hell out me he did. Scared me even more when he told me he was a leper. I was going to chase him away when he mentioned Arran's name."

"How did he get past the sentinels?"

"My guess would be that he blended too well with the night for them to see him. And he walks almost soundlessly, but then he's probably only a shadow of a man beneath that robe."

Royden nodded. "See it done and keep a good distance."

"I'm all for that," Angus said and took a wide berth around the monk. "This way and don't get too close or I'll shove my sword into you."

Royden saw then that Angus had his sword at his side. *Habit.* They had all learned to keep their swords with them or some type of weapon close by. It was a habit that would be hard to break. Or maybe they shouldn't break it.

He entered the keep anxious to find his wife. She wasn't in the Great Hall and he hurried to see if by chance she waited for him in his solar, but it was empty. He didn't think she would go to his bedchamber, but he looked there just in case. She wasn't there.

Her bedchamber. She had to have gone to her bedchamber. He took the stairs and saw that her chamber door sat ajar. A light flickered in the room from the fireplace and he eased the door open not wanting to wake her, though he was disappointed that he wouldn't be able to speak with her until morning.

The one side of the bed lay empty and the other side was swathed in shadow. He approached quietly, but when he could see the bed clearly he rushed to it, and glared at an empty bed.

Where was his wife?

He rushed out of the room and continued his search. Arran's room was empty and Raven's as well. He even went to his mum's small solar where she had done her stitching and sought solitude from two rambunctious sons. It was cold and empty as it had been since his mum's death.

Worry mixed with annoyance. Where could she have gone? He stopped at his bedchamber to fully dress for the day, slipping on his shirt beneath his plaid and covering his stump with the leather cuff.

He wasn't surprised to see Bethany in the kitchen readying food for the morning meal.

"Have you see, Oria?" he asked.

"No, sir, I haven't." Worry had her asking, "Isn't she in her bedchamber?"

Royden shook his head. "No. She was in the Great Hall not long ago."

"Does Oria know a leper beds down in the woods?" Bethany asked, turning anxious eyes on Royden.

"Angus was here to collect the food for the leper?"

"Aye, he left only a short time ago," she said.

Worry began to mount in him. If she had foolishly gone off into the woods, she would get a taste of not the grumpy, old man she had believed he'd become, but of the commanding husband she thought him to be.

"Any thought to where Oria would have gone off to?"

"You would know that better than me, sir," Bethany said.

"The years and distance between us have changed us both."

"Years and distance can't change the love you two have for each other. You both just need to find the way back there, back to the depths of your hearts. Think back to then."

Royden shook his head unable to go back there to that time and place where he and Oria had been so happy, so in love.

A memory rose up to jolt him. The shed by the oak tree. They had often slipped behind it to catch a few moments alone and steal a kiss or two.

He turned to leave and stopped, turning back to Bethany. "I owe you much."

"We are family," she said, an unshed tear lingering in one eye.

"Aye, we are family and I'm blessed to have you," Royden said and hurried off pleased that his sense of home was beginning to return to him.

A glimpse of dawn could be detected on the horizon. He approached the shed with rushed steps and called out as he did, "Oria!"

His heart hammered in his chest when there was no response and he rushed around to the back of the shed.

She wasn't there.

Chapter Nine

Royden was ready to roar his wife's name out. Where had she gone? He raced to the barn, thinking she had once liked going there to see the kittens with Raven. While he had seen cats around, he hadn't seen any kittens lately, but it was worth a try.

He grew more agitated when he didn't find her there. He headed into the village, the only place he hadn't looked. Fear soared in him when he saw Penn rushing at him, worry so strong on his face that all color was gone from it. Was he looking for him to deliver bad news about Oria? His heart pounded viciously in his chest, his stomach clenched so tight, he thought he'd double over.

Please. Please, God, don't let anything have happened to my wife.

"Mistress Oria—" he stopped out of breath from rushing and tossed his head back to catch his breath.

Royden almost reached out to grab him and shake the words out of him, but he regained his breath just in time.

"Mistress Oria sent me to tell you that she's tending to my wife's birth." Penn shook his head. "It's too early for the bairn to be born,"

Relief slammed into Royden and he sent silent gratitude to the heavens that his wife was safe. He did, however, feel for Penn, since he would have felt the same if it had been Oria delivering their bairn.

Royden laid a solid hand on Penn's shoulder. "My wife will know what to do. She'll get Emily through this." He had heard women talk that Oria had delivered a few bairns that had been born while he was gone. He trusted that she would know what to do. "Let's see if the women need anything, then we'll keep busy while the women see to your wife."

Sara, Angus's wife, was about to enter Penn's cottage when they approached it and Royden called out to her, "Sara, if Oria has a moment, I'd like to speak with her."

"Aye, sir," Sara said and entered the cottage.

Only a few minutes passed, agonizing ones for Penn, and Oria stepped outside.

Penn rushed to speak before Royden could. "How is Emily?"

"Emily does well. It's going to be a while. You should keep busy. I will send word when the time is near," Oria said, her voice soothing and reassuring.

Penn felt helpless and it showed with the way he looked from Oria to Royden.

Royden laid a strong hand on Penn's shoulder once again. "You can find us working on the new stone hut today."

Relief surged on Penn's face. He'd be able to see his cottage from where he worked and he was grateful.

Royden walked over to Oria. "Do you need anything? Are you all right?"

"All is good. Sara is here to help and Calla as well and with Calla having birthed five, healthy bairns she'll be of great help."

He reached out and tucked a long strand of her blonde hair, that had fallen along her face, behind her ear. "I want to know how you are."

She smiled softly, recalling how often he had tended to one of her stray strands and how it had always warmed her heart as it did now. "I'm good, Royden."

"You will let me know if you need anything," he said, though was acutely aware it sounded more like a command.

"I promise I will," she said and instinct had her leaning forward and kissing his cheek.

He stood staring after her as she entered the cottage, the door closing behind her. He shook his head and turned to Penn. "Come, we must keep busy."

Royden hefted stone after stone along with Penn and Stuart while Calla's youngest two sons played with little Stuart, their da, Innis also helping, while the three older brothers worked in the fields. Royden was glad for the mindless work, not that it kept his thoughts from straying. He hadn't had control of them since Oria had kissed him on the cheek—an innocent gesture that had touched his heart, the way her innocent touch had once stirred his loins.

He had never realized how much of a loving gesture it had been until that moment. A gentle kiss that demanded nothing but gave everything. That they loved each other wasn't in question, that he had changed was and he worried those changes might make a difference between them.

He was also still reeling from finding out that his wife had remained a virgin, though wed. He had fumbled his way through coupling at first, finding little pleasure in it. Then experienced women he bedded showed him a different way. He had learned more after that, trying things he never would have thought to do or was even possible. He had found more pleasure in coupling once he had gained experience, but still sensed he was missing something. If he introduced such intimacy to his wife, would she object and would he finally find what was missing?

"Don't worry, lad, she'll do just fine," Innis said.

"But will the bairn? She cried heavy tears that it was too soon, the bairn wouldn't survive," Penn said, his glance going to his cottage.

"Liam, over there," Innis said with a nod toward a lad of about four years running in circles with little Stuart. "He came sooner than expected. Not much frightens my Calla, but she feared for the little bairn. I did to when I saw him, small and skinny he was, and he fit in the palm of my hand.

But Lady—a mean Mistress Oria, she took good care of him. She made sure he was kept close to the heat of the hearth and she fed the little fellow drops of his mum's milk off the tip of her finger since he didn't have the strength to suckle. She saved his life, she did."

Royden got another glimpse of what it had been like for Oria the years following the attack. She had not forgotten his clan. She had made sure to visit here and tend those in need.

"I wish I could have been here when my son was born, but from what my Sara said, Mistress Oria got her through it and delivered little Stuart without a problem. She's a good woman. Your wife couldn't be in better hands," Stuart said. "Now get moving and stack those stones close. We want a good, strong shelter for our food this winter."

Royden worked side by side with his men, though he kept a silent tongue while they kept Penn occupied with talk. He thought on his wife and how she had never deserted his clan. She had seen to visiting his clan regularly and tending to those in need, in spite of entering the enemy's camp each time she did. He had always known Oria was a good woman, but he never realized how brave of a woman she was, and he wondered what else he had failed to see about her.

The men had half the hut built when Sara rushed out of the cottage and ran past them, Penn ready to pounce on her if she hadn't waved him off.

"All is good. I'm off to get a brew Oria wants made," Sara said, not breaking her fast stride.

Penn's whole body deflated, his shoulders slumping as he turned an anxious look at his cottage.

Innis practically knocked Penn off his feet when he smacked him on the back. "She'll be fine, lad. We men are made to plant the seed and the women are made to nurture and harvest it." He gave a hardy laugh. "After that it's anybody's guess what you do with it."

"You got that right," Stuart said, joining in the laughter as he looked at his young son drawing with a stick in the dirt.

"And if you're lucky," Innis said with a wink. "You'll get a wife who lets you plant your seed often."

Stuart grinned wide. "I'm a lucky man."

Innis grinned as well. "Five sons prove that I'm a lucky man."

"I'm sure our chieftain is as well and we'll be hearing about an heir to the Clan MacKinnon soon," Stuart boasted with pride that they had a leader who would see that the Clan MacKinnon would live on.

It hit Royden then that he had an obligation to his clan to see that Oria got with child. His clansmen wanted to know that what their clan had endured had been worth it. That the lives lost and all the suffering hadn't defeated the Clan MacKinnon. It had remained strong through it all and would rise once again a prominent and triumphant clan.

His da would expect him to tend to his obligations at all cost just as he had done when he'd been chieftain. Arran would expect it as well. And he had been seeing to his duties since his return home—all but one.

He joined Penn, his glance going to the cottage, his thoughts on his wife and how it would feel to make love with her. He turned away suddenly a memory rising to torment him. He could see it clearly as if he were there in the middle of it, reliving it all over again. He stood in a field, dead warriors all around him, blood covering him and dripping off his sword. And the odor, the horrible stench of battle that forever invaded his senses.

"Royden. Royden."

He heard his name, but didn't want to turn, didn't want to be told it was time to collect the weapons from the dead and look into the lifeless faces of all those warriors who had fought so heroically.

"Royden, we need help with a heavy stone."

He wanted to bless Stuart for pulling him out of the horrendous memory, and he turned.

Stuart nodded and kept his voice low. "The memories are the worst. They eat at your soul."

Royden nodded, though wondered if he had a soul left.

***

The hut was half finished when the men stopped, hearing Penn's name shouted.

Penn dropped the heavy stone he held, barely missing his foot, and ran. Royden followed at a slower pace. He changed his pace when he caught sight of his wife, her hair falling loose of its combs and the shine gone from her lovely eyes.

"Please. Please, I beg of you to tell me my wife and child are safe," Penn pleaded when he looked upon Oria.

Oria smiled. "I appear worn out because your son was a stubborn one, but your wife remained brave and she and your son are doing well. Come and see for yourself." She stepped aside for Penn to enter and before she could shut the door Royden sneaked past her.

Emily was sitting up in bed, smiling, her cheeks flushed red, and a swaddled bundle in her arms. "Come, Penn, and see your son."

Penn hurried to her and looked about to collapse, plopping down beside her on the bed. "I didn't think I would survive this birth."

Emily laughed. "I felt the same, but Oria convinced me I was strong and that I should let our son know who was in charge."

Penn peered over at the bundle, Emily easing back the blanket for her husband to have a look. "He's bigger than I thought he'd be."

"Oria thinks I miscalculated and he was born when he was supposed to be," Emily explained.

"He's a fine looking lad," Penn beamed with pride as his son's small mouth opened in a large yawn. "And a tired one too."

"He exhausted us both," Emily said, joy taking precedence over tiredness.

"We'll leave you now so you may enjoy your newly born son," Oria said. "Sara, Calla, and I will stop by over the next few days to help you with whatever you need, and I will have Bethany send food to you until you feel well enough to see to your own cooking."

"You are most generous, Mistress Oria," Penn said, turning to look at her.

"We take care of family, Penn," Oria said. "I'm sure my husband will agree and command you to spend the remainder of the day with your wife and son."

"I am lucky to have a wife who knows me so well. You can resume your chores tomorrow," Royden said. "And congratulations, Penn, on the birth of a fine son."

"Thank you, sir, and I can't thank you enough for your kind generosity," Penn said.

"I told you the Clan MacKinnon is a loyal and decent clan who never fail to look out for one another. That was why Oria helped us so much through the last few years. Though fate stole her wedding day from her, she was still part of the Clan MacKinnon and she never forgot it," Emily said, tears filling her eyes. "We're proud she's finally where she belongs, wife to Chieftain Royden and Mistress of the Clan MacKinnon." Emily lifted her arm, holding the bairn up. "Chieftain Royden, please come and see the first Clan MacKinnon clansmen born since your return home."

Royden walked over and peered down at the bairn. He was so small and yet he would grow into manhood as all lads do, and it was his responsibility to make certain he had a good and powerful clan to call family. And to produce a fine lad of his own to keep the MacKinnon clan strong.

"He is a fine bairn. You should be proud, Penn," Royden said.

"I am, sir," Penn said with a gleeful smile.

Oria and Royden left the cottage, Calla and Sara leaving shortly after them.

"You look tired," Royden said and took her hand as he used to do so often and instinctively. His fingers closed around hers and he felt a catch to his gut when her fingers gripped his, welcoming the clasp of his hand.

"I admit I was worried about mother and child," she said, relieved to voice her doubt.

"But it worked well," Royden reminded.

"Much better than I feared it would," she said with a sigh and rested her head on Royden's shoulder for a moment as they continued walking to the keep.

He'd never found himself at a loss of words with Oria, but at the moment he didn't know what to say since there was so much that needed to be said between them. Now was not the time, though. She was tired and no good would come of a discussion.

He thought of safer ground to be discussed, and said, "I received word on Arran."

She gasped and tugged at his hand. "Tell me. Is he well? Is he coming home?"

"Aye to all from what the leper told me."

"Leper?" she asked, tilting her head to look at him.

"A leper arrived here shortly after we spoke and delivered a message from Arran, letting me know he'd be home in a month or more."

"Why so long?"

"He has a matter that needs his attention?" Royden said.

"What matter?"

"The leper didn't say, though from what he did say I surmised it has to do with Raven," Royden said.

Concern sprang to her eyes and voice. "Any idea what that may be?"

"No, the leper gave no indication of any more information and I don't believe Arran would have offered any more in fear of not knowing if it would bring harm to Raven. My greatest hope is that when Arran returns home, he has Raven with him."

Oria hated keeping things from her husband, but she had made a promise. Though, part of the promise was no longer necessary. Unfortunately, both parts were connected. She had to find a way to slip into the woods and at least bring relief to one of his worries.

"You say a leper brought you this information?" Oria asked.

"Aye, he camps in the woods by the tangled tree for no more than two days. Does it bother you that I allowed him to rest here?" he asked, seeing a troubled look on her face.

"No, not at all. The poor man should have a safe place to rest. I just wonder…" She tilted her head and her brow scrunched as she looked upon him. "There was a leper who often stopped at Learmonth on his way to the Stitchill Monastery. He and Burnell would talk. I met him only once. His name is Noble, Brother Noble. I wonder if it is him."

"Odd that he travels the roads? He'd be safer and well cared for if he remained at the monastery."

"Gossip suggests he carries messages between the different monasteries. Another is that he searches for the witch healer in the hope that she will cure him."

"I recall the day the witch spoke to my sister and frightened her with her prediction of troublesome times and a long separation before our family would be reunited. Her prophecy has been accurate thus far. Has anymore ever been heard from the witch?"

It hurt her to continue to lie to him, but until she could be sure it was safe to break her promise, she had no choice. Though, she phrased it so it was no lie. "No more prophecies that I recall hearing."

"I wonder if Brother Noble ever found the witch and found she was no help to him."

"Some say she covers her home with a spell that keeps it invisible to all, except the ones she allows to see it," Oria said.

"That's nonsense. You can't believe that," Royden said. "The woods stretch far and wide. There are areas I have yet to explore or even wish to explore. She simply makes her home where few, if any at all travel. I think I will ask him if he's run across the witch."

"I'll go with you," Oria was quick to say.

"No, I'll not have you go near the leper," Royden commanded. "You'll go to your bedchamber and rest. And don't waste your breath in protest. You will do as I say." He released her hand. "Now go."

"Royden."

He turned to see Angus there.

"You're needed in the field to settle a dispute that can't wait," Angus said.

Royden turned back to Oria and raised a finger at her. "Go in the keep and stay there until I return and don't dare disobey me."

Oria grew annoyed that he walked off and was so confident that she wouldn't defy his order that he didn't even turn around to make sure she continued on to the keep. She waited until he was nearly out of sight, then turned and hurried toward the woods.

Chapter Ten

Oria stopped at the edge of the woods and shook her head. She was acting like a petulant child defying a parent. Royden was her husband, and while it was considered a wife's duty to obey her husband, her marriage to Burnell had taught her otherwise.

Burnell had allowed her to choose for herself, and he had made it clear that if anything troubled her she was to talk with him about it. He couldn't always promise things would work out as she wanted, but he would do his best to see that she understood why.

Refuse to look at a problem reasonably and you will never solve it, Burnell's words reminded.

Defying her husband's order would not solve his commanding attitude. She turned to go to the keep and stopped abruptly. Her husband stood not far from her, his arms folded across his chest and a stern look that far from marred his fine features.

She smiled seeing him there, his stance impressive. "So you didn't trust me to do as told."

"It hasn't taken long to learn that some qualities you once possessed vanished with the years. Besides, there is a defiance in your eyes when you intend to do as you like, a new trait I've discovered in you."

Now there was something she'd be wise to remember.

"You're observant," Oria said, another thing she'd be wise to remember. "What of the matter you were needed to settle?"

"I gave Angus clear instructions that would settle it fast enough. What kept you from defying me?"

"Common sense," she said and walked over to him, stretching her hand out to him. She was pleased he didn't hesitate to take it and was even more pleased when the strength of his hand closed around hers. "Your command was out of concern for me and it would have been rude of me to ignore it."

"I will not lose you again," he said, though it was more a command that warned of an unseen foe. "Even though you've become pig-headed."

His remark not only touched her heart, it made her laugh. "We shall make a good couple—me pig-headed and you commanding and grumpy."

He grunted rather than argued since she was partially right.

"Since you don't have to rush off, why don't we go see if the leper is Brother Noble?"

"It is me, Lady Oria."

Both Oria and Royden turned to see the leper keeping himself tucked behind a tree, his hood barely visible.

Nonetheless, Royden took no chance, he tucked his wife behind him.

"My condolences at the loss of your husband, my lady. I will pray for his soul." Brother Noble said.

"You were ordered to remain where you were told," Royden reprimanded.

Oria stepped out from behind her husband, but his arm shot out blocking her from going any farther. "Thank you, Brother Noble, that is kind of you."

"She is no longer Lady Oria, she is Mistress Oria, my wife," Royden informed him.

"My congratulations. It is good to know you are well looked after."

"What brings you so close to the keep?" Royden demanded.

His wife pushed at his arm to move past him.

"You'll stay put and hold your tongue," he whispered tersely.

"I am quite rested and wish to move on. I came hoping to get the food you offered so I can be on my way."

"I'll have it brought to you and—"

"Please feel free to seek food and shelter here on your travels," Oria said, her husband's head snapping to the side to glare at her. She paid him no heed, too anxious to ask, "I heard you were looking for the witch. Did you find her?"

"I've been warned against it by my brothers at the monastery. They tell me the devil will take my soul if I seek the witch's help. I wonder if the devil already hasn't claimed it with this plague that eats my body. I have heard many stories about the witch's power. I have heard the tale of how she healed your da, Chieftain Royden."

"What?" Royden asked, taking several steps forward. "You say my da is alive?"

The leper coughed and his gravelly voice became more of a growl when he spoke. "A tale I heard tell. Surely you have heard it."

"No, I haven't heard it. Tell me this tale," Royden demanded.

"The tale I heard was that your da was badly wounded in the wedding day battle that claimed many lives. He was thought dead, blood pouring from his chest. When the battle ended, his body couldn't be found. No one knew what happened to him. Some claimed the witch dragged him away and healed him, so he owes her his soul and cannot return home."

Royden glared with anger. "Why didn't you tell me this when we first spoke?"

"I assumed you had already heard it. Someone in your clan must have bared witness to it or how would the tale have gotten started?" the leper said.

"I'll see you have your food and I bid you farewell," Royden said, making certain the leper understood he was to leave. He turned and grabbed his wife's hand when he reached her, forcing her to walk along with him.

"You go to ask Bethany what she knows, don't you?" Oria said, taking two strides to his one to keep up with him.

"If anyone knows anything, she would," Royden said and approached the kitchen.

The kitchen extended off the keep and was connected by a narrow passageway. It was the busiest part of the keep, with constant food preparation going on.

Royden released her hand just before he entered through the open door. Oria came to a stop behind him and saw that all activity had come to a halt.

"Prepare a generous sack of food for the leper and leave it by the oak tree," Royden ordered. "Bethany, I will speak to you in the Great Hall.

Bethany had had only one person to help her in the kitchen, but with Royden's return that had changed. She now had two more people to help her and she left them to carry out his order.

Royden walked to the middle of the Great Hall, stopped, and turned his arms going across his chest. It was a purposeful stance, one meant to intimidate and Oria saw that it did just that since Bethany stood, her hands clamped so tight together that her knuckles turned white.

"Do you know about the tale of my da being alive and stuck with the witch since he owes her his soul for saving his life?" Royden asked and hearing himself thought how foolish it sounded, but tales existed in the Highlands with some ring of truth to them. That meant his da could possibly be alive.

"I've heard many tales these past few years, sir. But I can only speak to what I saw with my own eyes," Bethany said.

"And what is that?"

Oria cringed at the harsh command in his voice.

"I'm afraid not much, sir. As I told you, I don't know what became of your da," Bethany said. "When the battle ended the warriors who remained here ordered me to tend to the wounded that were brought to me. I asked about Chieftain Parlan, but was told he'd be brought to me if needed. He was never brought to me and I never saw what happened to him."

"Is there anyone here who might know?" Royden asked.

Bethany thought a moment. "Mildred was tasked with collecting all the weapons off the dead and wounded MacKinnon warriors. She is well aware of those who died, but she never mentioned seeing your da. A troop of warriors were sent out, I assumed to search for Raven, but perhaps they searched for your da as well. I can't say for sure since the warriors kept tight lips. But then we all kept tight-lipped not wanting to bring harm to anyone who may have escaped."

"Thank you, Bethany," Oria said.

"I will do anything I can to help reunite the family," Bethany said.

"You've done more than your share of keeping the Clan MacKinnon together, Bethany. I'm forever in your debt," Royden said.

Oria smiled softly hearing the old, strong, yet thoughtful Royden in his voice.

"I'll send one of my helpers to fetch Mildred to see if she can be of any help." Bethany bobbed her head and left.

Oria could see how frustrated her husband was, his hand roughly rubbing the back of his neck. She hated seeing him suffer when she could easily ease his hurt, but first she had to speak with—

"Do you think my da could have possibly survived?" Royden asked, interrupting her thought.

This was a chance to give him some hope and why not use a witch's words to do it. "If I remember right didn't the witch tell Raven you all would be reunited?"

"She did," he said, a bit of hope heard in his words.

"She was right about you all being torn apart, so I would think she would be right about you all reuniting."

Royden's brow narrowed. "I know it's been some time, but I don't recall telling you what the witch said to Raven." He shook his head. "Raven told you, didn't she?"

Oria nodded. "In the woods one day when she, Purity, and I met. She told me that you would probably tell me, but I didn't think you would."

He looked surprised. "Why?"

"Did you plan on telling me?"

"I asked first," he said, a command in his tone.

"That answers it for me and as for why? You tried to protect me from everything."

"It is my duty to protect the woman I love," he said his brief explanation enough.

"Aye, I understand that, but when you're not there, what do I do?"

Her question startled him, his brow shooting up.

"You wished to see me, sir?" Mildred asked.

He was glad for the interruption since he had no answer for his wife and that disturbed him. What if he wasn't there to protect her again? He had seen it for himself, the remnants of what happened to women in raids and attacks. It sickened him to see what some men were capable of doing and one thing that he actually admired about Platt was that he had forbidden the men to harm any of the women at places they attacked. They had looted places, stripping villages, but had left the women unharmed.

"Royden," Oria said, giving his arm a gentle squeeze.

He shook his head. "Sit, Mildred, I wish to talk with you."

"I didn't do anything wrong, sir," Mildred pleaded, tears glistening in her aged eyes.

"Of course, you didn't," Bethany cajoled, slipping an arm around the woman and leading her to the table nearest the hearth while her helpers placed a jug of ale on the table. Knowing Mildred favored ale, Bethany filled a tankard and placed it in front of her.

Oria filled a tankard for Royden and nodded for him to take a seat opposite Mildred, sliding along the bench to sit next to him.

Royden sat and was pleased when his wife moved to rest her arm against his and her leg against his leg as well. It felt good to be sitting close with her again and he found his frustration easing.

"Bethany tells me you were tasked with collecting the weapons off our dead warriors," Royden said. "I regret that you had to do such a horrible task."

Mildred's shoulders slumped, the worry draining off her that she had done something wrong. "It wasn't an easy task, sir, but I was glad for it, since I could treat our fallen warriors with respect as I took their weapons and I could say a prayer for each one of them as I did."

"I appreciate how brave you were, Mildred, and how kind and respectful you were to our fallen warriors. Bethany also said you never mentioned seeing my da among the dead."

Mildred downed more ale and looked about before leaning over the table closer to Royden and keeping her voice to a whisper, "I thought it best—safest—to say nothing to no one. I feared what might have happened if I did, not only to me and those told about it, but most of all to,"—she lowered her voice even more—"your sister."

"Raven? What has Raven to do with my da?"

"I saw her struggle to drag your da away and then that Macara lass, the one with the claw-like fingers, suddenly appeared and helped her drag your da into the woods. I don't know what happened to them after that."

"Did you see how badly my da was injured?" Royden asked.

Mildred nodded and wiped at her eyes with her sleeve. "He was bad, sir, blood covering his chest and he not moving as the two lassies dragged him away." She sniffled back unshed tears as she looked to Oria. "I saw how you fought those men, bit the one, and how he slashed your face, but you didn't stop fighting when the two men dragged you off to put you in that cart. Blood poured down your neck and covered your clothing, but you kept fighting the two of them. You were a sight to see and it gave me strength. I cried out when I saw that man who slashed you knock you out with one hard blow of his fist, then toss you in the cart. You're a brave one, Mistress Oria."

"No braver than any other who fought that day," Oria said, having felt the muscles in her husband's arm grow tighter and tighter as the tale unfolded.

"Bethany," Royden called out, having seen the woman lurking in the shadows by the passageway that led to the kitchen.

Bethany quickly approached the table.

"See that Mildred has food and drink to take with her," Royden instructed, keeping a tight rein on his mounting temper.

"You're most generous, sir, thank you," Mildred said and took a last swallow of ale before following Bethany out of the hall.

Royden stood and said, "My solar." He didn't wait for his wife. He walked off, leaving her to follow.

He entered his solar and went to the hearth pacing in front of it. Though Oria had told him what had happened, hearing it from someone who had witnessed it had enraged him. He fumed with heated anger that was difficult to control. He wanted to pound the man for what he had done to Oria until he couldn't stand, until he finally laid lifeless in the dirt.

Oria closed the door behind her and went to Royden.

His hand reached out, his fingers softly tracing along her scar. "I'm going to find him an—"

She placed her hand over his. "It's done, nothing can change that."

"I can't let this stand, Oria. The man who did this to you has to pay for it." He shook his head when she went to speak. "You waste your words. If it takes me years, I will see this done."

In time perhaps she could change that, fearing that his quest for revenge could bring more harm than good. For now, she would follow her heart.

She raised her lips to his and kissed him. His lips responded to her without hesitation and she was glad she had taken the chance that he wouldn't deny her. There was a deep hunger in their kiss that hadn't been there before. A need so strong that it almost frightened.

Her arms quickly wrapped around his neck, clinging tight, fearful their kiss would end far too soon. Her fear vanished when his hand cupped the back of her head, holding it firm. He didn't want her going anywhere.

His lips were a taste of the old and the new, softness mingling with a powerful strength she hadn't felt before and it sent a tingle down to her toes and up again, settling between her legs.

His arm coiled around her waist, the leather cuff pressing into her side as he lifted her enough so that her feet didn't touch the floor and hurried to brace her against a wall.

His palm flattened against the wall while his arm continued to hold her firm. His lips left hers, nipping with his lips and teeth down along her neck. Her pleasure erupted in repeated gasps and moans. He hefted her up a bit higher off the floor and pressed himself against her, settling his hard shaft against the apex of her legs.

She almost screamed aloud when he rubbed against her, a startling sensation shooting through her. Instead she buried her face in the crook of his neck, his name falling from her lips in a rushed whisper, "Royden."

"Lift your garments above your waist," he ordered in a harsh whisper, moving just enough away from her for her to do so. "Now push my plaid aside," he commanded impatiently.

Again she did as he said and when she felt his hard shaft rub against her, she cried out. Over and over and over his shaft teased her and she pressed against him, aching for much more.

"Royden," she breathed harshly in his ear, clinging to him.

"Look at me, Oria," he demanded.

She did as he said, lifting her head, their eyes meeting.

"I want to see your face when I bring you to climax the first time," he said.

His hand dropped down off the wall to cup her bare bottom and shove her hard against him, his manhood grinding against her and shooting a sensation through her that completely engulfed her and had her dropping her head back to hit the wall as she cried out his name.

The exquisite sensation ran through her and she pressed against him, demanding more from his manhood, refusing to let the pleasure fade away and then she felt it. He released his seed against her, thick and warm, and she wished, how she wished, he'd been inside her.

His strong fingers dug into her backside, squeezing tight and something flared in her, though faded much too quickly. She dropped her head on his shoulder and she was glad that he continued to hold her, her legs far too weak to keep her on her feet.

After her breathing calmed, he lowered her to her feet, her garment slipping down and covering her and his plaid doing the same to him.

"Don't wait too long to welcome me to your bed. I want my seed where it belongs, inside you, growing," he said and stepped away from her. "I won't enter you until then—until you welcome me, until you tell me you want me inside you, until you truly want to be my wife."

Oria stared after him as he walked out of the room, not looking back at her. He had changed. The thoughtful, mannerly man would have never braced her against a wall, never have ordered her to lift her garment or push his aside and done what he had done. The man she loved was far different now, far stronger, far more confident, far more commanding, and far more experienced when it came to coupling.

How did she handle such a man?

She wasn't sure, but she would find a way.

Chapter Eleven

Royden piled stone on top of stone on top of stone without stopping. Sweat covered him and his breath was labored, but he didn't stop, he wouldn't let himself. He hadn't been able to stop himself in the solar and it had all started with an innocent gesture—a caring touch.

Liar! The accusation echoed in his head.

Her touch had ignited what already burned in him. His anger at what happened to her, and how he hadn't been able to protect her, left him with an unrelenting need to fully make her his wife. He had failed to do that years ago and her father had given her to another man. And while he would have loved nothing more than to consummate their marriage, he wouldn't do so until she made it clear that she welcomed him, that she made her own choice to seal their vows forever.

Unfortunately, not only his need, but hers as well, couldn't be ignored or denied. He had done the next best thing to satisfy them both—and he feared what he had unleashed in himself.

He had gotten more satisfaction without having slipped inside Oria than he had gotten from any of the women he had poked. And he had enjoyed even more holding her after it was done. He'd never felt as content as he had at that moment and he was already thinking of when they would share such a moment again.

"You don't need to prove yourself to us, Chieftain," Angus said. "We've seen for ourselves what a strong, powerful warrior you are even though you have only one hand."

Royden stopped, the stone he held between his hand and stump, larger than he realized. He rested the stone in place, making sure it fit tight and looked to Angus, John, and Stuart. "I appreciate that, but it's more about what I have on my mind—"

"A woman," Angus said, nodding his head and the other men agreed, their heads bobbing along with his. "It's always a woman. And you're damned if you do and damned if you don't with them. Stop waving at me, Stuart, you know it's the truth. Not one of them makes a lick of sense."

"Is that so, Angus?"

Angus cringed, sending a glare at Stuart for not warning him sooner, and turned to face Bethany. "I didn't mean you, *mo ghaol*."

"So I'm different than the others, am I?" Bethany asked, a covered basket tucked in the crook of her arm.

"That you are, *mo ghaol*," he said with a confident smile. "And a lucky man I am to have you."

"You don't have me yet, Angus, and don't call me, my love. Don't think I don't know you're after me for my cooking skills. You have a long road to travel before you're a lucky enough man to be with me." Bethany turned to leave, then stopped, and turned around. "You made me forget where I was headed, Angus. Now you'll not get the sweet cake I was going to give you before taking the rest to Emily and Penn."

Angus grabbed his chest and stumbled back dramatically. "You wound me, woman. I favor your sweets, but I favor you more."

"That sweet tongue of yours isn't going to easily charm me like it does other women," Bethany warned. "And I'll hear no more of it."

A slight smile broke along Royden's face at the humorous exchange between the two. He was glad to see that his clan was healing, smiling, teasing, laughing. He had feared with the suffering and damage done to so many, they might never heal. But they were healing and he intended to make sure they remained strong and well-protected.

"Bethany, my love, let me explain," Angus said, hurrying to trail after her.

John laughed. "That man's got it bad and won't admit it."

"He talked about her endlessly while captive." Stuart shook his head. "I don't know why he's wasting time now that he's home. He should tell her and be done with it."

"I would if I had someone. When we were first presented with those willing women, I couldn't help but think how great it was, but then after a while it became meaningless. It was just a way to assuage a need. It didn't fill the emptiness inside of me." John turned a pleading look on Royden. "Please tell me you're going to find a way to have more women join our clan."

"We need both men and women. You've probably seen that some of our clansmen returned with Oria and me the other day. I'm assuming others from the clan were also dispersed to other clans. I'm going to see about getting them home."

John's smile beamed wide. "That would be wonderful."

"It would be nice to have our clansmen home," Stuart said, returning to stacking the stones.

Royden saw Penn approach, a basket in hand, and he kept his voice low when he asked with a nod toward the man, "What do you think of him?"

"Seems decent enough, but I still question who it is he's loyal to," John said.

"I agree. Was it truly love that kept him here or was he told to find a woman and claim this as his home?" Stuart asked.

The three men turned silent, Penn getting closer.

"Bethany sent me with some sweets and an apology that she hadn't offered you any. She says Angus is to blame for that," Penn said with a grin.

The men couldn't help but grin along with him, all but Royden.

John and Stuart waited for Royden to take a sweet cake. Royden realized out of respect they waited for him to take one first. He grabbed one, though not hungry, but once he bit into it that changed and he reached for another one.

He stopped before snatching another from the basket. "Emily and you have enough cakes?"

"More than enough cakes and food, sir. Bethany keeps us well supplied of which we are grateful," Penn said.

Royden took another cake, leaving what remained for John and Stuart.

"Tell me, Penn, how do I get my clansmen home?" Royden asked.

He had planned on talking to Fergus about this, thinking the man had more influence with the leader of the mercenaries. However, he was curious as to how Penn would respond to such a request.

"Sir?" Penn asked as if not understanding.

"You're no fool, Penn. You know what I ask," Royden said, a touch of warning in his tone.

Stuart took the basket from the man. "Our clansmen, you took them."

"We want them back," John said and grabbed another cake.

"And not only the warriors who were taken captive to serve your leader, but our women and children as well. I want them all returned home," Royden said. "If you can't help me with that, then tell me who can."

John and Stuart glared at Penn, waiting for an answer.

"Talk with Fergus," Penn said. "I can't say for sure that he can help, but he would be the one to talk to."

"Tomorrow you'll go and tell him I want to speak with him and I expect you to return with him," Royden instructed.

"And no telling him about what Chieftain Royden has to say to him," John warned.

"He'll expect me to tell him," Penn said and none of the men appeared surprised.

"Looks like his loyalty doesn't lie with the clan," John said, turning a threatening glare on Penn.

"I not only found love here but a happiness I never knew existed. I don't want to lose it. My loyalty lies here with my new home, my wife, my son. I'd do anything to protect it all. The man, the leader who built the band of mercenaries, has an unforgiving soul and I fear him more than anyone. So I do what I must to keep those I love and care about safe," Penn said.

"Then you'll tell me all I ask and all I need to know?" Royden asked.

"I know little since I was an insignificant warrior in a band of many. I became significant when I volunteered to remain here," Penn explained. "And I did that because I fell in love with Emily and couldn't bear the thought of leaving her."

"And your reward for sacrificing yourself?" Royden asked, "since I assume this leader commands you to remain here until otherwise told."

"My reward is being able to remain here with Emily forever," Penn said.

"And are you beholden to this leader forever?" Royden asked.

"If I want to live."

Royden seemed to grow taller as his shoulders spread and his chest expanded with each step he took toward Penn. When he reached him, he poked Penn in the shoulder with his cuffed stub.

"Are you telling me that your leader intends to always have a foot in my clan?" Royden demanded.

"As I've said, I know little. Fergus would know more. But I can tell you that he planned on claiming this whole area for himself and I've never seen him not get what he wants."

***

Oria paced in her bedchamber later that night, her thoughts not able to let go of what had happened in the solar. She had spent a good portion of her time since then thinking of nothing else but how she could handle the situation. Did she take time, learn more about the man Royden had become, or did she welcome the man he'd become into her bed without any thought or reservations?

And truly what difference did it make? He was her husband and would remain her husband. Did she want to waste time getting to know this man or would it take being intimate with him to better understand him?

She shook her head, tired of the constant questioning. All that truly mattered was that she loved Royden and that hadn't changed. If anything, her love had grown stronger through the years. There was never a time she doubted that he wouldn't return to her.

"He needs to know that," she said and rushed out of the room and down to Royden's bedchamber, not stopping to don her robe over her white nightdress.

She barely knocked before throwing the door open. "Royden—"

He stood completely naked in front of the fireplace. The flickering flames bathing his body in a glowing light. She had always thought him a fine looking man and felt herself lucky that his body had yet to go soft. But now staring at him, seeing the scope of his defined muscles that were everywhere, his chest full and broad, the ripples of muscle along his flat stomach, the curve of his waist, the strength in his firm legs, and the size of his manhood that sprang to life before her eyes, she was speechless, and she grew aroused.

"You come barging in here without permission, yet you have nothing to say?" Royden said snappishly, annoyed that his shaft responded like a young lad unable to control his desires.

She brought her legs closer together, hoping to stop the throb that had settled there. "I thought to tell you something. It can wait until you cover yourself."

"You're my wife. There's no need for me to cover myself in front of you," he said and knew it unwise to remain naked in front of her, but ignored the thought, since he couldn't help but see how she tightened her legs against the arousal that no doubt had snuck up on her.

She turned and closed the door and swallowed hard, thinking wisely on her words. While her body demanded that she didn't, that she do what she wanted to do, what she ached to do—make love with her husband.

Oria turned and tried to keep her eyes on his face and no place else. "You believe you failed me, but I knew you didn't, you wouldn't. The whole time you were gone, I never doubted you would return home. I was sure of your return and there was nothing that could change that. I knew you would come back to me. I know our love is that strong."

Royden wanted to go to her, scoop her up and lose himself inside her, but he stopped himself. "But that man is no more."

"You told me that you still love me."

"I do love you, more than ever," he admitted.

"Then you are the same man I love and I welcome you to my bed," she said, her quick decision a surprise, but one she didn't regret.

"You tempt me, Oria, my shaft already thick and hard, ready to plunge into you. But why do you really welcome me to your bed? Is it that you've grown aroused at the sight of me naked and aching for you? Is it that you got a taste of pleasure and want more? Or could it be that your wide eyes show surprise at your own words? When you welcome me to your bed, it will because you wish to be a wife to the man who has returned to you, the man you say you love, but don't truly know. So make sure the next time those words spill from your lips, you mean them."

"Don't you think there has been enough wasted time between us?" she asked, wondering what truly kept them from not consummating their vows, not finally bringing their love to fruition?

Royden took a step forward. "You think I want to waste time between us? I want to plant myself inside you every day, just as I planted myself in woman after woman after woman until I lost count of how many." His body stiffened seeing that she couldn't hide the shock in her eyes. "They meant nothing to me, I felt nothing for them. It was a need I had to satisfy just like the one that grows me hard now and just like the one that has you throbbing between your legs."

It hit her then and she spoke without thinking. "You fear making love with me."

Royden was at her side in three strides, planting his face close to hers. "I fear nothing. It's you who should fear the stranger in your bed."

She felt a chill run through her, but she kept herself from shivering. "You tell me not to wait long to welcome you to my bed and when I do you deny me and tell me I should fear you—a stranger. You are not a stranger to me.

You are the man I have loved for as long as I can remember and it seems you need reminding of that. And while you might be afraid, I'm not," she challenged. She walked boldly to the bed and climbed beneath the blankets.

Though she was foolish, Royden admired her courage. And while he didn't fear making love to his wife, he did worry what she would think of him once it was done. He was far from the mannered man he'd once been.

Not trusting himself, he went and grabbed his plaid off the chest.

"You refuse to make love to me and if you refuse to sleep beside me, then I'll surely know you're a coward." He turned a scowl on her that froze her. Otherwise, she would have jumped out of bed and hightailed it out of there to hide.

"You call me a coward?" he asked, not believing what he heard.

"If you don't remain here and sleep beside your wife, you are a coward." Good Lord, she said it again. Whatever gave her the audacity to say such a thing or demand he sleep with her?

He tossed his plaid aside and crawled slowly from the bottom of the bed up and over her. He almost smiled as she eased herself back to lay flat as he got closer and closer until he finally braced his stump and hand to either side of her head to keep his body hovering over her.

"So you invite me between your legs, do you?"

She did. Good Lord, she truly did, but... "No. You refused my offer so now you can wait."

He all but choked on his word. "What?"

"You heard me. You'll sleep beside me, but not make love to me."

"And what's going to stop me?" he asked, bringing his lips down to hover just above hers, then felt... "Did you just poke me in the chest?"

"I did," she admitted.

"A poke, a sorrowful one at that, is not going to stop me."

"It wasn't meant to stop you. It was my response to your question—you."

It took him a moment to comprehend, then he laughed. "I'm going to stop myself."

"Aye, you will, since Royden would never force himself on me, not ever," she said.

Damn, she was right, he wouldn't. But... "I don't have to force you, Oria, I know if I slip my hand between your legs I'll feel how ready you are for me."

"I won't deny that," she said, "but I will deny myself until you stop being such a stubborn arse."

A spark of anger fueled his words. "So I'm a coward and an arse."

"That will be up to you to prove otherwise."

"By sleeping beside you in bed without touching you?" he asked.

"Aye, and I'll have your word on it," she said, hoping this sudden show of courage—tinged with a bit of fear—proved wise.

"You have my word, but just for tonight," he said, capitulating, though he didn't know why. His shaft was still hard and with her sleeping beside him, it wouldn't soften anytime soon. And he wouldn't go back on his word not to touch her, so it was going to be an agonizing night. Why then had he agreed? It was simple. He wanted her there beside him.

She smiled and pulled the blanket up under her chin. "Good-night, husband." She turned on her side away from him, not trusting herself not to touch him when she ached to. But this was a start for them, here together in bed, and once in his bed, she didn't intend to leave it.

***

He couldn't get to her. No matter how fast or hard he ran, he couldn't reach Oria even though she was close. It was as if something was holding him in place. He could see the blood, running down her neck, soaking her garments. She fought the man, her fisted hands punching at him. He yelled for her to stop but she didn't and he made a fist, raising his hand and brought it down hard against her jaw, and she dropped to the ground.

He broke loose of whatever held him and ran, reaching the man before he could pick up Oria and throw her into a cart. His hand went to his throat and squeezed.

"I'm going to kill you. Kill you," Royden raged.

He felt the man grip his arm, fighting to break free, and when he looked down, it was Oria's hand he saw.

Royden woke to find his hand at his wife's throat.

Chapter Twelve

Royden woke with an ache in his neck. He unfurled himself from the wooden chair, stretching his neck and shoulders as best he could. He cringed not from the aches of sleeping in a chair in his solar, but with the memory of what he had done to his wife last night.

He got to his feet, stretching as he did, working the soreness out of his taut muscles. He'd been sickened by finding his own hand squeezing the life from his wife when he woke with a jolt from his nightmare. He was surprised she hadn't run from the room when he had quickly let go of her, though her labored breathing may have had something to do with that.

He had hastily slipped his arm around her waist and lifted her to sit up so she could breathe more easily. He'd been afraid to touch her after that. He had no right to, not ever again. Highlanders were great warriors, never fearing to fight, but he hadn't been prepared for the savagery that he'd had to embrace when with the mercenaries. He had feared becoming a savage himself and if he had had any doubt last night proved that he had become one.

Never again would he sleep beside his wife and he doubted she would disagree, since when he left the room she hadn't stopped him. He had grabbed his garments and boots on his way out and was glad he had. He wasn't prepared to face his wife just yet and he wondered if she felt the same.

Quick strides took him to the kitchen where he found Bethany starting to prepare the morning meal before her helpers arrived, a habit of hers since as long as he could remember. Her raised brow told him she was surprised to see him and he understood why. He rarely came to the kitchen since his return home.

"What's wrong?" she asked like a mum worried for her son.

He was going to remind her of her place, speaking to him so bluntly, but she truly was family and she had made sure to take care of the Clan MacKinnon in his absence.

"I'm not the man I once was," he said.

"None of us are who we were once. The attack and the passing years changed us, changed everything. We can't go back. We can only go forward," she said and handed him a slice of fresh baked bread. "There is one thing that hasn't changed, though, and never will. Our love for our clan, our family, and one another. It is what holds us together, what drives us to survive. You and Oria are a shining example of that love and the clan will rejoice and fill with promise for the future when the time comes for you and Oria to announce she is with child. It proves the Clan MacKinnon was not defeated. It lives on."

Royden ate the bread without thinking as he had done when captive. Food had been provided, but there had been occasions when it had been scarce and he had learned after that to eat when he could.

"The clan knows they now have a chieftain, much like his da, who they can count on," Bethany said.

Duty. He had a duty to his clan. He had had a duty to survive. He had had a duty to return home, but he didn't have a duty to love Oria. That was something he had chosen himself and she had chosen it as well. He did, however, have a duty to protect her and keep her safe. And after last night that meant keeping her safe from him.

"You were a good, honorable man before this happened and you're still a good, honorable man," Bethany said, tears glistening in her eyes.

Royden left the kitchen grateful for her words, but knowing they were far from the truth.

***

Oria hadn't slept since she woke with her husband's hand at her throat, squeezing until she barely could breathe. She understood it had been a nightmare that had driven him to do it. Still, it had been a frightening experience. From the profound shock and horror on his face, she knew he would never permit her to sleep beside him again. While the thought of his nightmare returning and it happening again frightened her, the thought of never sleeping by her husband's side frightened her even more.

She feared no amount of reasoning with him would work. The problem was he needed her and she needed him. They desperately needed each other.

She didn't bother to rush out of bed and find him. She was well aware that he would avoid her. She turned and moved over to his side, taking in his scent, a fresh scent since he had washed last night.

Oria was unable to resist hugging his pillow as she held it tight against her. It had her recalling how she had loved when he would hug her close and she would bury her face against his shirt and relish his scent, a mixture of earth, forest, and sweat blending into an intoxicating scent that was his and his alone.

Comforted by the familiar scent and memory, her eyes closed and she fell into a much needed sleep.

***

Royden met with Penn before he left to take the message to Fergus that he wanted to see him—today—to make sure he did as instructed. Then he went to see that chores were being seen to, not that it was necessary since everyone was eager to pitch in and do their share. It provided Royden with the time to talk with clan members, hear what they had to say and determine what he could do to improve things.

The one thing most complained about was that the clan didn't have the men and strength to survive another attack. The clan had to grow or it would never survive. He agreed with them and his hope was he could make that happen.

It was a fairly nice day, a mixture of sun and clouds, though more sun. A good day to be outside. And a poor excuse not to enter the keep and talk with his wife. He intended to make it clear to her that they would sleep in separate beds and he had not a sliver of doubt she would disagree.

"Whatever it is, it's best you talk with her and get done with it," Stuart said.

Royden sent a questioning look to him.

"I've been talking to you for the last few minutes and you haven't heard a word I've said. And I'm far too familiar with that look, since I've worn it enough on several occasions," Stuart explained with a grin.

Royden grunted, annoyed at himself.

"Go, all is good here," Stuart urged.

Stuart was right. He needed to get this done and over with without delay. Oria was probably in the Great Hall having the morning meal. It would be good to talk with her there. With servants about she would be less likely to argue with him.

He was surprised to find she wasn't there and stopped a servant. "Do you know where Mistress Oria went after she finished her meal?"

"The mistress hasn't been down for her meal yet," the servant said.

That worried Royden and he hurried up the stairs. Was she that upset about what happened last night that she still hadn't left his bedchamber? Or had she gone to her own, not wanting to remain in his bed?

He got his answer quick enough when he entered his quarters and walked over to the bed to find her sleeping on the side of the bed he had slept last night. She was entangled in the blanket, embracing his pillow as if she was holding tightly to him.

He shook his head. It wasn't going to be easy getting her out of his bed, especially since she was right where he wanted her. He had had endless dreams of sleeping beside her while away, their naked bodies pressed close, his arms tucked snuggly around her, the flowery scent of her tickling his nose. The worst part had been waking up and finding it had all been a dream. It had torn at his heart each and every time.

He went to leave but first stopped and added logs to the dwindling fire. He didn't turn to look at her again as he left, his mind too occupied with how he'd stop himself from keeping her in his bed.

***

Royden began to worry when he still hadn't seen his wife two hours later. Had she yet to wake up? Or was she purposely avoiding him? When he finally thought to go see for himself, he was notified that Fergus approached the village and would be at the keep soon.

He went outside to wait and greet the man, eager to confront him.

Fergus was barely off his horse, his face flushed with anger, when he said, "You summons me like a servant and dare make demands?"

"And yet here you are," Royden challenged.

"Watch it, Royden, your clan is not as powerful as it once was," Fergus threatened with a sneer.

"The very reason you're here," Royden said, angry at his threat, yet calling him out for it would do no good.

"So Penn told me," Fergus said, his top teeth rushing to grab his lower lip as if he could pull the words back.

"I figured he would, but I appreciate you confirming it for me." Royden nodded to the keep door. "Come, we have things to discuss."

They settled in the solar at the round table and Fergus didn't wait for a drink to be offered. He filled a tankard with ale from the jug on the table and took a seat. He did it with a familiarity that had Royden realizing that he'd been in this room many times before. That angered him. His home had been held captive just as he had.

"You have no leverage to make demands," Fergus said.

"This is their home and they have a right to return to it," Royden argued.

"It doesn't matter. A decision was made concerning them and it can't be undone."

"What do you mean a decision has been made concerning my clan, my family?" Royden demanded. "What decision? Who made this decision?"

"It was part of the negotiation for you and your brother's release. Your clansmen were to be returned home as well," Fergus informed him and emptied his tankard with a large gulp, then refilled it with more ale.

"Were you there for the negotiations?"

"No, I was informed about them afterwards and sent more warriors, so if you decided to retaliate, I'd be sufficiently prepared," Fergus said.

"There's only one person powerful enough to grant or take land away from chieftains and grant titles," Royden said, not quite believing his own thought.

"King David," Fergus confirmed and rested his arms on the table, his hand gripping his tankard as he leaned in closer toward Royden sitting across from him. "The King had no choice. He was wise in making this man his friend rather than his enemy."

"You're talking about the leader of the mercenaries," Royden said.

"I am. He's not a man you want to cross. He's wrath himself and only a fool would go up against him. You got a taste of the savagery he puts his men through. It's nothing compared to his personal troop of warriors. When he wants something, he doesn't stop until he gets it."

"How did you come to fight for him?"

"I had nothing. He offered me something. Anything is better than nothing," Fergus said, defending his decision. "And I'm not sorry I accepted his offer. I have a beautiful wife and two wonderful bairns and I'm a chieftain with land and influence."

"That you stole from someone else," Royden accused.

"And who did he take it from?" Fergus argued. "Battle, bargain, or marriage are the only ways to gain land and power."

"Is that what this man wants, land and power?"

"I don't know what he wants. I'm not privy to his private circle. I only know what he gave me—"

"You mean what you battled endlessly for," Royden said.

Fergus brought his fist down hard on the table. "And I'd do it again to have what I have."

"What is this man's name?"

"I don't know. Those that have seen him in battle call him the Beast. If you saw him in battle you'd know why—he's ferocious like a wild animal that needs caging."

"What does he want with this area?"

"I don't know. It's none of my business." Fergus jabbed a finger toward him. "And it's none of yours."

"He made it my business when he attacked my home, took me and my brother, and endless clansmen captive, killed my father, God only knows what happened to my sister and," —Royden kept tight rein on his anger as he raised his arm to rest his elbow on the table— "he took my hand."

Fergus had the decency to cringe at the horror that had been done to Royden. "I know it doesn't help, but it wasn't done on purpose and believe me when I tell you I have seen worse things cut off a man. I'm warning you as a friend—"

"I'm not your friend."

"Then as a fellow chieftain. What's done is done. Nothing will change that. He doesn't fail, Royden. Whatever it is he wants with this area, he will get. And when that day comes, you better be prepared to at least tolerate him or you won't be long for this life."

It wasn't long after that that Royden watched Fergus ride off. He had learned a lot from Fergus's short visit. This man Fergus spoke about, with a mix of fear and gratitude, had no intention of leaving this area without getting what he wanted. The question was, what did he want? He had laid claim to the Clan MacDonnegal through marriage. And while Fergus might be chieftain, he was answerable to this unknown man. Royden got the sense that the person who had somehow inherited the Clan Learmonth, along with its title was somehow connected to this man as well. That left the Clan MacGlennen, his wife's clan, that supposedly was also promised to someone, and then there was the Clan Macara, yet to learn its fate. He wouldn't be surprised if that hadn't already been fated for someone as well.

But why? What did this man want from this particular area? And why would the King negotiate with him? He would have to benefit from it somehow. Perhaps a guarantee that this area of the Highlands would be faithful to the King.

When Fergus finally disappeared from sight, Royden turned to enter the keep and caught sight of his wife. She looked to be coming from Mildred's cottage and when she spotted him, she smiled, waved, and rushed toward him. She didn't appear at all upset and his guard went up. Maybe it wasn't going to be as easy to talk with her about last night as he had thought.

Oria stretched her hand out to him as she got near. "Who knows how long this beautiful day will last. Come walk with me."

Habit or need, had him reaching out and taking hold, closing his hand snugly around hers. He caught a smile that almost slipped from his lips when her hand latched around his with a strength that warned she wouldn't let him go.

They walked slowly through the village. Many smiling generously as they called out greetings. Seeing the chieftain and his wife brought back some normalcy to the clan and promise of the future just as Bethany had remarked. It definitely was what they all needed.

Oria stopped and talked with some people as if she were a friend. But to them she actually was a friend, a good one. She hadn't deserted them after the attack. She had returned and given them what help she could.

Their walk brought them back to the keep, but at Oria's urging and a tug of his hand she led them to the large oak tree they had once spent time sitting under. Leaves were bursting in full bloom. Soon it would be a thick canopy providing shade and a perfect place to escape to. He looked forward to seeing it once again, having thought about this spot often while away.

She sat snug against him, not letting go of his hand and he could almost read her thoughts.

"You won't be sleeping beside me ever again," he ordered.

"I thought you'd say that, but that's not an order I intend to obey," she said, turning a bright smile on him.

"I'm not giving you a choice."

She laughed softly. "And I'm not giving you one either."

"And who do you think is going to win this?" he asked and while he thought himself sure of victory there was something in her smile that gave him pause to think otherwise.

"It would be a defeat for us both if we succumb to this." She squeezed his hand. "We've suffered enough defeat. It's time we stop fear from ruling our lives and taste victory once again."

Royden rested his head back on the tree trunk and closed his eyes. "I almost strangled you to death last night."

"But you didn't. You felt my hand squeeze your arm and woke." She smiled again. "From now on, I'll give you a good punch when you roll near me."

He brought his head forward and turned quickly to look at her. "You promise?"

He couldn't believe he was asking her such a thing. He should lock her in her bedchamber at night, that way he'd know she was safe. But, God help him, he wanted her in his bed.

"I didn't mean that," she said. Besides, he was too thick with muscle to ever feel her inadequate punch.

"Promise me it anyway and we'll continue to share a bed."

Oria couldn't refuse him since it would get her what she wanted—a chance to seal their vows.

"On one condition," she said and when he glared at her, she was quick to explain. "I want you to join me permanently in the master bedchamber. It's where you belong. Where we belong."

He had been avoiding that move, thinking that if his da should—by some miracle—return, he belonged there. But after seeing how the people regarded him and Oria today, he knew it was time.

"Aye, I'll join you there."

"Wonderful," she said and kissed him on the cheek. "Now tell me what Fergus told you."

She was as eager to know as he was what had caused this misery and what they had yet to face, and he wouldn't keep her ignorant of that. Besides, he enjoyed discussing the matter with her. She had a sharp mind and offered solid advice, much like his mum had done with his da.

He was about to detail his talk when someone screamed for Oria.

They both looked to see Penn rushing toward them. "Morgan is ill. Please. Please help my son."

Oria was on her feet in a flash and running right past Penn, her husband following behind her.

Emily was crying while rocking the screaming bairn in her arms. "Something is wrong. He won't stop crying. I've tried everything."

Oria took the bairn from her and laid him on the bed. He was whaling his head off and scrunching his little legs up while his arms flailed about.

Royden entered behind Penn and stood to the side, watching how tender his wife was with the baby and he couldn't help but think what he had always thought, that she would make a wonderful, loving mum.

Penn hugged his wife, comforting her, but tears were in his eyes as well. Royden didn't blame him one bit. He'd be frightened to death if that was his son.

"I believe I know what you need, Morgan," Oria said softly and lifted the bairn up in her arms and sat on the bed.

She rested the bairn's little bottom on her leg and with one hand cupping his tiny chest and stomach she tilted him forward some while her other hand rubbed his back.

He cried and fussed and suddenly—released a burp far too loud to come from such a small bairn and was followed shortly by another.

Oria smiled and when she eased him to rest in the crook of her arm, the little bairn smiled and snuggled against her.

She returned Morgan to his mum. "He probably stuffed himself at his last feeding."

Emily smiled and wiped at her eyes with her sleeve before she took the bairn in her arms to hold close. "He did. I didn't think he'd stop."

"Slow him down a bit next time," Oria suggested.

"He's all right then?" Penn asked and slipped his arm around his wife and stared at his son, his eyes almost closed in sleep.

"He's good. There's nothing wrong with him," Oria assured both parents.

"Thank you. Thank you so much," Emily and Penn both took turns offering their gratitude.

This time Royden didn't wait for his wife to reach for his hand, he took hers after stepping out of the cottage.

"How did you know what to do?" Royden asked as they walked back to the keep.

"Detta, the old woman at Learmonth who you met. She is an exceptional healer. I watched her treat many bairns," Oria explained.

"Why watch her treat bairns when you knew there was no chance of you having any of your own with Learmonth? Or did you think to wed again after his death?" He surprised himself with the question.

"I knew I'd wed again," she said. "As I told you and will keep reminding you. I never doubted you'd return to me. I wanted to be prepared to take care of our children."

The woman left him speechless far too often.

"Now if my husband would stop being a stubborn arse and plant his seed where it belongs, we could get started on the five or six bairns I plan to give him."

"So I'm not an *old*, stubborn arse anymore," he asked a joy overcoming him that he hadn't felt in a long time at the thought of having a large family with Oria. It had been something they had both once wanted and Oria hadn't changed her mind.

"No, you're just a stubborn arse now," she confirmed.

"I'll have to work on that."

"You have a lot to work on, husband," she said and poked him in the arm. "I want my own bairn to hold in my arms sometime this winter."

He had almost strangled her last night while in a nightmare. How would she feel after she coupled with a savage?

Chapter Thirteen

Royden stood by the side of the bed naked and turned a deep scowl on his wife snuggled comfortably beneath the blankets. "You will keep your promise and poke me if I get too close to you."

Oria thought about all the promises she had made and how some of them were causing senseless sorrow.

"You hesitate," Royden snapped.

She shook her head. "My mind wandered. I promise, but you must promise as well. If I get too close to you, you must *poke* me."

"It's not a poke I'll be giving you when the time comes. You have definitely changed, wife," he said, relieved he had seen to pleasuring himself before coming to her bedchamber. With his desire satisfied, it made it easier for him to sleep beside her. But then he hadn't counted on her playful words arousing him.

"I have," she admitted. "I'm not the young, innocent woman you once knew. And to be honest, I'm glad I'm no longer her. My da, God love him, protected me from far too much. Burnell encouraged me to learn as much as I could. He insisted I speak with the merchants that came to sell him their wares, to learn from them about distant lands they had traveled and even learn some of their languages. I found I quite enjoyed learning. It was why I accompanied Detta when she tended the ill. I wanted to learn all I could from her to be prepared for whatever the future held. What did you learn?"

His response came easily. "That there is a savage in every man."

"You fought rough battles here," she reminded.

"Aye and Highlanders can be a vicious lot, but they're kind compared to some of the savages I fought." He refused to detail what he'd been through. He hated having the memories in his head and he wouldn't put them in hers. "It often took being more than a savage to win against them."

"You're not a savage, Royden," she said, turning on her side and reaching out to lay her hand on his chest. She startled when his hand gripped her wrist, stopping her.

"Don't touch me," he warned with an underlying growl.

"Habit and instinct are difficult to control," she said and when he loosened his grip, she brought her hand to rest on her stomach.

It had taken her a while to understand how much of a toll their time apart had taken on them both and the depth of how much they both had changed. How could they resume what they once had together when they weren't the same people? Maybe they couldn't. Maybe they needed to start anew.

Nothing more was said between them. Oria turned on her side, her back to her husband and his back to her, having felt him turn. She didn't intend to sleep at least not yet. She was going to do her best to remain awake so that if Royden had another nightmare, she could comfort him and hopefully prevent it from going any farther. He may have demanded she promise to poke him, but nothing had been said about a comforting touch.

She kept herself alert by keeping her mind busy. There was still much to be done in the keep and she began to make a mental list. Engrossed in her task, it took a yawn to shake her out of it and that was when she heard a barely detectable sound. She listened a few moments and realized what she heard was a light snore coming from her husband.

Happy he slept, she turned over to lie on her other side facing his back. She would be ready to help him if necessary.

She sighed softly, content. She was where she wanted to be, where she needed to be. They couldn't forge a good and loving future together if distance was kept between them. She was here in his bed to stay and would help fight his nightmares with him.

***

The sword was heavy, blood thick on its blade, but it didn't matter. All that mattered was to survive. To fight until the last breath. The battle raged on, screams and moans filled the air, warriors dropped one after another. Women ran screaming. Chaos and madness reigned.

Would it never end?

Fight. Fight. Don't stop. You have to do this. You have to live. You have to find the one you love.

There were too many bodies. Too much blood.

Where are you? Where are you? I must find you! I must! I need to protect you, keep you safe.

More warriors rushed forward. Too many!

Run!

No, I have to find you. I have to.

"No! No! Let me go! Let me go!"

"Oria wake up. Wake up. I'm here. You're safe. I won't let anyone harm you."

Royden's strong voice yanked her out of her nightmare to find herself in his arms. Her arms shot out to wrap around his neck. "Don't let me go, Royden. Please don't let me go."

"Never!" he said, his arms tightening around her.

He had woken to her thrashing around beside him, her face a mask of fear, and whimpering like a wounded animal, then crying out, "I must find you. I must." He had grabbed her to wake her, but she had fought him. He was never more relieved when she woke, though she had yet to calm. Her body trembled against him and he held her so tight that he could feel her heart thumping madly against his bare chest.

"I couldn't find you," she whispered, though it sounded more like a gasp, her breathing still labored.

"I'm right here, *mo ghaol*, and I'm not going anywhere," he said, giving her a squeeze to confirm it.

Oria wanted to believe him, but the past warned that what we want isn't always what we get. Fate had a way of robbing you of things and leaving you to deal with the consequences. She was tired not only of others ruling her life, but Fate as well. It was time she took control.

Oria's cheek rested against, Royden's and she moved her head slowly so her lips brushed across his, then whispered, "We've wasted enough time. Let's not waste anymore."

A hundred reasons ran through his head why it was a bad idea, but no longer did any make sense and without hesitation his lips came down on hers in a crushing kiss.

He warned himself to go slow and easy that there was no reason to rush. It wasn't like after battle when sensations overwhelmed and he'd been desperate for relief. And yet he felt that desperation building in him now. He'd had a need for Oria that had never been satisfied and it had grown over the years. He had wanted her then and he wanted her even more now.

He moved his lips off hers, breathing deeply as he rested his cheek against her flushed one, needing to keep control. He jumped when he felt her hand take hold of his shaft and innocently run her hand along it, then grip it tight. He feared he'd explode there and then.

"Let go, Oria," he warned gruffly.

"I want him inside me," she whispered and nipped at his neck.

He felt his control slip a notch and he couldn't let that happen. He stiffened when she began to caress his shaft and continued to warn himself to hold on, keep control.

She breathed softly near his ear. "He's eager to finally settle where he belongs—inside me."

His control slipped another notch. One more and he feared the savage would break free.

Oria thought she would go mad with how badly she desired him, how badly her most intimate parts throbbed uncontrollably for him, and how wet she had grown in anticipation of him finally slipping inside her. He couldn't deny her. He couldn't. She wouldn't let him.

She slowly ran her fingers along his thick, wide shaft, admiring its size and anticipating the pleasure it would bring her, bring them both. Her finger caught a drop of wetness off the tip and pure desire and a dash of instinct had her bringing her finger to her mouth and licking it.

That was it.

Royden's control shattered and a deep growl rumbled in his chest. He rose up off her and with a forceful grip tore her nightdress off her, pulling it out from under her to fling off the bed.

Oria had waited forever for this moment to share with Royden, dreamt about, had been eager for it and yet there was something different—unfamiliar—in his dark eyes. It was as though she stared into the eyes of a stranger.

"Royden," she whispered suddenly, oddly needing to make sure it was him.

He straddled her waist and leaned down over. "Change your mind, wife."

Was that a rumbling growl she heard? And what was it in his dark eyes she failed to see?

His nose almost touched hers as he said, "Too late. I'll have you here and now and not just once."

Now she knew where she had seen that look in his eyes before—in the savage warriors the day the clan had been attacked.

Fear shivered her.

"Afraid, wife?" he asked, sitting up. "You should be."

"Royden," she said again softly hoping to calm the savage that had surfaced and reached out to touch him, her hand falling on his stump.

He swung her hand off him, his nostrils flaring in anger and the rumble in his chest growing. He shook his head and hurried off her and the bed, going to stand in front of the hearth, his back to her.

Oria hurried after him.

"Don't!" he commanded, swinging his arm out to the side, warning her away.

His powerful voice froze her and though he had spoken only one word, she could see he struggled to keep control of the untamed emotion that had risen inside him.

"Royden," she said softly, hoping by hearing his name again and again, he'd break free of whatever held him prisoner.

"Stay away," he ordered.

There was no mistaking the sneering growl in his voice, but she heard something else as well, just a hint, but she heard it. There was heartbreak there and it hurt her heart to hear it, to see him warn her away when it wasn't what he truly wanted. But he did it to protect her.

She didn't need courage to respond. She responded out of love. "No!"

He swerved around and Oria gathered her courage then, needing it when seeing the intense feral look in his dark eyes. She thought any moment that he'd reach out and—

She jumped and winced when his hand grabbed her arm, but he didn't loosen his grip.

"You'll do as I say, wife," he commanded and shoved her away from him. "Get out of here now."

She stumbled but remained on her feet and her chin went up defiantly. "I'm not leaving you. Not now. Not ever." She kept her defiant pose as his eyes roamed over her with a look so hungry she thoughts he'd—

He scooped her up so fast, her gasp got caught in her throat and for a moment she lost all breath. He carried her to the bed and dropped her down on it and she scrambled to right herself. She didn't even see his hand reach for her waist, though she felt his fingers dig into her and the next thing she knew she was on her stomach. She felt him straddle her and before she could turn her head to the side, she felt his teeth at her neck.

Her shoulders shot up as he bit along it, not harshly, but enough for her to feel the tug. It was what the she had seen the cats do time again and Purity had told her it was the way the male cat showed his love and dominance over his mate. A feral action for sure, but still a sign of love and she wondered if he realized that. At least she did and that made a difference to her.

It didn't take long for his nips to follow down along her shoulders and back. She pulled away when he nipped at her side, it tickling her, and he stopped.

"Spread your legs," he ordered.

She didn't have the will or wont to deny him, besides, her desire to make love with him hadn't wavered. It had heightened, realizing just how much Royden needed her, needed to be loved. She jumped when his fingers found their way inside her, igniting her passion, while his teeth returned to nip along her neck.

She wasn't surprised that her passion continued to mount. The combination of his loving nips and the teasing nature of his fingers made it impossible for her desire to do anything but grow, and in leaps and bounds. She only wanted to make sure that this time his seed was left inside her to grow.

She said his name repeatedly and softly like the purr of a kitten who enjoyed being stroked. It wasn't a savage who caressed her but a husband who loved her.

"Good Lord, Royden, I want you. I want you so badly."

Her eyes went wide when she suddenly found herself on her back staring up at her husband.

He shook his head and opened his mouth but no words fell from his lips. It was almost as if he'd awakened from a dream and was seeing that it wasn't a dream at all—it was real.

Oria hoped passion shined in her eyes and could be heard in her words. "Please don't stop, Royden. I love you and I so want to make love with you."

He brought his brow down to rest against hers. And when he went to speak, she captured his words with a kiss. It was what he needed and what she needed and while it was a tender kiss, it soon turned more urgent.

She almost cried out in protest when his lips left hers, but it turned to a passionate moan when his mouth captured one of her nipples. He suckled it, teased it with his tongue, and nipped at it with his teeth, and she relished every minute of the tormenting pleasure.

He couldn't get enough of her. He wanted to taste all of her, every inch of her. When he finished with each breast, he kissed and nipped down along her body. It was as if he needed to leave his mark everywhere on her, to claim every part of her, to know every part of her now belonged to him and him alone.

He looked up at her. "You're mine, Oria."

"Aye, always," she barely whispered, his dark eyes intense with such passion that it fired her own even more.

The need to warn her rose up in him and he brought his face close to hers. "You see the savage in me. He can't be tamed and he's never satisfied. His hunger is endless."

"Then I will make sure to keep him fed," Oria said and spread her legs farther apart inviting him before she kissed him.

Her unselfish response and loving kiss was like a beacon in the dark to him and he rushed toward the distant light, anxious to free himself of the empty darkness.

He returned her kiss, hungrier for her more than ever before. He covered her with his body, bracing himself to rest just above her and settling his shaft to rub between her legs.

She smiled softly when she saw a hesitation in his eyes. "I love you, Royden, and nothing on earth or in the heavens will ever change that. You're mine and always have been and will be."

"Hold on to me," he said thinking he didn't deserve her, but not able to let her go. "And let me know if I hurt you."

"You could never hurt me. You don't have it in your heart to hurt me."

"Damn, Oria," he said, resting his brow to hers, her words stinging his heart.

She gripped his arms. "I need you inside me. I want you inside me."

Royden wanted that just as badly as she did and he didn't waste another minute, since he was already close to climax. He rose up a bit higher off her and he warned himself to go slow. She was a virgin and he could hurt her. But when he felt how wet and ready she was for him and with how much he'd been delaying his own release, his passion having surged so quickly, he found himself rushing into her.

She cried out and he stopped, silently cursing himself.

"No! No! Don't stop," she pleaded.

And he didn't. His need, his love for her overwhelmed, and all he could think about was burying himself deeper and deeper inside her, going farther toward that light that teased him in the distance.

She moved along with him, her passion building as it had been doing, slow at first. Now it was hurtling so rapidly she couldn't control it, didn't want to. She had waited far too long to share this moment with Royden and she didn't want to wait another minute.

Royden groaned deep as he drove in and out of her. "Oria," he growled, sounding like the savage he had thought he'd become.

"Aye. Aye, Royden," she said, her breathing growing more rapid.

He pounded into her, though he warned himself to go easy, be careful not to hurt her, but it was Oria who urged him on, thrusting her hips up and demanding he go deeper. And he did.

He took her soaring to unimaginable heights of passion that it almost brought her to tears. God, how she loved this man, her husband.

He brought his face down close to hers and urged, "Now, Oria, now."

She nodded and screamed out as she splintered into a thousand pieces of pure pleasure.

Royden let go with a roar that exploded in the room as he burst with such an intense satisfaction that it shattered the darkness and a brilliant light consumed him, filling him with a pleasure he had never known.

When it finally faded, he collapsed over her barely able to breathe and though he didn't want to move off her, he feared his weight too much for her and rolled off her onto his back. He felt her hand slip around his and he squeezed it tight.

"I didn't know it could feel that wonderful," she said, her breath still a bit labored.

"Either did I," he said and he did something that he didn't think he'd ever do again—he smiled.

Oria released his hand and turned to snuggle against him and her heart swelled with joy when she saw the smile on his face. The smile she had put there.

"Truly?" she asked, though his smile said it all.

"Aye, wife, truly," he said. "I've never known it to feel this satisfying." Worry suddenly creased his brow. "Oria, if I did anything that yo—"

She smiled. "I enjoyed everything you did to me. You made our first time together a beautiful memory I will forever cherish." She poked him in the chest. "Though you must promise me it won't be the last time we do it."

"I know now why I fell in love with you. You have the kindest, most unselfish, and loving heart I have ever known." He rolled her onto her back. "And you're mine, all mine, and I'll never let you go, not ever." He kissed her gently and he wrapped himself around her, something he'd been longing to do.

It wasn't long before she fell asleep and he laid there thinking how he'd protect her if they ever suffered another attack like the one that had separated them. It stirred in him again—the savage that lurked in the darkness—and he was glad to feel him. He'd never go away and oddly enough he didn't want him to. He'd let him loose when necessary and never again would anyone harm Oria or take her from him.

He fell asleep, glad the savage still lived.

Chapter Fourteen

Royden woke with his wife tucked snugly against him. He kept his eyes on her, thinking if he looked away he'd wake and find it all had been a dream. Given time, he knew he'd accept the fact that he was truly home and that Oria was his wife, truly his wife now.

He smiled and almost touched his face to feel it. His wife had been the one to make him truly smile again and it was another debt of gratitude he owed her.

She stirred beside him, her leg moving over his to rest near his groin and since he'd woken already aroused it didn't help any.

He had been woken in the middle of the night when Oria had stirred restlessly in her sleep. Fearing it was the beginning of another nightmare for her, he had stroked her gently and whispered reassuring words. The next thing he knew they were making love again and it had been more than amazing. It made him realize that the many women he had been with through the past years had soothed a need, but never had he known true satisfaction until Oria.

Thinking on that flared his desire for her. He told himself to leave her be. She had to be tired and possibly sore since this was new to her. Then he felt her hand on his shaft and he smiled again.

He turned his smile on her. "Can't keep your hands off me, wife?"

She was already smiling broadly. "Do you want me to?"

"No. Never," he said with a light laugh. "I'm glad you like to touch me, but you know what will happen if you keep touching me."

"Why do you think I'm touching you, husband?" she said with a light laugh of her own.

Royden rolled over her, pinning her on her back with his body. "You're sure about this? You're not too uncomfortable?"

"If you're asking me if you've left me worn out and sore from last night, the answer is no. And you should be aware that I'm no delicate flower you need to treat carefully."

"So I'm beginning to realize," he said.

Oria ran her hand gently over his shoulder and down along his arm and gave it a gentle squeeze. "You may have changed some, but you're no savage I need to fear. There are new things we need to learn about each other and we have the time to do so. One thing that hasn't changed about either of us is that we still love each other and that—dear husband—is all that matters and is something I'll keep reminding you about."

He kissed her. "I do love you, wife."

She ran a finger faintly over his lips. "Show me."

And he did.

***

A cart meandered through the village later that day, Penn waving a welcome to the man holding the reins.

"Who is he?" Royden asked, brushing his hands free of debris after placing another stone on the hut. It was almost finished and would soon be ready to use. He had wanted it done, that and the fields ready for planting, so that his clan would see that winter would pose no problem for them.

"Clive. He's a merchant of sorts. He comes through here every now and again. Sometimes he has things of interest, other times not so much," Penn explained.

"Where does he get his wares?" Royden asked.

"He tells tall tales of knowing wealthy merchants and such, but I think he gets them whatever way he can."

"You mean he's a thief," Angus said.

"I'd be careful calling him that in front of Bethany," Penn warned. "Clive always has something for her when he shows up."

"Of course she'd be appreciative of cooking ware," Angus said.

Penn shook his head and grinned. "It's ribbons and babbles he brings her. Last time it was a fine wine he brought her and they shared the bottle together before he left the next day."

Angus glared at Penn. "Go on with you, Bethany didn't do that."

"She did, and if you truly favor Bethany you'd best watch out. Clive has an eye for her and he keeps saying he's getting old and needs himself a good woman to settle down with.," Penn said.

"You better watch it, Angus," John said with a chuckle. "Old Clive there will snatch her right away from you."

"The devil he will," Angus said, straightening tall and drawing his shoulders back as the cart got closer.

"I tell you, Penn, I'm getting too old for this endless traveling. I need to find a good woman and settle down," Clive said as he pulled to a stop by the stone hut.

Penn smiled, the old man confirming his words.

Royden turned a curious eye on the man. If his white and gray beard and his hair the same color, though sparse, was any indication of his age you'd say the man was old, but there was a spryness to his blue eyes that told a different story. Though the wrinkles around them begged a different tale as well as did his body that had barely a belly to it. He appeared right fit.

"You should talk to Old Mildred. She could use a good man," Angus said.

"She's a good woman, but I got my eye set on one already and I brought something special for her," Clive said with a gleeful smile.

Angus muttered under his breath.

"Clive, this is Chieftain Royden," Penn said with a nod toward Royden.

"It's good to see you made it home, Chieftain Royden," Clive said with a bob of his head.

"I'm glad to be home," Royden said and caught a gleam in the man's eyes, as if the news more than pleased him.

"Is there a mistress now that might be interested in my wares?" Clive asked.

"Aye, there is and you'll find Mistress Oria at the keep," Royden said and saw the gleam grow brighter in the man's eyes.

"I'll take myself right off then and present my wares to the fine mistress," Clive said and, with a nod to the men, the cart rolled away at a slow pace.

"How long has he been coming around here?" Royden asked Penn.

"About two years now."

"He's a harmless old man that walks with a limp and likes his ale, wine, and women," Penn said. "He's no threat."

Royden didn't know about that. Those blue eyes of his told a different tale and he wondered what it was. He returned to work, no more than an hour's worth of it left, but his eyes kept going to the cart meandering toward the keep. He was surprised when he saw his wife come around the corner of the keep and when she caught sight of Clive, she waved at him enthusiastically.

That she waved and acknowledged him before he waved to her meant that Clive was no stranger to her. And that made him all the more curious about Clive.

***

Oria hurried toward the cart with a smile. "I'm so glad to see you, Clive."

He bobbed his head. "Mistress Oria." His voice turned to a whisper. "Be careful, I fear your husband may be watching us."

Oria had to force herself not to look toward the hut where Royden had told her he'd be working today. She had been foolish not to consider that, but she had been so excited to see Clive that she hadn't even given it thought.

"These bones are getting old," Clive said, climbing down off the cart and limping around to the side to glance casually in the distance. His voice turned low again. "He does watch."

Oria pointed at the cart. "What wares do you have to offer?" She peered over the cart, her voice turning to a whisper as well. "You must deliver the news that Royden is home and that Arran will be home in a month or so." She kept a smile on her face, but sadness filled her voice. "It's time for the secrets to come to an end."

"Some yes, unfortunately, some no," he said quietly.

"How is everyone?" Oria asked.

"They do well, but I think this news will bring joy to many."

"I often wished for life to be the same as it once had been," she said and shook her head. "But I've realized life will never be the same. It must start anew." She made a fuss about looking at the items in his cart. "It's time to start fresh. Please tell them I can't keep their secret much longer. I won't continue to lie to my husband."

"But one may still be in jeopardy," Clive warned.

"I know and I will say nothing about that. You know the ones I mean. Please see it done," Oria all but pleaded.

"I will deliver your message," Clive said.

"I will hold my tongue for one week no more," Oria cautioned. "That should be more than adequate time to see it done."

"Patience, Oria," he cautioned as well.

"I have no more patience left for this. It is time this is settled. It is time for life to begin anew. See it done or I will," she ordered.

"You have grown brazen," Clive said.

"No, I have grown wise," she said. "Now show me what you have so that when my husband asks, I can show him what I found that had worth to barter for food and a night's worth of lodging."

Clive laughed. "I'm sure he's learned by now that Bethany has provided me with food and shelter out of the goodness of her heart. You'll need to find something he'll find more believable."

"Promises are nothing but headaches," Oria complained.

Clive laughed again. "Only if you keep them."

"If you're honorable, you have no choice," Oria said and foraged through his cart, stopping suddenly when she tugged on the corner of a tapestry. "Let me see this?"

Clive piled items aside to get to it, finally yanking it out and sending things tumbling. He draped it over the side of the cart so she could have full view of it.

She stared at it, shaking her head. "Where did you get this?"

"Where do I get anything? Here, there, and everywhere."

"I need to know, Clive," she insisted.

The urgency in her voice had him capitulating. "Truth be told, I gave fair trade to the merchant for the whole cart. I have no idea where he got any of this stuff. Why do you ask?"

"This tapestry once hung here in the Great Hall."

***

Oria got busy beating the tapestry with a thick stick, sending dust and dirt flying off it. Clive had left it draped over the side of the cart for her while he went to see Bethany. She beat it over and over again, eager to see it looking as grand as it once had. The keep was beginning to feel like home again and this piece done by his mother and several women in the clan would make the Great Hall feel even more like it once had. She couldn't wait to see it hung.

"I hope you don't take a stick that hard to our children."

Oria looked up at her husband and shook the stick at him, standing on the opposite side of the cart. "You know I would never do such a thing. One scowl from their da and they'll obey fast enough."

"So my scowl frightens, does it?"

"It would take more than a scowl from you to frighten me," she said, walking around the cart to poke him in the chest with the tip of the stick. Recalling a few of his scowls, she might have to amend that.

"You think that puny branch would stop me?" he asked with a laugh.

"I warn you, husband, I have hidden skills," she challenged and swatted his arm as if she brandished a sword.

He laughed again, hardier this time. "That will not keep me away, wife." He pushed the stick away and took a step toward her.

Oria was quick and swatted at both of his arms more than a bit playfully.

Royden stopped and rubbed one arm. "You wound me, wife."

She smiled. "Then keep your distance, sir, or suffer for it."

"Are you really challenging me?" he asked with another laugh.

"By all means, no." Her grin grew. "I'm saving you from disgrace since you'll not win against me." She brandished the stick not far from his face.

He laughed even harder as he stepped right at the whipping stick and Oria quickly swatted at his arms, but it didn't stop him.

"I warn you to stay back," she said, continuing to swat at his arms and seeing he paid no mind to it.

When his hand shot out to grab the stick from her, she threw it at him and ran.

Royden ran after her laughing. "Where is your courage? Stand and fight. Or surrender."

"I'll never surrender," she called out, and turned around to run backwards, laughing. "And you'll never catch me." The next thing she knew her foot caught in something and she went flying backwards. Her hands shot out to her husband. "Royden!"

Royden rushed forward, fearing he wouldn't reach her on time. He had to bend over to catch her around the waist and the momentum sent him tumbling as well. He had just enough time to twist his body so that he took the brunt of the fall with her landing on top of him.

Oria clung to him for a moment too shocked to move.

"Are you all right?" he asked, fear for his wife's safety evident in his rushed words.

She lifted her head off his chest. "I should be asking you that. You took the hardest of the fall."

"I'm good, wife, it is you I'm concerned about."

"I'm good as well." She grinned. "But I'll have you know this is no surrender."

"I don't know about that," he said with a smile and shake of his head. "It looks like surrender to me."

"It's a capture," she said and moved up and placed her lips just above his. "This, dear husband, is a surrender." She kissed him and not gently.

After only a minute, Royden forced his mouth away from hers. "If you don't get off me and we don't hurry into the keep the whole village is going to see us making a bairn."

Oria scrambled off her husband, urging him to "Hurry!"

Royden was almost on his feet when his wife stood, winced, and almost toppled over. He grabbed at her side to stop her from tumbling and once on his feet he took hold of her arm.

"What's wrong?" he asked anxiously.

"My ankle. I must have given it a twist," she said and was suddenly scooped up in his arms. "I can walk."

"I didn't ask you if you could and don't bother to tell me to put you down. That's not going to happen." He turned and headed toward the keep and stopped suddenly.

Oria turned her head, realizing he had seen the tapestry. "I asked Clive where he got it. He bought everything in the cart off another merchant. He never asked the man where he got everything."

"You were cleaning it to hang in the hall again," he said.

"Aye. I wanted it in fine shape before it once again graced the wall of the Great Hall."

"Does he have any more of what is ours?"

Ours.

How one word could touch the heart so much and bring such joy startled Oria. She shook her head, needing a minute to form her words. "I looked through the cart myself. I saw nothing that once belonged here. But you might want to check yourself, since I might not be familiar with everything." Oria could tell what he was thinking. "Put me down, Royden, and have a look. It's nothing more than a light sprain. I'll be fine."

"You'll tell me if it pains you?"

"I will," she said and bit her lip before, *I promise*, spilled out. Some promises served no purpose and this was one of those times.

Royden placed her gently on her feet and didn't let go of her arm until he was sure she could stand without difficulty.

Oria stepped carefully to the side and smiled. "The pain is minor. As I said, nothing more than a light sprain. I will keep off my feet the rest of the day and it should do well."

Royden grinned. "I know how I can definitely keep you off your feet."

"Hurry and look," she encouraged with a soft laugh.

Royden rummaged through the cart, pushing items aside in search of anything familiar. He was almost finished when something caught his eye. He hurried to clear things to the side, revealing a wooden handle.

Oria could tell with the way her husband looked at the small wooden sword he had yanked out of the cart that it meant something to him.

"It was Arran's," he said and turned the sword handle for her to see a fairly straight line carved in the wood and running from the top of the handle to almost where a blade would start and two lines crossing over the top of it. "He carved that into the handle, marking it as his own. I remember the day my da gave it to him. He was so happy. He started practicing with it right away and never stopped. He was proud of this, his first sword."

"It is good it will be here for Arran's return home," Oria said.

"Found something else you like?' Clive called out, walking toward them.

Royden turned, pointing the wooden sword at him, a hard glare in his eyes. "I found two things that belonged to me."

"I didn't know and you can't blame a man for trying to survive," Clive said. "I have no fight with you, Chieftain Royden. Take what is yours."

Oria was about to place her hand on her husband's arm, hearing the familiar rumble of anger in his voice and stopped when he spoke.

"You're welcome to sup with us and shelter here the night if you wish," Royden offered, his glare not as hard, but not completely gone.

"I gladly accept your generosity," Clive said with a nod.

"Good," Royden said, "It will give us time to talk about the merchant from whom you stole this merchandise."

Chapter Fifteen

Royden woke annoyed to find himself in bed alone, not that he wasn't already annoyed from last night. The night had gone nothing as he had planned. Clive had begged an ailing stomach and hadn't joined him for supper and when supper was nearly finished, he'd been notified that a small group of warriors had been spotted in the nearby woods. He had taken a few men with him, including Penn and Angus, while leaving Stuart and John to watch over the village along with the other men there.

Angus hadn't been happy about it. He had complained the whole time, insisting Clive wasn't sick at all. He believed it nothing more than an excuse to spend time alone with Bethany, especially since Bethany had turned down his offer that they sup together.

They'd found no sign of the warriors, but Royden hadn't wanted to take any chances. He doubled the night sentinels and had sent notice to his wife that he'd be taking the first shift. He had thought to wake her when he finally joined her in bed, but she'd been sleeping so soundly he hadn't wanted to disturb her. He figured one of them would wake in the middle of the night and they'd soon be making love.

That hadn't happened and when he woke to find himself wrapped around her pillow instead of her, he got even more annoyed. Where had she gone off to? Why hadn't she woken him? And why did he feel that it had something to do with Clive, the merchant? If he were a merchant.

Royden got himself dressed quickly and went in search of his wife and some answers.

***

"Remember what I told you, no more than a week," Oria reminded Clive as he climbed up to sit on the cart's wooden seat.

Clive looked to Oria after taking the reins. "I can't promise—"

"Once it is made known that Royden has returned home, it will no longer be for you to decide," Oria said. "Deliver the news, the rest will see to itself. And please give them my regards. It has been far too long."

"From what I've been told, you had no choice but to stay—"

"Clive!"

Clive and Oria turned to see her husband at the top of the keep steps.

Oria's breath caught slightly at the sight of her husband. She had always thought him a man of fine features and body, but now years or perhaps circumstances had added to his features defining them in a way that made him all the more appealing, from the lines that crinkled at the corner of his eyes and the bridge between them, to the tight set of his jaw, and the commanding lift of his chin. And after making love with him, seeing the hard definition of his muscles, the ease in which he lifted her, he was beyond stronger than he had been.

He took the steps down to them with a confident, quick pace and she saw Clive tense, intimidated by Royden's approach.

"I need to be on my way, kind sir," Clive said with a forced smile.

"Where are you off to next?" Royden asked, his arm going around his wife's waist when he came to stand next to her.

Clive hesitated, then grinned. "Learmonth. Detta might need something."

"Give her my regards," Oria said.

"That I will," Clive said, keeping his grin wide as he went to snap the reins.

"A moment, Clive," Royden said, his sharp tone making it clear he was not to be refused.

"What can I do for you, sir?" Clive asked.

Royden watched as his mask slipped briefly and he caught sight of a man who didn't take kindly to commands. A strange trait for a merchant.

"You told my wife you don't know where the tapestry or wooden sword came from, but tell me where was it you acquired the items?"

"I got them from an old merchant who, like me, grew tired of the travel and wanted nothing more to do with the trade," Clive explained.

"And where was this?" Royden asked.

"Where?' Clive scrunched his brow as if confused by the question.

Royden patiently clarified. "What area here in the Highlands did you come across this merchant?"

Clive turned his glance up at the sky, scrunched his brow again, then looked at Royden. "I'm afraid age has robbed me of a good memory. I don't recall."

Royden would have to be blind not to see that the man lied. The question was—why did he lie? "Were you in the woods at all last night, Clive?"

Royden's question caught Clive unaware and he wasn't able to hide his surprise. "Why would I go into the woods?"

"You tell me," Royden said, keeping his dark eyes focused intently on Clive.

"I kept company with Bethany," Clive said.

Royden's brow went up. "I thought you had a bad stomach?"

"I did," he was quick to explain. "Bethany was kind enough to bring me a broth that helped settle it."

"So she did not stay long with you," Royden said.

Oria couldn't help but tense. Bethany made it known to many a man that she would not be free with her favors. That was meant for marriage alone and she'd have it no other way. And if Clive lied, Bethany would make the truth known.

Clive shook his head. "Nay, Bethany stayed until I finished the broth, then left."

"Then my original question remains. Did you go into the woods last night?" Royden asked, more of a demand in his tone and once again he watched Clive's mask slip.

Oria saw it too. He was obviously annoyed and obviously about to lie and she wondered if the men spotted in the woods had been there to meet with Clive.

"What reason would I have to go into the woods at night? I slept after Bethany left and didn't wake until dawn," Clive said, his smile gone.

"Maybe you saw to your nightly duties before falling asleep and perhaps spotted the men we searched for last night," Royden suggested and turned to his wife. "And why do you tense at these questions? Is there something you both keep from me?"

Oria had had enough. She turned to Clive. "I won't lie to my husband any longer."

Royden stepped away from her. "Any longer?"

Oria looked to Clive.

"To my solar, the both of you," Royden ordered and turned away to climb the stairs, not waiting for them to follow, but expecting them to. And they did.

Once in the solar, Royden turned to his wife and ordered, "Tell me."

Clive responded, "She can't. She swore to keep her word and she has, even as difficult as it has been to do so."

Though annoyed, Royden admired his wife for honoring her word. Now, however, since they were husband and wife, he expected no secrets to be kept between them.

"I wanted to tell you so badly, but it meant the safety of others," Oria said.

Royden could easily see that it had troubled his wife and that troubled him.

"I need someone to explain, *now*!" Royden demanded.

"That's the problem," Clive admitted. "We can't."

"You aren't a merchant, are you?" Royden more stated than asked.

"No, but that cannot be divulged or others will suffer, for while I would like to think that I could withstand torture, I fear everyone has a breaking point. Oria's breaking point is lying to you."

Royden reached out and took his wife's hand from where they sat beside each other at the round table.

"I made a promise," she explained. "One I was honor bound to keep for the good of many. I never meant to intentionally keep anything from you."

Clive went on to explain. "She gave me an ultimatum. A week's time no more or she would reveal—"

Oria interrupted, wanting her husband to know, "What was safe for you to know while continuing to keep the deepest of trusts, the deepest of promises."

Royden knew the cost of promises. He had one he had yet to keep. "There is much I wish to ask you—"

"I ask that you don't," Oria said, squeezing his hand.

"This has been a burden for you," Royden said, seeing the torment in her eyes.

"Not until you returned home. You should know—"

"But it is best you don't," Clive finished.

Royden looked from one to the other. "I don't like not knowing."

"I don't know everything myself," Oria admitted, leaning in to press her shoulder against his, needing to be as close as she could to him, needing his strength.

Royden sensed and felt her need for him. It stirred in his gut and tore at his heart. He moved his chair closer to her and wrapped his arm around her shoulders to keep her tight against him.

"Is there anything you can tell me?" Royden asked.

Oria couldn't keep it from him any longer. "Your da is alive."

Royden's heart slammed against his chest, catching his breath.

"He was severely injured in the attack, but he has healed well," Oria said.

Clive shook his head. "You should have waited."

"His da would want him to know just as he would want to know his son has returned home," Oria argued.

"My wife is right," Royden said. "When will my da return home?"

Clive appeared reluctant to say.

Oria spoke up. "Your da will not want to leave Wren."

"Wren?" Royden shook his head, the name unfamiliar.

"The witch in the woods," Oria explained.

"What has the witch to—" He shook his head again. "She healed my da."

"If it hadn't been for her, he would have never survived," Oria said and looked about to say more but stopped.

"Tell me," Royden encouraged, thinking he was indebted more than he ever thought possible to a witch.

"Your da fell in love with Wren and she with him," Oria said. "And I doubt he'll want to leave her."

"Then let him bring her home with him," Royden said and Oria voiced his own thought.

"The clan might not accept her."

"I will take the message to your da that you are home and wish him to return home as well," Clive said.

"You are a messenger then, not a merchant?" Royden asked.

"I am whatever I need to be," Clive said.

"Tell my da to come home and bring Wren with him," Royden said. "Her skills will serve the clan well." He looked between the both of them. "What else do you keep from me?"

Oria shook her head. "I have sworn an oath and, as much as I want to tell you, I cannot break it."

"And you?" Royden asked, turning to Clive.

"I know nothing more," Clive said.

"I don't believe that, but something tells me to let it be for now," Royden said.

"You're a wise man, Chieftain Royden," Clive said with a nod.

"Don't mistake wisdom for patience that will last only so long," Royden warned.

"Time will reveal what you need to know," Clive offered and stood. "I need to be on my way. If all goes well, your da should return home in about a week's time."

"And if he doesn't?" Royden asked.

"Then he will have made his choice," Clive said and with a bob of his head left the solar.

"I'm sorry," Oria said as soon as the door closed behind Clive.

Royden placed his hand on the back of her neck while he brought his brow to rest against hers. "You have no reason to be sorry. You gave your word and it protected my da and for that I am grateful. It took courage for you to keep that oath when you knew what it would mean to me, yet you kept it, continuing to protect my da. I'm proud of you, Oria."

She didn't know what to say, the guilt of knowing more that could further assuage his pain, hurting her.

He kissed her lips gently. "When the time is right, you will tell me the rest. What matters now is that my da is alive and Arran will return home soon. Then we will search for Raven together." He drew his face away from her when he felt her tense again. "It's Raven. You know about Raven."

Oria nodded, knowing she could say no more.

"You fear for her."

Oria didn't answer.

Royden smiled. "That means she's alive, which means Arran and I can find her, return her home, and finally keep her safe. This is good, so good. Da will be relieved to learn that his only daughter is alive. And I am overjoyed that our family will one day be reunited."

He kissed her, a strong and solid kiss, then rested his brow to hers once again. "I missed you there beside me when I woke this morning."

"It was difficult for me to leave you when all I wanted was to," —she smiled— "wake you and hurry you inside me."

"The place I most want to be," he said and kissed her again.

She loved when they kissed. Their lips strong against each other's. The way he would nibble along her bottom lip or tug at it with his teeth. It was when his tongue entered her mouth or hers entered his first that all but guaranteed they'd soon be making love. Like now, his tongue having pushed wickedly fast past her lips.

She tore her mouth away from his with reluctance. "If you don't stop kissing me, I will expect to find you inside me very soon."

"Then you won't be disappointed, wife," he said, pushing her chair out from the table and snagging her around the waist to hoist her off the chair and onto his lap.

Oria rushed her hands to his shoulders to steady herself, her smile spreading. "I wondered how it would be to ride you."

He was a lucky man that she had given thought to the possibility and that she didn't shy away from different ways or places to make love.

"You're about to find out," he said and smiled when her hands left his shoulders to reach down and yank her garments up.

A knock at the door had a mumbled curse leaving his lips and a scowl settling over Oria.

"Chieftain Galvin demands to see you," Bethany called out.

Royden seriously wanted to kill the man and it took great restraint to stop himself and not to stop his wife from slipping off his lap.

"Later," she said and kissed her fingers to press against his lips.

Royden stood and turned his back to his wife, knowing if he looked at her his shaft would never soften. With his anger getting the better of him, he stomped to the door.

Oria's hand covered his when it settled on the latch. "You look ready to kill."

"I am," he said, staring at her slender fingers that should be wrapped around his shaft and guiding it in her just about now.

"Duty before pleasure, husband," she said. "Besides, I'd rather a longer ride than a short one."

He turned and looked at her, his anger dissipating. "Then it's our bedchamber we'll seek right after Galvin leaves."

"With great anticipation and pleasure," Oria said and with her hand still rested on his, opened the door, not trusting either of them to leave the solar—just yet.

"Wise move, wife, since a thought struck me that a short ride now would suffice until you could enjoy a longer one later," he said as they walked to the Great Hall.

"I was thinking the same myself, husband, and was the reason I opened the door so fast," Oria admitted.

He laughed. "I'm glad we think alike."

"You must help me, Royden," Galvin said as soon as the couple entered the Great Hall.

Royden hid his shock at seeing Chieftain Galvin. He was not the man Royden had remembered. He had been a sizeable man, thick in the chest and waist with dark hair that hadn't showed a sign of age. No more, though. He was half the man he'd once had been, His cheeks were hollow and there was a darkness beneath his sunken eyes that didn't bode well. And his hair had turned completely gray, not a shred of darkness could be seen.

"Sit, and we'll talk," Royden offered, pointing to the table close to the hearth, thinking the frail man needed its warmth.

Galvin stared at Royden's stump. "I had forgotten you lost your hand, perhaps you'll be of no help to me."

Oria left her husband's side to step toward the man. "How dare you enter our home without so much as a greeting and congratulations for our marriage. And then you insult my husband implying he isn't the man he once was," —she shook her head— "it is beyond offensive. Royden is a more skilled warrior than he had been when he had two hands. Now you will apologize to my husband or take your leave and never return here."

Royden was shocked, impressed, and proud of the way his wife defended him, not that Galvin would think so. Any minute he expected to hear the man's booming voice reprimand Oria for daring to chastise him like a child and order her to leave the talk to the men. He was taken back by Galvin's response.

"Forgive my rudeness, Mistress Oria. I was pleased to hear not only of Royden's return, but your marriage to him as well. It is good you both have been reunited."

"Thank you, Chieftain Galvin," Oria said with a nod. "Now please sit and enjoy a hot brew while we discuss what help you need from my husband."

Royden waited for Galvin to object that his wife would join them and when he didn't, Royden knew the man definitely wasn't the man he had once been.

"What can I do for you, Galvin?" Royden asked once they were all seated at the table.

"I am not a well man, Royden. I fear I don't have much time left and while death is inevitable, I more fear being the last of my line, that no one will follow me. That I have failed my ancestors. A new chieftain will be named, but he won't be of my seed. My only hope to continue the true Macara name is through my daughter. I need you to find her and I need Arran to wed her when he returns home."

"Have you even heard from Purity in these past five years?" Royden asked.

"No, but I believe my daughter was either wise enough to stay away or too fearful to return home," Galvin explained. "I don't care which, either way, kept my land from being claimed. Now that I am ill, I need my daughter returned home and wed so I can die with the knowledge that my blood will run through the bairns she eventually will birth. And with her husband taken over as chieftain, the Clan Macara will rightfully live on. I know Arran would make sure of that."

"I can't speak for Arran," Royden said. "And you don't even know if your daughter survived."

"Purity survived. She was in the woods. I saw her sneak there with Raven before the attack came. She knows those woods better than most around here, always preferring to be alone or with animals," Galvin said, shaking his head as if still trying to understand it.

"It's been five years," Royden reminded. "That's a long time for Purity to last in the woods on her own."

"I don't believe she's alone. Some of your women and children were never accounted for and many believe they made a safe escape. Somewhere my daughter is alive and along with her possibly some of your clansmen. As chieftain it is your duty to see they are brought home safely."

"That I can do, but I can do nothing about your request that Arran wed Purity," Royden said.

"You're chieftain now, you can order him to wed," Galvin reminded him.

Actually, he wasn't chieftain, not with the news that his da still lived, though that wasn't news he would share with Galvin.

"I won't do that, Galvin," Royden informed him. "Arran has a right to choose who he weds."

"Even when our land is at stake?" Galvin argued. "What if I die with no heir? Does this mysterious man who has taken so much from us sweep in and take my land and disperse my clan? And what of your clan, Oria? It should belong to your husband now with your father gone and yet you are told you have no right to it? And what of Clan Learmonth? We are told that a distant relative will inherit, yet Burnell had mentioned time and again he had no family. So who truly is laying claim to his land? Then there's the Clan MacDonnegal that now has—Fergus—forced upon the old Chieftain Thurbane. And what of the warriors left among the clans, like Penn was left here and Freen was left with my clan? Is this man who swept in here and tried to lay claim to all the land in the area actually succeeding? Will he eventually surround your land, Royden, and you will have no choice but to pledge your allegiance to him?"

Royden detested the thought and was annoyed that Galvin actually made some sense. Was this man that Fergus had said many called the Beast, biding his time to eventually get what he wanted?

He always gets what he wants.

The memory of Penn's remark sounded clear in Royden's head.

"Your words certainly have relevance and are well worth considering," Royden said.

"Aye, but we don't have sufficient warriors to stop him and there's something else we should consider. King David continues his desire to control the far north, Orkney and Caithness is already in his control. What if he has hired the mercenaries to take control of our land so they will swear allegiance to him and fight with him against the Highlanders if it comes to that?"

"I don't think the Norse people will give up that area they have settled so easily. He will continue to have his hands full there," Royden said. "As for the King hiring mercenaries, I suppose it's possible, since he's been spread thin with trying to get a foothold into northern England."

"I tell you the King has made a pact with the devil," Galvin insisted. "Please, I beg you, find Purity and explain the importance to Arran of him marrying my daughter when he returns. He'll be chieftain of an established clan and have land and the wealth and importance that goes with it."

"I will discuss it with Arran when he arrives home, but as I've said, it will be his decision. I will not force him to wed," Royden said, making it as clear as he could to Galvin.

Oria sat contemplating what had just been discussed while Royden saw Galvin to his horse. By her da having had her wed Burnell, and Raven and Purity unable to be found, it had no doubt upset the plan of whoever had devised the whole plot. Elsewise, she, Raven, and Purity would have been married to men that had been chosen for them and the clans and their lands would have been lost to the chieftains. But whose rule would the chieftain then had been under?

Royden entered the keep and went straight to his wife and kissed her. "I don't want to think any more on this. I just want to be with you, feel you naked in my arms, and know it's real and not a dream."

Oria smiled. "I'll race you to the bedchamber."

Royden laughed. You always lost when we raced."

"I think this time you just might let me win."

He laughed again. "You're right. I will."

Oria got to her feet and was about to run when Angus hurried into the Great Hall. Her husband looked ready to kill him until he spoke.

"Some of our warriors and women return home," Angus shouted with joy.

Chapter Sixteen

"Have you a count?" Royden asked as he watched the group of people enter the village to smiles and warm welcomes.

"Fifteen of our warriors have returned and all are in fine shape," Angus said. "A few brought women they've wed. I was glad to see Cadell, the metal worker, among the group."

"Aye, that is good, we need his skills," Royden agreed.

"He brought a wife with him, Huberta and their two children, two lads three years and one year," Angus said, nodding at the woman standing beside Cadell, a sleeping bairn lying against her chest and a little lad clinging to her tunic. "Lona, the lass who spun such fine wool returned with a husband, Wilfred." Angus nodded toward a tall, thin man.

"He appears uncomfortable and not at all sturdy," Royden said, the man's eyes wide and darting about as he kept close to his smiling wife, who barely reached his shoulder.

"Lona boasts that he's an exceptional arrow maker and the finest of marksmen," Angus said.

"If true, he would prove a good addition to the clan."

"They are also expecting a bairn just before winter," Angus informed him. "So the clan now grows."

That pleased Royden and he hoped that he and Oria would add to that growth, though he'd need more time alone with his wife to see that done. He spotted her then approaching Lona, a basket on her arm, and the two women hugged. His wife's welcoming smile grew along with the young woman's when she placed her hand on her stomach, announcing the news. There was no hiding how thrilled his wife was over the news. Oria held the basket out to Lona and her husband and both took some of the offered food. She then leaned down and coaxed the bairn clinging to his mum to take some as well.

Royden kept his eyes on his wife as he spoke to Angus. "Do you have a total yet?"

"Last count was thirty, that doesn't count the children, but I believe there's more," Angus said. "Once things settle and they all have lodgings, we'll be able to get a better count."

"Any suspicious to you?"

Angus looked out over the sea of people. "You're thinking what I am, that some were sent among our own to keep an eye on us."

"That is exactly my thought. Do you know where each of them have been?" Royden asked, seeing Penn and his wife, their newborn bairn tucked in the crook of her arm walking through the crowd.

"I heard one mention something about the Clan MacDonnegal."

Royden turned to Angus. "Fergus had some of our people?"

"I heard it in passing."

"See what you, John, and Stuart can find out," Royden ordered and turned his attention back to his wife. But his glance settled on Wilfred first and seeing his look of surprise, Royden followed his line of sight to see what had caught him unaware.

Penn. He had spotted Penn and it was obvious he knew him. That was a good indication that Wilfred could have been planted in a clan just as Penn had been. But why in Fergus's clan when he was loyal to the enemy and why would a skilled arrow maker be sent here? He could have insisted his wife remain where they were, unless he'd been ordered otherwise.

Royden wasn't only surprised, but Wilfred was as well when Penn went to him and didn't hide that he knew him, greeting him with a firm slap on the back and a bear hug, like old friends who hadn't seen each other in a while.

Royden had to smile when he saw his wife point to either man and with a smile appeared to be questioning them. He'd have some news on the two soon enough.

"It's a good thing we got most of the cottages repaired, though the common hut for the warriors might be crowded now," Angus said with a huff.

"Thought you'd be in Bethany's bed by now?" Royden asked with a grin.

"I was doing good until that merchant showed up," Angus complained. "Do you know what he brought her and she was beyond happy about? *Spices*. He brought her spices."

Where had he gotten spices? They were not easy to come by in these parts, though trade with the far north could get you them. Royden wondered how truthful Clive had been with him. Had the merchant he bought the cart from have them or had he acquired them himself? There definitely was more to Clive than he had said.

"I thought Clive brought her some baubles and ribbons or some type of trinket women enjoy receiving," Royden said.

"He gave her some of that too, but it was the spices that brought her the most joy."

Royden didn't want to make it worse for Angus, but he figured he'd voice what the man already knew. "It would seem that Clive knows what makes Bethany happy."

Angus snorted in disgust. "And here I thought I knew women."

"You do know women. You just don't know Bethany," Royden said.

Angus's eyes went wide as if just realizing something. "You're right. I treat all women the same. I don't know Bethany at all." He nodded to himself. "I need to get to know her before that fool merchant returns and steals her away from me." He gave a quick glance around and spotted Bethany. "She could use help handing out food and drink and it would give me a chance to see what I could find out from some of the arrivals."

"Then go," Royden said, knowing Angus waited his command. His advice to Angus had him thinking he should pay heed to it as well. Oria and he had said time and again that they weren't the people they once were. It was time he made an effort to get to know the woman she had become.

He went to join his wife and she stretched her hand out to him as soon as he was close enough for him to take hold of it, and he did.

"Isn't this wonderful, Royden, Penn and Wilfred know each other," Oria said.

Royden saw the touch of fear in Emily's and Lona's eyes and watched Wilfred pale. It was Penn who bravely, though nervously spoke up.

"Wilfred and I met in one of the mercenary camps and spent a few years together," Penn explained. "He fell in love with Lona like I did with Emily. There is something irresistible about the women of the Clan MacKinnon. Wilfred brings his exceptional skill as an arrow maker to the clan."

"Lona met Wilfred at the Clan MacDonnegal, where she'd been moved to shortly after the attack," Oria said.

Royden settled a glare on Wilfred. "Why would Chieftain Fergus part with such an exceptional arrow maker?"

Lona responded before her husband had a chance to. "I wanted to come home. I missed my clan, my family, the people I love."

"It is good to have you home, Lona.," Royden said, keeping a calm voice yet a commanding tone. "We have need of a skillful spinner."

"I am here to serve the clan, sir, as is my husband," Lona said, clinging tightly to her husband's arm as if she feared he'd be taken away from her.

"Fergus gave you no argument about that, Wilfred?" Royden asked and Lona went to respond again for him. "Your husband can speak for himself."

Uncertainty flared in Wilfred's eyes and he looked to Penn.

Royden didn't wait, he ordered, "Both of you come with me."

"Wilfred has done nothing wrong, sir," Lona begged, keeping hold of her husband's arm.

"Then he has nothing to fear," Royden said and looked to his wife. "Settle Lona in one of the cottages."

"I know one that will be perfect for you and Wilfred," Oria said and she let go of her husband's hand to take Lona by the arm. "Come, Emily, the cottage is not far from yours."

Emily squeezed her husband's arm, a worried look in her eyes, before going off with the two women.

Royden took note of the way his wife had reassured Lona that there was no need for worry, that her husband would be returning to her. She wisely understood that he would not turn away a skillful arrow maker, though if time proved he could not trust the man, he would not hesitate to be rid of him.

"My solar," Royden ordered and without being told directions the two men led the way right to it. His chest tightened with anger that strangers had been in his home and knew it almost as well as he did. How many attacks on innocent people had been planned in what once had been his da's sanctuary? A place where he had once fought for more peaceful ways to settle disputes and accusations that could have easily led to battles.

Royden pointed at the table for them to sit. "When was the last time you were both in this room? And why would a warrior and an arrow maker even be brought here?"

Penn spoke up first. "Warriors were brought here now and again and asked if we had learned anything, from those in the clan, about your sister Raven."

"And you didn't think to tell me this?" Royden asked, his voice raised in annoyance.

"What was there to tell?" Penn shook his head. "No one, not one person, knew anything about Raven's whereabouts or if they did, they never said a word. It was a worthless effort. It was always the same when I came here. Where is she? Who has seen her? Where does she hide?"

"They believed her alive?" Royden asked and realized why his wife had kept quiet about what she'd known about his da and sister. His da would have survived only to find his life taken from him if the enemy had discovered his whereabouts. And his sister? He hated to think about her fate. Oria had lived with a hefty burden over the years.

"I assumed they did since they encouraged me and others to try and find out anything we could. But I heard and saw nothing that pertained to your sister," Penn admitted. "As I told you, this is my home now, here with my wife and son, and I will do whatever is necessary to see it remains so."

"I will too," Wilfred said quickly. "I was only in this room once. I was brought here after I delivered arrows to a man called Trevor. He was so pleased with them that he brought me here for a drink. I had joined the mercenaries of my own accord, though it was soon obvious I wasn't cut out to be a warrior. I don't like to kill."

"None of us do," Royden said. "Unfortunately, there are many who enjoy it, which leaves us no choice but to defend ourselves. I assume you were protected because of your skills as an arrow maker."

"Aye, I wasn't forced to fight. I spent my days and many nights making arrows," Wilfred said. "I was glad when I was left at the Clan MacDonnegal. And even more glad when I met Lona. She didn't mind that I wasn't a warrior."

"Why would Fergus let you go when you have such skill?" Royden asked.

"That baffled me," Wilfred said, shaking his head. "I think it baffled Fergus as well, since he appeared angry at letting me and Lona leave. And it wasn't only me he didn't like losing. Lona is a fine spinner, the best one he had."

"The other people you journeyed here with, they came from the Clan MacDonnegal as well?" Royden asked.

"No, they all arrived at the clan about four days ago. Lona was surprised to see members of her clan and when she found out they were returning home, she demanded to be returned home as well. I accompanied her when she went to see Fergus, since I wasn't about to be separated from my wife. That was when the chieftain told us we'd be returning here as well."

Royden thought about his talk with Fergus. He had already known that some of the Clan MacKinnon were being returned home and he hadn't said a word. Or had it come as a surprise to him that Lona and Wilfred would be among the group?

"I told Penn he'd have to earn my trust. The same goes for you, Wilfred," Royden said.

"My wife is thrilled to finally be home with her people. I'd rather die than see that taken from her. Besides, it would be nice to finally have a clan—a family—to belong to."

"Prove you're worthy of being part of the Clan MacKinnon and you have a home for life. Betray my clan and I'll kill you both myself," Royden warned.

***

It was a day that seemed never-ending. People needed to be settled in cottages and fed. As soon as Wilfred returned to Lona and she learned all was well, she immediately offered to help any way she could. She was sent to the kitchen along with others since help was needed in preparing food for so many. Wilfred and Penn got busy finding a hut where Wilfred could make his arrows, Royden ordering him to set his skill to work within two days' time. And through it all, people were sharing stories where they had been and what they had gone through the last five years. Some had coped well, others hadn't. But one thing everyone agreed upon was that they were relieved and happy to finally be home.

Every chance someone had they would thank or bless Royden or Oria for bringing them home. Royden didn't feel right accepting praise for something he hadn't done. This had to have been arranged all before he had spoken to Fergus. So who was deserving of the praise?

It was late by the time Royden climbed the stairs with his wife to their bedchamber. Watching the way her rounded hips swayed so temptingly as he climbed behind her, aroused his loins, but her slow steps reminded him how tired she was.

"It's been a tiring day," Oria said, going to the fireplace and raising her arms above her head in a good stretch and an equally good yawn.

The urge to go to his wife and wrap her in his arms overwhelmed him, but if he did, he'd have her stripped in no time and on her knees on the bed so he could take her with rapid speed. He could almost feel himself ramming into her sweet wetness over and over and over until—he shook the vision away. He cursed his thoughts, his shaft having responded swiftly to the vision.

It didn't help that she moaned and stretched her body as if in the throes of coupling.

He snarled quietly and shook his head again. He didn't know how he was going to get through the night. When another loud yawn came from her, he knew she was too tired for anything but sleep.

Tomorrow morning, he promised himself as a way of compensating for his disappointment.

Then she did something that brought him far too close to the edge. She stripped off her garments, tossing them aside. He couldn't take his eyes off her round hips and backside. And the vision returned of her on her knees on the bed and grabbing that gorgeous backside of hers in his hand and slamming into her to pleasure them both.

She turned, her arms still stretched in the air as she moved her shoulders, in an attempt to work out the soreness.

Good Lord, she was beautiful and so damn tempting. Maybe he'd enjoy taking her from behind for a while then flip her over and settle in her again so he could feast on her plump breasts.

Stop! Stop! Stop! He silently warned himself when yet again she yawned widely.

Her arms suddenly dropped to her side. "Why aren't you undressed yet? While I would love to take time and make love, I just don't think I'd last. We need to be quick about it tonight. We can always take our time in the morning."

Royden never got undressed so fast in his life and he was surprised when his wife hurried to take his leather cuff off his stump. He went to pull his arm away.

"Please don't," she said softly. "My heart aches for you that you lost your hand, but better your hand than your life. You are no different to me with one hand then you were with two." She took it and placed it between her breasts. "You're here with me. That's all that matters."

Royden's arm shot around her waist and he yanked her close and before his lips came down on hers, he said quickly, "Good God, Oria, I love you so much."

Her arms went around his neck and as they kissed with an urgent need, he lifted her so her feet faintly brushed the floor as he walked to the bed.

She tore her mouth away from his. "I can't wait."

"Either can I," he admitted and dropped her on the bed. "On your hands and knees," he ordered with a smile that was far from playful.

Oria didn't hesitate to do as he said, far too eager to have him inside her.

He fit his shaft easily between her legs, a wetness greeting him, letting him know she was more than ready.

"Hurry, I've been waiting all day for this," she urged, wiggling her backside against his poking shaft.

That did it for Royden—he plunged into her.

"Oh!" she cried out, digging her hands in the blankets as he slammed against her with the most exquisite pleasure.

Royden feared he'd explode there and then, she clamped so tightly around him and when she began to meet his powerful thrusts with her own, rocking her backside against him, that was it. There was no way he'd change positons now on them. It felt too damn good and they were far too close to climax to ruin it for either of them. Besides, he loved watching her round, firm bottom smack against him with unbridled passion.

"I can't wait! I can't wait!" Oria cried out, her passion having soared so fast she had no control over it.

Royden was relieved, since either could he.

Her scream was cut short as a tremendous wave of passion smacked into her stealing her breath.

Royden let out his own roar as he was devoured by the most powerful burst of pleasure he'd ever experienced and it didn't stop as he continued to plunge into her drawing out every bit of pleasure for the both of them. When he heard her gasp—as if catching her breath—and she began to moan again, he knew she was on the verge of another climax and he made sure not to stop, but to feed her mounting passion with more hard thrusts.

After the waves of pleasure faded along with their strength, they both collapsed beside each other. Their bodies were damp with sweat and their breathing heavy, yet a slight smile tickled at the corners of their lips.

"It gets,"—she paused for a needed breath— "better and," —another breath was needed—"better."

"Aye," he agreed, his labored breathing not letting him say any more than that, so he reached out for her hand. He smiled when she clasped onto to his hand as soon as he touched hers. It was important to him to hold on to her, never let her slip away from him again. It was a fear that lingered too often in him. Even when she was here beside him in bed, he worried she could be taken from him again.

Oria released his hand and turned to cuddle against him, pleased when his arm went around her to keep him close. "Never again will we be separated," she said, her breathing having slowed.

They had often thought alike and he was pleased that that was something that hadn't changed between them.

"Aye, never again," he said with such resolve that it sounded like a decree.

They drifted off to sleep, Oria waking from a chill and left her husband's arm to grab the blanket at the end of the bed.

Her movement woke him from a dead sleep and his hand shot out to grab her arm. "Where are you going?"

"To get the blanket. I'm chilled," she said, a shiver running through her.

He released her arm and she pulled the blanket over them, settling against him once again.

"I'll warm you," Royden whispered as he slipped over her.

"It may take a while. I'm really cold," she said with a soft laugh.

"Don't worry. I promise you'll be hot in no time," he said with a chuckle and kept his promise.

Chapter Seventeen

"Those who have returned have settled in well this past week," Oria said, looking out on the village from the top step of the keep.

Royden nodded in agreement. "They're happy to finally be home,"

"Aye, and don't we know how that feels," Oria said with a smile and hugged her husband's arm, her hand traveling down to take hold of his wrist, no hand there for her to grab.

He looked down at her hand, amazed that she hadn't flinched. Not once had she done so since that first time she had learned he'd lost his hand and that had been out of pain for what he had been through. She had accepted what fate had dealt him much easier than he had. But then he hadn't told her the half of what he'd been through while healing from the awful wound. There had been times he could have sworn his hand was still there. Then there had been times the pain would get almost as bad as the day he'd lost it. It still pained him at times, but he refused to surrender to it or let anyone know.

"The village is coming together well," Oria said. "Lona spins a fine wool with her spindle and whorl, and Colina, your warrior Sefton's wife he brought home with him, has the same skill as well. Though we will need more sheep, the few left will not be enough."

"There is a gathering soon for the various clans to sell or trade livestock and such. We'll get sheep from there and whatever else we need before winter arrives."

"You wear a scowl. What's wrong?" Oria asked.

"Some of our clan has returned, but far more are absent and I wonder how many are lost to us forever."

"And you worry how we will defend ourselves if ever attacked again," Oria added when he didn't.

"You read my thoughts well, wife."

"My thoughts are much like yours," she admitted. "How can we not worry about being prepared for an attack after suffering and losing so much on that horrendous day?"

"It will take years to rebuild the clan, leaving us vulnerable," Royden admitted.

"Not if we acquire more warriors."

"And how will we do that?"

"We do as the mercenaries do, only we invite warriors to join the clan, not capture and force them, who are tired of battle and look for a different life," Oria explained.

"How do we trust they aren't ordered to come to us to infiltrate our clan and then fight against us if the time comes again that we're attacked?"

"Why would you and Arran be released if only to be attacked again? And why were we forced to wed as a condition of your release? It would seem someone wants the clan to survive."

"I was told a high price was paid for my release and I would think Arran's as well. I have wondered endlessly over who had sufficient coin and power to do that," Royden said, the thought having troubled him since he'd first learned about it.

"You worry you'll be beholding to someone who will make demands on you?" Oria asked, thinking the same herself.

"Aye, and what those demands might be is what concerns me," he said.

She hugged his arm, then pressed against it. "Right now, I only care that you're home and we're together. And together we'll face whatever comes our way."

He bent his head and kissed her brow. "And together we will stay."

"Always," she said with a soft smile.

He hoped his fear of losing her again abated with time or else he feared he'd never let her go far from his side.

"Go and find out from Penn and Wilfred their thoughts on seeing if others like them would consider joining the Clan MacKinnon," she urged.

The cry of a bird interrupted Royden's response and his eyes went to the woods. "I have not heard such a clear cry of a gowk in years and it's a female's cry, which means a male is near. It's a reminder that life continues no matter what."

"Then go and see if we can improve the quick growth of our clan," she urged once again and gave him a playful shove.

"What plans do you have that makes you so eager to be rid of me?" he asked with a feigned scowl, though it was important for him to know so if anything should happen he could get to her quickly.

"I will be helping in the kitchen garden today," she informed him. "Now go and see to your duties." She gave him another playful push. "And make sure you relate to me all that Penn and Wilfred have to say. We can meet later in your solar to talk." She went to turn away, his response halting her.

"It won't be talking we do in my solar," he said.

Passion flared so hot in his dark eyes that it more than sparked her own and she wanted to grab his hand and drag him to his solar, but she couldn't.

"I will hold you to that, husband," she said and it took tremendous willpower to turn away from him and hurry off.

Royden watched her go, surprised that she hadn't rushed him into the keep and to his solar. Any mention of a possible quick poke and she was ready and willing. He had actually been wondering when her eagerness and frequency to coupling would come to an end and hoping it never would. But it looked like it just had. Or perhaps she thought it more important he not wait to speak with Penn and Wilfred. He'd rather think that than the other, but he couldn't help but see and sense her eagerness to leave him.

***

Oria cringed, as she ran toward the woods, at the thought that she had just rejected her husband's veiled invitation for a quick poke. Never did she deny him, though it was more like she didn't deny herself since she so enthusiastically enjoyed coupling with her husband. But she had recognized the call of the female gowk bird for what it was—a call to meet her friend in the woods. And it had to be extremely important if she had taken a chance to come so near the keep.

With a quick glance around to make sure no one saw her, Oria slipped into a section of woods not far from the kitchen garden. Hasty steps had her to the spot where her friend would be waiting. The area was empty except for the squirrel that stared at Oria when she came to a stop, as if angry with her intrusion, then hurried off.

Oria waited, not daring to take the chance and call out.

"I'm here."

Oria smiled, not only hearing Purity, but seeing the movement to the side of one of the trees. She was wrapped in a cloak, the hood pulled down so that only her mouth showed. She couldn't take a chance of revealing herself, letting anyone know she was there. There was still worry that if found she'd be forced to wed someone and her da's clan and land claimed by another. With her brother Bayne dead, she couldn't let that happen.

"You've taken an awful chance in coming here," Oria said.

"I know, but I needed to speak with you after learning that Royden has returned home and that you and he have wed. I am so happy for you and him. I know how very much you've always loved him. All goes well with you both?"

"It does, though not at first. Royden has changed some."

"Haven't we all?"

"Aye, we have and it's to be expected. If it wasn't for our love remaining strong, things could have turned out differently. Thankfully our love was a bond that no one, not heaven or earth, could break or take from us. I honestly believe our love grew even stronger and more determined than ever to survive the years we were separated."

"You're so very lucky," Purity said, happy and envious of her friend.

"Arran will be returning home as well," Oria said, always remembering how much Purity loved Royden's brother.

"That matters little to me now," Purity said.

Oria thought differently, hearing the sadness in her friend's voice and tried to offer what comfort she could. "Your da talked with Royden and asked that Arran wed you when he returns."

"A foolish request years ago and a more foolish request now," Purity said.

"It is a safe way for you to return home," Oria offered and intended to make sure Arran saw that as well as soon as he arrived home.

"If I could, I would make the woods my home for the rest of my life," Purity said.

"Please don't say that. I miss you and—" Oria bit her lip.

"I miss her too, but she's the one who must be the most careful," Purity warned.

"You think they still search for her?"

"If we can't be sure, then we can't take a chance," Purity said, wishing things were different.

"You're right," Oria agreed.

"I don't have much time, though I wish I did. I wish we could sit and talk without worry of time or being caught, like we once did." Purity laughed. "Though we did hide away, so I wouldn't be seen. Some things don't change."

"They will. The three of us will be together again one day," Oria assured her, praying it would be so.

"Listen, for I must leave soon. When it was learned that Royden was home and leading the clan, those who were part of the Clan MacKinnon decided to return home with his da. They have given their word not to betray my location."

"How many are left with you?" Oria asked, worried her friend would be left alone.

"Worry not about me, Oria. I am content where I am. See to those returning to you and there is one other thing you should be aware of—Wren is returning with Parlan. He refused to leave without her and, unselfish as she is, refused to let him leave his family for her. I don't know how she'll be received so watch over her. She has been good to us."

"I will and I'm sure after everyone gets to know her they'll see what a good and gentle woman she is," Oria reassured her.

"I must go," Purity said.

You didn't tell me, how is King?" Oria asked, curious about the cat that had stolen Purity's heart and wanting to linger a bit longer with her friend.

Purity laughed lightly. "His name is most appropriate since he rules all the other animals and humans as well. Take care, Oria. I do miss you."

"And I you, my friend, and I will send word when Arran returns home."

"It matters little. He can do nothing to help me."

Oria watched, tears stinging her eyes, as Purity swiftly disappeared deeper into the woods. She had rejoiced when she had discovered that Purity had survived, though it had been a full year before she had managed to get in touch with Oria. It was a short, wiry fellow who had appeared too far into his cups to even stand who had delivered the first message from her, garbled as it was. She barely understood it, though later realized it was in case anyone heard, they'd make no sense of it. It took another year after that for Oria to finally meet with Purity in the woods, more often near Learmonth since none of the warriors paid her much mind there.

It had been through Purity that Oria had found out that Raven had survived, though to keep her safe, Oria and Purity knew only that she was alive. Nothing more was told to them for their own safety.

Oria continued to pray as she had from when it had all started that everyone would one day be reunited and all would be healed. Her familiar prayer fell softly from her lips as she walked home through the woods.

***

"I'll talk with you both," Royden ordered when he reached Penn and Wilfred talking outside of the cottage that was now home to Lona and Wilfred.

He couldn't help but think of the two men as the enemy, especially when he saw them together like this talking or more whispering, their heads bent close. This is what he feared if more of their kind joined the clan. If they remained loyal to whoever they once had pledged allegiance to, then how could he ever trust them to defend the Clan MacKinnon.

Royden had passed Angus just before reaching the two men and he saw that Angus had followed him and stood to the side, his presence letting Royden know he was there if needed. That was clan loyalty, being there to help without being asked.

"What can we do for you, sir?" Penn asked.

It wasn't lost on Royden that Wilfred kept to Penn's side, but more behind him as if Penn was a shield that protected him.

"You both tell me you love your wives and want to stay here and make this your home."

Both men nodded, each voicing the same, "Aye. Aye."

"Had you wanted that before you met your wives and fell in love?" Royden asked and kept a firm eye on them both, waiting to catch the slightest reaction that could contradict their responses.

Wilfred surprised Royden by speaking up first.

"I ached for a more peaceful life before I met Lona. Falling in love with her made me want it even more."

"I was glad to be left here. Constant battle wears on you, tormenting your dreams, filling your head with godless thoughts until you don't know who you are," Penn said.

"Aye," Angus agreed, walking over and joining the discussion. "Sometimes I don't want to go to sleep at night, not wanting to be held captive by my dreams."

To hear others say what Royden himself felt made him realize how many more must feel the same. Five years had taken a toll on him, leaving him scarred in so many ways and thinking that some of those scars would never heal. But being home now made him think it just might be possible to heal those scars he had believed permanent.

"Do you think there are others who feel as you do?" Royden asked.

Penn nodded right away. "I talked to many a warrior who wished an end to the battles."

"Penn's right," Wilfred said. "Many told me I was lucky to be an arrow maker and away from the battlefield."

"Then there are those men who live to battle. They can't get enough of it. It's like a hunger that can't be satisfied," Penn said. "Couple them with the greed of powerful men and wars will never end."

"How do I reach these men who no longer wish to battle so I may offer them a home—a family?" Royden asked.

Penn and Wilfred exchanged a quick glance of surprise and possibly a hint of suspicion.

Royden crossed his arms over his chest and waited for one to answer.

"The men owe him," Penn explained. "I don't believe he'd let them go."

"So this man, the one you call Beast, didn't let either of you go. You are still beholding to him?" Royden asked.

They both nodded.

"You don't walk away from him without permission," Wilfred said.

Angus spoke up, his anger flaring. "How can men remain loyal to him when he takes them captive and forces them to fight for him?"

"He doesn't force most of them. They come to him," Penn said.

Angus pounded his chest. "He forced us."

"Aye, Penn said. "He took a good portion of men from this area, but I don't know the reason why. It was strange to see and strange that he's left a hold on this area, which can only mean his job here is not finished."

"What do you mean?" Royden asked.

"He's paid to do a job. Once it is done, he leaves," Wilfred said.

"So his job isn't done here," Royden said. "I suppose neither of you know who paid him to attack this area or why?"

Both men shook their heads.

"The warriors are never told that information," Penn said. "But it is surprising that this has gone on so long here. He is usually swift in seeing a job over and done."

"Which means something has prevented him from finishing," Royden said.

"Someone must want this land bad and have an overflowing coffer to keep this going for five years," Angus said and rubbed his chin. "Unless…"

Penn and Wilfred turned scrunched brows on Angus.

But it was Royden who satisfied their curiosity. "Unless it's revenge someone is after and if so until he gets it, he'll never stop."

***

Royden headed toward the kitchen garden to see his wife. He wasn't sure what to make of his discussion with Penn and Wilfred. Was it possible this whole thing had been brought about because of revenge?

Penn and Wilfred had both made it clear that they didn't want to reach out to other warriors about joining the Clan MacKinnon for fear of what trouble it might bring them. They were too afraid of losing what they had and it went without saying that Royden couldn't offer them protection against this man his warriors called the Beast.

He thought it might be for the best, since he was doubtful that warriors who'd been loyal to this man would ever go against him in battle.

Royden rubbed the back of his neck, an ache having settled there. He had thought himself free of battle once he was freed, but he was in the middle of an even bigger battle. A battle against an unseen and unknown enemy who appeared to want not only the majority of the land in this area, but complete control over it as well.

He continued to rub his neck. He'd discuss it with his wife, though not before he gave her a good poke that would leave them both well satisfied. He smiled at the thought as he rounded the corner of the keep.

It vanished in a flash when he didn't see his wife in the garden.

He was about to hurry to the kitchen and see if she was in there. Actually, he was praying she was there, since fear had gripped him when he hadn't seen her where she'd said she'd be. But just before he did, he caught a rustle of movement coming from the woods.

Could someone have taken his wife? Fear slammed into him, stealing his breath but he ran anyway, straight toward the sound. Before he reached it, his wife appeared, her eyes going wide like an animal's eyes when caught in the sights of a hunter.

She appeared frozen in place, as if shocked to see him, and he rushed to her. His hand closed around her arm like a shackle, gripping her tight, and he dragged her out of the woods.

Oria winced from her husband's strong grip and tripped a few times, but had no fear of falling since he held her firmly.

Royden swung her around to face him once out of the woods almost slamming her against him, but stopped just shy of her hitting his hard chest.

His dark eyes burned with fury and there was an angry growl to his tone. "What were you doing in the woods? Are you that foolish? Anyone could have grabbed you and abducted you. Never! Ever! Do that again!" he warned, not realizing he was shaking her.

"Stop, Royden. Please stop," she cried out, growing dizzy and pain shooting through her arm. She feared he didn't hear her, seeing in his eyes the savage side of him that rose on occasion. She placed her hand against his chest. "Please, Royden, Please."

Her plea had him halting immediately and shaking his head, forcing the savage in him to retreat.

"My arm," she said, the pain making her wince.

He let go of her and stepped away and took hefty breathes, finally able to breathe.

Oria rested her hand on his back.

He pulled away. "Don't touch me."

She ignored his protest and rested her hand on his back again. "I can't. I need you."

Her soft plea had him turning around and she tucked herself under his arm and against his chest. His instincts took over, his arms going around her, and his lips pressing a kiss on her brow.

"You frightened the life out of me," he said, trying to explain.

"I'm truly sorry, I didn't mean to," she said, slipping her arms around his waist as far as they could fit.

"I thought someone took you," he said, keeping her tight against him.

"You would hear me scream for you from far off if anyone attempted to do that," she said.

"Your word on that, wife," he demanded.

"Even if my life was threatened, I would never hesitate to call out to you. I'm all too familiar with the foolishness of not screaming out for your help."

He heard in her voice and saw the guilt in her eyes that she felt for not having called out to him during the attack.

"I would have come for you, saved you if I had known," he said.

"I know that, but I so feared distracting you from the battle," she admitted.

He shook his head and rested his brow to hers. "The past is done and can't be undone. I'll have your word now that from this day forward you will not hesitate to call out to me for help—not for any reason—if ever the need should arise. I promise I will be there for you."

"You have my word, husband," she said, his promise providing a sense of safety and a bit of worry since after what they both had been through, each of them would do whatever it took to see the other safe.

"Now you will tell me what you were doing in the woods," he said and saw the worry and hesitation in her eyes. "I will have the truth, wife."

"I gave my word and I will have yours now that what I tell you, you will share with no one, and I only do this because I know you are a man of your word," she said and shivered with the intensity of the strength in which he spoke.

"On my honor, you have my word, Oria."

She went to explain all to him when…

"Hurry, Royden," Angus yelled, running toward him. "Your da returns home."

Chapter Eighteen

Royden hurried through the village, Oria keeping pace with him. He came to an abrupt halt when he caught sight of his da, people crowded around him welcoming him home with smiles and tears of joy.

"He looks good," Royden said after Oria came to a stop beside him.

Royden had feared that his da might be a shell of the man he had once been, but he looked well-healed. He even had a bit more weight on him than Royden remembered and more wrinkles crinkled near his eyes from his broad smile, but he was far more fit than expected and Royden was grateful.

"From what I've been told, Wren has taken excellent care of him," Oria said happy for her husband and wishing her own da was there to see the reunion.

The reminder that his da had not returned home alone had Royden searching the crowd for the woman who had predicted his family would be reunited. He spotted several women who had been members of the clan, some now widows. One was Flora, a woman more familiar to Arran and one whose company his brother had enjoyed on occasion.

"Is that Wren?" Royden asked, pointing to a gray-haired woman not far from his da.

"I wouldn't know. I never met Wren," Oria said, though curiosity had her looking where her husband pointed.

When Emily hugged the gray-haired woman, Royden shook his head. "Can't be Wren, Emily knows her. Does she look familiar to you?"

"Five years can be harsh or easy on a person, depending on the circumstances," Oria reminded him.

Royden nodded, understanding all too well. All those who returned today would be grateful to have things returned to the way they'd once been, but Royden understood what would take time for them to understand—nothing would ever be the same again.

His da's eyes finally met with his and Royden didn't wait, he hurried to him, people moving aside. Their arms shot around each other in a tight hug that brought tears to most of those surrounding father and son.

When they finally released each other, reluctantly, Royden shouted, "Our Chieftain Parlan has returned."

A cheer filled the air, but Parlan shook his head and waved his hand for the people to settle and when they finally did, he spoke. "It is time for me to pass the torch. Royden has been your chieftain in my absence and he shall remain so. He deserves to lead this clan and the clan deserves a younger man with his strength and bravery to do so."

A loud roar echoed over the land, agreeing with Parlan.

Royden went to protest but his da's strong whisper stopped him.

"You will see when we talk that this is for the best." His da looked to the leather cuff covering Royden's stump. "You more than earned this."

"What is the witch doing here?" a man called out, pointing.

"Shut your foolish lips, Coyle," Flora called out. "Wren saved our old chieftain's life and others as well."

Royden half-listened to the two bicker, his attention drawn to the woman his da rushed to. She was nearly as tall as his da and had flaming red hair sprinkled with white, yet her pretty face showed little signs of age. Her green eyes brightened with joy when she looked upon his da, the way Oria's did when she looked at him. The woman loved his father and from the way his da took the witch in his arms and held her close, it seemed his da felt the same way.

Royden wasn't surprised when his da's voice took on the tone of one in command, and he was glad to see his da still commanded with strength and confidence.

"Wren is not a witch, she is a healer, and will soon be my wife."

Gasps mingled with cheers and Royden didn't hide his own surprise. He turned when his wife's hand closed around his.

"How wonderful that your da has finally found love again. Your mum would be so happy that he isn't alone."

Oria was right. His mum would want that for her husband, though it had Royden thinking and asking, "If anything should happen to me—"

Oria's smile faded and she leaned against him to whisper, "I have loved you since I was a young bairn. I could never, would never, love another as I love you." Her smiled returned and she kept her voice low. "Besides, I doubt there's a man alive who is as talented as you are in bed."

Royden gave her a quick kiss on the cheek and whispered, "I wouldn't want you to be alone, but I can't stand the thought of another man touching you. Like you, I've loved you since we've been young. There could never be another woman for me. And you're not so bad in bed yourself."

"I think there's more you could teach me," she said with a teasing smile.

"I'll teach you something new tonight," he whispered and felt her shudder against him.

His da's booming voice echoed over the people and had Royden and Oria listening. "You will give Wren the respect you give me. I will not tolerate anyone treating her poorly or intending her harm."

Heads bobbed throughout the crowd, while some skeptical faces could be seen.

"Wren saved my da's life," Royden called out. "I'm sure we all are grateful to have such a skilled healer among us."

The approving nod his da sent him, like the many he had done in the past, had Royden feeling—for a sheer moment—that life, at least a glimpse of it, was returning as it once was to the clan. And that was a huge sign of hope.

"Now it's time to get everyone settled in homes and fed, and in a few days we will have a fine feast to celebrate," — Royden raised his voice with strength and pride— "the return of the Clan MacKinnon."

The people cheered and when all quieted, Royden didn't need to issue orders. Angus let him know he'd take count and help John and Stuart with seeing everyone settled and to the cart that had followed behind them with their belongings. This time, however, he motioned Penn to him.

"You'll help John and Stuart, then report to me how things go."

Penn looked surprised, but pleased. "Aye, sir, I'll see it done."

Royden looked around for his wife, not realizing she had left his side, and smiled when he saw her with his da and Wren. He went and joined them.

"I can't tell you how pleased I am that you and Oria have finally wed," his da said. "I only wish the whole family could have been here for it."

"We'll wed again and hold a huge celebration when the whole family is reunited," Royden said.

"That will be wonderful, a joyous day indeed," Wren said.

Royden didn't know if he heard what he wanted to hear in Wren's remark or if she spoke to let them know that it would be so. That one day such a celebration would take place.

"It is a pleasure to finally meet you, Royden," Wren said. "Your da spoke often of you and Oria, and Arran and Raven as well. I feel I already know all of you."

"I hope to get to know you as well as you know all of us," Royden said, her gentle voice quite soothing to the ear.

"Let's get you some food and settled in the keep," Oria said.

Royden wasn't surprised that it took a while to reach the keep, since many in the clan stopped his da to personally welcome him home. He was well-loved and well-respected by the clan that he'd led with honor, and seeing him well and in fine shape had surely been a sign of hope to everyone.

Oria had seen to food and drink once in the Great Hall and when it was placed on the table she said, "I'll leave you to talk. It's my duty to see to the people who have returned home."

Royden looked ready to disagree, but quelled his response. He wouldn't stop his wife from doing what was right.

"I'll join you. Some may need my healing hand," Wren offered.

"You haven't eaten and you're tired from the journey," Parlan said, taking hold of Wren's arm when she went to stand.

"You need to talk with your son," Wren said softly, covering his hand with hers. "I will sup with you later."

"You love her, don't you?" Royden asked as his da watched Wren leave the Great Hall with his wife.

"I never expected to fall in love again. Your mother stole my heart and took it with her when she died. I didn't think I had an ounce of love in me for another woman. Wren was..." He shook his head. "It was like my heart suddenly came alive and I felt things I hadn't felt since the day I lost your mum." He took a swig of ale. "Wren is a good woman."

"You don't have to explain yourself to me, Da," Royden said. "You love Wren and that's all that matters."

"News got back to me about you and Arran. My heart broke when I heard you lost your hand, though I was relieved you survived it."

"I wouldn't have if it hadn't been for Arran."

"I wouldn't have expected anything less from him. He may be all smiles and charm, but Arran is a superior warrior and most of all a devoted brother," Parlan said with pride. "I heard mentioned that he will be returning home as well. Pray tell it is true."

"He's been released and I got word that he must see to something before coming home. I pray it has something to do with Raven."

"Have you heard anything about her?" Parlan asked anxiously.

Royden cupped his tankard tightly with his one hand. "I only know she has survived, nothing more than that."

"I heard the same, but wonder if it was nothing more than wishful thinking. I know of no one who has seen or spoken to her." Parlan reached out to grip his son's wrist. "I can't bear to think what may have happened to her or that I failed to protect her."

"We're all to blame. Arran and I discussed this and we both agree that one of us should have seen to her safety. I believe she survived and she remains in hiding for fear of what might happen if she shows herself."

"What has she got to fear now?" Parlan asked. "You have returned to the clan. You are wed and no doubt soon will have news of a bairn on the way. The Clan MacKinnon is secure."

"It could be that Raven hides so well that she doesn't know what goes on here," Royden suggested.

Parlan laughed. "Your sister had her nose in everything. She's been a little sneak since she was young. I doubt that has changed."

His da was right about Raven. She had listened more times than not on discussions held in their da's solar without ever being caught. And she spied on Arran when he and Flora met for a poke or two in the barn.

Parlan's brow suddenly drew together. "How was it you managed to return home?"

"I was released and you should know that my release was conditioned upon me wedding Oria."

"Why? You would have wed her anyway," his da asked.

The thought was like a slap in the face. His da was right. He might have been foolish upon returning home, but in the end he would have wed Oria. He would have never chanced losing her again. It just would have taken some time to realize it.

Everyone knew he and Oria wished to wed, so why had it been a condition of his release? Who would think they wouldn't wed?

"Not much is making sense right now, Da. I was told a high price had been paid for my release."

His da shook his head. "It's not only coin that would be needed to secure your release. It would have to be someone with power or influence or both." He shook his head again. "You're right, not much makes sense. There was no strife among the clans in this part so why the attack? Who paid the mercenaries for it?"

"Arran and I tried to find out what we could, but it was useless. No one talked and no one seemed to care," Royden said. "It's a puzzle I intend to solve."

"You have to have all the pieces to solve a puzzle. I don't believe we have enough pieces to do that just yet," his da said with a bit of annoyance.

Royden understood what his da meant without saying it. Until Arran and Raven were home there'd be no solving the puzzle.

Royden talked, ate, and drank with his da and the years they'd been separated seemed to melt away. They were once again back to the way it had been, only it really wasn't, not without Arran and Raven there. Not without their family completely reunited.

"I was thinking that maybe I should assign one of the warriors to shadow Wren, since it might take time for everyone to come to see she is an asset to the clan and accepts her," Royden said.

"I appreciate the consideration, but don't waste a warrior's time. Wren has a way of protecting herself and I'll be with her a good portion of the time. I miss her far too much when I'm away from her too long."

"Is that why you keep glancing to the door?" Royden asked with a laugh.

"I'm an old fool in love," Parlan said as if it were a fault.

"It doesn't only take being old to be a fool in love," Royden said with a laugh.

Wren returned excited. "I found the perfect cottage for us," she said, rushing to Parlan.

"Cottage?" Royden questioned. "You'll be staying in the keep. Oria and I will return to my bedchamber and you and my da will take the chieftain's quarters."

Wren looked to Parlan and he in turn looked to his son. "The chieftain's quarters belong to you and Oria."

"Then you and Wren take my bedchamber," Royden said, not wanting to argue with him. "You belong here in the keep with family, not in a cottage."

"Once people realize what a fine and exceptional healer Wren is they will waste no time seeking out her skill. You don't want them coming to the keep all hours of the day and night. Besides, I'm not only used to sharing a cottage with Wren, I prefer it."

"It is close to the keep," Wren said, "though uninhabitable at the moment."

"Then we will reside in the keep with my son and his wife until it is habitable," Parlan said.

Royden saw that his da was trying to appease him and Wren, and he would not make it any more difficult for him.

"It will be good to have you here in the keep with us for a while," Royden said, looking at his da before turning his attention to Wren. "Do you know where my wife is?"

A pleasant smile graced Wren's face. "Your wife is tireless. She bounces bairns on her hips while issuing orders for things to be moved from cottage to cottage, even moving things herself if someone doesn't respond fast enough. She also scrubs and sweeps and still has time to make a child laugh. She makes sure everyone gets food and drink and orders, pleasantly, the weak and old not to lift a finger. She is quite loved by the clan."

"Oria always gave more than others and many times more than she got in return," Parlan said. "I was sorry to hear about her da's passing. He was a good man and wise to wed her to Burnell before she was claimed by a stranger."

"How did you know that?" Royden asked.

"We got word of what was going on," Parlan said.

"How did you get word?" Royden asked. "Actually, I don't know all that happened to you. I only know you were dragged into the woods and taken to the wi—" Royden quickly corrected himself. "Taken to Wren for help."

His da explained, "I was told that Raven got the women inside the keep to safety, seeing that the battle was not going well. They are the ones who got me to Wren. It took a long time for my wound to heal and for me to fully recover. There were times I didn't think I'd make it, but with Wren's skills and encouragement, I did."

"How did word reach you so deep in the woods since it was believed that Wren's home was where many didn't go?" Royden asked baffled.

His da looked around and after satisfied no one was close, motioned for the only servant in the room to fetch more ale even though the jug was half full. Then with a faint whisper said, "Purity."

At that moment, Royden knew who his wife had met with in the woods.

Chapter Nineteen

It had been a long day, supper even lasting longer than usual. Oria was glad that talk was mostly reminiscent of good times and avoided the harsh memories of the past five years. It was good to laugh with family again and good that she now had a family. Times like these, though, were when she missed her da and mum the most.

The unusually long day had brought on fatigue, so by the time Oria entered the bedchamber she wanted to drop into bed and sleep.

"You never did tell me who you met in the woods," Royden said, slipping his shirt off before unwrapping his plaid.

Oria turned and sighed softly. Even half naked her husband managed to spark her passion. And while she was too tired to discuss her trip into the woods or partake in coupling, she got the sense that that wouldn't matter. And not because her husband would make demands, but because her own body would dictate her actions.

She folded her arms across her chest and tilted her head slightly as she asked, "Do you trust me, husband?"

"Of course I do," he said as if insulted she should ask.

"Then why ask me what you already know?"

"You've grown far to wise, wife," he accused.

"You haven't grown wise enough," she said with a laugh. "Did you mean to catch me in a trap? Expect not to hear the truth? Or was it that you were annoyed because I hadn't confided this to you?"

He tore off his plaid and went to the chair near the hearth to slip off his boots.

"Do you need to think of a response or is it that I'm right that annoys you?" she asked.

"Are you looking for praise for knowing your husband so well?" he said a sharp bite to his tone and turned his annoyed expression to the flames in the hearth.

Guilt stabbed at her. They were still finding their way with each other and the remnants left of the years they'd been apart didn't help any. They each had been left with seen and unseen scars. The unseen ones could be poked without realizing it, the pain returning to suffer them all over again.

Today an unseen scar had jabbed at her heart. Seeing Royden reunited with his da had brought both joy and heartache. It had made her miss her da terribly. And now she was regretful for whatever scar she had unintentionally opened on Royden.

Oria slipped off her garments and shoes and went to her husband and, with his knees parted just enough, she slipped between them to stand close to him.

"I didn't mean to make you angry," she said softly.

He turned his head and looked up at her. "You didn't. I made myself angry." His one hand went to rest on her hip and his stump rested on the other. "I worried day and night about everyone here. Who had survived and who hadn't. What had been forced on those who had survived? It tore at me that I was helpless to do anything about it. I don't want to feel that ever again. I know we were interrupted when you were about to trust me, confide in me about who you met in the woods, but I was annoyed that it had taken you time to do so. That I learned more from my da than you about Purity."

"I didn't want to keep anything from you, but I gave—"

"Your word, as you said, and I can't fault you for that. And I should have taken your response for how it was meant—playful teasing. It would seem you were not only right about that but right about me being grumpy. Forgive me?"

Her heart hurt seeing the hurt in his eyes. They'd both been hurt enough. She wouldn't let the past dictate their future.

"There's nothing to forgive, though…" She tapped her finger to her lips for a moment. "If you feel the need to make it up to me, you could always keep that promise you made earlier."

Royden scrunched his brow, not recalling, then suddenly he smiled. "I think I remember."

"I remember it clearly and there has been something I've wanted to try," she said.

"Whatever you want, wife," he said, eager to couple with her any way she wanted to. He wasn't, however, expecting her to kneel down in front of him.

"I've wondered what it would be like to taste you."

Before he could say or do anything, her face disappeared between his legs and he groaned when her mouth settled on his shaft. He'd already sprung to life when she had stood naked in between his legs and it didn't take long for him to swell in her mouth.

It didn't take long for him to fear that he'd climax far too soon and he definitely didn't want that.

She stopped suddenly and looked up at him eagerly, "Am I doing it right?"

A strand of her blonde hair had fallen over her eye and he reached down and brushed it away as he said, "Perfect. Absolutely perfect."

She smiled. "Good. It's more enjoyable than I imagined."

And once again her head disappeared between his legs and he dropped his head back against the chair and thought the same. It was beyond enjoyable. It was real and not one of the many dreams he would have, when captive, only to wake and find she wasn't there. Not so now. She was here, wanting to taste him, enjoying the taste of him. Good God, but he was a lucky man.

Passion soared in him, chasing away all his worries and misery, and as it did, his need for his wife grew in leaps and bounds. While he could easily sit there and enjoy, he needed more. He needed to be inside her.

"Oria," he said and when she looked up at him, her tongue tracing her lips, licking the taste of him, that was it. "Straddle me," he ordered impatiently.

Oria didn't protest, her need had turned to an ache that she knew only having him inside her would ease. She hurried over his lap and being as wet as she was, he slipped easily inside her and she let out a moan of satisfaction that rippled around the room.

She braced her hands on his wide shoulders and planted her feet firmly on the floor, then she began to move. The pace came naturally, starting slow so that she could enjoy feeling him slide in and out of her, then the tempo changed and she was moving faster, her moans no more a ripple but full and robust.

His hand and stump found their way to her backside and he forced the pace to change once again, fast and with a force that demanded from the both of them.

"God, wife," Royden groaned. "You're going to kill me, but I'll die happy."

"You're not dying without me," she said and dropped her had back and moaned loudly.

It truly felt like he was on the precipice of a tremendous fall he didn't know if he'd be able to survive and he didn't care. And he didn't intend to go alone. "We'll die together."

Oria brought her head up, her eyes going to her husband's. "Aye, together. Always together."

She gripped his shoulders and rode him hard and fast and in seconds they both fell off the edge together, tumbling down and down in an endless, explosive climax that had Oria collapsing against him in a near faint.

Royden squeezed his eyes and let his groan fade away as the last sparks of his climax drifted off. That's when he realized his wife felt much to lifeless against him.

"Oria," he said anxiously, his hand moving up along her damp back to shake her shoulder gently. When she remained lifeless, his heart began to pound in his chest and he shook her harder. "Oria!" Relief flooded him when he heard her groan softly.

With effort and keeping her head rested on her husband's shoulder, she looked up at him. "We're alive?"

Royden laughed. "Aye, we're alive."

"I thought I'd died and gone to heaven," she said. "It felt that great."

He hugged her and laughed again. "On that we agree."

She yawned, then said, "I could sleep right here."

He felt the same, but knew that wouldn't last. Besides, the light, sheen of sweat covering them both would have their bodies cold in no time.

"The bed would be more comfortable," he said.

"You inside me is when I'm most comfortable," she said and yawned again.

It continued to startle him as to how much he loved his wife. He gently maneuvered her off him and up into his arms and carried her to bed, pulling the blanket over her.

"Where are you going?"

"To stoke the fire since once I join you, I'm not leaving your side again."

"You better not," Oria ordered and watched him tend the hearth, then pulled the blanket back when he got near the bed. "Hurry, I need warming."

They were soon wrapped snug around each other and sound asleep.

***

Oria made her way to the cottage Wren had chosen for her and Parlan. More hands than needed helped with the repairs. Still though, Royden and his da pitched in to help. It was what made them such fine leaders. They worked side-by-side with the clan and the people appreciated it.

A day or more and the cottage would be ready. Oria would miss having the couple at the keep. This last week, having them in the keep, had been wonderful. Oria imagined it must have been similar to when Arran and Raven had been there. She had been envious of Royden's family. It had only been her and her da since she'd been eight years. It was nice to have a larger family, which was why she hoped that Royden and she would have many bairns. The keep would always be filled with talk and laughter.

She smiled when she spotted her husband and his da working together to attach the repaired front door. He returned the smile when he saw her and not wanting to disturb him, she went and joined Wren by the side of the cottage, staring at a plot of freshly turned soil.

"I'm not sure if this size will suffice for my garden," Wren said before turning to look at Oria.

"That would depend on how much planting room you have need of," Oria said, though thought the plot sizeable.

"I had a large garden at home in the woods. It was difficult for me to leave it." Wren smiled. "But it would have been more difficult to bid Parlan farewell. He helped me dig up some seedlings to bring along and I must get them planted since they won't do well much longer in their temporary home."

"There's a small section in the kitchen garden where some herbs grow if you should require them and the area can be extended if needed," Oria offered.

"Bethany offered the same," Wren said and chuckled. "She told me she has a large patch of comfrey that she had needed more for Raven than Royden and Arran since Raven constantly got scrapes and bruises from climbing trees and doing a number of things that weren't meant for a lass."

"That's Raven all right and curious as well. If she were here now she would be asking you endless questions about the different plants you use to heal." Oria's question stirred her own curiosity. "How did you come by all this knowledge?"

"My mum was a healer. Most women in my family were healers. I learned from a young age about the plants and all they could do to heal or to kill."

"Did your mum have your other skills as well?" Oria asked and realizing the question wasn't polite of her to ask, offered an apology. "Forgive me, I shouldn't have asked."

"No. You have every right to ask. You have opened your home, accepted me as a healer and not a witch, though I think some are still skeptical of me."

"I doubt that will last," Oria said. "The clan members who have returned home with you have had nothing but high praise for your skills and once the others see the truth in those words, there'll be no more skepticism."

"I hope so, though I am glad to have Parlan. I feel safe with him. I've seen what can happen to healers when fear ravages a village. It's why my mum chose never to remain long in one clan."

"You moved around a lot then?" Oria asked.

"We did and wisely so, until my mum grew too old to keep moving. That's when we settled in the woods. It was where my mum and I knew I'd meet the man I was destined to love." Wren smiled gently. "Just as you were destined to love Royden and he you."

A huge smile lit Oria's face. "I knew it as soon as I met him. My dad teased me about it, but I was glad he also took me seriously and made sure that one day Royden would be my husband." She caught a strange look in Wren's eyes. "Is there something wrong? Does something happen to Royden?"

"No. No. All is fine. You and Royden will have many children and share a long life together. My mind drifted for a moment that's all."

Oria breathed a sigh of relief and yet she couldn't help but feel that Wren hadn't been completely truthful with her. However, something had her holding her tongue and she wondered if it was because she didn't want to know what Wren didn't want to tell her.

"Shall we get those seedlings in the ground?" Oria offered.

Excitement replaced the strange look in Wren's eyes. "You don't mind helping me?"

Oria held up her hands, wiggling her fingers. "I've loved digging in the soil since I was young. It always made me feel so good."

"The soil enjoys the touch hands bring to it and returns it in kind," Wren explained. "Now I will show you how to plant with care so that the seedlings feel safe and welcome here, accepting this spot, this soil as their new home."

Oria enjoyed the time she spent with Wren and listened and learned what Wren taught her about the plants that seemed to take well to the soil.

Wren was planting the last seedling when Royden and his da joined the two women.

"Two more days and it will be done," Parlan announced, reaching out to help Wren to her feet.

Royden's arm went around his wife. "Are you sure you and Wren don't want to remain in the keep, Da? You know how cold the winter can get around here."

"We'll be warm enough," his da said, sending Wren a wink. "Besides, you're going to need the room for all those grandchildren you're going to give me."

"Excuse me, Royden."

Royden turned to see what Angus wanted. "Something wrong?"

"Two more of our warriors entered the village, not in good shape at all," Angus said.

Wren stepped forward. "I will tend them. Take me to them."

"They're more in need of food right now. I sent them to Bethany," Angus said.

"Perfect. I'll tend them in the Great Hall," Wren said more to herself than anyone else and off she went.

"What have you yet to say, Angus?" Royden asked, seeing an unease in the man's eyes.

"It's Lunn and Evan who've returned and Lunn was quick to tell me that they spotted a troop of about twenty men headed this way and wouldn't be far behind them."

"Did either have any idea who they could be?" Royden asked, worried there wasn't enough time to prepare and even if they did, they didn't have enough men to defend against the troop.

"None at all. Lunn did say that they didn't seem to be in a hurry and while they didn't appear ready for battle, they did carry many weapons with them," Angus said.

"Alert the village and make sure everyone keeps a weapon near," Royden ordered and Angus nodded and took off.

"We'll greet them at the entrance to the village, Da," Royden said when he turned to his father.

"Aye, son. A wise choice not to let them enter the village," Parlan said.

"Wait for me in the keep, Oria," Royden said, stepping away from his wife.

"I'm coming with you," Oria said and her husband's hand went out to stop her from taking another step.

"No, you're not," he ordered firmly.

Oria pushed his hand out of the way and stepped up close to him. "You'll not be sending me to the keep like you did the last time. If anything should happen, it's by your side I'll be, and don't dare try to tell me otherwise." She poked him in the chest. "And don't think that scowl on your face will change anything."

"You've changed, Oria," his da said.

"Aye, I have and for the better. Now let's go see to our visitors," she said and stepped around her husband.

"We'll discuss this later, wife," Royden said, following after her.

"Aye, unless we're too occupied to do so," she said and heard Parlan chuckle just before her arm was grabbed and she was yanked back against her husband.

"I'll give you this, this time, wife, and you'll stay close to my side unless I *command* otherwise," he ordered with a fierceness that sent a shiver through her that he felt. "And we will definitely discuss this tonight."

"You want to make a wager on that?" Oria challenged.

Her smile softened his fierceness. "No, I don't care for the odds."

His da slapped him on the back as he walked past him. "Wise man."

Several men followed Royden, Oria, and Parlan to the entrance to the village.

"Penn!" he called and the man hurried to his side. "You'll stay close and let me know if you recognize any of the men."

"Aye, sir," Penn said and kept to his side, though back a couple of steps.

The troop was approaching at a slow pace by the time the group took position in front of the village. Royden could see that they rode fine horses and that their garments were in good shape with not a sign of repair or wear to them, and their weapons gleamed, which meant they were well tended.

The man who led the troop rode straight and tall on his horse and as he drew closer, Royden could see the confidence and courage in his posture. He was a man who wasn't afraid of battle. His light brown hair fell past his shoulders and one side was braided. He had intense dark eyes and fine features and he looked fit. He was not a man to take lightly and Royden would keep a sharp eye on him.

Before the troop came to a stop, Penn leaned in close to Royden and whispered, "That's Trevor, the Beast's right-hand man.

Chapter Twenty

The troop stopped not far from Royden, the horses pounding the ground as if annoyed they'd been brought to a halt. Had the animals fought that many battles that they assumed every village was to be pillaged?

Royden kept his eyes on the man, seeing that he could easily intimidate with his imposing posture alone. His striking features also caught the eye. One would think him born of royal blood the way he held himself and he dismounted and walked toward Royden, his commanding stride adding to the notion. His plaid was more a dark cloth with threads of a ruby color running through it, and leather straps crisscrossed his chest and circled his waist with two sheaths at each hip, and sizeable knives tucked in each.

Royden spoke before the man could. "You ride on my village as if ready to attack it."

The man stopped a few feet from Royden. "My apologies for the fright, but I was eager to meet my new neighbor. I am Trevor, the new chieftain of the Clan MacGlennen."

Oria caught her gasp before it could escape and her heart grew heavy with sadness. With this man's arrival the clan her da had led was now lost to her. It was as though in that instant her past had vanished, gone along with her da.

"How do you lay claim to the Clan MacGlennen?" Royden asked.

"That's a story better saved for when we have time to share a hardy drink or two," Trevor said. "My visit is a short one meant to make you aware of my arrival. And to let you know that I bring a sizeable group with me to the Clan

MacGlennen, warriors, craftsmen, and families. If I can be of any help to you in any way, please reach out to me. I hear you have an exceptional healer among you. Our healer fell ill and died on the journey here. I have sent for another but it will take time for her to reach us. I would be in your debt if your healer could help us if needed. My wife, Demelza, carries our first child, due in a month or more, and while she does well, I would rest easier knowing a healer is available to her if necessary."

"I'm only too pleased to help in any way I can," Wren said, coming up behind Parlan and slipping her hand in his.

"I am grateful for your generosity," Trevor said.

"I will give you a few days to settle in, then pay a visit to your wife and see to anyone else in need of tending while I'm there, with my chieftain's permission, of course," Wren said with a nod to Royden.

Royden was pleased that Wren acknowledged it was his decision whether she would go or not, though he didn't show it.

"We'll see you in a few days, Trevor," Royden said, not only letting him know Wren wouldn't be coming alone, but also dismissing him.

Trevor turned a decent smile on him, but it was the flare of anger in the man's dark eyes that alerted Royden to the truth behind the smile.

"A *braw* day to you," Trevor said.

Royden couldn't hold his tongue any longer. He wanted answers to the endless questions that haunted him. The words rushed in a demand from his lips as Trevor turned to leave. "When do I get to meet the man who leads you and the mercenaries, the man who attacked my clan and surrounding clans, and claimed land he had no right to, and who took so many men captive? I believe he's called... the Beast."

Trevor turned around slowly and Royden saw the fierce warrior in him then. The look in his dark eyes brought back memories of how men looked when going into battle, ruthless and determined.

"You'll meet him—when he's ready to meet you," Trevor said. "And be warned, my friend, the name suits him well."

Royden watched him ride off and a dread fell over him, and his da said what he thought.

"This isn't finished yet, son."

"Aye, Da, I agree," Royden said and hearing the soft whispers rush around him, others agreed as well.

"It a good time to rest and have a spot of ale," Oria suggested. "Take yourselves off to the table under the tree and I'll see a jug brought there." She gave her husband a quick kiss and hurried off.

"Oria has changed, but she is a good wife to you," Parlan said.

Royden laughed. "That she is, but don't think that she sends us to sit at the table and drink out of wifely duties. She intends to join us and discuss our meeting with Trevor."

"I never thought Oria to be strong-willed—kind and gentle—but never strong-willed," Parlan said.

"Then you never truly knew her, Parlan," Wren said. "Oria hasn't changed, she has simply found herself."

A young lad approached them slowly, looking to Royden, though his eyes kept drifting to Wren.

"What is it, Tad?" Royden asked, knowing the lad, though not recognizing him when he had first returned home. Tad had been around three years when he had left. Now at eight years he was far from the little lad he'd remembered. "Are you in need of the healer?"

Tad stepped closer to Royden, dropping his head back to look up at him, his brown hair falling back off his face as he did. "Is she a witch?"

Royden dropped down on his haunches to speak with the lad. "No, Tad. I can assure you she's not a witch. She heals people. Do you need her help?"

Tad nodded, his hair falling in his face again and held up his hand. His one finger was red and swollen.

"We need to take care of that right away," Wren said with a gentle smile, though didn't make a move toward the lad.

Tad moved closer to Royden and whispered, "You sure I can trust her?"

"My word on it," Royden said as seriously as the lad.

"Follow me to the keep," Wren said, "And when we're done I'll see if Bethany has a sweet cake for you."

Tad's smile covered his whole face. "Let's go." He took off ahead of her and she hurried along after him.

"She'll win over the whole clan eventually," Parlan said with a prideful smile.

Royden grinned. "How long did it take for her to win you over? Or was it you who needed to win her?"

His da's smile softened and a sudden sadness filled his eyes. "I was racked with fever and in so much pain when I was brought to Wren that I thought she was your mum come to take me with her. I was so happy to see her. I remember telling her how glad I was she came for me and how I'd missed her more each day since she'd died and how I never stopped loving her. Every time Wren touched me, I thought it was your mum and I welcomed her touch." He sniffled back tears. "I was so devastated when the fever broke and saw it wasn't your mum. Wren told me later that it was thinking your mum was there with me that saved my life. That I responded and listened to all she said and did whatever she asked of me. It also made me see that some of the qualities Wren possesses are the same qualities I loved about your mum."

Royden felt his da's sorrow and hated that he suffered so much without his family there to help and comfort him. He was, however, grateful that Wren had been there for him.

They just sat down at the table outside when Oria and Bethany arrived with a jug of ale, tankards enough for four, and a serving board with some meat on it that Royden and his da didn't waste any time enjoying.

Royden's arm went around his wife's waist after she sat down beside him. "This is your clan now and always."

Oria kissed his cheek, appreciating that he understood how the news of her family clan having a new chieftain had upset her. "I thought I was prepared for it. I knew it was coming, but it still hurt some."

"We're going to gather all the pieces and put this puzzle together and when we find out who was the cause of all the pain and suffering so many of us have shared, we're going to make him pay," Royden said.

"It's not a puzzle," his da said and took a swig of ale.

"What do you mean, Da?" Royden asked.

"I've realized this is a game to someone," his da explained. "He set up his pieces with precision, moved them wisely, and plays the game with exceptional skill. This is a man who calculates his every move and only makes the next move when he knows he can win."

Oria shivered and leaned against her husband, his arm at her waist hugging her close.

"Perhaps Wren can tell us something," Oria suggested. "She had seen what was coming before, perhaps she can see what comes again."

"I learned that Wren doesn't see everything and the visions are sometimes foggy when they come to her. Then there are times a vision is as clear as day like the one about the attack and its eventual outcome."

"Has she seen anything about Raven?" Royden asked.

"My first question to her when all was finally clear to me was about Raven, you, and Arran. She told me all of us would be reunited. You're home and from what you've told me Arran will be home soon—it is Raven I worry about. Wren can tell me nothing about what happened to her. And I can't help but worry how she survived all these years."

"That is all I know as well, and I didn't inquire about her from anyone in fear that in searching for her, I could bring her more harm," Oria said.

"Burnell said nothing about her to you?" Parlan asked.

"He told me the search continued for her a few times, but that stopped about two years before he died. I sometimes wondered if he was warning me in case I did find out anything, but I couldn't be sure. And I would never put Raven's life in jeopardy."

"If this is a game, then the man called the Beast would have collected all the pieces and set them up to fall as he planned and if one didn't fall as planned," —Royden shook his head— "How does he win the game?"

"Or two pieces, since Purity hasn't been found as well," Oria said.

"The thing is," his da said, refilling his tankard. "This scale of a game can't be played alone and while we've seen his many pieces, I wonder about the pieces we haven't seen."

"You're suggesting he had help from someone within one of the clans." Royden turned to his wife. "It's something Oria has given thought to herself."

"Burnell and Thurbane were the only ones who didn't attend our wedding that day," Oria reminded. "Though I've wondered if the warriors who arrived on Burnell's land had prevented him from attending. He had no strength to fight or the will. Age and illness had weakened him."

"I do recall him sending his regrets that he wouldn't be able to attend," Royden said.

"This had to have taken much planning and as I said, all the pieces moved into precise place, so that everything lined up perfectly," Parlan said.

"And how could the pieces be moved if someone wasn't inside helping maneuver them?" Royden asked.

The thought did not sit well with Oria that someone they all possibly trusted had joined forces with the enemy. "Who would be selfish enough to betray us all?"

Parlan raised his tankard. "A question when answered that could change the outcome of the game."

***

Oria rolled from her back to her side and into her husband's arms once he joined her in bed later that night. She rested her head on his shoulder and snuggled close to him.

"I didn't think I would ever say this, but I'm too tired to make love tonight," she said with a heavy sigh.

Her warm breath sent an enticing whisper along his neck, but he had known before he'd gotten into bed how tired she was. He had never seen her climb the stairs to their bedchamber as sluggishly as she had or seen her remove her garments with such painstaking slowness. She had worked hard finishing planting the seedlings for Wren, since she'd been called away to help several people. Tad had been singing her praises throughout the village, letting everyone know what a great healer Wren was. It had been enough for a few skeptics to let go of their doubt and seek her help.

After Oria had finished with that she had helped Wren clean the inside of the cottage. He'd been surprised to see her freshly washed when she sat for supper in the Great Hall and had learned she had helped the servants carry water to the tub she had them set up in Raven's old room to bathe.

Halfway through supper her eyes were closing on her, so by the time supper was finished it was obvious she was far too exhausted to make love.

"We're both tired," he said, not wanting her to feel guilty. He felt her body rumble against him with laughter.

"You say one thing but your stirring shaft says another."

"Ignore him," Royden ordered.

She yawned, her eyes beginning to close. "I fear I have no choice but to do just that."

Royden watched her slip into a peaceful slumber and feeling sleep creeping up on himself as well, fell asleep thinking how he'd stroke his wife gently and intimately awake in the morning.

***

Oria's eyes sprang open, her naked body still snuggled tight against her husband's. She didn't know what woke her or how long she had been asleep. She peeked over his broad chest at the hearth and seeing that the fire burned boldly assumed it hadn't been long. How was it then that she felt so awake?

She closed her eyes intending to return to sleep and after a while realized that sleep wasn't forthcoming. With sleep eluding her, she laid there awake and her mind soon spun with endless thoughts and worries.

If Trevor served this man called the Beast, what did that portend? Did the Beast intend to make his home here in the Highlands as well? Could he be searching for Purity to wed her and take ownership of the Clan Macara?

Restless, Oria eased herself away from her husband and out of bed. A chill greeted her when she slipped out from under the blanket and she hurried her husband's shirt over her head, it falling well past her knees. It warmed her and his scent, heavy upon it, made it feel like she was wrapped in his embrace. She went to the hearth and stood in front of it, so the heat would continue to keep her warm.

Her thoughts returned to what the future could hold for all of them if the Beast should make his way here and claim—what land? Would he search until he found Purity? Or was he the one who would lay claim to her deceased husband's title and lands? But if he was a distant relative of Burnell's, why would he have attacked this area? He would already have a title and land. And how would they protect themselves against him when they had failed to do so the last time?

Was this truly a game to play or a puzzle to solve? Perhaps a puzzle needed to be solved in order to play the game. She wished Raven was here. She was good at games and puzzles, always figuring things out before most others. But that was probably because she asked endless questions and didn't stop until she had the answers.

Her head drooped, far too heavy with endless thoughts of things that would not be solved tonight or worries that would not help solve the problem. She should sleep. Her mind would be clearer in the morning and she could tackle her heavy thoughts then.

Oria turned and saw that her husband was awake and looking at her. He threw the blanket off him and walked over to her. He didn't say a word. He slipped his shirt off her, scooped her up, and carried her back to bed.

"When I get done making love to you, I promise you'll sleep soundly," he said and buried his face in the crook of her neck to tease her sensitive skin with endless nibbles.

She ran her fingers through his hair, taking hold of the sides of his head and tugged it away from her neck so she could look into his eyes. "Promise me that we'll always love like this."

"That's an easy promise to keep, my love," he said and his mouth came down on hers in a kiss filled with a passion that wouldn't be sated swiftly.

Much later, their unrestrained passion leaving them spent and a light sweat covering their bodies, they fell into a sound slumber just as Royden had promised.

Chapter Twenty-one

"It's as though I'm seeing spring burst in full bloom for the first time in years," Oria said, riding her horse at an easy pace beside her husband. "The hills are greener, the trees fuller, the flowers more vibrant. You brought the beauty of the Highlands back to me." A smile caught at her lips as she pointed. "Look, the white wind-flowers and the blue fairy flowers are in abundance."

Royden looked where his wife pointed and took note of the dense green grass that sprouted around the flowers, then looked around at the towering trees, thick with leaves, and how the sun shined brightly touching everything with its warmth.

"Life blossoms everywhere," Oria said with glee, her hand going to rest at her stomach.

Royden's eye widened. "Are you—"

"It's too soon to tell anything." She laughed. "Though I'd say there's a good chance with as much as we couple."

"We'll keep at it to make sure," Royden said with a playful smile, though meant every word.

"That we will, husband," Oria agreed.

"Are you all right with returning home?" he asked worried that seeing her clan with a new chieftain and mistress might upset her.

"It troubles me that my clan and land rightfully belongs to you, once we wed. I also feel for my clan since they were so pleased that one day you would lead them. I feel helpless that somehow I failed them."

Royden regretted asking her, the joy that only moments ago shined across her face now gone. "You didn't fail them.

None of what happened is your fault. And I shall discuss with Trevor the release of at least some of your clan members who do not wish to stay with him."

"While I appreciate that, do you think it wise to ask such a thing?" she asked.

"Strangers have confiscated our lands and made demands of us. It is time we begin to make demands on them and defend our people."

"What if Trevor won't release them?" Oria asked worry for all concerned churning her stomach.

"Then the people will know his true nature and loyalty will not come easy for him."

"You are a wise leader," Oria said, her smile returning and her stomach settling.

"I know you will help Wren tend those in need of her skills, but you will give me your word that if you feel threatened at all, or the least bit uncomfortable, you will come to me right away," Royden said with a stern eye on his wife.

"You have lectured me on this since the invitation arrived yesterday and I have repeatedly given you my word. I will take no chance. You have no reason to worry," she assured him.

If her repeated word hadn't assuaged his worries, she didn't know what would, though she did understand his concern. All had been going well the last week. Repairs to the village had continued, another stone hut was being built to store food, the fields were almost ready, and news of several women getting with child had spread joy through the village. Like the land blossomed so did the clan. So it was only natural that Royden worried about keeping everyone protected and safe.

Oria stretched her hand out to give her husband's arm a reassuring squeeze. "No worries, husband. I will come to you posthaste if anything should upset me."

"Then my worries are eased... a little," he said, his dark eyes warning it better be so.

As soon as they entered the village, Oria was surrounded. So many crowded around her after she dismounted that Royden feared he wouldn't be able to reach her if she needed him.

"Let her be!" Trevor shouted and the people hurried away from Oria. "Mistress Oria will visit with you later."

Oria's voice was as strong as Trevor's. "It has been too long since I have seen them. I will visit with them now." Oria fought to keep calm, after spotting bruises and unhealed wounds on some and hearing Trevor order her people away from her didn't help. It angered her to the point that she wanted to lash out at the man, but she was wise enough to know that wouldn't help the situation.

"I will join Oria and offer what help I can."

Trevor's hand shot out, stopping the petite woman that went to walk past him. "You were to remain in the keep, Demelza."

"Nonsense, Trevor. The day is far too beautiful to stay in the keep and I am looking forward to talking with Oria and the healer Wren. So go take yourself off with the men and do what you will."

Royden almost laughed seeing the petite woman with blonde hair, a pretty face, and round with child speak to the mighty warrior not only without fear but also order him to take himself off.

"Demelza," Tremor said, a warning in his tone.

The petite woman went up on her toes to reach her husband's face, though he quickly bent his head down, and she kissed him on the cheek and whispered something to him. He didn't stop her when she stepped away from him and turned to Wren, who had remained by Parlan's side, a pleasant smile on her face.

"You must be the healer," Demelza said and stretched out her hand. "Come, I've arranged a cottage where you can tend those in need and where Oria can speak with her people."

Demelza walked off with Oria and Wren flanking her and those who had crowded around Oria followed them.

"Women," Trevor said, shaking his head as if the one word was explanation enough. "Come and have a drink while the women do what they will do."

"I see a lot of changes here," Royden said, looking around and seeing huts housing craftsmen and stone work being done

"I will show you what's been done after we drink and talk," Trevor said.

Royden nodded and sent one last look his wife's way to see where she was going in case he needed to find her fast.

"Your wife is safe here. No one will harm her," Trevor said, seeing where Royden's attention had been drawn.

"My wife is safe when she is with me. Is that not the same for you?" Royden challenged.

"You're right," Trevor said without hesitation. "I would kill anyone who would dare harm my wife."

"I would do the same without an ounce of regret," Royden informed him, and so it was made known between the two men that they would defend their wives with their lives.

"Let us drink, talk, and become friends," Trevor said.

"Friends? That remains to be seen," Royden said and he and his da followed Trevor to the keep.

***

Wren looked around the sizeable cottage, amazed at all the dried plants hanging from racks and the many crocks that sat on a high chest. She gently touched the stone mortar and pestle on the table in the middle of the room.

"It takes years of use to form a mortar as deep and smooth as this one," Wren said.

"It belonged to Hilda, our healer, and her mother before her and possibly her grandmother," Demelza said. "Hilda told me on the journey here that she was not long for this world but she assured me that a wise, local healer would help until another healer could be fetched."

"I will do all I can," Wren said, pleased the old healer hadn't viewed her as a witch. "Before I tend to those waiting outside. Tell me, how are you feeling?"

"I feel good. My stomach protests some mornings, but not as badly as it first did, and if I feel tired I rest."

"But your husband worries about you regardless of how much you reassure him," Wren said, having sensed the man's worry when his wife had appeared. "Why is that?"

"You sense things," Demelza said with a smile and a nod as if that knowledge comforted her. "Hilda did too."

"Did Hilda sense something that worried your husband?"

"No, my husband worries because I miscarried once. I wasn't far along, but I bled heavily and there was worry I might die. Trevor fears what could happen with this delivery."

"And when he asked Hilda about it, she was honest and told him that there is no telling what will happen with any birth."

"You are as wise as Hilda said you'd be. I am pleased you will be around to help, and I beg my husband's forgiveness now since I know there will be times he will not be as cordial as he should be."

"Most men aren't," Wren said with a laugh. "Is there anything else you'd like to tell or ask me before I begin tending the ailing?"

Demelza hesitated, then shook her head. "No, I'll leave to your task."

"Demelza," Wren said when she reached the door. "Your worry is not for the bairn and you appear well and rested. So what is it that worries you?"

She kept her voice low, almost to a whisper. "He will come here and I worry what will happen when he comes. He is a man who wins at all costs."

"He brings more trouble here?" Wren asked.

"I hope not," Demelza said and stepped outside.

Wren followed Demelza out and called out to Oria, "Send whoever you think needs to see me first."

Oria walked with Ross to the door, his arm wrapped with a cloth, the blood on it dried. "I tried to tell him, Oria, I'm a farmer not a warrior. I could grow him good crops and lift a sword if necessary, but I'm no warrior. Please, I beg you take me and Aine and our two sons home with you. Please, I fear what will happen if we remain here. You should talk with Old Henry. He wants to leave here too."

That Ross begged her for help tore at her heart and that Old Henry wanted to leave worried her as well. If she remembered correctly, he was the oldest person in the clan. That he wanted to leave the only home he had ever know was unthinkable. She was tired of feeling helpless, tired of watching good people suffer—her people suffer.

"Get your things together when you're done here and be ready to leave with us," she ordered.

"He won't let you take them," Demelza said after Ross entered the cottage.

"Your husband stole this clan. These people rightfully come under my husband's rule. If your husband has an ounce of honor in him, he'll let those go who wish to leave with us," Oria said, it was growing more difficult to hold her anger. She had listened to complaint after complaint about how every man had to spend so much time on the practice field learning to be a warrior, learning to battle.

"My husband is a good man with good intentions—"

"Intentions of what? Battle? Are these forced lessons in preparation of something to come? Will you attack and take our lands from us once again?" Oria accused.

"It is what my husband knows—"

"Then he needs to learn it is different here," Oria snapped.

Demelza paled and placed her hand on her stomach.

Oria went to her and hurried her to the bench that sat against the cottage. "Stay here, I'll get Wren."

"No, please, I'm all right. The nausea comes and goes. It has already past."

Color began to return to her face so Oria did as Demelza requested, but guilt had her offering an apology. "Forgive me, I should not have spoken to you like that."

"I can't believe you have been as pleasant as you have, coming here to the clan that had once been yours, seeing the people who appear to truly care for you unhappy. I have tried to come to know them, make friends with them, but I believe they fear my husband too much to even acknowledge me at times."

"Were you forced to wed Trevor? You seem far too kind to have wed such a man of your own accord," Oria said and gasped at her audacity to say such a thing. She was sounding like Raven, who often failed to temper her words. She was shocked when Demelza laughed.

"Everyone wonders the same," Demelza said. "But I saw and continue to see the good in my husband. Given a chance, I think the people here would see that as well."

Oria saw herself in Demelza. She would defend Royden no matter what, but then all knew Royden was a good man, grumpy and commanding as he may be at times, he was still a good man. And Demelza believed the same of her husband.

"I suppose that is a possibility, but how long will that take and how many will suffer?" Oria asked worried for her clan.

Demelza sighed. "I don't know. Trevor can be stubborn until he realizes what I offer him is actually sage advice."

Oria had a thought. "Perhaps he needs to hear it from me."

"I don't know if that would be wise," Demelza advised.

"Wise or not, I can't let those I care for suffer," Oria said and offered her arm to Demelza. "Will you come with me?"

Demelza smiled. "I wouldn't let you go alone and I wouldn't want to miss what you have to say to my husband."

They passed Parlan on his way to see how Wren was doing and he told them that Trevor was showing Royden the practice field. Both women hurried along after hearing that, each not saying a word, but both thinking the same thing.

***

"What are you doing?" Oria shouted when she and Demelza caught sight of their husbands' wooden practice swords in hand and both about to enter the practice arena.

"A friendly joust," Trevor said.

Planting her hands on her hips and with a terse tone, Oria said, "I don't think so." She was quick to cut Trevor off before he could remark. "There are more important things to see to than a game best left to young lads." Her hand went up to stop Trevor again. "The most important thing being that whoever in my clan wishes to come home with me will be leaving here with us."

Trevor's eyes narrowed and a scowl spread across his face.

"My people. My clan. My family," Oria said, pounding her chest as she spoke. "I will not leave them here to be treated poorly by you. You cannot force a farmer to be a warrior or a craftsman to neglect his skill. You have no idea how to be a clan chieftain."

"You dare insult me in my own home?" Trevor asked and took a step toward Oria.

Royden stepped in front of his wife. "Remember what we said about our wives."

Trevor took a step back.

"Why don't we settle this in the practice arena," Royden suggested. "I win and you let those go who wish to leave with us. I lose and none leave with us."

"I won't let all of them leave," Trevor said. "If you win, you may take ten, no more."

"Not counting their children," Royden said.

Trevor nodded. "Not counting the children."

"Let's see this done then," Royden said and turned to his wife. "I may not be able to see all of your clan released now, but it's a start."

"You be careful, husband. I don't want my foolish anger bringing you harm," Oria said, worried she had not considered the consequences before letting a sharp tongue loose.

"Worry not, wife. You gave me the perfect excuse to see this done." He kissed her cheek and entered the practice arena.

Oria turned, hearing Demelza raise her voice. "I will not go to the keep. I will stay here and watch."

"I gave you an order, wife," Trevor said sharply.

"That I refuse to obey," Demelza said and walked away from him to slip her arm around Oria's. "Let's watch our husbands act like foolish young lads."

"Let's go, Trevor, unless you wish to surrender," Royden called out with a laugh.

Trevor sent his wife a scowl as he walked past her and snapped, "Later."

"He will not hurt you, will he?" Oria asked.

"Never," Demelza said. "Never has he or would he raise a hand to me. As I said, he's a good man."

Royden and Trevor positioned themselves in the center of the field and as the wooden swords clashed, it drew people to watch the two mighty warriors fight.

Oria had watched her husband when he practiced at home and she'd been amazed then how skillfully he handled a sword. Seeing him now fight against a real opponent, she was amazed even more of how talented he'd become and with only one hand.

It was Trevor who stepped back a moment. "You learned well to fight with one hand."

"I had no choice and when choice is gone, so goes loyalty," Royden said.

"You think to teach me a lesson?" Trevor laughed.

"One can try and teach, but learning is up to the pupil." Royden raised his sword, ready to resume the fight.

The wooden swords slammed against each other and people watched in awe, more gathering as news spread of what was at stake.

The ending came so swiftly that a silence fell over the area as if everyone could not quite believe it had ended with such a quick thrust. It stunned everyone and gave thought that the winner had been teasing the loser all along and brought the fight to an end in his own good time.

A cheer suddenly rang out. "Royden!"

Trevor stared at Royden, his sword gone from his hand and the tip of Royden's sword pressed to his chest.

"You can thank your leader for your defeat today. He made me who I am now," Royden said for their ears alone. He lowered his sword. "I'll see those people gathered now who return home with us."

"I will have a cart made ready for their possessions and if any can't walk the distance," Trevor said. "But I also expect a rematch one day."

"Gladly," Royden said. "I will enjoy besting you again."

Demelza hurried to her husband, his arm going around her to draw her close. "You are all right?"

"My pride is a bit scarred, but it will heal," Trevor said. "This did not upset you?"

"I am not fragile, Trevor."

"I know, but you are with child and—"

"I am fine. Stop worrying. Wren says she will be here if or when needed. Now let's help those who wish to leave and see about making sure we don't lose anymore," Demelza said in a whisper.

Oria hugged her husband and couldn't help but hear what Demelza had said. She hadn't thought she would like Trevor's wife since she didn't care for Trevor, but to her surprise she liked Demelza and thought she just might be good for the clan if given a chance.

"You did well, husband," Oria said, giving him a quick kiss.

"Do I get a prize for my victory?" he asked with a playful smile.

"Aye, you do," she said and leaned up to whisper in his ear.

"Damn, Oria, you can't say that to me here," he scolded.

She grinned. "I just did and you better walk close behind me since he's rising to the occasion."

"Damn," Royden mumbled and kept his wife close in front of him as they walked away, not so wise to do since the sway of her hips didn't help the image any she had put in his head.

It was difficult choosing those that would return with Oria and Royden. Most wanted to go, but it was decided that those most in need would be chosen. Ross and his wife and two sons were first since Oria had given her word. Oria insisted they all work together to decide and she told them she would work to get more of them released. She also spoke kindly of Demelza and urged those staying to give her a chance. Old Henry made the choice to stay this time so that others, more in need, could be chosen. Oria promised him he'd be in the next group to go.

It wasn't long before all were ready. Wren had seen to everyone and had shared a brew and some food with Demelza while she waited and now with it all done, it was time to leave.

Royden was speaking with Trevor. Wren was saying a last few words to Demelza. Parlan was talking with Ross, having remembered him when he was just a lad. Oria stood watching it all, happy she could bring some of her clan home with her, though sad for the ones she had to leave behind.

She heard a woman say, "He's an evil one."

Wondering who the woman meant, she turned and all color drained from her face. There, a short distance away from her, stood Firth, the man who had taken a dagger to her face.

Chapter Twenty-two

Royden went to his wife, seeing her pale and worried she might faint. His arm went around her and when she pressed herself tightly against him, he knew something was wrong.

"What is it, Oria?" he asked softly.

She heard her husband, but she was too lost in the memories of that moment. She could almost feel the dagger slice across her jaw and the blood pour down her neck. The pain and helplessness also returned to assault her. But her husband's arm tight around her reminded her that she was no longer helpless and no longer alone.

She raised her head and abruptly held her tongue, thinking of the possible consequences of telling her husband.

Royden saw the uncertainty and worry in her eyes. "Tell me, Oria."

"You'll hold your temper?" she asked worried what could happen if he didn't.

For his wife to ask that of him meant she knew how he'd respond and was concerned what could happen. Anger began to rumble deep inside him. "Tell me *now*."

There was no keeping it from him. "He's the one who gave me the scar." Her eyes went to Firth.

"Is something wrong?" Trevor asked, approaching them.

"I have a score to settle with that man," Royden said, pointing to Firth, a brawny man with dark hair and eyes.

"What score is that?" Trevor asked.

Firth stepped forward. "I gave his wife that lovely scar she carries during the attack on Clan MacKinnon and she was well deserving of it."

Oria was surprised when her husband didn't lurch for the man, but she did feel his body tense.

"So you admit you're a coward," Royden said loud enough for all to hear.

"I'm no coward," Firth spat.

"Only a coward uses his weapon on a helpless woman," Royden argued.

"She was far from helpless," Firth said with a huff.

"She had a weapon?" Royden asked.

"No, but she fought like a wild banshee. Three of us couldn't control her."

Royden fisted his hand. "Three men and one woman who possessed no weapon and you don't think yourself a coward?"

"She bit me," Firth yelled. "Left me with a scar she did. He pulled back his shirt sleeve to prove it.

"So she uses her teeth to fight you and you slash her with a knife." Royden glared at him. "Sounds like you're a coward to me."

Oria realized what her husband was doing. He was goading Firth into attacking him, giving him reason to fight the man.

Firth went to step forward, but Trevor's sharp command stopped him.

"Enough! I will see to this matter."

"And what will you do?" Royden demanded.

"That is my decision and one I will not explain," Trevor cautioned. "Be satisfied with your small victory today, Royden, and take your leave."

Oria feared her husband would ignore Trevor's warning and then what? Her stomach roiled at the thought of what could happen to him here among their enemy. She was surprised and relieved when Royden responded calmly.

"Another time then."

"Another time," Trevor said, though the look in his eyes was enough to know that time would never come.

"Let's go, wife," Royden said and eased her away from him.

Oria should have known her husband would not be put off from retaliating, but it still came as a shock to how fast he moved. His dagger was out of its sheath and he slashed Firth across his face before anyone knew what was happening.

Firth roared out and stumbled, blood pouring from the cut that ran below the corner of his right eye down to his chin just missing the corner of his mouth. His hand flew to his cheek cupping it, the blood flowing around his hand and along his neck.

"If I ever see your face again, I'll kill you," Royden threatened and turned to Trevor as he slipped the dagger back into the sheath. "You would have done the same or worse if it had been your wife. But then your wife didn't suffer through a battle. Now we'll take our leave."

Wren looked ready to step forward and help the man when Royden turned around.

"Don't!" Royden commanded, taking hold of Oria's arm and sending a scowl at Wren that had Parlan taking her arm and directing her to the horses.

Oria was glad her husband had hold of her arm, her limbs having gone weak, so shaken was she from what happened. She thought to protest when he lifted her in his arms and placed her on his horse, ordering one of the warriors who had accompanied them to take charge of her horse, but thought better of it. In his arms was exactly where she needed to be.

Royden held her close as they rode off and wondered if she even realized her whole body trembled. "He won't hurt you ever again."

Oria understood all too clearly. Her husband intended to see Firth dead. She thought to argue with him but realized it would do little good. She'd wait and talk with him when the time was right.

She did, however, voice another worry. "Won't Trevor retaliate?"

"Firth isn't worth a battle. Besides, from what I could tell of our visit, Trevor is here to establish a home for himself, or he never would have brought his wife along. He's also here to try to build a modicum of peace with the locals and not cause any unrest."

"In preparation of his arrival," Oria said.

Royden nodded. "The man responsible for all that has happened."

"Demelza told Wren she expects him and she worries what will happen when he comes. She says he wins at all costs. He's already taken so much. What more is there for him to take?"

"That's what we need to find out," Royden said.

***

Royden left his bedchamber before Oria woke the next morning and went to the practice field. Anger had stirred him awake and the more he had laid there, the fouler his mood had turned. He didn't want his wife waking to that nor did he want it to follow him throughout the day.

He practiced against an imaginary opponent. It was easy. All he had to do was recall in his mind the many battles he'd been in and the many opponents he had fought. He could hear the clang of the swords, the screams of the fallen, smell the blood, the sweat, the fear.

He stopped as if emerging from a nightmare, glad he had taken his shirt off, his chest damp with sweat and heaving from the strenuous practice. He'd been a fool to think raising a sword would calm him. It only angered him more like it had done after every battle he had fought. He was a Highlander and battle was part of survival, but not a constant as it had been the five years he'd been away.

A quick movement caught his eye and he looked to the section of woods that bordered the practice area on one side. The movement came again and with his sword clamped firmly in his hand, Royden went to see who was spying on him.

"Don't come any closer."

Royden stopped, recognizing the leper's raspy voice and catching sight of his outline that almost blended in with the tree he looked as if he clutched.

"What are you doing back here?" Royden asked.

"I have messages that need to be delivered."

"For who?" Royden asked.

"Other monasteries."

"Then you best be on your way," Royden said and turned.

"You fight well with only one hand."

Royden turned around. "You watched?"

"It is not every day one sees a warrior with one hand swing a sword with such skill. It was good to see that the loss of a hand doesn't condemn a warrior."

Unlike the leper who was condemned no matter what he did. Royden couldn't imagine how lonely life was for the man. No one would go near him. He would never feel a comforting touch or a hardy hug, or even share a meal with friends. He'd always be removed from others—alone.

"I did what I had to do to survive, just as you do," Royden said.

"Aye, and both lives were forced upon us by evil hands," the leper said.

His accusation had Royden thinking. "Fate would be the evil hand that touched you, and I have yet to discover the evil hand who touched me. In your travels, perhaps you heard of the man responsible for the attack on my home."

"I've heard some about him," the leper said and offered freely what he knew. "He's a Northman, a Viking, a brutal beast. I suppose that's why many refer to him as the Beast. I heard someone say his name was Wolf, but I don't know if that was in jest."

Royden thought out loud. "What would a Viking want in these parts? They've settled farther north. They no longer come to this region."

"King David would disagree with you on that. His appointment of a Scot to be first Bishop of Caithness did not sit well with King Eystein of Norway. King David is foolish to think that King Eystein will sit idly by and do nothing while King David tries to regain the area for Scotland."

"With the King so busy defending land that far north, no wonder he has little care of what happens in this area," Royden said.

"More land more power," the leper said.

"True enough," Royden agreed. "And the reason so many battle. What else do you know about this Northman?"

"Heard he's a fierce warrior and demands that his warriors be the same. He also hates defeat."

"He wins at all cost," Royden said, recalling what his wife had told him.

"Defeat comes to everyone, one time or another," the leper said, his throat growing raspier.

"Do you need a drink?" Royden asked, concerned for the condemned man. While he would spend the day with family and friends, the leper would go off alone… always alone.

"A gentle brew if you please. Ale hurts my throat or what's left of it."

Royden almost shuddered. He may have lost a hand but the leper's body was being eaten away at each day.

"Wait here. I'll get you a brew to take with you." Royden went to the kitchen and in no time Bethany had one of the hide skeins filled with an herbal brew Wren had asked her to keep ready when someone was in need of soothing. She also wrapped food in a cloth and Royden returned with both to the leper.

"Place it on the ground just inside the edge of the woods," the leper said.

Royden saw his hooded head peeking out from behind a tree and did as asked, then stepped a good distance away.

"Again I thank you for your generosity," the leper said.

"As my wife offered and I agree, food and drink will be provided for you whenever you pass this way and if you should hear any more about this Northman—"

"I will tell you all I learn about him," the leper said.

"Take care, my friend," Royden said.

"You are a good man, Royden, and you have a good wife. May the Lord always bless you both."

Did he hear the leper sniffle back tears? Royden's heart went out to the poor man and recalling his name said, "Safe journey to you, Brother Noble."

Royden walked away. It wasn't until he got to the far side of the practice field that he glanced back. The food and drink were gone and so was Brother Noble.

He went to the rain barrel and washed the sweat from his chest and face before slipping his shirt back on. The village was just beginning to stir to life when he entered the keep. He hoped to find his wife still abed. He had a need for her that couldn't wait. It was a deep need born of a love that had stirred, grown, and strengthened through the years, and would continue to grow ever stronger. He wanted to wrap himself around her, plant himself deep inside her, and join with her in that love.

His quick pace had him up the stairs in no time and he lifted the latch on the door as quietly as he could so as not to wake her—yet.

"Where did you go off to?" Oria demanded when he stepped in the room.

Royden had to smile. His wife stood by the fireplace, stark naked, her shift dangling from her hand, her blonde hair in wild disarray around her head and shoulders, and her green eyes sparked with a touch of anger.

Oria dropped her shift and reprimanded him as she approached. "Never do we leave our bed in the morning without waking the other. *Never. Ever. Never!*" she emphasized, shaking her finger at him. "What are you smiling at? This is not humorous."

"You. You're beautiful and I love you with all my heart," he said and his hand hurried to the back of her neck to take hold as his lips came down on hers.

His kiss not only stirred her passion, but his words touched her heart, and she was swept up by the kiss that easily sent her desire soaring. Though, when the kiss ended she jabbed him in the chest.

"Don't ever do that again—leave our bed without waking me—not the kiss. I love when you kiss me," she said and rubbed his hard chest where she'd jabbed him.

He laughed. "You didn't hurt me."

"You hurt me by not waking me the usual way you do," she said. "I sprang out of bed when I realized you weren't here, fearful something terrible had happened that took you away."

"I didn't mean to worry you," Royden said, his arm going around her and his hand, stroking delicately down along her cheek.

Oria shivered at his faint touch. "Well you did and I'll have your promise now that you'll never do it again."

"You have my word, wife," he said.

"Good," she said and stepped out of his embrace and took his hand in hers, tugging at him as she walked toward the bed. "Now you will see to your husbandly duties that you failed to see to this morning."

"Will I now?" he teased with a laugh.

"Aye, you will," she commanded and when he laughed again, she gave him a shove that sent him tumbling down on the bed, which made him laugh even more. She crossed her arms over her chest. "We'll see how much you laugh when I refuse to couple with you."

Royden sprung up just enough to grab her arm and yank her down on top of him.

Oria tried to squirm free, but he held her too tight and besides, all her squirming was growing him hard against her.

"Still you grin at me," she said, annoyed.

"Because we both know that you'll never refuse to couple with me. I'm too irresistible to deny."

Oria laughed, she couldn't help it.

"And you're too kind to make your poor husband suffer like that," Royden said.

"He wouldn't be the only one suffering," Oria admitted. "I love the feel of you inside me."

"I love being inside you." His hand drifted down to cup her bottom and give it a squeeze.

"Then what are you waiting for?" she asked.

Royden rolled to his side, slipping Oria onto her back. His hand went to her breast to tease her nipple with his fingers as his lips touched hers playfully at first, but not for long since her response was more demanding.

His hand slipped down along her slowly, enjoying the feel of her soft skin before his fingers disappeared between her legs.

He pulled away from their kiss. "You're more than ready for me."

"I've been ready for you since I woke this morning, so do not keep me waiting or this will be done before you enter me," she warned. "Now get those garments off. I want to feel you naked against me."

He was all too willing to oblige her, moving off her to shed his garments when a knock sounded at the door.

"No. No. No," Oria cried.

"An important message," a servant called out.

"Go away," Oria commanded.

"It's from Arran," the servant said and footfalls could be heard rushing away.

"Go!" she ordered frustrated, his brother's message more important than coupling.

"No, wife, I'll not leave you like this." He spread her legs and dropped down over her, his shaft falling perfectly at her entrance. He plunged into her, knowing it wouldn't take long for either of them to climax, though he was determined to see to a lengthier and uninterrupted coupling later.

Oria grabbed onto her husband's arms, his quick thrusts bringing her rapidly to the edge of an explosive climax. She wished she didn't have to let go. She wished she could linger a bit longer.

Later, she promised herself. Later they would linger.

Oria let go, digging her fingers into her husband's muscled arms and releasing a shout she was certain the whole keep heard.

Royden joined her, though he let loose a quieter groan as he emptied himself into her.

Normally, they would have lingered, but any news from Arran was important, so they both were up not long afterwards. Oria rushed to dress and raked her fingers through her hair as they hurried out the door.

"Your da should hear this," Oria said as they entered the Great Hall.

"I sent for him," Bethany said, standing beside a table where a man, slim and of good height, though dirt covered and weary-worn, sat shoveling food into his mouth.

"You have a message from my brother Arran?' Royden asked.

The man nodded, his mouth stuffed with food.

His da and Wren rushed into the Great Hall, both appearing a bit disheveled and he wondered if their coupling had been interrupted as well. He shook the thought away, not wanting to think about it.

"What's the message? Has Arran found Raven?" his da asked anxiously.

Royden wondered the same. All the inquires he had sent out about his sister came back with no news of her. They at least knew she was alive, but where had she gone? Where was she hiding?

"What word do you have from my brother?" Royden demanded.

The man took a swig of ale and wiped his mouth on his sleeve, then slowly looked to each one.

"If the news is painful, then deliver it and be done with it," Royden ordered.

The man was quick to oblige. "Arran can't be sure, that's why he'll be later returning home than he had planned. He's making more inquires."

Royden shot him a scowl.

The man hurried to say, "Arran heard that Raven is dead."

Chapter Twenty-three

Royden asked the man endless questions, most of which he couldn't answer.

"I wish I could tell you more, but that's all I was told," the man said. "Your brother is cautious when discussing your sister and I don't blame him. If the Beast is after her, he'll find her, unless he already has."

The pain on his da's face tore at Royden's gut. He, his da, and Arran had sworn to keep Raven safe and they had failed and continued to fail. And what had he done to find his sister? Sent out inquires? He should be searching for her just as Arran was doing.

"Arran says I'm to wait here for him," the man said.

"Of course you will. You must be a friend of Arran's or he wouldn't have entrusted the message to you. You are most welcome here," Oria said.

"I am grateful and the name is Halvor. I fought alongside Arran for the last two years."

"Bethany," Royden said and the woman stepped forward sniffling back tears, the news of Raven upsetting her. "Take Halvor to Angus and tell him to see Halvor settled."

"Aye, sir," Bethany said and waved at the man to follow her.

Wren slipped her arm around Parlan and ushered him to the table to sit and pour him a tankard of ale. When she placed it in Parlan's hand, she said, "Raven isn't dead."

Oria took her husband's hand and they joined the couple at the table.

Parlan turned pleading eyes on Wren. "Are you sure about this?"

Wren closed her eyes for a moment and all remained silent. She opened them slowly almost reluctantly. "Aye, Raven is alive."

"Where is she? What's happened to her? Why didn't you tell me?" Parlan asked anxiously and with a touch of annoyance.

Wren took Parlan's hand in hers. "I can't see beyond that she's alive. I can't tell you if she's well or ill or suffering. I only know that she isn't dead and my vision five years ago of you all reuniting tells me she will return home."

"You don't know when or if she—" Parlan shook his head, thoughts of what may have happened to his daughter causing him unbearable pain.

Wren held tight to Parlan's hand. "I wish I could see more, I truly do. That I can't worries me for it sometimes means the future has yet to be decided."

"But you saw us all reunited," Royden reminded.

"Aye," I did," Wren said with a nod. "But I can't see anything beyond that for Raven and that troubles me."

"But that might be good," Oria said. "It means once she arrives home we can help see to a good future for her. No matter how she returns to us we are all here to love and help her any way we can."

"That is true," Wren agreed.

"So the most important thing is to get Raven home," Parlan said. "Hopefully, Arran will see to that."

Royden was glad his da didn't look at Wren when he said that or he would have seen the flash of sadness that he had caught in the woman's eyes. She knew Raven wouldn't be returning with Arran and Royden wondered what more could be done to help find his sister.

***

Later that day rain moved in and everyone took shelter inside. Royden searched for his wife once he entered the keep and no one could tell him where she was. He hadn't found her in their bedchamber like he had hoped he would or in his old bedchamber. He was a bit surprised to find her in Arran's bedchamber.

The bedding lay on the floor in the corner and she was busy wiping dust off most everything while a small fire burned in the hearth. He stood in the open doorway and watched her. She was so intent on her task that she didn't know he was there. She worked with enthusiasm, a smile on her face, sneezing when a plume of dust rose around her.

She jumped when she turned and saw him. "You sneak around as quietly as your sister did."

Royden shook his head. "No one surpasses my sister when it comes to sneaking around."

Oria laughed. "Raven was good at hiding where no one would find her." Her smile remained after her laughter faded. "That skill no doubt serves her well now."

"I pray it is so, but what are you doing in Arran's bedchamber," Royden asked, stepping into the room.

"Seeing that it is clean and fresh for your brother's return home," she said, looking around the room at the work already accomplished.

"Someone else could see to that," Royden said.

"True, but I am his sister now—family—and I will see it done as I will with Raven's room as well."

Royden went to her and brushed a piece of dust out of her hair. "Arran and Raven will be grateful."

Oria's smile vanished. "I should have tried to find out more about what happened to Raven and where she was. I might have been able to help her."

Royden gave her arm a tender squeeze. "You did the right thing. There was no telling who was watching you.

You might have been tortured for the information and Raven would have been found. You both would have suffered. You made the right choice."

"It was so difficult, knowing she was out there somewhere, possibly in dire need, and doing nothing to help her."

"You did do something. You protected her the only way you could and by doing so you saved the Clan MacKinnon as well." Royden took her in his arms. "You did right by Raven, by us all. Don't ever question that you didn't."

"Did you ever question your decisions?" she asked, wondering if he too punished himself with doubt and what ifs.

"I did. I fear I wallowed in it for a while until the anger pushed aside everything. The anger drove me, sustained me, helped me to see what mistakes I would never make again," he admitted.

"You didn't make any mistakes," she admonished. "You fought like a true warrior."

"The mistakes came before the attack."

"Tell me," she urged, eager to know, eager to help him heal from all he had suffered.

"Not here," Royden said and took her hand.

He led her to his old bedchamber and sat on the bed, bracing himself against the wood headboard, then reached out and took her hand, tugging her down to sit across his lap. He had often dreamt about a day such as this, where they sat in his bed and talked and eventually made love. An unexpected joy filled him that part of his dream had finally come true and he planned on making sure the latter part came true as well.

"Tell me," she urged again, cuddling against him, the pleasant scent of fresh rain on him rushing up to tingle her nose.

He had avoided talking to her about anything to do with the horror of that day. Now, however, comfortable with her safe in his arms, he found he wanted to discuss some of it with her. "One thing that troubled me about the attack was how the warriors got past the sentinels we'd posted. My da had doubled the sentries. Some of them surely would have lost their lives, but some should have been able to alert us to the approaching troop long before they arrived at the keep."

Oria's brow wrinkled. "You're right. How could they have gotten past so many of them?"

"The only answer that seems feasible is that someone knew where every single sentry had been posted."

"Who would know that?"

"A number of people, the sentries themselves included," Royden said.

"Do you think one of your own betrayed the clan?" Oria asked astonished. "Have you discussed this with your da?"

"Betrayal seems likely and, aye, my da and I have talked about it. It's not something we want to believe, but it's something we can't ignore. It is also something I will never let happen again."

"How will you prevent it?" she asked, relieved to know he'd taken precautions and curious as to what they were.

"I change the sentries' positions throughout the day and night. They never remain in the same area. I've assigned the task to Angus and John. They go and move the sentries around so even the warriors themselves don't know where they'll be posted or for how long."

"That's brilliant," Oria said. "I feel safer already."

"It wasn't my idea. I learned it from Platt, the man whose command I served under and who led the attack here that day. I hate the man, but he has a brilliant mind for strategy. He had men infiltrate areas and garner information long before we attacked."

"You think that could have happened to the Clan MacKinnon? You think someone might have been planted here long before the attack?" she asked, a slight shiver racing through her, thinking how easily she had trusted everyone in the clan.

"If not, the answer points back to a friend who betrayed us all," Royden said, the thought of it sparking his anger.

"It troubles me to think that someone we trusted, we called a friend, could betray us," she said.

"And it leaves you wondering who around us can truly be trusted," Royden said.

Oria rested her head on his shoulder. "I'm so glad we can trust each other."

"Didn't you trust Burnell?" It still rankled him and probably always would that she had been married to another man before him even though their marriage hadn't been truly sealed, a relief to him. But odd as it was he was also grateful she'd been wed to Burnell. That marriage had kept her safe.

"There are only two people I can say who I trust without an ounce of doubt. You and my da."

"What about my da, Arran, Raven?" he asked, curious that she didn't count them among her most trusted.

"I trust them as well, but it's a deeper, different type of trust I feel with you and felt with my da. The kind I never questioned, never doubted. A trust that would never fail me, knowing both of you love me unconditionally and would always be there for me," she said, feeling that deep security now there with him.

He tried to tame the anger, aimed at himself, that bubbled up inside him. "But I did fail you."

Oria sat up with a sudden jolt and a startled glare. "I don't know how many times I must tell you this. You did not fail me."

"I told you I would keep you safe and I didn't," he argued. "You carry that scar because of me. You were forced to wed another because of me. I failed you, Oria, and I sometimes wonder how you can love me."

"You doubt my love for you?" she asked, shock sending deep wrinkles running across her raised brow.

"No. That's just it. I'm amazed that you still love me after all you have suffered because of me," he said. "I always knew you had a kind heart, but I didn't know you had such a forgiving one."

"There's nothing to forgive, Royden. You didn't fail me and not once did I ever think you did. You did what you were supposed to do that day, fight to protect me, your sister, your clan. And I've often wondered if I had made it into the keep with the other women would I have jeopardized their lives just by being there, since those men purposely came looking for me." She rested her hand against his chest. "It's useless to rehash what might have been if either of us had done something different. The one thing that never changed, that remained constant through it all, was our love for each other. Never did I question my love for you and never did I doubt your love for me. I always knew you'd come back to me no matter how long it took. And I intended to be here waiting for you."

"A married woman," he reminded.

"Burnell told me when we wed, and I could see it for myself, that he was ill and didn't have much time left. When he lay dying he told me to stay strong that you'd return to me." She turned a tender smile on her husband as she poked him in the chest. "You're mine. You always have been and I'm keeping you."

He barely broke a smile, but passion rushed to his dark eyes. "Are you sure you don't want to toss me back?"

"Never," she said softly. "Though you said something to me once, a promise of sorts, and you haven't kept it."

His brow narrowed as he tried to recall. "Tell me and I'll rectify it."

"You told me that it was in this bed we'd make bairns together."

He smiled, remembering that day. "Then it's time I kept my word."

Oria was off the bed in a flash and had her garments off just as fast.

Royden swung his legs off the bed and rested his one hand and the stump of the other to either side of her waist, then kissed just above her navel.

"You never deny me, wife," he said, looking up at her.

She rested her hands on his wide, thick shoulders. "Why would I? I love you and I enjoy making love with you."

He pressed his cheek to her flat stomach, then kissed the soft flesh again, loving her female scent that drifted up to tempt him. He looked up at her. "I'm going to plant my seed deep inside you and we're going to make a bairn, wife, and in the months to come I'm going to enjoy every moment of watching you round with our child."

His arm went around her waist while his hand remained at her side as he pulled her down on the bed. He stood and was out of his garments as fast as she had shed hers.

He laid down on his side next to her and he ran one finger gently over her face, like the delicate touch of a feather. When his finger traced across her lips, she tried to capture it in her mouth, but he was too quick. His finger remained faint on her naked skin, moving down along her slender neck, across her shoulders, over her firm breasts, teasing her nipple with the pad of his thumb until it was hard, solid like a pebble, and aching for his tongue. His finger moved to her right arm, tracing along it, barely skimming her skin and when he reached her hand his finger traced delicate circles around her palm, and she moaned from the sheer pleasure it ran through her.

"Royden," she said on a whispery breath.

"I'm going to touch all of you," he said and lowered his mouth to suckle hard at her nipple.

Oria groaned with the tantalizing sensation that rushed a wetness to settle between her legs.

He kept his word, faintly touching every inch of her and when his finger finally grazed that most intimate spot she nearly bolted off the bed.

"I'm not going to last long with you torturing me like this," she warned.

"Then I'll make you come again," he said the play of his fingers intending to do just that.

"You promised me we'd make a bairn. I need you inside me for that," she reminded and reached down to touch his shaft and guide him where she needed him to be. He grabbed her hand and she smiled. "You're just as ready as I am."

He brushed a light kiss across her lips. "Aye, but this time I want us to linger until—"

"We both go insane—"

"With pleasure," he finished and his mouth went to one of her nipples.

How could making love be so tortuously blissful? Oria didn't know and didn't care. She simply allowed herself to get lost in every exquisite touch, in how his lips and teeth rose sensations along her flesh and deep inside her that were foreign yet so welcoming. She ached for him to be inside her, yet she didn't want him to stop touching her, kissing her, loving her.

She gasped when he turned her over and proceeded to touch her and kiss every bit of her quivering flesh. When he nipped at her bottom, a surge of desire shot through her so strong she thought she'd burst in climax.

Oria dug her hands into the bedding and buried her face in the mattress, fearful her passionate scream would echo throughout the keep when his fingers found their way inside her to tease and torment.

She barely had a rationale thought in her head and as for a breath? She didn't think she had a breath left, passion strangling her senseless.

It was too much. She was going to burst any moment and she was too breathless to warn him.

Suddenly, she was on her back and ever so grateful when he shoved her legs apart and entered her with a hard thrust that had her crying out and gripping his arms. He rammed into her hard and fast and she met his every thrust with her own. He couldn't go deep enough for her and she arched high and hard, hearing their flesh slap wildly against each other.

His rumbling groan grew and she knew he was near. She was already there, another thrust, just one more and...

Oria screamed, pleasure consuming her like a fit of divine madness that tossed her about and consumed her over and over and over again.

Royden thought for certain he stood on the precipice of death, endless, blissful pleasure devouring every inch of him as he emptied into her. He dropped his head back and groaned as her muscles tightened around his shaft, as if squeezing every last drop of his seed out of him.

He dropped forward over her and went to roll off her, but she wrapped her arms around him, not that they fit all the way around, or that she was strong enough to hold him there, but then he was too spent to stop her. And truth be told he didn't want to pull out of her yet, or move off her.

Her hips wiggled slightly beneath him and he raised his head and the look on her face told him that she needed to climax again. He'd realized, quite happily, that she rarely had one climax. Sometimes it was a brief second one and other times it was as strong as the first.

He didn't hesitate. He might not be as hard as he'd been but he was lucky enough to have a sizeable shaft and a few thrusts had her sighing with pleasurable relief.

When her sigh drifted off completely, he rolled off her, bringing her to rest against him.

They laid there, their flesh damp with sweat, and their bodies quenched with pleasure. It wasn't until Oria shivered that Royden hurried to retrieve the mangled blanket at the end of the bed and spread it over the both of them.

Oria cuddled against him, placing her head on his shoulder and looking up at him. "This may not be the time to ask, but after the exquisite way we made love, I have to know how you learned all the wonderful things you do to me. Did a woman teach you such skill?"

He ran his thumb over her lips, plump from kissing. "I never touched another woman like that. It was meant for you and you alone. I would dream about the different ways I wanted to make love to you. That was one of them." He smiled. "And believe me when I say it far surpassed my expectations."

Oria smiled softly. "Mine too."

"Those women meant nothing to me, Oria," he said, needing her to understand. "It was a need born of frustration and endless battle. I felt nothing for any of the women, except..."

Oria waited, knowing guilt had him confessing to her and though it sometimes pained her to think he had known other women intimately, it also helped to know that it had been out of need and no more, except... she continued to wait.

"There was one woman, a bit older than me, who sought me out. She liked that I wasn't rough with her or hurt her. She taught me some things and she listened when I talked about you. She asked me how I could be sure you'd be waiting for me. I told her that we loved each other since we'd been young and nothing would ever change that. We knew we'd be together always. She would ask me to tell her stories about us and I always obliged her. She said the stories made her happy to know that a love like ours existed."

"What was her name?" Oria asked in an odd way grateful to her for bringing a bit of comfort to the hellish life he had been forced to live.

"Avena," Royden said.

"You had feelings for her?" Oria asked, hearing a sadness in his voice he didn't try to hide.

"I was grateful to her for letting me talk about you. It helped ease the pain of missing you."

"It must be a terribly hard life for her."

"Not anymore. She died. One of the warriors, in a drunken fury, beat her to death."

Oria didn't believe her husband a savage, but there were those times she saw a rage in his eyes that frightened her. She saw it now.

"I wasn't in camp at the time. When I returned and found out what happened—I killed him."

"No one stopped you."

"They tried. Avena didn't deserve that, but I made sure he got what he deserved." He shook his head. "You didn't need to know that."

"I do need to hear it," she said. "And you need to tell me if we're both to heal."

"I could stay like this the rest of the day with you, lying here talking while the rain beats against the keep, warm and snug in each other's arms, just the two of us."

Oria hurried out of bed, grabbing her garments.

"I guess you don't like the idea," he said a bit startled by her reaction.

"I love it," she said as she slipped her shift on. "But we can't survive the rest of the day here without food." Her stomach grumbled to prove it. "I'm going to fetch us food and tell Bethany we're not to be disturbed." She rushed to the door.

"Good Lord, but I love you, wife," he called out, a broad smile filling his face.

"Or course you do." She laughed softly like a gentle breeze whispering in the trees. "I will be only a moment. Don't dare get out of that bed."

"As you command, wife," he said with a nod.

Oria hurried off, eager to return and have her husband all to herself.

And she did.

Chapter Twenty-four

Royden stood on the keep steps looking over the village with pride. The last two weeks had seen much improvements. The most successful improvement had been with the people. Smiles were widespread as was laughter. Children played carefree again and women gathered in gossip. He was glad his brother and sister would come home and see that the clan flourished.

He made a habit of walking through the village, making himself available to the people, listening to their problems or concerns so that he could settle any issues before they turned difficult. When he had spoken of it to his da, he thought it a wise choice of Royden to do so. That it would avoid escalation of problems. It had amazed and also baffled Royden that his da hadn't minded relinquishing the status of chieftain to Royden. That was until he had seen how happy and content his da was with Wren.

Royden was pleased for his da and pleased that he still had his da around to go to for advice. Rarely did a chieftain relinquish his position. Death usually took it from him or he lost it in battle. Royden was relieved that neither was the result for his da.

Soon he was talking with various people and settling small issues, which pleased him since it meant things were going well. Until Penn approached him.

"A word with you, sir?" Penn asked and looked around, "in private."

Royden obliged him, walking off away from the village a bit where they could still be seen but not heard.

"What is it, Penn?" Royden asked. While the young man had continued to be an asset to the clan, Royden still didn't completely trust him. Penn feared the man who he had once battled for and who left him here so he would have eyes on the clan. And though he claimed allegiance to the clan, Royden couldn't be sure what Penn would do if confronted with a choice of who to fight against.

"Rumors have been stirring that you should be aware of," Penn said.

Were there? Or was Penn stirring some of his own accord? Royden ordered him to continue. "Tell me."

"The attack that left the clan decimated also left some more than curious. It seems many believe that it was a betrayal by a chieftain."

"Not my da," Royden was quick to defend his father, though he wasn't surprised by the news. If he and Oria had suspected someone guilty of betrayal, certainly others would have as well.

Penn hurried to say. "No. No. Your da is beloved and respected by the clan."

Hearing that he wondered not only what the rumors were saying, but why they seemed to disturb Penn.

"Who then?" Royden demanded.

Penn hesitated only briefly, Royden's sudden scowl forcing the words out of his mouth. "Chieftain William MacGlennen."

"Oria's father?' Royden asked, not believing what he'd heard.

"Aye, sir. Many are saying he helped to plan the attack."

"That makes no sense," Royden said, shaking his head. "He was pleased Oria and I would wed. He had insisted we get married sooner not wanting his daughter's fate to be that of Thurbane's daughter."

Royden's mind started spinning. Could the attack on Thurbane's clan have been a prelude to the whole plan? Had it been meant to force he and Oria to wed sooner so that all the chieftains, would gather together in one place where an attack would be made easier?

He didn't want to believe it, even conceive it possible. If it were true it would devastate Oria.

"Do you know if there is any truth to this?" Royden demanded of Penn.

"No," Penn said, shaking his head. "I was nothing more than a warrior. I followed orders and did what I was told. I knew of no plans in advance."

"Yet you were left here to feed your leader information. Why?" Royden's question was punctuated with such force that it sent a shiver through Penn.

"I could only guess," Penn said.

"Then guess," Royden ordered.

"I couldn't hide my feelings for Emily. I wore my love for her for all to see. She became my world. I had asked about leaving the mercenaries so that I could remain here with her. I was refused and when I heard we would be leaving, I never felt such pain," Penn admitted.

"I have," Royden said.

"I understand now. I didn't before I met Emily. If I were to guess, I would say that my love for Emily was used to my leader's advantage."

"How so?"

"If I wanted to remain here indefinitely, I was to keep an eye on what went on here," Penn confessed.

"Is that what you've done? Kept him aware of all that has gone on here? Or is it all a ruse and if the time came you would raise your hand against this clan?" Royden asked, since against his better judgment he had come to believe that Penn truly loved Emily and he didn't want to see her hurt.

"I would say nothing that would bring harm to the clan and I would fight to the death alongside the Clan MacKinnon if it came to that," Penn said with all honesty.

Royden found trust difficult, knowing most lied for selfish reasons. He wanted to believe Penn, but only time would tell.

"The Beast wants something from this area," Penn said. "And he'll get it, which means he's going to return here. That can also mean it's why he placed Trevor in the home of Chieftain William of the Clan MacGlennen… an ally."

***

Royden sat in his solar waiting for his da. He wanted to discuss the situation with him. He didn't think his da had heard the rumors or he would have brought them to Royden's attention. And he doubted his da would believe them. He and William had been friends for a long time and had fought more than one battle alongside each other.

He couldn't help but wonder what or who had started the rumors. Penn had had no idea when he had asked him. He had simply wanted to make Royden aware of the situation and he was glad Penn had. He didn't want Oria hearing the gossip until he could at least find out how they had gotten started. He didn't want to believe there was any truth to them, but they had raised speculation.

Why, though? Why would William have done such a thing?

His da asked the same thing after Royden explained it all.

"Why?" Parlan asked, shaking his head. "It makes no sense. What reason could he have had to betray us? To betray everyone?" He posed a reasonable explanation. "Perhaps the guilty one is trying to lay blame at William's feet to keep from being discovered."

"A possibility," Royden agreed.

"Yet you sound doubtful."

"I'd rather sound hopeful, but I fear proving William's innocence isn't going to be easy with him being dead," Royden said. "And I worry what this news will do to my wife."

"You need to tell her right away, before she gets wind of the rumors herself," his da said with concern.

"I was hoping to learn something about this rumor, some hope of sorts, before laying such a hefty burden on her."

"I wouldn't take the chance, son," Parlan advised. "If she hears it herself and discovers you knew and didn't tell her, it will prove even more of a burden for her."

Royden thought about what Oria had told him, how she trusted him and her da. If it proved that her da hadn't been the trustworthy man she had believed him to be that left only him who she trusted with such a deep conviction. Besides, if this was reversed and he was the one who needed to be told, he'd expect her to come to him right away.

"I understand that instinct and love have you trying to protect Oria from the pain of this news, but she'd suffer far greater pain if you waited to tell her. Also, ask yourself what you would expect from Oria if she heard it was me who stood accused."

"My thoughts as well, Da," he said, hoping he'd be as wise a father to his children as his da was to him and his siblings.

Parlan rubbed at his chin. "I don't even know where to tell you to start in tracking down the origin of this claim. Or who to trust will tell you the truth. This is a conundrum of massive proportions, especially since William isn't here to defend himself."

"People want answers to what happened that day. Why we were attacked? Who attacked us?" Royden said.

"In hopes that somehow those answers will prevent another attack," Parlan said. "The wild Highlands can't be tamed or explained. It is a land that has been robbed and raped by many. By those born of its soil and foreigners as well. But the Highlands will be the only winner in an endless battle. It dominates man while remaining wild and free. Warriors, battles, clans will come and go, but the Highlands are here forever."

"I felt the pull of the Highlands when I was taken off its shore to fight in a foreign land. The pull to return home was an ache like no other. It was worse than losing my hand. It was like losing my soul."

"It's been said that if you're born of Highland blood you'll find no peace anywhere but the Highlands. You fought to come home. Arran fought to come home and I have no doubt that Raven fights to come home." His da stood. "I'll see that Oria knows you wish to see her here in your solar."

Royden nodded, his da knowing him well enough that he'd waste no time in doing what needed to be done.

Royden got up from the table and went to the fireplace, a fire keeping at bay the chill that always seemed to penetrate the stone walls. He stood gazing at the flames. How did he tell his wife that her da, who she loved dearly, could possibly be responsible for the attack that destroyed not only many lives, but their lives as well?

"Da said you wanted to see me," Oria said, bursting into the room with a smile.

She caught him off guard for a moment hearing her say da and thinking she meant her da. He was caught off guard even more seeing how her cheeks glowed red and more strands of her blonde hair fell loose than were contained in her braid and her smile beamed with delight.

It was a smile he was about to destroy and it ripped at his heart.

"Something's wrong. What is it?" she asked, hurrying over to him.

He used to be able to keep things from her for her own good, or so he thought. It was what a husband did to protect his wife, or so he thought. For a moment, he wished he could do so again, or so he thought.

Instead, he did what she would want him to do. "Sit, Oria, we need to talk."

Oria's stomach churned. Something was wrong, terribly wrong. She could hear it in his voice, see the concern in the way his dark eyes looked at her—with sorrow.

"Tell me, Royden," she said, her hand going to rest at her stomach.

He wished he could spare her this hurt that was bound to grow, but at the moment all he could do was make her aware of the wagging tongues. "Rumors are going around that your da is the one who betrayed everyone."

Oria stared at him, taking a moment to comprehend his remark. Had she heard him correctly? She shook her head. "My da betray his family and friends? She kept shaking her head. "Impossible." Her shock quickly turned to anger. "You can't believe this nonsense."

"No, but it seems that some do or this rumor wouldn't have taken root."

"I can't let his good, honorable name be tarnished. I won't let lies destroy my da's legacy. I have to prove his innocence. Who claims this? I want to talk to him? Tell me now."

Royden reached out to take her in his arms and was shocked when she stepped away from him.

"Tell me now, Royden," she demanded, avoiding the comfort of his arms. It would be too easy to surrender to the comfort he offered when strength was called for.

"I don't know who claimed it. I just learned of it myself."

"From who?" she demanded.

He wondered if he should tell her, but only for a moment. She had a right to know. "Penn."

"And you believe him, a man who owes allegiance to your foe?"

"Penn only alerted me to the rumors. He knows nothing beyond that."

"And how do you know this? Did you speak with anyone who heard the rumors?"

"No," he said and held up his hand before she could accuse him of anything. "I spoke with my da. He hadn't heard anything and he was shocked at the news himself."

"Because he knows it's a lie," Oria said. "He was and still is a good friend to my da."

"As am I, Oria, which is why I wanted to tell you before doing anything," he said, wishing it didn't feel like she had placed a distance between them.

"What do you plan to do?"

"I want to track down the origin of this claim and find out the reason for it," he said.

"The reason? It's a lie, plain and simple," Oria argued.

"Aye, but why the lie? Who is besmirching your da's good name?"

"The coward—the guilty one," Oria said.

"Then we will find him," Royden assured her and reached out once again wanting to hold her and let her know he was there for her. But again she stepped away from him and began to pace.

"Could the rumor have come here with some of the people we brought back from my clan?" she wondered aloud.

It bothered him that she didn't seek solace in his arms. He had to remember that she had learned, out of necessity, to tackle many problems on her own while he'd been gone. But he was here now and they had each other. She wasn't alone anymore.

She stopped pacing. "I need to go talk to them."

She turned to leave and he felt a catch in his chest along with a spark of anger that she would say nothing more to him or invite him go with her. He was about to call out to her when she stopped and turned.

Oria rushed over to her husband and placed a hurried kiss on his lips. "I am so grateful I won't have to do this alone. That I have you, your love, your trust, and you will help me prove my da's innocence. I love you, Royden." She kissed him again, not lightly this time. "I will return and tell you everything I find out."

His hand latched on to her arm when she quickly turned to leave. "I won't forbid you from doing this."

Her brow went up. "You would dare forbid me?"

His brow narrowed in response. "I dare anything when it comes to protecting my wife, whether she likes it or not. You can ask your questions, but you will be careful, wife, and take no unnecessary chances. And I will speak to those who I believe may be helpful in finding the truth." His brow lost its scowl. "Trust me when I say I feel your pain in this matter and I share it with you. But your da would not want you placing yourself in harm's way because of him. Remain the wise and patient woman I know you are and remember you are not in this alone. I am here for you."

As tears tugged at the corner of her eyes, his words born from the depths of his love for her. She gave him a hug, pressing her face to his chest and letting his linen shirt catch the persistent tears. Worried more tears might fall, she hurried from the room.

Royden stared after her, feeling guiltier than he had ever felt in his life since he couldn't help but think what would happen—if the rumor proved true.

Chapter Twenty-five

Oria found Ross easily. He was busy in the planting fields. She had told Royden that Ross had an exceptional touch when it came to farming and he'd immediately assigned him to the planting fields. He had also allowed him to settle in one of the small farms just on the outskirts of the village that had sat empty since shortly after the attack.

She caught his attention with the wave of her hand and returned the smile Ross sent her when he spotted her. Gone were the harsh lines that had marred his pleasant features and his shoulders no longer slumped with the weight of his worries.

"Mistress Oria, I can't thank you enough for what you have done for me and my family," Ross said when he stopped in front of her. "Aine prays for you and Chieftain Royden every day. It was generous of him to assign us a fine cottage and some land to plant once again. The lads are happier than they've been in a long while. We are forever grateful. Life here is good. Very good."

"I am pleased to hear that, Ross, truly I am. But now I need a favor from you," Oria said.

"Anything, Mistress Oria, anything," Ross said eagerly.

She glanced around and comfortable that no one was close enough to hear their conversation, though keeping her voice low to be sure, she asked, "Have tongues been wagging, not so kindly, about my da?"

The sudden, tense change in his demeanor and that he appeared lost for words told her what she needed to know.

"Please tell me what you've heard and from whom," she said and braced herself for what she was about to hear.

Ross nodded, worry filling his eyes. "I can't say who I heard it from since I don't recall. You know how wagging tongues are. You hear a little from one person, more from another, and before you know it, you can't recall who was the first to whisper in your ear. It was little bits of whispers at first. There was mention of your da meeting with a dark figure late at night, curiosity as to why he pushed for a quick wedding between you and Royden instead of sending you away until the trouble passed. Inquisitiveness grew when your da, not given to fits of anger, got furious after learning that a chieftain wouldn't attend your wedding. He even went as far as to go speak to that chieftain and get him to change his mind."

That puzzled Oria. She had believed all had accepted the invite of their own accord except Chieftain Thurbane and Lord Learmonth, who had declined for obvious reasons.

"That hardly speaks of betrayal," Oria said even more puzzled.

Ross appeared hesitant to say more.

"Please, Ross, I trust my clan to be truthful to me and I can't defend my da's good name if I'm blind to what is being said about him."

"You're right and I will help you however I can," he said. "But I can only venture to guess that when people have questions, which they did, and no answers are offered, which they weren't, curiosity grows. Somewhere someone couldn't resist to ask the obvious. How do you explain that our clan continued on unscathed compared to others? Few enemy warriors were left behind. And none of our warriors were taken. Your da continued to lead the clan without interference and he continued to meet with that dark figure."

It took a few moments with Oria searching back in her memories to put together what others already had. She spoke her thought aloud. "Why now? Why do I hear this only now?"

Ross shrugged. "I can only surmise that people who returned here with you feel safe enough to discuss it with those outside our clan."

Was that it? Or had someone purposely wanted the speculation made known?

"Do you believe my da betrayed his friends?" Oria asked.

"Your da was a good chieftain and good to his clan and I will always remember him that way."

Oria wasn't sure of his response. Did Ross mean that regardless of what her da had done, he would remain faithful to the man? She thanked Ross for his honesty and walked away. How had she been so blind to what had been going on? Why hadn't she known that her da was meeting with someone he didn't want known? And why had he gotten angry when a chieftain had turned down the invitation to her wedding?

She stopped suddenly, turned, and ran back toward Ross, calling out, "A moment, Ross."

He turned and walked toward her.

"Who was the chieftain my da got angry with?" she asked.

"Chieftain Galvin of the Clan Macara."

***

Royden went in search of Penn shortly after his wife had left his solar. He would have summoned the man there, but he didn't want to chance his wife returning while he spoke with him. He intended to keep private what he discussed with Penn. It was too dangerous a task he sought for anyone to know except him and Penn. He would rather chance Oria's wrath than see harm brought to anyone over his decision.

Not seeing Penn anywhere as he walked through the village, his task was delayed when stopped by a few seeking help or a friendly chat. He took the time, since he didn't want anyone to know he was intent on a mission. When he failed to spot Penn anywhere, he went to his cottage.

Penn's eyes went wide when he opened the door and saw his chieftain standing there.

"A word," Royden commanded.

Emily pulled the door from her husband's hand to swing it open. "Is something wrong, sir?"

"Emily!" Penn admonished. "We don't question our chieftain."

"When it comes to my husband, I do," Emily argued, tears clouding her eyes. "I'll not be losing you, Penn."

Penn slipped his arm around his wife and before he could comfort her, Royden spoke up.

"Rest easy, Emily, you're not losing your husband," Royden said, though offered no more.

"It is good to know our chieftain is a man of his word," Emily said.

Penn waited until he was a distance from the cottage so his wife wouldn't hear him apologize. "Please forgive, Em, sir. She worries I will be lost to her."

"As long as you remain faithful to the clan she will have no worry," Royden said.

"I take it that my faithfulness is about to be tested?" Penn asked.

"It is," Royden said and turned toward the edge of the woods to talk with him.

Penn stopped. "Too much lurks in the woods that can't be seen."

Royden turned and Penn followed as he led them both away from the village.

"You are to find out if Oria's da helped the Beast," he ordered as they walked.

"I am nothing more than a warrior, expected to fight not ask questions—"

"You refuse to obey me?" Royden snapped.

"No, sir, I tell you the truth and while I might be able to discover a small, most likely irrelevant piece of information, there is one who knows the information you seek."

Royden went to ask who when it struck him. "Trevor."

"Aye, sir. He is trusted by the Beast. They may not be brothers by blood, but they are brothers nonetheless. Trevor would know if Mistress Oria's da helped the Beast with his plans."

"Do you supply Trevor with information?" Royden asked.

"No. I report to Fergus," Penn said.

"And what do you report?"

"Your status on warriors and weapons," Penn said and when an angry scowl surfaced on Royden's face, he was quick to continue. "I feed Fergus enough for him to believe I adhere to my task. I've made no mention of the many arrows you have Wilfred making or the iron work that keeps Cadell busy. It is good to know we will be well prepared if attacked."

"Do we need to worry about that?" Royden asked, still hoping that in the end his love for Emily and his son was enough for him to remain loyal to the clan.

"With Trevor having brought his wife here, I doubt it. He, and definitely not the Beast, would ever put her in danger," Penn said.

"Why would the Beast care about Trevor's wife?" Royden asked, odd that the Beast who seemed to care for no one would be concerned about the woman.

Penn kept his voice low as if revealing a forbidden secret. "Trevor's wife is the Beast's sister."

***

Oria rushed to catch up with her husband as he approached the keep, calling out, "Royden."

He stopped, turned, and waited for her to reach him, his hand going out to take hers.

"We need to go talk with Chieftain Galvin. I discovered that he wasn't going to attend our wedding and my da got angry and spoke with him and he changed his mind. Why hadn't he wanted to attend?" She shook her head. "Purity never mentioned anything about it. She had looked forward to the wedding. Bayne as well. Why would their father refuse to attend? Could he have known of the attack?" She shook her head again. "But why let your son and daughter attend if you knew of the danger? And why attend yourself? We need to speak with him."

It wasn't until she stopped speaking that she caught the troubled look in his eyes.

"What's wrong? You found something out and fear to tell me," she said, providing her own answer.

"No, nothing about your da. Penn told me that Demelza is the Beast's sister."

That news brought Oria to an abrupt halt. "What could it mean that his sister now resides in the area?"

"I wonder the same," Royden said. "I would only send my sister to an area that I knew was truly safe for her to reside."

"That would mean he plans no more attacks here," Oria said with some relief.

"Why though?" Royden asked. "He didn't get all of what he wanted. Our clan and land is lost to him as well as Clan Macara."

Oria had her own question. "And why after five years accept defeat?"

"From what I've learned about the Beast, he's not one to accept defeat."

"Either are we," Oria said with a toss of her chin in the air.

He leaned down and kissed her cheek. "It's a good day for a ride, wife."

Oria grinned and squeezed her husband's hand. "I could do with a good ride, then we can go visit Chieftain Galvin."

Royden laughed, shaking his head. "You truly are a gem, wife."

Realization struck Oria. "Oh, you meant a ride to Clan Macara."

"Aye, but we'll see to your ride first, then we'll ride to Clan Macara."

"Nonsense," Oria said. "A visit to Clan Macara is more important."

Royden shook his head and with a firm hold on her hand eased her arm behind her back while he drew her close against him. "Nothing is more important than making sure you get a good ride."

Why did his words have to ignite her passion that seemed to always stir just beneath the surface?

As much as she didn't want to, she said, "Later."

"No. *Now*," Royden insisted.

"I need to prove my da's—"

"His innocence will still be there for you to prove," Royden said.

She didn't want to refuse her husband, especially since the thought of him nestled between her legs was far too enticing to put off. But it was important she put a stop to the wagging tongues before they ruined her da's good name.

Royden watched the play of passion versus duty to her da's memory spar in her eyes. It disturbed him to see her struggle like that when she shouldn't have to.

He brought his lips near her ear to whisper, "I'll make it quick now and we'll linger later."

Oria smiled and threw her arms around her husband's neck. "You are a good husband."

***

"Keep grinning like that and everyone is going to know what we were up to in the barn," Royden warned as he rode alongside his wife. "Not that they probably don't already know since it was difficult keeping you quiet."

Oria's grin vanished. "You think I was heard?"

Royden laughed. "When are you not heard, wife?"

Oria's cheeks stained red. "I tried to keep quiet. What must they think of me?"

"They think you love your husband and you're keeping him very happy." He reached out and gave her arm a reassuring squeeze. "Worry not, I caught your loud moans with a kiss."

Oria grinned again. "You're my champion."

"And you're mine."

They continued on, the day pleasant, and it wasn't long before they reached the Macara keep.

Oria looked around as they entered the small village and the sour faces on the people reminded her of how sad Purity always appeared. From what Oria had gathered, Chieftain Galvin had been a commanding parent rather than a loving father. And from the looks of the people here it appeared it was Galvin's way with everyone.

The village was well kept and Oria wondered if it was more from fear than pride that kept it that way. She didn't see a smile or hear a bit of laughter, though people did bend their heads in whispers. A good place for wagging tongues to flourish.

Royden took his wife's hand as they entered the keep and were shown to the Great Hall by an elderly man. It was a room of good size and kept well, a pleasant scent wafted in the air. The keep wasn't as large as MacKinnon keep, though not as small as Learmonth keep.

"Do you have news. Tell me," Galvin demanded, rushed steps bringing him into the room.

"That's not much of a hospitable greeting," Royden said.

"What do you expect when I've heard nothing from you regarding my request?" Galvin argued. We're the only two clans to keep our holdings. We should be defending each other and Arran should not even have to think about my offer. He should accept marriage to my daughter without question."

"That will be up to Arran," Royden said, annoyed that he once again had to remind the man.

"Ridiculous," Galvin said with a sharp dismissive wave of his hand. "Your father should make him wed my daughter."

Royden's brow narrowed. "You know my da has returned home?"

"Of course I do. That's not news to stay quiet. And I heard he brought a witch with him," Galvin said smugly.

"Yet you didn't think it would be nice for a—supposedly—old friend to visit to see how he's doing? Or to even be curious about the so-called witch? Or perhaps demand from him that his son wed your daughter?" Royden asked with a sudden anger.

"I don't answer to you," Galvin shouted at Royden. "And why should I visit with *supposed* friends when they do nothing to help me save my clan and land?"

Oria stepped forward, they all yet to have taken a seat. "Did you decline to come to our wedding, the one that was first to take place?"

"I certainly did," Galvin said without shame. "And your father argued over it with me, though he never did make good on the promise he made me if I attended your wedding."

"What promise and why didn't you want to attend?" Royden demanded.

"Why should I attend when your father refused to see my daughter safely wed to his son?" Galvin argued, shaking a fist at Royden, then turned to Oria. "And your father was a liar."

Royden's hand clamped around Galvin's wrist and wrenched his arm back when he went to shake his fist in Oria's face. "You'll respect my wife or I'll beat you senseless."

Galvin yanked his arm to free it of Royden's grip, but Royden's hold was like a shackle.

"Release me," Galvin demanded.

"Raise a fist against either of us and you'll find what it's like to lose a hand," Royden warned.

Galvin paled, his eyes darting to Royden's stump, and he backed away from him. "I want no more, no less then you have—I want my clan and land safe." Galvin tempered his tone when he looked to Oria. "Your da assured me he would get Arran to wed Purity." He shook his head slowly. "He was so convincing. I almost thought he had already seen it done, he spoke with such confidence. I was a fool to believe him."

"My father was no liar," Oria said. "The attack changed everything for all of us. Otherwise he would have done his best to keep his word."

"Done his best? He was supposed to see it done by your wedding day. He promised me that Parlan would have good news for me that day and so I agreed to go to the wedding. When I got your father alone that day,"—Galvin nodded to Royden—"he told me William hadn't said a word to him about a marriage between Arran and Purity. He lied just to get me to attend your wedding. What kind of friend does that?"

On the return ride home, Oria remained silent, lost in her troubling thoughts.

Royden attempted to comfort her. "Maybe Galvin is lying. We'll ask my da when we get home."

"And if he confirms what Galvin said, what then?"

"What possible reason could your da have for helping a man, from all accounts, who is more beast than man? It isn't something your da would do," Royden said.

With a sharp turn of her head, she looked with wide eyes at her husband. "Unless he was forced to."

Chapter Twenty-six

When they reached home, they went straight to Royden's da and he confirmed what Galvin had told him. Oria's da never talked to him about Arran and Purity.

"There would be no reason for William to talk to me about it. He was well aware the choice was Arran's," Parlan said. "I don't know why Galvin would claim such an outlandish thing." He turned a quick glance on Wren, busy at the table in their cottage crushing herbs in her mortar and pestle. "Do you see anything about this, Wren?"

"Please do tell us if you have seen anything concerning my da," Oria pleaded.

What she had discovered so far had proved more detrimental to her da than helpful. And no matter what anyone said she couldn't believe her da guilty of betrayal.

Wren stopped grinding the herbs and let the pestle lay free in the mortar as she turned sympathetic eyes on Oria. "I wish I could offer you something, anything that could ease the worry you have for your da. Unfortunately, nothing has been revealed to me and I can't see anything even when I try to have a look. That usually happens when I find the situation so steeped in secrets and promises that it clouds everything. Or I'm not meant to know. I'm truly sorry. I wish I could offer you more."

Disappointment stabbed at her, but Oria didn't let it show.

"You should sit and have a nice soothing brew and let your thoughts rest," Wren advised. "It will help you to see things more clearly."

Royden could see his wife had no intention of doing as Wren had recommended. He thought differently. He hated seeing his wife hurting like this. If he could take the pain from her, he would. Since he couldn't, he'd be right there beside her offering all the strength and love he could.

He slipped his arm around her waist like he'd done so often since returning home, needing to keep her close, feel her there against him, know this was all real and he wouldn't wake to find it nothing more than a dream.

"I could use a brew," he said and led her out of the cottage.

They settled on a bench in the Great Hall, the heat of the hearth at their back and Royden glad they had since his wife shivered once seated.

"This can't be true," Oria said. My da was a good man. He would have died before betraying anyone."

"We'll find the truth," Royden said with a firmness that had his wife turning a sad smile on him.

"I so want to believe that, but I can't help but wonder how." She shook her head. "Who do we trust to tell us the truth?"

Royden worried when his wife sat drinking the hot brew and not saying a word. He expected her to be voicing her thoughts, bouncing them around to see if any could be pieced together and made sense of or discarded as nonsense. Her silence unnerved him, since she rarely kept quiet.

Finally, he could take no more. "You are far too quiet, wife."

Oria sighed. "I am at a loss."

"You've run out of words?" he teased and he was glad he got a smile from her and that she returned the tease.

"You wish."

"Never," he said with a hardy laugh. "I love when we talk. I used to talk with you in my dreams. Have conversations in my mind with you. It's such a pleasure to finally be able to truly talk with you."

Oria's eyes brightened. "I did the same. I would talk with you in my head night after night."

"What did we talk about?"

"I would tell you about my day, make light of some things that happened, and always I would tell you how much I loved you and missed you and how I couldn't wait until you returned home to me and we would build a life together."

Tears filled her eyes and Royden pulled her into his arms. "I heard your words, Oria. Every night I heard you tell me you loved me and missed me and I said the same to you. Our love helped us then and it will help us now. We'll see this problem through together."

Oria hugged him and kept her face pressed against his chest. It was warm and hard, his scent comforting as well as the strong, steady beat of his heart. She wanted to linger there in his arms. Actually, she wouldn't have minded if they snuck off to their bedchamber and got lost in making love. It was the one time her mind was so consumed with passion that there was no room for other thoughts. But that wouldn't do right now. She needed to address this problem. She needed to find the truth.

She reluctantly and slowly moved out of her husband's arms, though she could feel his reluctance to let her go. He held her firm and she was about to surrender to the comfort his embrace offered when she heard the creak of the Great Hall door opening.

"I'm sorry to disturb," Aine said, looking hesitant to approach.

Oria sat straight, though didn't move completely out of her husband's arms, which pleased Royden. He wanted everyone to know how strong their love was for each other.

"Not at all," Oria encouraged. "What brings you to the keep?"

"Ross told me that you spoke with him about your da," Aine said, measuring her words as she went.

"Do you know something?" Oria asked eagerly and was disappointed when Aine shook her head, though hope returned when she spoke.

"I don't, but I might know someone who does."

"Who?" Oria asked, excitement in not only her response but her eyes that widened at the news.

"Do you remember Old Henry, Mistress Oria?" Aine asked.

Oria nodded. "I do, I had hoped to talk with him when I was at the MacGlennen keep, but I never got the chance."

"Old Henry is a good man. He wanted to come here with you. But so many families wanted to go with you, he felt it was only right the younger ones went before him. Anyway, I lose myself when I should be telling you that if anyone would know anything about your da, Old Henry would. He and your da talked often. I think it was because Old Henry was around when your grandfather was alive and your da could talk to him about old times and family. Many believe Old Henry knows all the MacGlennen secrets or so the wagging tongues say. I would agree, though, since he's never been one to reveal much of what anyone says to him. I don't know if this helps, but Ross said I should tell you."

"It helps greatly, Aine, and I'm glad you told me," Oria said.

Oria turned to her husband after Aine left. "I need to talk with Henry."

"Why don't I have him brought here," Royden suggested, knowing if he saw Firth again, he'd kill him.

"Trevor might object, which would delay me being able to talk with Henry." She never called him Old Henry, having grown accustomed to hearing her da simply call him Henry.

"The man is of no value to Trevor. I don't see any reason why he would object to Old Henry coming here," Royden argued.

"What if he does out of spite? You beat him in a sword match and people lined up to leave there, then you slashed Firth's face. I don't think he's going to be too keen on obliging you."

She had a point and it was important they find out the truth about her da before the rumors grew so large they couldn't be stopped.

"We'll go tomorrow," he said.

She smiled with glee though it faded fast. "You won't make trouble with Firth?"

"I won't make trouble, but I will inquire about the man and if he's still there I'll make certain he keeps his distance from you."

Oria hoped that was so, but the scowl on her husband's face warned otherwise.

***

Oria was impatient to speak with Henry. The weather had delayed their visit for three days, the rain appearing as if it would never end. Concern for Demelza had Wren joining them and Parlan as well.

Oria and her husband were surprised when Trevor greeted them with enthusiasm.

"I'm so glad you've come. I was going to send for Wren today since my wife isn't feeling well," Trevor said, after rushing down the keep steps upon their arrival.

"I'm feeling fine, Trevor. You worry too much," Demelza called out from the top of the keep steps.

"Don't you dare come down those stairs," Trevor ordered.

Wren hurried up the stairs when it appeared that Demelza wasn't about to obey her husband and together they entered the keep.

Royden thought it a perfect time to inquire about Firth, seeing Trevor relieved that Wren hadn't hesitated to go to his wife.

"Where is Firth?" Royden asked, though he was aware it sounded more like a demand.

"Not that it concerns you, but since you generously share your healer with me I'll tell you he was sent away and he won't be returning," Trevor said.

"I'm glad to hear that," Royden said and saw the relief on his wife's face.

"I'd like to visit with some of the people while you and my husband talk," Oria said, seeking permission this time so she didn't hinder her chance to speak with Henry.

"No one else from this clan leaves here today," Trevor ordered sharply.

That didn't sit well with Oria, knowing Henry had wanted to go with her, and she couldn't hold her tongue. "There is only one person I wish to take with me today and he's an old man. He has nothing to offer you. He knew my grandfather. He belongs with me."

"Old Henry," Trevor said, shaking his head after realizing who she referred to. "My wife has taken a liking to him. He talks with her when others won't." He shook his head again. "I can't let you take him, at least not now. Maybe after the bairn is born."

Oria was disappointed but she could understand his reasoning.

"Go and talk with him. He is treated well here and does not suffer at my hands, none of your clansmen do," Trevor said. "I should say they do better since my wife has convinced me they all aren't meant to be warriors."

Oria was glad to hear that, but she also heard his annoyance that he had yet to win favor with the clan. She couldn't feel sorry for him. He had robbed her of her clan, of her family, though she was grateful that her clan hadn't been mistreated. Still, he was a stranger to them.

"Henry still resides in the cottage that has been his home for as long as I can remember?" Oria asked.

"He does," Trevor confirmed.

She took hold of Royden's wrist above where his hand would have been. He would think she did it to show Trevor that his lost limb didn't disturb her in the least, but that wasn't so. She often took hold of his arm there, as if she actually was holding his hand and it always pleased him, more so now. Though she hadn't done it on purpose, he was glad Trevor had seen her do so, glad that he saw that she wasn't repulsed by it. That the loss of his hand made no difference to her.

"Henry's cottage sits off by itself some, nearer to the woods than the other cottages. Anyone can point you to it," she said.

Royden nodded again, pleased that his wife let him know where she'd be and that she wouldn't be far. He watched her walk off and waited until he saw the direction she went, then he turned to follow Trevor up the steps.

"While we enjoy some fine wine, you can tell me what truly brought you here today," Trevor said and continued up the steps.

Royden decided then that it would be a good time to confront the man about Oria's da.

***

"Mistress Oria, you're a sight for these old eyes that are glad they can still see a beautiful woman," Old Henry said as he struggled to get off the bench he'd been sitting on in front of his cottage.

"Sit, Henry, please sit. I'll join you," Oria said, rushing to his side and keeping a hand to his arm so he would remain seated, she joined him on the bench.

"How are you doing, Henry?" she asked. His many wrinkles attested to his advanced age, though he had worn those wrinkles for as long as she could remember. He had always worn a smile, just like he did now. He never had a bad word for anyone. He was the most peaceful soul she'd ever known.

He chuckled. "I must be doing good since I've lived long, so long that I can't remember how old I am." He chuckled again.

She laughed lightly and placed her hand gently on his arm. "I heard you wanted to come home with me. I'll see about that."

"I appreciate that, I truly do, Mistress Oria, but I think I'll stay here. I've lived my entire life here and it's not so bad. We're treated better than at first. Besides, the new mistress is in need of a friend. She visits me every day and we talk. She makes sure I have plenty to eat. She's a sweet, kind woman like you, though a bit lonely. She'd miss me if I left and I'd miss her and the others who come and talk with me."

"I agree with you, Demelza is a sweet, kind woman," Oria said, glad that Henry was content. "If that's what you wish, Henry, so be it."

"Is something wrong, Mistress Oria. You seem troubled," Old Henry said.

There were no hiding things from Henry, which was probably why people talked with him. They also confided in him since he never repeated a word of what anyone told him.

"Something does trouble me, Henry," Oria said. "I know my da trusted you and talked with you often, you being the oldest member of the clan and knowing him since he was a wee lad. When I discovered tongues wagging about my da, I thought you might know something about it."

He nodded his head, his smile fading.

"You've heard?" she asked, saddened to see his smile disappear and worried what it might mean.

"I have and sadly I expected it."

"You did? Why?" Oria asked.

"Because your da confessed all to me and I knew that time would not keep his secret."

***

Royden took a seat in Trevor's solar as did Parlan. He'd been here often enough through the years, though it had changed some since the last time. It was obvious a different man occupied it now and if he had time he'd inquire about the many different weapons hanging on the walls. But he wanted answers to questions that couldn't wait.

"Did William MacGlennen betray his people and help the Beast?" Royden asked.

"That's a question I can't answer," Trevor said.

"Or you refuse to answer," Royden corrected.

"No. I believe it's a question Wolf would prefer to answer."

Royden leaned forward in his chair. "Wolf is the one known as the Beast?"

"He is," Trevor confirmed.

"What an appropriate name for one referred to as the Beast," Royden said, wondering why Trevor chose now to relieve the man's name to him.

"Wolf takes pride in his birth name. It's the name of an old, respected tribe and he does it proud."

"From your prospective he may, but not from mine," Royden said again, wondering why he divulged more information about the man that had caused so much damage and loss to his clan. "I believe it would be wiser if you told me about William MacGlennen's connection to Wolf?"

"Why do you believe there's a connection between the two?" Trevor questioned.

Parlan answered, "Because nothing else makes sense. William was a man of his word. He would never betray his clan. But wagging tongues always start with a grain of truth to them. What did William have that Wolf wanted?"

Chapter Twenty-seven

Oria was eager yet afraid to ask Henry. She believed her da a good, honorable man and no one would persuade her otherwise. Her concern was that the lies had been allowed to go on unchecked and no amount of the truth would save her da's good name.

"What did my da confess?" Oria asked, her heart beating wildly.

Old Henry took her hand. His aged hand didn't hold the strength it once did, but he used what he had left to give her hand a comforting squeeze. "Your parents aren't your true parents."

Oria stared at Henry. Had she heard him correctly? She shook her head. "Did you say my parents aren't my true parents?"

Old Henry bobbed his head. "I did."

"That's nonsense," Oria said. Why would he make such an outlandish remark? When she saw the sadness deepen on his face, her stomach knotted.

"I promised I'd breathe not a word of what your da told me. But, like the wise man he was, he knew the time would come when you needed to know and he made me swear I would tell you all if I outlived him. Before I do, I want you to know that to your mum and da, you were their daughter and they loved you so much."

Tears welled in Oria's eyes and she almost stopped him from telling her the truth, but like her da had known, she also knew—she couldn't hide from the truth.

Old Henry kept hold of her hand. "Your mum had suffered three miscarriages. The fourth time she learned she was with child, she was doing well. When she was eight months along, she started feeling ill. Your da learned of an exceptional healer at least a week's time from here. Your da thought to bring the healer here, but her clan would not permit it, though invited your mum and da to go there. They did." Henry got teary-eyed. "She delivered the bairn but it never drew a breath and the healer told her she'd never carry another child. They both thought it a miracle when on their return home they came upon a merchant with a bairn who was no more than a few weeks old. He told them the bairn's mother had perished from an illness and he couldn't tend the bairn and offered to sell the wee lass to them. He did, however, warn them that the mother had been a Norseman slave. They immediately paid the merchant and gladly took you from him. The timing was perfect. When they arrived home, your da proudly announced his wife had given birth to a beautiful, wee lass, and we all celebrated."

Oria sat staring at Henry. This couldn't be true. This was a bad dream—a nightmare. It had to be. How could she have gone to bed last night and woke this morning a different woman?

The thought had her asking, "I'm not a Scot?"

The way Old Henry squeezed her hand again and the tears that clouded his eyes told her there was much more to the story.

"Your da was told you are the image of your true mum."

"Someone recognized me?" Her heart felt like it slammed against her chest. "Trevor?"

Old Henry nodded. "Trevor was scouting the area and came across you here. He met a few times with your father in the dark of night, and asked about you. Your da denied it at first, insisting you were his daughter. Trevor didn't believe him and told him how a slave woman had abducted the daughter of a chieftain of a powerful Norse tribe. They were never able to find the child until now. Trevor told your da there was no denying who you were and he threatened to snatch you away from him as you'd been snatched away from your true family. Your da finally admitted the truth. I think your da felt guilty when he learned the truth. All those years, he believed your mum dead and that he was protecting you. But knowing you were stolen from your true parents disturbed him."

Oria didn't know what to think. Lies upon lies, secrets upon secrets. Promises upon promises. Was there truth to anything? At least one of the questions about her da had been solved. The dark figure he'd met with had been Trevor. It had nothing to do with betraying the clan and that brought a small bit of relief to her.

"So I'm not a Scot, I'm a Norsewoman?"

Old Henry looked hesitant to continue.

"Please, Henry, I need to know," Oria encouraged, though wondered if her painful heart could take much more.

"You're the daughter of a Norsewoman from a powerful tribe that once owned this land and all the land around it," Old Henry said.

Shock almost robbed her of her breath as an unbelievable thought slammed into her. It couldn't be, it just couldn't be, she silently told her. Why then did it seem like a piece to the puzzle had suddenly fallen into place?

Oria shook her head. "Tell me it isn't so, Henry, tell me Demelza isn't my sister and—God help me—please tell me the Beast isn't my brother."

A tear slipped down Old Henry's cheek. "I wish I could, but I can't."

This couldn't get any worse. Good Lord, her brother was responsible for all the suffering brought on the clans and worse, he had been the one responsible for tearing Royden and her apart.

"Your da was warned not to let you wed Royden," Old Henry said. "But he knew how much you loved Royden, always loved him, and he wanted you happy and safe. His only thought was to keep you safe and with the one person he knew would protect you with his life."

"Royden," Oria said as pieces to the puzzle continued to connect. "That was why my da wanted so many chieftains and some of their warriors at my wedding. He wasn't betraying them. He needed their help. He feared an imminent attack." She shut her eyes, holding back tears and the horrific memory of that day. "Chieftain Galvin Macara and his son Bayne were fearless warriors. That's why he was upset when Galvin refused to go to the wedding."

"Your da feared the attack would come on your wedding day, but he couldn't be sure," Old Henry said. "He wanted as many powerful and skilled warriors there just in case."

Oria turned a confused expression on Henry. "Why didn't my da just tell everyone?"

"Lies and secrets have a way of growing with time. Your da was trusted by all, as was his word. If the truth were known, he feared all the clans would demand you be given to the Beast in exchange for him to leave them in peace. But worst of all, he feared once Royden learned the truth he might have second thoughts about taking you as his wife. Or worse, his da would forbid him from marrying you. Your da wanted you protected and safe. With all the years you'd been gone from your true family, your da didn't think they would be so cruel as to kill your husband, the man you loved since forever," Old Henry said. "Your da also worried what might happen if the Beast managed to stop the wedding and take Royden prisoner."

"So my da devised the plan for me to wed Burnell," she said, then shook her head. "They could have easily made me a widow. Why let me stay wed to him?"

"Demelza could probably explain that to you and also tell you all about your true family," Old Henry said.

Another wave of shock slammed into her. Demelza had known from when they'd first met that they were sisters. How long did she intend to wait to tell her the truth? Another thought rushed fear through her. What would her clan, Royden's family, and the other clans think when they learned of this? And Royden. What would he think? Was their love strong enough to survive this news?

Oria got to her feet. "I have to go, Henry."

"Remember one thing, Mistress Oria. This changes nothing. You are who you've always been. A good, kind soul who loves her family, her clan."

"Thank you, Henry, and thank you for being a good friend to my da. I only hope others feel the same as you," she said and took off for the keep.

She entered the Great Hall to find Wren and Demelza talking. She thought to go straight to what had once been her da's solar, knowing that's where she'd find her husband. She had to talk with him, had to let him know, had to try—she shook her head, a sudden thought interfered and brought her to a stop near the table where the two women sat.

Wren looked about to wave her over to join them, but stopped seeing the angry glare Oria sent Demelza.

"You know," Demelza said.

Oria couldn't acknowledge her as her sister and never would she accept the Beast as her brother. What she did want was everything made clear to her. Her thoughts came fast and furious, connecting more and more pieces to the puzzle.

"I understand why your brother couldn't let me wed Royden. He'd inherit this land through our marriage and be chieftain when my da passed, giving him ownership of a large swath of land and the power that goes with it. But why let me remain wed to Burnell?" Oria demanded, anger flaring in her eyes, turning the color a sharp green.

Demelza stood. "He was wise enough to know you wouldn't want to leave the only home, only country you have known. When all was done, he planned on finding you a good Norseman to wed and return you to your clan where your husband would rule."

She might believe that but Oria didn't. "You mean he'd keep me safely tucked away wed to an old man while he made sure to see that his plan was carried out successfully."

Demelza remained silent, giving Oria her answer.

"The Beast planned to take MacKinnon keep for himself, wedding Raven." Oria smiled, realizing what Raven's bravery had done. "He didn't count on Raven escaping him, did he?"

"Raven is a prickly thorn in my brother's side," Demelza admitted. "But *our* brother—"

"He is no brother of mine," Oria spat.

Demelza remained calm, though her hands trembled. "Wolf had no intention of residing at MacKinnon keep or marrying Raven. He intended to wed Raven to a Norsemen and have him rule over Clan MacKinnon, but that is no more. Our brother will reside in our ancestral home with a Norsewoman as his bride."

"Learmonth," Oria said. "Burnell told me time and again that his ancestors had once owned all the land as far as one could see from the top of the keep. The land stretches out endlessly. But time and battles lost much of it." She shook her head. "Of course, the distant relative of Burnell's that inherits the title and clan is your brother. That's another reason your brother left me wed to Burnell, my deceased husband is somehow related to you. Couldn't your brother be satisfied with Learmonth? Why come after all the other clans?"

"*Our* brother wants what is rightfully ours—the land that had belonged to us far longer than anyone else." Demelza said. "It was a promise he made to our grandmother, born of this land, and our brother always keeps his promise."

Promises. Oria hated promises. They often hurt more than helped.

"You must understand what it meant—how it felt—that after all these years of thinking you were lost to us forever, you were found. Mother and Father were elated. They cannot wait to see you," Demelza said.

"Yet they let five years pass without acknowledging me," Oria reminded.

"That was Wolf's order," Demelza said.

"And you always do what he orders," Oria said.

"Everyone does. He's earned his position, his power, and though he can be harsh at times, he is a good man," Demelza said.

"Not in my eyes," Oria argued. "How can you even say that when he takes men captive and forces them to battle for—" It struck Oria then. "Why didn't I see it? Thinking back to Penn, Fergus, Wilfred, they all willingly joined the group of mercenaries your brother formed. He only took warriors captive from the clans he attacked to leave the clans vulnerable and unable to defend themselves so he could easily take command of them. He never had any intention of letting any of the captured warriors return home, including Royden and his brother. He formed the band of mercenaries for just that reason, to hold all those warriors' captive and prevent them from ever returning home to help free their clan."

"You have a sharp, intelligent mind just like our mother," Demelza said.

"My mother is dead as is my father," Oria shouted. "I will never acknowledge you and especially the Beast as family." She shook her head. How could she face her husband with such news? How could she even accept it herself?

The sudden urge to flee gripped her. She didn't want to run, didn't want to seem a coward, but at the moment she didn't think she could be rationale. She had to get away from everything and everyone. Her feet paid her thoughts heed and she turned and ran out of the keep. She heard Wren's voice call out for her to stop, but she ignored her. Once outside, she ran to her horse, mounted, and took off. She needed to ride, just ride, not worry, not fear, not think. She simply wanted to feel free of—everything.

The wind stung her cheeks and tore at her braid, the strands that fell free whipping around her face, she rode so hard. Tears stung at her eyes, but she wouldn't let them fall. She wouldn't let herself feel. She was tired of the pain, the endless hurt, and suffering. The lies, secrets, promises had done her so much damage that she didn't know if she'd ever recover from them.

She didn't realize anyone had followed her until her husband was there beside her. The pain, the hurt, the fear of what this news might bring tore at something inside her and she burst into tears.

Royden thought his heart would break when he saw the pain that devoured his wife's face, but when she exploded in tears, his heart completely shattered. He didn't waste a minute. He judged the distance and when the time was right, he jumped, landing perfectly behind her and took the reins from her to slow the horse to a stop. Not comfortable with being out in an open field, he guided the horse to a tree near the edge of the woods, his horse following.

He dismounted, his feet barely touching the ground when he reached up and lifted her off the horse. Her arms immediately went around him and when her feet touched the ground, she buried her face against his chest.

Royden locked her tight against him. She said something that he couldn't understand, her voice muffled by his shirt. "What did you say, Oria?"

She turned her face away from his shirt, but didn't look up at him. "Don't hate me. Please don't hate me."

"I could never hate you, Oria," he said, keeping a tight hold on her, the quiver that ran through her running along him, and her tears and words shattering his heart even more.

Oria didn't want to leave her husband's arms, didn't want to face the truth, didn't want to believe that her whole life had been a lie. She laid no blame on her parents. They hadn't known she had been abducted. They had seen a wee bairn in need and had taken her and given her all the love they had to give. She couldn't imagine, and she didn't want to, the heartache her true parents must have suffered at losing her. But she simply could not accept a new family, not now, and not one who had caused the man she loved such harm and such suffering.

"I'm here. I'm not going anywhere. I love you and nothing will ever change that," Royden assured her.

His words eased, a bit, the ache in her heart. As long as she had Royden's love nothing else mattered to her. She had always trusted his word and now more than ever, she had to trust that he loved her enough for their love to survive this news.

Oria felt like a fool for crying. She wiped at the tears that had fallen before looking up at her husband.

"No matter what, I love you," he whispered.

Tears threatened again, hearing him reassure her, letting her know that nothing could come between them, and she trusted him that it was true.

She plunged ahead needing to be done with it. "My da told Henry a family secret. It seems I'm not who I thought I was." She stopped, took a heavy breath and forced the words from her mouth that she still couldn't believe. "I'm Demelza and the Beast's sister." She felt the shock of her words tense his body, but he didn't let go of her, didn't shove her away. She hurried to explain all Old Henry had told her, adding what she had surmised herself, and the little Demelza had told her as well.

Some of what she told him stabbed at her heart and she finished the only way she could—with an apology. "I'm so sorry, Royden. This is all my fault. You suffered horrendously because of me."

"That's nonsense," he said without hesitation while pushing the loose strands of hair tenderly off her face. "You weren't what drove the Beast to do what he did. His plan all along was to take back his land. You accidentally fell into his plan and he altered it some because of you. You're not at fault. You did nothing wrong. Your parents did nothing wrong. They took a wee bairn and gave her a loving home. I just wish your da had confided in me and that he had had enough confidence in our love to know that it would have made no difference to me. I would have married you regardless. I can, however, understand how the other clans may have felt and what they may have done. So in that regard, I'm glad he didn't tell anyone. Your da did the best he could to protect you, even having you wed Burnell."

His words brought a rush of relief to her and she hugged him tight, grateful for his love, his understanding, and for the honorable man she had always known him to be.

"What now? What happens when other clans discover who I am?' she asked, only just considering what it might mean.

"Who is there left to complain but Galvin. The Beast has already moved his cohorts into the area. Trevor has the Clan MacGlennen, Fergus has the Clan MacDonnegal, I would think someone loyal to him will have Clan Macara, Clan MacKinnon remains mine, and he takes Learmonth for himself."

"He surrounds us, Royden," Oria said. "How do we ever get free of him?"

Royden responded honestly and with his own misgivings. "I don't know if we do. He planned well and played a good game as my da suggested. He established himself here, planted roots or nourished his roots that were already here, digging in deeper. As much as I want revenge against him, I don't think it's going to be possible, not unless we want more bloodshed and loss. And I don't believe anyone wants any more of that."

"Are you saying we need to befriend the Beast?" she asked.

He tightened his arm around her waist. "I'm saying that I will do whatever is necessary to make certain no one takes my wife from me and that she remains my wife. I won't lose you again, Oria, and if I have to make friends with the Beast to assure that, then I will."

Oria opened her mouth but nothing spilled out. His words had stunned her and made her realize the depths of his love for her.

Royden kissed her when she failed to speak. He couldn't help it. Her partially open mouth was just too tempting to ignore. His tongue slipped past her lips and at first he felt her surprise and then she responded as she always did as if she'd been given a gift to enjoy, and she did.

He stopped the kiss, his desire mounting much too fast and while he had a brief thought to take her quickly behind the tree, knowing her desire mounted as fast as his, he warned himself not to. There was no telling who lurked about. He was glad he'd decided against it when his wife spoke.

"I want to go home. I want to make love. I don't want to think of anything but you and me. I don't want to feel anything but the love we have for each other."

Royden responded by scooping her up and placing her on her horse, then mounting his own.

Oria was surprised that he didn't join her on her horse.

Royden smiled. "Let's see who makes it to the keep first, though I warn you I—"

Oria took off, her laughter trailing behind her.

Royden took a moment to listen to it, the joyous sound swirling around him and filling his heart with relief, then he followed after her. He'd let her win, wanting to remain behind her or at her side to keep her safe. He'd pull ahead for a bit, so she wouldn't figure out his plan.

That was until he realized she actually was beating him. That's when the race became real.

Oria was waiting on the steps to the keep when her husband caught up with her. She was smiling. Her husband wasn't.

"I'll race you to our bedchamber," she said with a laugh.

And when she saw that he didn't laugh, she took off.

Royden caught her before she reached the door. He scooped her up and threw her over his shoulder. "You rode hard and fast and got your victory, wife. Now it's my turn to ride hard and fast and—"

"Victory will be mine once again," she declared with a laugh that grew louder when her husband swatted her backside.

Chapter Twenty-eight

"What do you mean no?" Oria asked, surprised and annoyed.

"What further explanation of no is necessary? No is no," Royden said, tucking his plaid in place.

"You're refusing to make love to me?" she asked, not believing her own words. It wasn't possible. Neither of them ever refused the other.

Royden walked over to the bed, trying to ignore the way her taut nipples pleaded with him. Or was that his aroused shaft pleading with him to get busy making love to his wife? He fought the urge, standing beside the bed, not trusting himself to sit. This had to be done. It couldn't be put it off any longer.

"I've lost count of how many times in the last three days that we've made love, not that I'm complaining. But it's time for you to stop avoiding what needs to be done." Royden raised his hand when his wife went to argue. "You need to talk with your sister." To Royden's relief, his wife pulled the blanket up to cover her breasts.

"I haven't avoided it. It's been an endless thought that I can find no answer to," Oria said.

"You'll find no answer in your swirling thoughts and perhaps you won't find one when you speak with your sister, but this revelation cannot be ignored. Your parents will want to meet you and one day the Beast will come here."

She bristled at the thought. "I don't want to meet any of them."

"Ignoring them isn't going to make them go away," Royden said and sat on the bed, his desire having abated enough for him to trust himself. Besides, it was more important for them to talk. "Tell me why you don't want to acknowledge your true family, Oria."

She hesitated at first, not wanting to openly admit what she'd been thinking.

"Tell me, Oria," he coaxed. "I'm here to listen, not to judge."

He'd been patient with her since their return home. They had agreed that it would be best if no acknowledgment was made of her true heritage. The wounds of the attack had begun to heal and this might open them again. They had spoken with his da and Wren since they had witnessed and heard what had been said and both had agreed that the secret wouldn't remain a secret for long, since servants in MacGlennen keep surely must have heard Oria and Demelza. Tongues would start wagging soon enough.

Wren had told them all would be revealed when the time was right. And Oria hoped her remark had been because of a vision and not just to ease her concern. They had spoken little of it since then and her husband was right. She couldn't continue to ignore it. It wasn't going to go away. It was there to stay.

She reached for his hand, hooking his fingers with hers, to hold on to them, needing that small connection with him and said aloud what had haunted her. "Once I acknowledge, accept, my true birth, I won't be the daughter of William and Claire of the Clan MacGlennen anymore. I won't be born of the Highlands, of its beauty and strength. I won't be me anymore."

Royden laced his fingers with hers and held tight. "I know who you are and who you will always be—my wife. But I also understand what you're saying. So tell me who you think you will be if not you."

"That's just it, I don't know," Oria confessed, her heart heavy with sadness.

"Then it's time to find out—together."

He reminded her time and time again she wasn't alone and she did the same for him. They both needed that reminder after having been torn apart for five long, empty years. They no longer needed to do things alone, they had each other once again.

"I guess I have been avoiding it," she admitted.

"Trevor has sent me endless messages that started out demanding you return and speak to his wife to his last one yesterday, pleading for you to return and talk with a heartbroken Demelza."

"She's all right, isn't she?" Oria asked, worried for the petite woman. "I should have never yelled at her, especially with her not feeling well and being so close to delivering her bairn."

"You had every right to feel as you did and I doubt Demelza is as fragile as her husband believes. She couldn't possibly be, being wed to Trevor."

Oria smiled and unlocked her fingers from his, then hurried out of bed. "I'll get dressed and we can be on our way."

Royden admired his wife's nicely curved backside, the gentle sway of her hips, though her sway was anything but gentle when his shaft was buried deep inside her.

He stood, his shaft feeling as if it stood before he did, he had grown hard so fast. "We have time for a quick roll in the bed."

"No, we best get going," she said, not looking his way.

He took hurried steps to her, grabbing her shift from her hand. "You say no to me?"

"This is important. We must see to it right away," Oria argued.

"Aye, you're right, we must." He scooped her up in his arms and had her down on the bed and slipped inside her before another protest could slip from her lips. It was when she grinned at him that he realized she had tricked him into getting what she wanted.

"Damn, wife, you did that on purpose," he said, annoyed but much too snug inside her to deny either of them.

"Aye, I got you right where I want you," she said and began to move against him.

Royden had no willpower to deny her or himself. "It will be a quick one."

"Aye, a quick one," she agreed with a wider smile.

It was an hour later that Royden picked his garments up off the floor and got dressed yet again and with Oria's stomach grumbling, it was another hour before they took their leave.

***

Parlan and Wren once again joined them and as they neared MacGlennen village, Oria drew her horse near Wren.

"You seem worried for Demelza. Have you seen something? Does she have a difficult delivery?" Oria asked.

"There's something that precedes the delivery I cannot see, which could mean any number of things," Wren said. "I sensed when I met her that she would have five bairns, but that doesn't mean she won't lose any bairns, just that five bairns would survive."

"I didn't help by arguing with her," Oria said, feeling guilty.

"Demelza is far from a fragile woman. She was far more upset with the way you learned about your true birth. She had hoped you and she would become friends first and that would ease the burden of the news. She was born two years after you were taken. Her mother had told her stories about you and they both hoped that one day you would be reunited with the family. There is much she wishes to tell you."

"I will listen, though I don't know how I will feel about it," Oria said.

"Listening is all you need to do right now," Wren said.

"What else did Demelza confide in you?" Oria asked.

"Give Demelza a chance to tell you. She has longed for the day she could do so and longed for the day she would get to know her sister. This was not her family's fault nor the family who claimed you as their own, loved you, and kept you safe."

"Then whose fault is it?" Oria asked, looking for an answer.

"The slave who took you? Those who made her a slave? Your true mother who let a slave care for you? Or had fate simply intervened? There is no definitive answer, nor an answer that would satisfy the pain and hurt that stirs in you. The most important thing for you to remember is that you were loved by the parents who raised you and you're loved by the parents who lost you."

Wren's words remained with her as they entered the village that had once been her home, a loving home with loving memories. People smiled at her, waved, called out greetings and she returned them in kind as she had always done.

"Are you all right, Oria?" Royden asked, his horse plodding along beside hers.

Her smile remained as she turned her head to face him. "Aye, I am. I can do this. I want to do this."

Royden was glad to see her eyes spark with renewed confidence and he was relieved and happy that she'd regained it for herself.

Trevor and Demelza stood at the top of the keep steps and Oria almost chuckled seeing the tight arm Trevor kept around his wife's waist to keep her from rushing down the stairs.

Oria was grateful for the snug fit of her husband's hand around hers as they climbed the stairs. She was also glad for her returned confidence that had her speaking before anyone else could. "I hope you can forgive me for my rude behavior the last time I was here. I'd like for us to talk. I'd like to get to know you, Demelza."

Demelza broke free of her husband's arms and flung herself at Oria, tears running down her cheeks.

Oria hugged her not because it was the mannerly thing to do, but because she felt the need to hold her sister tight.

"I am so happy to hear that. I want so badly to know you better," Demelza said, easing the hold she had on Oria. "We can talk in my," —she stopped abruptly to correct herself— "your mother's solar."

That Demelza acknowledged the woman who raised her as her mother touched Oria's heart. "It is your solar now just as Royden's mum's solar is now mine." She smiled. "And one day will be our daughters. Time doesn't stand still for anyone."

"Then let us not waste a minute," Demelza said and took Oria's hand.

Wren stepped forward from where she stood to the side with Parlan. "If you have need of me, I will be tending those in the clan who require my help."

Demelza nodded. "I will see you later, Wren." Then she sent her husband a smile as she hurried past him with Oria and entered the keep.

Trevor looked to Royden. "I appreciate this."

"I do this for my wife and for your wife," Royden said.

"You still have my gratitude and I am in your debt."

"Good, then settle the debt now and tell me what the Beast has planned for this area."

***

Happy and loving memories welcomed Oria like a comforting embrace as soon as she entered her mum's solar.

"My mum died when I was only eight years, but I have wonderful memories of her. I hope I can be as good and loving mum as she had been to me," Oria said, needing Demelza to know how much her mum meant to her.

"I'm glad a good woman found you and raised you with such love," Demelza said and pointed to a chair worn from use, for Oria to sit.

Oria didn't hesitate. It had been her mum's chair and she recalled sitting on her lap and listening to endless tales of brave Highland warriors and strong Highland women.

"Our mother is a good mother as well. Every day she prayed to the gods that you were kept well and that you were loved. She was so pleased and relieved to know that her prayers had been answered."

It was strange to hear her say *our* mother, but Oria made no comment. She took Wren's advice and listened.

"She so looks forward to meeting you and is quite upset that our brother, Wolf, forbid it until things were settled here. He felt it wouldn't be safe for her or me to travel here until then. Our father agreed with him, the plan to reclaim our land having taken years to execute and with you being safe, neither felt there was any reason to risk failure."

Oria was actually grateful for that decision. She didn't know what she would have done if she'd been swept away from the only place she'd known as home and risk Royden never finding her.

"I must admit I was thrilled when plans were suddenly changed and Trevor was ordered to come here and establish a home with me. *Móðir*, mother in our language, and I talked endlessly about me meeting with you. The one thing she wanted you to know was how her heart broke when you were taken from her. How she missed you suckling at her breast and the way you would curl your tiny finger around hers and hold on tight even as you slept, as if you knew you didn't have much time with her. She so loves you. We all do."

Oria fought back tears, hearing the pain her abduction had caused her family, that was foreign to her yet loved her so much.

Not knowing what to say, she let her thought speak aloud for her. "I don't know any of you."

"I realize it will take time for you to accept us as family and so does *Móðir*, not so much Wolf. To him you are family and he was more than upset when your King and our King ordered him to release your husband, his brother, and the clan warriors that had been taken captive."

"I didn't know that," Oria said. "Why did they do that?"

"Wolf refused to say. I only know that plans changed after that and while our brother will get what he wants—the land that is ours—how he obtains it won't be as he planned."

"You know nothing of why that is?" Oria asked.

"No, and neither does Trevor or so he says. It seems Wolf was sworn to secrecy by both Kings."

"You think your husband keeps the truth from you?" Oria asked.

"Trevor and Wolf have been friends since they could walk. They confide everything in each other. I can't believe Wolf didn't tell him all of it, but I also know if he gave our brother his word not to say anything, then Wolf's secret is safe with him."

"Secrets, promises," — Oria shook her head— "I've had enough of them."

"I've always resented being sent from the room when the men gathered to discuss things," Demelza said. "Mother wasn't. She'd entered whether invited or not and Father never chased her out. She told me one day I would be given the same respect, but that day hasn't come. I believe it's because my petite size makes me appear fragile and so everyone thinks they need to protect me. I may be petite, but I'm not weak. I am like our grandmother, the one born here in the Highlands. She was petite and stronger than any woman I have ever known. She dared to love a Norseman and dared to believe that one day the land that had belonged to her clan and had been unjustly taken away, would one day belong to her family once again."

"*Seanmhair*, grandmother in our language," Oria said, a strength rising in her that Scot blood still ran through her.

"I believe our *seanmhair* would be proud of us both," Demelza said.

"I believe you're right," Oria agreed with a smile. "I also believe our husbands are discussing things right now that we should hear for ourselves."

Demelza sighed. "I agree, but Trevor would never permit it."

"I have a friend who taught me how to sneak and have a listen without being caught. Shall we see what we can find out for ourselves?" Oria challenged with a grin.

"I never got to sneak about on my own when I was young. Wolf always kept a watchful eye on me." She chuckled. "Though when Trevor and I fell in love we found a way to keep it from my brother, certain he wouldn't approve."

"What happened when he found out?" Oria asked, knowing how ruthless the Beast could be.

"At first he looked ready to kill and Trevor shoved me behind him ready to battle. Then Wolf laughed, not a sound often heard from him. He'd known all along what we'd been up to and was glad that I had fallen in love with a man strong and brave enough to keep me safe. And Trevor certainly has done so—to a fault."

"Then let's change that. I'll teach you the skill I learned from one who was a master at it," Oria said and stood, stretching her hand out to Demelza and going to her side to help her out of the chair when she saw her struggle to stand.

"Finally, I have a sister I can plot with just as Wolf plotted with Trevor," Demelza said with excitement.

Oria thought how she hadn't wanted to like Demelza even before she had met the woman. But that had changed quickly and she had found she liked the petite woman who handled her demanding husband with strength and patience. She hadn't known what to think when she had discovered Demelza was her sister, though anger had reared its head. But for some reason, she continued to like the woman. There was something about her that made her feel like she'd known her longer than the short time since they'd met. Perhaps it was the same blood that ran through them both, that connected them, that made them sisters.

They walked to the door arm in arm, smiling. Oria opened it and quickly rushed Demelza behind her when they were met with a dagger pointed at them.

Chapter Twenty-nine

"Firth?' Demelza said from behind Oria.

Oria hadn't recognized him at first, the scar her husband had left on him red and angry, not fully healed and leaving him difficult to look upon.

"Shocked I managed to escape my guards?" Firth asked with a sneer. "There's one thing I learned fighting for the Beast. Trust no one and always be prepared for the worst. I've built myself a sizeable troop of disgruntled warriors. Ones the Beast himself discarded."

That alarmed Oria. If the Beast had rejected them there had to be something seriously wrong with them. She couldn't let him take them out of the keep. If he got them out, they were as sure as dead.

"I heard you talking in there. I wasn't going to take you," he said with a nod at Oria. I intended to leave you with your throat slit and your face slashed for your husband to find you."

The thought turned Oria's stomach and Demelza's as well since she heard the petite woman gag.

"I only wanted the Beast's sister, but now I have his two sisters. That should get his attention," Firth said, the scar making his grin appear grotesque.

"You don't want to do this, Firth," Demelza said. "The Beast will make you suffer horribly for it."

"I'll have my revenge and he'll pay well to get his sisters back," Firth said. "Though he won't know until it's too late how much me and my men enjoyed them."

Oria felt Demelza's hand rush to her stomach, concerned for her unborn child.

"Let's go," Firth ordered and gave Oria a good poke in the chest with the tip of his dagger. "And if you think to fight like you did the last time, know that as soon as you do, I'll slice your sister's stomach open and let the bairn spill out."

Demelza gasped in fear.

"I won't fight you," Oria said, having stifled the pain she'd felt from the jab of his dagger and now feeling the blood soak into her shift and tunic from the wound he'd left.

"Move," he ordered, stepping away from the open door to let them out.

When Firth pulled his hood up, Oria saw that he wore the brown garment of a monk and surmised that was how he had gotten past everyone. It was how he would make it out of the keep with them, no one paying a monk mind, if she didn't do something.

Firth stepped in front of them to go down the stairs and ordered Demelza to go behind him.

Oria kept herself protectively in front of Demelza. "She is uneasy on her feet. She may fall into you and then what. Alert everyone to your presence? Let her follow me so I may help her."

He didn't argue, but he ordered them to hurry.

They entered the Great Hall and Oria was disappointed no one was about. At least someone would have seen them, but then what did it matter. She had to stop them from leaving the keep. Once outside, he probably intended to take them around back where they wouldn't be seen and into the woods. His men were probably waiting for him there, and if he managed to get them there, all would be lost.

Oria recalled something she had promised her husband, that she would call out to him if she was ever in danger. She didn't hesitate. She turned quickly wrapping herself around Demelza, to protect her and the bairn, and screamed out her husband's name.

"ROYDEN!"

She felt the blade slash along her arm, but she didn't release Demelza. Her head was suddenly yanked back and the dagger was at her throat.

"Let her go," Firth ordered.

Demelza pushed at her, urging her to do as he said and when she did, Oria was yanked back.

"Release my wife now!" Royden demanded, his heart pounding wildly and his anger soaring along with fear for his wife.

Even with the knife at her throat, Oria felt safer now that her husband was there.

"Come to me, Demelza," Trevor ordered.

"Go to him and I'll slice your sister's throat and I'll have just enough time to slice your belly before your husband can reach you."

"You're a dead man," Trevor warned, fighting with all his strength not to charge at the man.

"Maybe, but these two will be dead as well if anyone dares to make a move," Firth threatened.

Royden saw the spot where the blood soaked at his wife's chest and that her sleeve had been sliced open, blood soaking the material around it and running along her hand. He wanted to rush the man and strangle the life out of him, but Firth would slice her throat before he could reach her. He had failed Oria once, he wouldn't fail her again.

"All will be well," Royden said, his eyes on his wife.

"I know," Oria said without an ounce of doubt in her response.

"Your husband lies," Firth said, raising his voice in anger. "You both will come with me or the three of us will die right here."

"Oh, goodness!" Demelza cried out and looked down. A pool of liquid was gathering at her feet.

"Demelza!" Trevor shouted and went to rush to her,

"Stop!" Royden warned, seeing Firth ready to slice his wife's throat.

Trevor forced himself to heed Royden's words.

Oria seized the opportunity to help her sister. "She's going into labor. She's no good to you now. Let her be. Besides, your revenge would be more satisfying taking me, since I'm the sister the Beast has yet to meet."

Demelza let out a groan and doubled over, her arm wrapping around her stomach.

"See, she will only slow you down," Oria said and saw the hope in Trevor's eyes that he would leave Demelza behind.

Firth nicked her neck, a small river of blood flowing down her smooth skin. "I see you follow us, hear your horses following, spot a tracker, and I'll slice her piece by piece. I have a sizeable troop who have eyes on the village. Follow me and I'll know it and she'll suffer for it. Understood?"

Royden nodded, his face pinched tight and his eyes on his wife. "Understood."

"You want her back, then let the Beast come for her." Firth backed slowly out of the room.

"I love you, Royden," Oria called out just before they slipped out of the keep.

Trevor was at his wife's side in an instant, scooping her up in his arms.

Royden looked to his da and without a word spoken, his da nodded, and Royden hurried out of the Great Hall to leave the keep through the kitchen.

"Go get Wren," Trevor ordered.

"No!" Demelza warned. "They see him leave the keep and they'll think he's following after Oria.

"I'll find a way to get her here," Parlan said and took the same path as his son, through the kitchen.

"Put me down, Trevor, and go get Wolf. You know you have to and I know he's close," Demelza said.

"I'll see you safely to our bed first," Trevor insisted, annoyed he had to leave her yet knowing she was right. Wolf had to be told as Firth had demanded.

"No. There is no time to waste. Wren will see to me. You must help rescue Oria. I cannot lose my sister when I've only just found her. And I can't bear the thought of what Firth has planned for her, a fate I would have suffered, not to mention what would have happened to our child, if not for Oria not only shielding me from Firth's dagger, but convincing him to leave me here." She stopped him before he could protest. "I am not some fragile flower you need to always protect. Go do what must be done and I will do the same."

Trevor thought his heart was being ripped out of him when after he kissed her and told her he loved her, he turned and walked away from his wife. He was never so relieved to see Wren and Parlan enter the room.

"Take care with my wife," Trevor ordered Wren.

Wren took no offense to his sharp command and soothed the fear that she knew had caused it. "Don't worry, all will be well."

"And while I protect your wife, you take care to help my son," Parlan said as he passed him.

Trevor nodded and hurried out of the room.

***

Royden squatted down on his haunches behind a bush, separating the branches just enough to see past them. He had watched Firth shove his wife to the center of the small clearing where they'd stopped. He had given her a hard push, ordering her to sit. She had stumbled and fallen, landing on her wounded arm. He had wanted to charge at the man, snap his neck, and be done with it. But Firth remained too close to Oria and his blade could do far too much damage to her before Royden reached her.

His wife remained brave and was busy tending her wound. She tore off part of her other sleeve to wrap around the wound that still oozed blood. She hadn't paid her chest wound any attention and he assumed her garment had soaked enough blood to stop the bleeding. Her neck wound was minor, nothing more than a dribble of blood. It was important he get her to Wren, concerned any of the wounds could eventually prove deadly if not tended properly. But first, he was going to make Firth suffer for what he'd done to her. He wasn't going to let him get away this time. He intended to make certain Firth never got to hurt his wife again.

"It's a good thing Firth doesn't have a sizeable troop, or any skilled warriors with him, or they would have captured you by now," Royden whispered without turning around.

"I was soundless. You couldn't have heard me," Trevor said, keeping his voice to a whisper as he hunched down beside Royden.

"I could smell you."

Trevor lifted an arm to sniff his sleeve. "My wife," he said, her sweet scent lingering on him, then quickly peered past the bushes. "So you realized Firth had no troop with him?"

"He wouldn't have warriors wait this close to your keep. Your men would have decimated them. But he's not foolish enough to come alone. There's a good chance he has a troop nearby, so time is not our friend here."

"You should let the Beast handle this. Firth would suffer far more at his hands than yours."

Keeping his eye on Oria, he asked, "And what would you do if it were Demelza?"

"That would depend on if I could reach my wife before the Beast did," Trevor said, his eyes on Oria as well.

"How long before the Beast arrives?"

"Not long," Trevor said. "Firth doesn't stand a chance against Wolf and his men."

"Either will my wife, if Firth reaches her first," Royden said and stood.

"What are you doing?" Trevor asked.

"I'm going to get my wife before someone gets her killed," Royden said and was about to step past the bushes when he stopped and dropped down to peer through the bushes again.

That got Trevor to turn his head and do the same. "It's that damn leper."

"You know Brother Noble?" Royden asked.

"Is that his name?" Trevor shook his head. "We call him leper. He begs for food sometimes. What is he doing approaching those men?"

"My guess would be that he's trying to help my wife, since she has been good to him," Royden said and watched.

Brother Noble entered the clearing, leaning on a sturdy branch that Royden assumed he used as a walking staff. His gait was slow, his body stooped, and the hood of his brown robe hung over his face.

"He's a leper," one of the two men with Firth said and though he wasn't close, the man moved farther away.

The other man went to the edge of the woods, looking as if he would dash away any minute, and Firth stepped away from Oria as Brother Noble approached her.

"Stay where you are, leper," Firth ordered.

Brother Noble paid him no mind. His feet continued to shuffle along the ground as if it was too much of an effort to lift them as he moved toward Oria. "Mistress Oria is my friend and I see that she's hurt. I stopped to pray for her."

"We don't need your prayers, be gone," Firth demanded, waving his hand trying to shoo the man away.

"I don't mean to of—" A hacking cough robbed the leper of words and it was a minute or so before he could talk once again. "I don't mean to offend. A prayer or two, then I'll be gone."

Royden almost yelled out for the leper to stop, he was getting far too close to Oria, but he held his tongue, realizing what the leper was doing. He was shielding Oria from Firth and the other two men. They wouldn't dare approach her with the leper standing between them.

Royden owed Brother Noble for his bravery and for giving him the chance he'd been waiting for—Firth far enough away from his wife that he couldn't harm her. He stood and entered the clearing.

Firth rushed toward Oria when he spotted Royden, but stopped abruptly the leper blocking his way.

"I warned you," Firth shouted at Royden, then looked to the leper, his shout even stronger. "Move!"

"I'm not finished praying," the leper said.

Royden thought to order Oria to come to him, but being closer, seeing her more clearly, he saw that her wounds and the days' events had begun to take a toll on her. She was pale and the cloth around her arm was soaked with blood, and he didn't know the extent of her chest wound. She needed Wren. But at the moment, she was safer where she was, behind the leper.

She sent him a smile and he caught the cringe she tried to hide. She was in pain and he cringed along with her, though it resembled more of a scowl, he was so angry that she suffered. Her forced walk through the woods certainly hadn't helped her. Or that he hadn't gotten to her faster.

He could almost hear what her smile was saying. "I've been waiting for you."

She never doubted he would come for her just like she had never doubted he'd return home to her.

"Leave, leper, now!" Firth screamed at him and raised his dagger, taking the tip in his hand, ready to fling it at the man.

"That is not a wise thing to do, my son—" A cough interrupted him for a moment, a reminder of the danger of his illness. "You will have to retrieve it from my body and you don't want to be that close to me. Even from that distance you must smell the stench of my rotting flesh. Then you'd have to retrieve the dagger awash with my blood. And during the time it would take you to do that, you would be left weaponless, thus vulnerable."

"You didn't plan this well, Firth," Trevor said, stepping out of the woods, his sword drawn. "You may have escaped my warriors, a lucky moment, but there isn't a chance you'll escape the Beast."

The two men with Firth looked around, then at each other. Their decision didn't take long, without a word, they took off into the woods.

"You're done," Royden said, Firth's unexpected laughter sending a chill through him.

"You think I learned nothing while fighting for the Beast," Firth flipped the knife and caught it by the handle.

A rumbling noise in the woods caught Royden's attention and he worried whose arrival it portended. Suddenly warriors emerged on horses, one by one, from the woods behind Firth. They were a ragtag group and from the many scars on most of their faces and along their necks, they looked to be a vicious lot and fought for one thing and one thing only—coin. This was never about revenge for Firth. It was about coin.

"Who was it that didn't plan well now, Trevor?" Firth asked with a smug laugh.

Fear choked Royden and twisted his gut. He couldn't let Firth take Oria. She was exhausted and in pain. He had to get to her. He couldn't wait. He ran to his wife. His only thought was to get her safely in his arms.

Her scream tore through him and when he saw two arrows had landed on either side of her, he stopped dead.

"Back away, Royden, and you too, leper, or I'll order the next arrow through her wounded arm," Firth warned.

For a brief second Royden thought to lunge himself at the man, but he'd do his wife no good if he died. He reluctantly did as Firth ordered as did the leper, backing slowly away from Oria.

"I would put you out of your misery, leper, but I prefer you suffer for interfering with my plans," Firth said and with a sharp snap of his hand, a horse was brought to him. He mounted and the warrior that brought the horse, yanked Oria to her feet.

Royden cringed but again it was more a deep scowl when he saw his wife's face tighten in pain.

The warrior lifted Oria none to gently and dropped her carelessly in front of Firth on the horse.

Royden made sure to mark the man's face in his memory so he could make certain he suffered for causing his wife even more pain.

"Tell the Beast it will cost him to get his sister back," Firth said and laughed, his dagger appearing suddenly in his hand. "I can't promise in what condition. Though, I do think she needs a scar like the one her husband gave me. Tell the Beast he'll hear from me when I'm ready to make the exchange."

Royden wanted to roar with rage as his wife sent him the same smile she had sent him before. She would wait again for him to come for her. He failed her again and he had to fight with himself not to take off after her. But he'd never be able to keep up with the fast pace they were sure to set. He needed a horse to go after them and he could use the help of a good tracker just in case, and he didn't have a minute to spare.

"He set a fine trap," Trevor said, shaking his head. "I underestimated him."

Royden was aware that he had done the same thing. He'd been so intent on getting to his wife that he hadn't considered all the probabilities of the situation. All he had thought about was that he had to get to Oria, just as he did now, her life being in even more peril.

He turned to Trevor and as he did he was glad to see the leper was gone. He didn't want to see Brother Noble hurt when he had bravely protected Oria.

"I need to get my horse and a tracker," Royden told Trevor.

"You need to wait here. Both will be here soon, the tracker exceptional, the horse well trained, warriors to help you fight, and the Beast who will not rest until he finds his sister."

Royden didn't argue. All that mattered was that he got his wife back safely and if he had to rely on the man who had caused all the heartache and damage to his family and clan, then so be it. He would do whatever it took to get his wife back without her suffering any more harm.

He didn't bother to look to the sky when he thought it was a roll of thunder he heard. He knew what it was—horses, lots of them.

The Beast was about to arrive.

Chapter Thirty

Royden stood, his feet planted firmly on the ground, his sword in his hand, ready to meet the man who had brought endless heartache to his family, but now was the one person who could help save his wife.

Warriors fanned out along the edge of the woods, circling the clearing, some wore helmets, some didn't. A section parted and into the clearing rode the Beast.

He sat his horse tall and straight, not a slump to his body. A fur cloak was draped over broad shoulders and some type of leather hide covered his chest. He wore a helmet, a narrow piece running down the center to cover his nose, leaving a portion of his cheeks and beard-covered jaw exposed. Long black hair fell from under his helmet to rest past his shoulders. But it was his eyes that drew the most attention. They appeared as black as the darkest night, not a spark or twinkle of light to them, empty eyes, soulless eyes, and Royden understood why men feared him.

Royden, however, was not one of them. He had suffered enough because of him. He would suffer no more.

"I need a horse and your tracker, now!" Royden ordered.

Every single one of the Beast's warriors drew their weapons.

Royden cared little for their display of strength. He knew the Beast would not hurt him, for if he did, he'd be hurting his sister as well.

"A horse, now!" Royden demanded again.

Trevor stepped forward. "They left only moments ago. If we pursue now, there's a good chance we'll catch them."

"Firth demands coins in exchange for my wife's life, though he doesn't know what condition he'll return her in," Royden said. "We don't have time to waste. Oria has suffered three wounds. She needs a healer."

The Beast snapped his hand and one of his warriors disappeared and reappeared quickly with two horses in tow.

"Firth is mine," the Beast commanded, his deep voice full of strength and the confidence he'd be obeyed without question.

"We'll see about that," Royden said and took the reins of the horse handed to him and mounted quickly. He didn't wait for orders or instructions. He took off after his wife.

***

Oria's arm pounded with pain with every hoof beat of the horse. The wound needed serious attention. Her shift and tunic had served as a good covering to stop the bleeding of her chest wound. She didn't believe it as serious as her arm wound and for that she was grateful. She had been shocked and beyond thrilled when she had laid eyes on Royden when he had returned home, but it couldn't compare with the relief she felt when her husband had walked out of the woods. Seeing him, she knew all would be well. Even though Firth had spirited her away, she had no doubt her husband would follow and find her. Her only hope was that it didn't take him long. She feared what Firth would do to her.

Firth brought his horse to a sudden stop and the jolt sent a pain shooting through her arm. It didn't help when she was yanked off the horse and placed on another to ride alone. Her first thought was that it gave her a chance to escape.

Firth brought his horse next to hers. "I can almost hear your mind thinking on how you can escape. Try it and I promise you that you will be caught and when I get done with you, your husband will never want to look upon you again."

The thought sent a shudder through her, remembering the pain of healing from the slash to her jaw that he had given her. But what fate awaited her if she didn't try to escape?

"Any attempt not to keep pace and you'll suffer for it," Firth ordered.

She watched as he rode over to a group of warriors. A slim warrior hurried to a horse that a warrior already sat and mounted behind him. They talked with Firth briefly then took off with several other warriors following.

Firth returned, two warriors keeping pace with him and drawing up on either side of her while the one warrior who had remained near her directed his horse to a position behind her.

"I'm going to have some fun with you this evening while your beloved husband follows in the wrong direction. Firth laughed as he positioned his horse in front of her and with a wave of his hand took off. She had no choice but to follow and keep pace, but there was something she could do that would help Royden find her. She would suffer for it, but if he didn't find her, she would suffer anyway. She had no choice but to take the chance.

***

Royden joined the tracker on the ground when they came upon an area where Firth and his men had separated. Royden could clearly see for himself what had taken place.

He stood before the tracker did. "He tries to deceive us."

The tracker nodded to the Beast. "It could be either trail."

Royden took the reins of his horse and walked down the one trail, looking for any sign his wife might have dared to leave him. When he spotted something on the ground, he dropped down and touched the spot.

"Blood," he said, smearing it between his fingers and walked farther down to find more. His wife's blood. She was letting her arm drip blood so he could easily follow her. He mounted his horse and took off. He had to get to her. She was risking her life so that he could find her.

He rode fast and hard. They couldn't be that far ahead. Firth might think he tricked them, but he doubted the man would take a chance. He had probably ordered some of his warriors to lag behind and that had him slowing his horse. The Beast was soon beside him, exactly what he had wanted.

"Firth probably left warriors along the way to deal with us and I can't spare the time to fight them when my wife lets her wound bleed so I can track her."

"Keep riding, my warriors will see to it, but know that I ride directly behind you," the Beast said. "I will not lose my sister."

"Something we both agree on," Royden said and once again took off. This time not intending to stop until he caught up with Oria.

Several of the Beast's warriors rode past him and it was only a short time later that he passed three dead bodies tossed aside to leave the path clear. He kept going, thinking only of getting to his wife, glancing down to make sure he followed the blood trail and with every sizeable drop of blood he saw he worried that his wife wouldn't survive.

Royden pushed the horse harder and when they broke out of the forest into a field, he spotted them. His wife was flanked by two warriors and Firth rode in the front. The Beast's warriors were busy taking down more of Firth's men. He had to get to Oria. He had to reach her before Firth realized he couldn't escape them and he made Oria suffer for it.

The Beast was suddenly beside him, two of his warriors passing them. They would dispose of the two warriors flanking his wife.

"Your choice," the Beast shouted to him.

Royden understood. Firth or his wife. There was no choice to make. "My wife."

The Beast gave a nod and rode past him.

Royden went straight for his wife and when he saw her body slump to the side, then pop back up again, he knew she was fighting to stay alert, stay on the horse.

Royden was grateful when the Beast's warriors got rid of the two warriors to either side of his wife with ease. The warriors followed along behind the Beast as he went for Firth, who had taken off when he had seen his plan collapse. It left the area open for Royden to reach his wife. He saw that she was trying to slow the horse down, but he doubted she had any strength left to do so.

The horse did begin to slow some and that made it easier for him to do what he needed to do as soon as he got close enough.

Jump!

He landed behind her, his arm going around her waist to rest her back against him. "I'm here, Oria. I've got you."

"Royden," she barely whispered and her body went limp against him as if knowing she was finally safe and could rest.

He slowed the horse and brought the animal to a stop. He yanked her tunic up to grab at the hem and ripped off a piece, then wrapped it snugly around her wound, and couldn't help but wince when she did.

Oria fought the darkness that was slowly devouring her. She had to tell him before it was too late. She couldn't die without telling him one last time. "I love you… always."

Her head lolled to the side and her body felt as if it drained of life. Fear slammed into him. "You're going to be all right. You must be all right. I can't lose you, Oria. I won't lose you."

He turned the horse around as a horrific scream pierced the air.

Firth was kneeling on the ground, staring at his arm that had been severed from the elbow down, the Beast standing over him the blade of his sword stained with blood.

Firth pleaded desperately with the Beast. "Please. Please. I'm sorry. Mercy! Please have mercy on me, I beg you."

Royden gave the Beast a nod as he rode past him. He was indebted to the man. Without his help, he feared Oria might have been lost to him. Realizing that, he knew he'd have no choice... he'd have to make peace with the Beast.

Another horrific scream filled the air and Royden thought how right Trevor had been. Firth would suffer far worse at the hands of the Beast than he would have with him, and he was glad for it.

***

Royden yelled for help as soon as he entered the Clan MacGlennen village. People came running when they caught a glimpse of Oria lifeless in his arms. They helped him get her off the horse and he held his wife snug against him as he took the keep stairs two at a time, someone holding the door open for him so he could rush inside.

"Wren!" he shouted, his voice echoing off the stone walls.

He hurried up the stairs, recalling that Demelza had gone into labor. Oria needed Wren, Demelza would have to wait. Not knowing where exactly Wren would be, he shouted out her name as he climbed the stairs.

"Wren! Wren!"

Parlan's worried face greeted him on the second floor and his eyes shot wide seeing his son clutching Oria. "Good, Lord, what happened?"

"Wren, Oria needs Wren," Royden said and she suddenly appeared. "You have to help her, Wren." He heard the plea in his words and he would continue to plea. He would do anything to save his wife.

A gasp came from the open doorway and Demelza hurried over to Royden, her hand on her rounded stomach. Her pleas were even stronger. "Help her, Wren, please help her. Don't let my sister die."

Wren remained calm in the chaos that ensued. She had Royden follow her to a bedchamber and ordered Demelza back to her room. The woman refused, following them.

Royden didn't want to let go of his wife. He feared if he did, he might never get to hold her again, but he did as Wren ordered him to do and placed her on the bed. His da's firm hand on his shoulder eased him away, leaving Wren to tend his wife.

"You need to return to your room," Wren said to Demelza.

"No. You said I had time yet. I will stay and help you with my sister while I can."

Wren turned to Royden.

"I won't leave her," he said, knowing Wren would tell him to leave.

Wren didn't argue. She went to work on Oria while keeping an eye on Demelza.

"Royden."

It was a soft plea, but Royden heard it and hurried to his wife. When he saw how bad the wound was to her arm his gut wrenched. He took her hand, Wren giving him room to get close.

"I'm here, Oria," he said, squeezing her hand.

"Don't leave me," she pleaded. "I want your face to be the last one I look upon before I die."

"You're not going to die," Royden ordered as if he commanded it so.

"Your husband is right," Demelza said. "You won't die. We won't let you."

Oria wanted to believe that, but she had known the risk she took with leaving a trail of her blood for her husband to follow. And feeling as she did, as if life was slipping away from her, she found it difficult to believe death wasn't hovering nearby.

Royden's eyes went wide, a sudden thought striking him. "You're not going to die. Wren saw us having many bairns. You are going to live and we're going to have lots of bairns. Right, Wren?" He turned pleading eyes on the woman.

Wren ran a tender hand over Oria's brow as she spoke to her. "I think that's already started."

Royden was stunned and Oria smiled weakly.

"I wasn't quite sure, so I didn't want to say anything yet," Oria said and looked to her husband. "I wanted to be sure when I told you that I carry your bairn."

He pressed his brow to hers. "The first of many precious bairns to come." He looked to Wren for her to confirm it.

"Your healing will take time and it won't be easy, but you have a loving husband who will do anything to help you and that makes all the difference," Wren said.

"Anything. I'll do anything," Royden hurried to say. "Just tell me what I need to do."

"You may need to hold your wife while I stitch her wound."

Royden nodded, though his stomach clenched even tighter knowing the pain she would suffer. He brought his wife's hand to his lips and kissed it. "I'm here with you and here is where I will stay until you're so sick of me, you will chase me away."

"Never would I chase you. You're where I want you, beside me," Oria said, her smile appearing a bit stronger.

"I will help too," Demelza said. "And how wonderful that our children will grow, be close, like brothers and sisters."

Oria turned, surprised that her sister was there. "You need to be in bed. You're about to have a bairn."

"I will know when it's time to seek my bed. For now, I help you," Demelza said.

"It's time to get to work on Oria, then we'll see about delivering that bairn," Wren said.

They all got busy following Wren's every word. Parlan directed the servants in getting whatever she requested, even running off at times to fetch things himself.

Demelza worked with Wren, doing whatever the woman instructed her to do and that included taking time to breathe through her labor pains.

When it came time for his wife's wound to be stitched, Royden pressed their clutched hands to his chest to hold her firm and rested his brow to hers. He talked softly to her about their future together, hoping it helped to distract her from the pain. It pained him to see tears roll down her cheeks and feel her hand squeeze his with what strength she had. He wished a faint would take her so that she didn't have to suffer so. But she was a strong woman and fought gallantly.

Never was he so relieved when the ordeal came to an end for her and he felt her body ease with relief.

Demelza was helping Wren wrap the wound when a strong pain struck her and while she attempted to muffle her cry, it was still heard.

"Time for you to return to bed," Wren ordered.

"What are you even doing out of bed?" Trevor demanded from the open doorway, looking with alarm at his wife.

"Helping my sister," Demelza said. "And don't think to order me to bed."

"If you won't listen to me," Trevor said with a glare, "then one word to your brother, who waits downstairs, should do it."

"He's here?" Demelza asked, a touch of fear in her voice.

"He waits to hear about both of his sisters, and the birth of his first niece or nephew," Trevor said.

Oria clutched her husband's hand tightly. "I don't want to meet him yet."

"You don't have to," Trevor said, hearing her. "Whenever you're ready will be soon enough."

Another pain struck Demelza and she grabbed her stomach as she let out a cry.

Trevor didn't wait, he rushed over to her and scooped her up in his arms.

"I'll be right with her," Wren said, and with a nod Trevor hurried out of the room. She turned to Parlan. "Can you get that brew I asked the kitchen to keep ready?"

Parlan nodded and went to do as she asked.

Wren hurried around picking up bloody towels and cloths and dropping them outside the room along with the buckets of dirty water.

"A servant can do that," Royden said.

Wren shook her head and came to stand by Royden and looked down at Oria her eyes so heavy with exhaustion she lost the battle to keep them open. "Oria needs rest, and I don't want a lot of people in and out of her healing room. She cannot travel until I'm sure the wound does well and no fever shows itself. Four to five days at least. Now I must go and see to Demelza. Call out if you should need me for any reason. Give her some of the brew that Parlan returns with, but rest is what Oria needs now."

Royden remained by his wife's side and when she woke hours later it was to the news that Demelza had delivered a son and that the Beast had taken his leave, assured that both his sisters did well.

It was later that night when all were asleep, the keep silent, Royden still at her side that Oria woke.

"Do you need, Wren?" he asked anxiously.

"We never sleep apart," she said softly and winced when she attempted to move and make room for him.

"Don't," he ordered quietly and gently eased his hands under her to move her enough so that he could join her, and he did. Once in bed, he settled her gently in the crook of his arm and she slept once again.

He didn't. He still feared losing her and now their bairn. He had placed her so that his one hand would be free to help her if needed and he placed that hand on her flat stomach. He worried that he still may lose the both of them and that he couldn't bear. He fell asleep begging God to keep them both safe.

Chapter Thirty-one

Three months later

"You're not doing this alone. I'm here with you and this day had to come eventually. You couldn't delay it forever," Royden said, keeping hold of his wife's hand and feeling her anxiousness.

"I know, but how do I accept them as my parents when all I've known are the parents who raised me?" Oria asked, looking in the distance at the approach of several riders.

"You don't."

Her brow wrinkled in question.

"You don't need to accept these people unless you want to. What matters is that you give them a chance. Give yourself a chance," Royden said.

Oria smiled at him. "I do believe I will keep you now."

Royden laughed. "So you changed your mind about getting rid of me after I told you that your parents were arriving today?"

"Actually, after I finished arguing with you and stomped out of the Great Hall like a petulant child, your da explained to me it was you who made certain my parents didn't come to visit until today. That you argued endlessly with Trevor over it and the Beast himself. He told me it wasn't until you were satisfied that I was completely healed, even though Wren had claimed me sufficiently healed to receive visitors weeks ago, that you would allow this meeting to take place. So forgive me for arguing with you when it was you who allowed me time before having to face this moment."

"There's nothing to forgive, Oria. I only did what I knew you would want, even if you're too stubborn to admit it at times," he said with a grin.

"Stubborn, you say?" she said with a playful jab to his chest, reminded of how good his hard chest had felt waking up on this morning.

"Aye, you insisted on making love when you still hadn't fully healed."

She laughed softly. "You expected me to wait until I was fully healed?"

He laughed as well. "Actually, I was counting on it that you wouldn't."

Oria gave her husband a quick kiss. "I do so love you."

"And I you," he was quick to say.

They stood side by side as the horses approached. Oria was glad the Beast wouldn't be among them, having been called away on an important matter. She wasn't ready to meet him and didn't know if she ever would be, no matter how many times her husband reminded her that he had helped save her life.

Oria gripped her husband's hand tighter as he guided her down the stairs to greet the group that came to a stop there. She was shocked to see just how much she resembled her mother, their blonde hair and green eyes the same color, their faces almost identical if it wasn't for the scar she carried. Her father was a tall and broad man with shocking white hair that fell past his shoulders and a white beard and moustache. His eyes were dark, far too dark to Oria's liking. Her da had dark eyes, but there was a pleasantness in them that she didn't see in this man.

Demelza was all smiles and hurried to Oria as soon as Trevor helped her off the horse and took their sleeping son, Aric, from her. She waited until her parents dismounted, then quickly introduced them.

"Oria, our mother and father," Demelza said, nodding to each.

"Your proper name is Astra," the large Norseman said.

"Thorald," the woman admonished. "There is time for her to learn her true name."

"We've wasted enough time, Freya. She is our daughter and needs to know that," Thorald chided.

"My name is Oria, and I am pleased to meet you, Freya, and, Thorald," Oria said, letting them both know she wasn't ready to call them mother or father.

Anger rose on Thorald's face and he went to step forward.

Royden quickly stepped in front of his wife. "I gave you the courtesy of inviting you to our home to meet your daughter. If you intend to make demands of her in any way, then take your leave and don't return here."

"Astra was taken from us," Thorald said, his voice bold and loud. "We were robbed of her all these years."

"And you will be robbed of her forever if you think to command her like a daughter you have raised all these years," Royden said, his voice just as bold and more strong than loud. "And while she is your daughter, take care to remember that she is *my wife*."

Freya placed her hand on her husband's arm. "We are pleased that our daughter has such a strong husband to protect her."

"We'll still see about that with him having only one hand," Thorald argued.

Oria almost rushed around her husband to remind Thorald that it was his son who had done that to her husband, but stopped when Demelza spoke.

"We should go inside and talk," Demelza suggested with a cautious smile.

"You will hold your tongue, daughter," Thorald ordered with a shake of his finger at her.

Trevor went to step forward, but Oria had had enough and she sped around her husband to come to a stand in front of Thorald.

"You do not command Demelza or me and do not dare ever remark about my husband having only one hand since it was your son's fault he lost it. And if you think I will ever call the likes of you Father, then you are a fool." She turned to Demelza. "Bring your son and while he sleeps, we'll share a brew and talk." Oria waited until Trevor handed their son to his wife, then she turned to Freya. "You're welcome to join us, Freya."

Freya stepped forward to follow.

"Don't you dare go with them," her husband ordered.

Freya turned an angry glare on her husband. "I lost my daughter once. I won't lose her again." She followed her daughters into the keep.

"Do something about your wife," Thorald ordered Royden.

Royden laughed. "I'd say my wife is much like her father. So you go try and defy her."

"She does have a strong manner and much courage about her," Thorald said, his chest puffing with pride.

"More than you'll ever know," Royden said, his pride for his wife obvious. "It's a fine day. We'll share a brew outside while the women talk. And maybe, just maybe, they'll take pity on you and speak with you later."

"I don't need their pity," Thorald snapped. "Though I don't want my wife hurt again. I don't want to hurt again. Astra—Oria—didn't sleep well unless she fell asleep in my arms. She was so small. She fit perfectly in the crook of my arm and would snuggle there, stare up at me, and smile, as if letting me know she was content, then she would drift off to sleep. Her eyes would pop open every now and then to make sure I was still there. I would sit staring at her, thinking of all I wanted to teach her, all I hoped I could help her become.

Then I would rest her in her bed and she wouldn't stir all night. I missed her being in my arms. I missed her eyes looking up at me so content. I missed her growing into the strong, brave young woman she looks to have become." He turned his head away, sniffling back tears.

"You need to tell Oria that. But first, come and have a drink and we'll talk, and I will tell you all about how your daughter became the brave woman she is," Royden said, placing a hand on Thorald's shoulder to lead him away from the keep, Trevor trailing behind them.

***

Oria laid snuggled against her husband in bed that night. "They weren't the only ones who suffered a loss, I did as well. I lost the chance to love parents I didn't even know I had. Yet if I never had been abducted, I would have never met you and I can't imagine life without you."

"I feel the same," he said, hugging her tight, the thought of never having her in his life frightening.

"They want me to come visit what they call my home."

"I know, but I made it clear that you wouldn't be going anywhere since you're with child," Royden said. "Though I also made it clear they are welcome to visit us anytime."

"You have been most gracious and generous with them. Freya was impressed with you," Oria said. "If only she knew how impressive you truly can be."

Royden laughed. "I take it you're tired of talking since your hand is inching down—"

"To arouse you, but I'm pleased to find out you're already more than aroused." She chuckled, stroking him.

"You knew I would be since you made a point of walking around the room naked, swaying those gorgeous hips of yours and stretching your arms above your head and groaning, like you do when you're in the throes of pleasure, while bringing them down slowly along your body."

She chuckled again. "And here I thought I wasn't being obvious."

Royden laughed and rolled her onto her back. "Now that's a lie, wife, but I love you anyway."

Oria ran her finger lightly across his lips. "I pledged my heart and love to you long ago, Royden, and that's a pledge I'll keep forever."

He kissed her. "Aye, you're pledged to a Highlander and he'll never let you go."

THE END

Watch for book two, Entrusted To A Highlander, Arran & Purity's story

&

Book three, Highlander Oath Of The Beast, Raven & Wolf's story.

Titles by Donna Fletcher

Highland Promise Trilogy
Highland Oath Prequel, Highland Promise Trilogy
Pledged To A Highlander
Entrusted To A Highlander
Highlander Oath Of The Beast

Macardle Sisters of Courage Trilogy
Highlander of My Heart
Desired by a Highlander
Highlander Lord of Fire

Macinnes Sisters Trilogy
The Highlander's Stolen Heart
Highlander's Rebellious Love
Highlander The Dark Dragon

Highland Warriors Trilogy
To Love A Highlander
Embraced By A Highlander
Highlander The Demon Lord

Cree & Dawn Series
Highlander Unchained/Forbidden Highlander
Highlander's Captive
My Highlander A Cree & Dawn Novel

For a full listing of all titles and to learn more about Donna go to her website

www.donnafletcher.com

Made in the USA
Monee, IL
28 June 2020